W9-CEG-508

ANNO DRACULA 1899

ONE THOUSAND MONSTERS

ALSO BY KIM NEWMAN AND AVAILABLE FROM TITAN BOOKS

ANNO DRACULA
ANNO DRACULA: THE BLOODY RED BARON
ANNO DRACULA: DRACULA CHA CHA CHA
ANNO DRACULA: JOHNNY ALUCARD
ANNO DRACULA: 1899 AND OTHER STORIES
ANNO DRACULA 1999: DAIKAIJU (OCTOBER 2019)

ANGELS OF MUSIC
THE SECRETS OF DREARCLIFF GRANGE SCHOOL
THE HAUNTING OF DREARCLIFF GRANGE SCHOOL
AN ENGLISH GHOST STORY
PROFESSOR MORIARTY: THE HOUND OF THE D'URBERVILLES

JAGO
THE QUORUM
LIFE'S LOTTERY
BAD DREAMS
THE NIGHT MAYOR
THE MAN FROM THE DIOGENES CLUB

VIDEO DUNGEON

ANNO DRACULA 1899

ONE THOUSAND MONSTERS

KIM NEWMAN

TITAN BOOKS

ANNO DRACULA: ONE THOUSAND MONSTERS

Mass-market edition ISBN: 9781781165652
E-book edition ISBN: 9781781165645

Published by Titan Books
A division of Titan Publishing Group Ltd
144 Southwark Street, London SE1 0UP

Mass-market edition: April 2019
1 3 5 7 9 10 8 6 4 2

This is a work of fiction. Names, characters, places, and incidents either
are the product of the author's imagination or are used fictitiously,
and any resemblance to actual persons, living or dead, business
establishments, events, or locales is entirely coincidental. The publisher
does not have any control over and does not assume any responsibility
for author or third-party websites or their content.

Kim Newman asserts the moral right to be identified as
the author of this work.

Copyright © 2017, 2019 Kim Newman

Visit our website:
www.titanbook.com

No part of this publication may be reproduced, stored in a retrieval
system, or transmitted, in any form or by any means without the prior
written permission of the publisher, nor be otherwise circulated in any
form of binding or cover other than that in which it is published and
without a similar condition being imposed on the subsequent purchaser.

A CIP catalogue record for this title is available from the British Library.

Printed and bound in the USA.

For Cath

Yoru bakari
Miru mono nari to
Omou-nayo!
Hiru sae yume no
Ukiyo nari-keri.

Think not that dreams
appear to the dreamer
only at night:
The dream of this world of pain
appears to us
even by day.
Lafcadio Hearn,
In Ghostly Japan

'Immortal powers!' cried Roderick, 'what a vision! In the name of transcendent perfection, who is she?' He sprang up and stood looking after her until she rounded a turn in the avenue. 'What a movement, what a manner, what a poise of the head! I wonder if she would sit to me.'

'You had better go and ask her,' said Rowland, laughing.

'She is certainly most beautiful.'

'Beautiful? She's beauty itself – she's a revelation. I don't believe she is living – she's a phantasm, a vapour, an illusion!'

'The poodle,' said Rowland, 'is certainly alive.'

'Nay, he too may be a grotesque phantom, like the black dog in Faust.'

'I hope at least that the young lady has nothing

in common with Mephistopheles. She looked dangerous.'

'If beauty is immoral, as people think at Northampton,' said Roderick, 'she is the incarnation of evil.'

Henry James, *Roderick Hudson*

1

Medical Log of the S.S. Macedonia, kept by Geneviève
Dieudonné (Acting Ship's Doctor)

At anchor in Tokyo Bay, December 6, 1899

'There are no vampires in Japan,' said Baron
Masamichi Higurashi. 'This is the position of the
Emperor.'

The emissary nodded. A bow with the effect of a sneer.

I respectfully lowered my gaze, lips tight over sharpening
fangs.

The wind blew. The deck creaked. Seabirds squawked.

Christina Light, the Princess Casamassima, smiled
graciously, as if Higurashi had complimented her pretty
hat. Sparks in her eyes – deep in the irises, like reflections
of distant stars – betrayed her annoyance. She can no
more understand Japanese than read tea leaves. He might
as well have barked at her like a dog.

'What did he say?' she asked.

Besides doctoring, I'm expected to be the *Macedonia*'s
official translator. For the benefit of my shipmates, I
rendered the Baron's statement into English.

9

Kostaki's dead face gave away nothing. Christina's frown let everyone know she was irritated.

'But what did he *mean*?' asked the Princess.

'There *should* be no vampires in Japan,' I said, in Italian. I suspected Higurashi understood English. 'If the Emperor states something, it's a fact. If the Emperor happens to be wrong, it's the duty of this official to address the situation... not to correct the Emperor, but to correct the world.'

The Princess was impatient, as well she might be. The *Macedonia* has carried us a long way. This is a Voyage of the Foolishly Hopeful.

'The Emperor *is* wrong, by the way,' I continued. 'There were vampires – of a sort – in Japan when I was last here.'

Three hundred and fifty years ago, admittedly.

It's unlikely that *kyuketsuki* have died out like the great auk. The Meiji reforms can't even rid this country of unemployed samurai. I daresay ancient blood-drinkers have survived any pogroms. Should Yuki-Onna, the Woman of the Snow, lower herself to take a title, she could claim to be Vampire Empress of Asia. Which would aptly make her Queen of the Cats. Japanese shapeshifters favour cats (*bakeneko*) or nine-tailed foxes (*kitsune*) over the bats and wolves of the *nosferatu* bloodline. By rights, we should present *cartes de visite* to Yuki-Onna, not Emperor Mutsuhito. He is at best a temporary throne-warmer. She is as eternal as the white cap of Mount Fuji. It's said her court can be reached from the earthly plane on but one night in a century, which would make securing an audience problematic if it weren't smoke and nonsense put about to puff up her reputation.

Sunset in the Land of the Rising Sun. The sky crimson over Chiba Prefecture, to the west. Higurashi's launch had steamed from the east shore, where the city rises and spreads.

I remember Tokyo as Edo, bustling military camp of

the Tokugawa shogunate. The name changed thirty years ago when the new emperor moved from Kyoto to take Edo Castle for his palace. The young imperial capital is bent on becoming the mercantile-political-cultural centre of the Pacific. London, New York or Paris with earthquakes and bath-houses. The Japanese probably dismiss London as Tokyo with fog and vampires. Cities are cities – each thinks itself centre of the universe.

We met on the open deck of the *Macedonia*. Three European vampires petitioning for safe harbour and a warm Japanese making a show of parlay with creatures he deems ugly demons. If we were not vampires, he'd think us just as hideous. In Japan, we may well be despised more for big noses and round eyes than undead pallor and sharp teeth. That two women were doing the talking did our cause no favours – especially since Christina is a *terrible* diplomat.

The Princess sat on a little folding chair as if it were a throne. A scene arranged with her as centrepiece. Her white silk dress had pearls inset in the bodice. Her train wound tight round her legs, lest it catch the wind and unfurl like a banner of war. She posed like a mermaid on a rock, fluttering eyelashes and playing with a parasol to draw attention from her tail.

Higurashi ignored her anyway.

The emissary spoke to me out of necessity, expressing no surprise or pleasure that I knew his language. He treated Kostaki as our chieftain.

When drummed out of the Carpathian Guard, the Moldavian elder put away all decorations. In a greatcoat stripped of insignia, he seems a ghost of himself. His shako is obscenely naked without hackle and badge. He even cut off his moustaches and shaved his head. A phrenologist might say he has a fine skull. A doctor – me! – says the rest of him is too meagre, even for a vampire. His skin is almost transparent, a rice-paper wrapper for his bones.

His veins are as visible as an anatomy diagram.

Kostaki kept his eyes on Higurashi, hand casually on his sword-hilt. He didn't give up the weapon with his medals and honours. It is his own property, not the Guard's; a Portuguese black carrack. Originally, the blade was a dull black, so as not to catch the sun and alert the enemy (should Kostaki do any daytime fighting); now, it's silver-coated for use against vampires. The weapon has a peculiar-shaped pair of claws in the hilt, to trap an opponent's blade so a wrist-twist can disarm in a clash. It's politely called a crab sword, but crudely known as a *colhona* ('big balls') – in profile, the claws look like caricature testicles. It may have a name Kostaki hasn't shared with us – Gut-cutter, Raven-brand, Skull-splicer. We might be scorned as barbarians, but the sword will be welcomed in Japan. Here, everything sharp has a coat of arms, an official birthday and secret and public names.

'Is he a monk?' asked Higurashi.

I saw why he might think that. Buddhist bonzes are bald. Fasting gives many a lean, ascetic look. When did Kostaki last feed?

Japanese has a precise word for what Kostaki is.

'Not a monk,' I told the Baron. '*Ronin.*' A masterless samurai.

Under the Meiji Restoration, steps have been taken to curtail the samurai class, seen by the regime as relics of the displaced shogunate. Since the suppression of the Satsuma Rebellion, many former retainers of noble houses are unemployed or in disgrace, following the warrior's path (*bushido*) without direction. Some turn to freelance heroism. Others to banditry. France was the same after the Crusades. A bad time to be the sort of person who gets robbed at swordpoint.

Like all in our party, Kostaki seeks more than shelter. He needs a cause.

Higurashi bowed to the Carpathian. Properly.

In something of a pet, Princess Casamassima twinkled. Sparks danced in her aura like dying fireflies. No one elevated her to any position of leadership, but she assumes command by divine right of Christinaness. After marrying into a title, she spurned all it entails to espouse the cause of revolution. Her late husband could hardly have been delighted. She gave him other reasons to be unhappy. She declares social rank obsolete and insists she not be called 'Your Highness'. She is particularly sure to tell people who don't know she's a princess not to treat her like one. Yet her offhand manner hints at dire consequences if she isn't recognised as *special*.

She *is* a rare creature. Christina *shines*... a vampire trait I'd heard of, but never before directly observed. You can't look away from her. Her skin glows with a lustre like her pearls. Her golden eyes hold white flames. Her fine hair ripples with violet luminescence. Like a dweller in sea depths beyond reach of the sun, she is her own candle. Something is very *fishy* about the Princess. Kate Reed, always well-informed, tells me that the way some vampires can become mist, Christina can turn into moonbeams. That, I've not witnessed – but she lights up like a lantern when exercising her power of fascination and burns white-hot if she's resisted.

That *glamour* is a property of the vampire condition not shared by my bloodline. Life would be simpler if I could make people do what I want... but getting one's way all the time is bad for the character. I can instance many examples, warm and undead, of this lesson. Princess Casamassima is at the head of that list. Prince Dracula is on it too. And Mr Mycroft Holmes of the Diogenes Club, who is at least as responsible for me being a woman without a country as Dracula himself. Britain has too many puppet-masters at present; the rest of us get our strings tangled.

I had to admire Higurashi. Christina's fireworks didn't jar his composure. He kept talking to me as if I were a trained monkey and keeping his eye on Kostaki as if he were the organ grinder.

To meet the foreign vampires, the Japanese emissary wore European formal dress – tailcoat, starched collar, red stock, diplomatic sash, top hat, ceremonial sword. He might have been the Mayor of Middlesbrough visiting a trade council. Like Kostaki, he kept a hand near his sword-hilt by studied accident. Was his German sabre a subtle mark of contempt? *Gaijin* aren't worth Japanese steel.

The *Macedonia* has steamed across the seas with its strange captain and stranger cargo. We've been turned away from ports like a plague ship. Gunboats kept us out of San Francisco Bay and followed at respectful distance until we quit US waters. No sanctuary for turncloaks in the Americas. We do not count as 'huddled masses yearning to breathe free' for it is popularly supposed we do not breathe at all. Canada and Australia welcome *warm* refugees from Dracula's England, but not us – not vampires.

If any of our party were to show their face in London, they'd be impaled in public, beheaded with silver and have their ashes strewn on Rotten Row. We are against the Crown Prince, and escaping his dominion... but in America the Kane papers scream that we're secretly his murder-missionaries, spreaders of his vile bloodline. The *Inquirer* ran Jedediah Leland's sensationalist serial *The 'Viper' Invasion of New York* and half the country took it for news. In Kansas, spinsters pulled white pickets from fences to sharpen for stakes and bothered priests to bless their wells. Leland dreamed up the notion that splashes of holy water burn vampires like vitriol. In the final episode, Teddy Roosevelt turns a fire hose on 'the King', a thinly disguised Dracula, and washes him down a sewer.

Dracula is undisputed King of the Cats, and we're *cats*

– so we *must* bow to him and plot the subjugation of the whole warm world. Even on the other side of the globe, his stench is on us. When Higurashi says *Dorakyura*, he scowls.

I assume the Japanese Navy has guns trained on the *Macedonia*. Not that there's much point. The ship is held together by rust and rancid seal fat, more likely to be sunk by a squall than enemy action. It is all we could get and Death Larsen the only captain, warm or undead, bloody-minded enough to take us on. Without him, we would have to cross the ocean in open coffins, paddling with our hands. At that, sharing a nightly table with Larsen is high price for a passage. Many warmfellows are disgusted by the way vampires feed... but the most ravening rat-fanged *strigoi* is refined next to Captain Larsen.

Yet the brute has vanities. He is proud of his nickname. We came to the Americas on the clipper *Elizabeth Dane*, another ill-starred ship, then crossed the Isthmus of Panama by mule train. When we met Death in Panama City, none of us were impressed by his sinister soubriquet, or curious enough to ask how he came by it. His scarred lips twitched in a childish moue.

'I have read of the *Demeter*,' Larsen told us as our cargo of caskets was winched aboard the *Macedonia* as Dracula's earth-boxes were once stowed in the hold of the ship that brought him to England. 'On that voyage, there was but one fat leech and a whole crew to feed him. My ship has a hundred and twenty *vampyrer*, a pack of thirsty bastards. And me. I am not the fool who skippered the *Demeter*. I shall not tie myself dead to my own wheel. My crew are not meat and drink to living corpses. My men are mine alone. I own their lives and deaths. They call me Death Larsen. Death. What a name! *Death*. You wonder why that is so, perhaps? Many times have I earned it. My own brother gave it me first. He was one of your sort – a wolf inside a man. At full moon, he turned his skin hairy-side out and howled. Captain of the *Ghost*. Wolf Larsen is no more. If I am Death Larsen, he is Dead Larsen. A fine joke, hah hah. Dead, for he is dead, at the bottom of the sea. And my silver harpoon through him. Thus I treat my own kin. You, I know not and care not for. A warning, that is all. It would be best if you kept to your boxes. Or the ship arrives in port free of leeches, and my brother has company down below – so many bats to follow one wolf.'

Fifteen years ago, perhaps, Death Larsen was the most terrifying person in his world – then Dracula came out of Transylvania to conquer London, bringing with him horrors most of Europe didn't believe in or had forgotten. A warm man merely *called* Death commands little fear when people who *are* Death cast such long shadows.

Most of us are still hibernating. The *Macedonia* isn't a passenger vessel or even really a cargo ship. Its usual trade is seal hunting and its guts are foul with a carcass stink which won't wash away. Larsen's battered crew stay clear of the coffins below decks, for vampire sleep is not always restful. Many of us have nightmares of Dracula, spreading black wings over us. Or the mob, with fire and silver.

Remembering the slaver trick of jettisoning human cargo when a revenue cutter hoves in view, Kostaki volunteered to be supercargo. With the Carpathian on watch, Larsen could not just rob us and consign us to the sea. He's survived worse than silver harpoons.

Christina would not sleep away an opportunity to speak for us all, so she also stayed out of the hold. She swanned around the *Macedonia*'s narrow walkways as if enjoying first-class passage on the White Star Line's *Majestic*. The crew were in awe, and sometimes mooned about behind her like small boys seeing their first horseless carriage. When bleeding a man, she leaches colour out of him. Those she has visited are identifiable by white patches on their hair, formerly tanned skin and even their clothes.

Kate mentioned that too. She has no idea how it works. A quirk of the Oblensky bloodline.

I happily left Kostaki and the Princess to represent us on the voyage. I was roused from my padded trunk after Dr Doskil cut his throat. One night, Larsen took it in mind to tear strips off the bald-pated, meek little man. The ship's doctor might have done something to offend his captain, who inflicted a severe dressing-down in public… or perhaps Death hadn't killed anyone in a month and was seized by his own brand of red thirst. Starting quietly, Larsen trapped Doskil into contradicting him on trivial points, then let fly a stream of inventive, vicious taunts. Kostaki − late of the Carpathian Guard, famous across Europe for savage cruelty − professed to be appalled at the way the Captain set about murdering the doctor, throwing words like harpoons. In the end, Doskil fled the table and took out his razor.

A ship must have a sawbones. Kostaki remembered I had worked in a clinic in London. So, I was roused from weeks of lassitude. I inherited Doskil's cabin. It has been scrubbed but is to my senses permeated with spilled, spoiled blood. Lying on the bunk forces my fangs from their gumsheaths, which is painful and frustrating. I fight red thirst as a warm drunk sleeping on a whisky-soaked mattress would struggle with the bottle.

Many of the crew's minor injuries were caused by the Captain. He likes to lash out with the tarred end of a rope, often at table. Something about eating sharpens his cruelty, though he knows better than to go after Eddie Joe, the Negro cook. If anyone is well-placed to murder Death, it's Eddie Joe − he could easily sauce a fish supper with jellyfish sting.

At one meal, Larsen suddenly took against Popejoy. The American tar was piling too many greens on his plate, but any excuse would have done. The rope-end flicked out, and made a mess of his face. I saved the patient from having to wear a patch, but he'll squint for life.

'You'll have to find a new deck name,' laughed the Captain. 'We can call you Hawk-Eye the Sailor Man no more.'

That's what it was really about. Taking away the name.

Even a captain as cruel as Larsen could only go so far in tormenting his crew. He dare not cripple or kill more than one or two on each voyage. Even if he had no fear of mutiny, he must worry about having too few able bodies to keep the *Macedonia* afloat. The passengers were another question. At sea, seven vampires turned to dust and bone in their boxes. I have an idea how that might have happened. Death wanted us to show him the respect of fear, even if it killed us all – which it might.

Defying Dracula means having interesting associates. Some I would steer clear of if given the option. In the hold are many choice specimens. For one: Mr Yam, the *jiang shi* elder who once tried to pull off my head. The Chinese assassin – not a political animal – accepted too many contracts to eliminate (understandably unpopular) cronies of the Crown Prince. In our company are committed opponents of the regime (like, to give her credit, Christina Light) and criminals who'd be wanted by Scotland Yard no matter who sat in Buckingham Palace. We also have former Dracula loyalists. Most who fall from his favour are selfish rogues or fools whose mistake is getting found out for dereliction of duty or conniving in treasonous plots – though Kostaki is in exile for abiding by a military code that embarrasses superior officers and frightens the troops.

We are a pond stocked with sharks. When all are awake, there's no guarantee we won't turn on each other. Christina collects (and selectively disseminates) information with a genius that rivals Mycroft Holmes. She tattles about those among us who are old enemies or have recent affronts and betrayals to avenge. With tart sweetness, she points out that I am not exactly popular with some vampires.

Daniel Dravot is in the hold too, implacable agent of the Diogenes Club. His duties still include keeping watch on me. Hard as it is to be accepted into the club, membership turns out to be practically impossible to resign. The Sergeant doubtless has sealed orders for every occasion sewn into the lining of his coat. Even in the Far East, we are Mycroft's pawns. He foresaw our wayward course would wind to Japan, a country he has lately given some thought. The war with China over Korea marked this as a coming nation – insular still, but no longer isolated. Mycroft ponders how Asian realignments affect the interests of the Ideal Britain he is devoted to – a phantasmal, misty realm not to be confused with the red map stain ruled by Prince Dracula. I've been used by the Diogenes Club before and did not much relish the experience. It has cost me a man I might love. For him, I am still just about willing to stay in Mr Holmes's Great Game. Our little circle – Charles, Mycroft, Dravot, myself – once dealt a blow to Dracula's legitimacy as monarch, but it is taking an age for the Prince to topple and Mr Holmes's Britannia to rise again.

A smart steam launch ferried Higurashi to the *Macedonia*. All brass trim and tight lines. A brand new flag flying from its aft pole. A red circle on white, like a spot of blood on your best tablecloth. A Maxim gun mounted on the prow, the lid off the ammunition box, so we could see the gleam of silver shells.

The Japanese are loaded for vampire.

In modernising his armed forces, the Emperor has a passion for buying – or copying – from Western powers. The launch's keel will have been laid in a British shipyard. Japanese sailors look like Dartmouth sea cadets in white uniforms. Skin smooth, as if they've just shaved for the first time – tiny razor nicks above fresh collars.

Delicious little beads of red.

It's been a long time since I drank anything but ship rat's blood.

'We... wish... to... come... ashore,' said the Princess to the Baron, enunciating each English word like an American ordering a steak and potatoes in Paris.

Higurashi gave no sign of understanding.

'We're in need of urgent repairs and provisions,' I told him, in Japanese. 'We can pay.'

Ironically, one thing we aren't short of is money. Vampires tend to get rich over the centuries. Well, other vampires do. I am perpetually stony broke, and among the few elders obliged to work for a living. I am drawing wages from Captain Larsen – or, at least, getting partial refund of my passage.

The widow Casamassima's credit is good at any bank in the world, thanks to the fabulous fortune she inherited. The Prince, frail scion of a distinguished but enfeebled Italian family, tried to turn when she did. His noble blood was too thin. Christina rose from death as a shining vampire angel. Her husband shrivelled into something like a human-sized vole, which coughed and shat for a few nights then became compost. He had to be shovelled into the Casamassima vaults in Rome. Christina Light, of American and Italian parentage and the strange airy-fairy Oblensky bloodline, is a relative newborn, but conducts herself like the breed of elder who looks down on Dracula as an ill-mannered parvenu. Just the type to become a revolutionary. She thinks the ruling classes – and, indeed, everyone else – are beneath her, and would rearrange the world to prop up that belief. Much like an Emperor of Japan.

If she gets ashore, she'll probably become Empress. Hikari-Onna, Woman of Light.

In London, the Princess was leading light – *ahem* – of a series of short-lived factions, unions and parties which tended to fall apart through internal squabbles well before

Mr Caleb Croft's Special Branch or General Iorga's Carpathian Guard got round to infiltrating or raiding them. Christina sat with Kate Reed on the Council of the Seven Days, an anarchist cell that made a splash during the Jubilee Year. It is her useful habit to be a sole survivor. Useful for her – not for anyone else in her playrooms. Katie barely got out of the council alive. I hope we of the *Macedonia* fare better.

'We are refugees,' I continued. 'We seek sanctuary.'

Higurashi nodded. I couldn't tell if it was a yay or nay nod.

The emissary came aboard the *Macedonia* alone. Considering that we're a ship of monsters, that showed courage. I did not sense a death wish or foolhardy confidence. He was more than just a messenger.

The way he stood, at ease yet coiled… just like Kostaki. That touch with the lid of the ammunition case. One item out of place on the ship-shape launch – just the thing to draw the eye, send a message. We could be cut down at any time. We were above water only because this man refrained from having us sunk.

At a guess, Higurashi is a member of the Black Ocean Society.

Black Ocean have influence with the Emperor – perhaps even *over* the Emperor. They feel an emperor should have an empire, and agitate for the accumulation of overseas possessions in Korea, China and elsewhere. They may have supplied the ronin assassins who killed Korea's Russian-leaning Empress Myeongseong in 1895, and run a chain of brothels across Asia to finance patriotic endeavours and harvest useful information.

Even Mycroft Holmes would draw the line at that. With India in turmoil after successive mutinies against Dracula's viceroys – the atrocious Sir Francis Varney, the ruthless Hymber Masters, the disgusting Lionel Roach – Black

Ocean might even consider the sub-continent achievable territory. Like the British, the Chinese and the Russians, the Japanese drink tea… tea-drinkers always thirst for empire. Even bloodsuckers are less rapacious. Blessed with time, we care less for space. We don't even own our graves. Except Dracula, of course. He wishes to be King of Space and Lord of Time. Which is why I have sailed to a hemisphere where he holds little sway.

Higurashi was sizing us up. That was why he had come aboard. Not to talk, but to pass judgement.

After tiresome debate between Christina and me, with Kostaki grunting every half hour or so, we had decided all three of us should meet the Emperor's man. The Princess tactfully ventured that it might be best to keep Kostaki in the shadows, 'for he is the kind of vampire the Japanese would take fright at'. She allowed that I present 'at least an unthreatening face'. She was confident her own charm would carry the day, as it has so often before.

In the event, Christina found it impossible to fluence Higurashi. Exercise of a power of fascination entails first getting a person's attention and the Baron affected not to notice her. It's as well she relented and let Kostaki on deck with us. Otherwise, the emissary might have treated us as invisible, inaudible gnats, and waved us into insignificance with a hand flap.

Still, the former Carpathian Guardsman kept quiet.

There seemed nothing more to be said. I wondered about Indo-China, Madagascar or East Africa. Could the *Macedonia* survive another ocean crossing?

From inside his coat, Kostaki took a large white handkerchief. He used his left hand, leaving his right on his sword.

The gesture caught Higurashi's eye the way all the Princess's smiles, moues, coughs, flutters and sparkles had not. The Baron stared at the flapping cloth.

Kostaki handed the handkerchief to Christina and stood well back. Higurashi faced him.

The Carpathian and the Japanese shared no spoken language, but understood each other. I didn't try to intervene.

The bay was calm, but the deck still shifted a little. I am now so used to sea voyaging that I seldom notice the motion. The breeze rippled the handkerchief.

Warm men might feel the winter cold. Higurashi's breath frosted. Kostaki's did not.

'Heh, mateys, *look*,' said Captain Larsen, who had kept an eye on our conclave from his wheelhouse.

The crew paid attention. I've been treating their gashes and bruises, resisting the temptation to lick a welling cut for fear of a marlinspike through the heart. Few would sail on the *Macedonia* if they could get berths on less cursed ships. Now, the sour lot were an audience for… what? A duel?

Higurashi and Kostaki closed their hands around sword-hilts. Their elbows kinked and their shoulders angled.

Christina held up the handkerchief, which streamed like a ribbon.

Were we declaring war on Japan?

Christina let the handkerchief go. It flew away.

Quicker than the human – quicker than the *vampire* – eye can register, Higurashi and Kostaki drew swords. The shiver of steel sliding from scabbards set my nerves on edge. I felt it in my sharp teeth, and the salt tang of blood from my gums…

They struck poses.

The point of the Baron's sabre dimpled the Carpathian's coat, over the heart.

The edge of Kostaki's carrack rested against the inside of Higurashi's thigh.

They stood like a stage tableau. Christina was puzzled. She knows what a thrust to the heart means to a vampire, but not what the severing of the *profunda femoris* artery is to a warm man.

It always surprises me that people who live off human blood don't trouble to learn more anatomy. As a warm girl, I was apprenticed to my father, a battlefield surgeon in the service of the Dauphin. I had enough schooling in the ways men bleed and die before I turned vampire. I've had centuries to keep up to date with fatal wounds and how they are inflicted.

The duellists stepped back and sheathed swords.

I knew now the real reason why Higurashi brought a German sabre. It is silver-plated. Since there are (by imperial decree) no vampires in Japan, few local swordsmiths manufacture weapons to kill us. So they must be imported. I'm not surprised silver bullets and swords reached Japan before we did. The best vampire-killing implements are made in Sheffield, with Dracula's mark stamped on them. British arms are bought around the world.

Higurashi and Kostaki each had the measure of the other. In the *Ittō-ryū* style – the duel of the single stroke – they were at stalemate, and neither would survive. They did not need to press the matter further.

'What is this silliness?' Christina asked.

'It's been settled,' I told her.

'You may come ashore,' said Baron Higurashi, in English. 'But you will be permitted only in a certain district.'

2

BEFORE DRACULA

As the curtain falls on the nineteenth century, memoirists and historians will fall over each other to chronicle the last fifteen turbulent years. I do not expect to join them in print. Sergeant Dravot will ensure this notebook finds its way to you, Charles. Once you have read it, and removed certain personal pages of no interest to anyone but ourselves, you will deliver it to Mycroft Holmes – who will secure it in his private files. Consider it a report. Intelligence, collected by the Diogenes Club.

To be used against our great enemy.

In filling pages unused by the late Dr Doskil, I shall become an imitator of journal-keeping Jonathan and letter-writing Mina in Bram Stoker's strange half-novel. No longer welcome in Fleet Street, Kate Reed writes for the underground press – pamphlets printed off in East End basements, distributed by inky-fingered children. Jack Seward muttered into his dictagraph till the end. Mycroft, like Jonathan Harker, uses a shorthand of his own devising. If posterity needs to know what is in his diaries, only his clever brother will be able to crack the cipher. Everyone who takes part in the dance around Dracula becomes an author, *lettriste* or diarist – except the Crown Prince. He dictates telegrams or scratches curt notes signed with a bold D. Until he mesmerises G.A. Henty or Marie Corelli into transcribing his yarns of foes impaled and ladies loved, we won't have Dracula's side of his story.

I shall try to be truthful, at least as I remember the truth.

Charles, I concede I have been a poor correspondent, but neither of us have recently had fixed addresses. I don't even know if you are in England. I hope you aren't, though it's ridiculous to ask you to be somewhere safe. For us, there is no such place. Even if there were, you wouldn't be there. We're lucky not to be in unmarked graves or Devil's Dyke. I can scarcely complain that life 'on the run' hampers maintenance of a social calendar. Murder brought us together. Murderers keep us apart.

The only picture I have of you is on the 'wanted' poster issued by Special Branch. I keep it folded in this log as a place-mark. They use a studio portrait taken on the occasion of one of your engagements. You are handsome, if stiff. A photographer's brace pinches your neck. A sliver of Penelope's shoulder edges in. Or is it Pamela? Penelope, I think. I discern incipient irritation. That's it for Penelope, as usual: cut out of the picture. I trust she remains an ornament of night society, prospering all the more for being thoroughly disengaged from you. Also, I hope you've altered your appearance since the photograph was taken. Caleb Croft won't forget your face. I'd regret the loss of your whiskers less than I should the loss of your head.

As for the picture on my wanted poster… I don't recognise myself. In photographs, as in mirrors, I show as a wedge of fog – so I am a problem sitter. Who did the sketch of me? Some lightning-fast scribbler who specialises in studies of brazen baggages in the dock for the *Police Gazette*. He makes me look a perfect horror. For all I know, it's a fair likeness.

This – written in quiet moments between crises – is the story of my wandering.

Like every story in this age and in all the years to come, it is about Dracula.

He is a meteorite, fallen from the sky. A rock, tossed into a pond. Arriving in England, he made a splash. Ripples will radiate for all time. Everyone and everything will be affected. At the beginning of the nineteenth century, a volcano erupted in the Indian Ocean and robbed Europe of a summer. As the century ends, the Vampire Ascendancy has clouded the world. Even Japan.

Will historians of the future reset the calendar, marking 1885 as the Year Nought, Anno Dracula?

I was in Paris, relearning medicine from first principles for the sixth time. For any professional, an extended lifetime mandates periodic returns to the well of knowledge. One generation's forward-thinking genius is the next century's hidebound dunce. Before Lister and Pasteur, doctors didn't wash their hands before surgery or after autopsy – as efficient a means of horribly killing patients as Dracula could conceive.

Unlike France's first women doctors, I didn't need permission from a husband to study medicine. But, in the years before Dracula, a convincing recent past was required for any official undertaking. In my long experience, it was simple enough to find people to pose as husbands, parents or children – human furniture for the imaginary houses vampires had to build.

Less fastidious bloodsuckers enslaved coteries of the warm, dressing them up and parading them like marionettes. Van Helsing said Dracula had a 'child-brain'. An acute insight. Many of the Prince's bloodline suffer from the condition. Vampires who play ringmaster and stock life-sized toy circuses. You know the ones. Emil Mitterhouse or J.C. Cooger – never-grown-up elders with motley retinues of hunchbacks, dwarves, pretty girl acrobats, gypsy riders, kohl-eyed harlots, strongmen and clowns.

Skills I learned – which all vampires before the modern age *had* to learn – are now obsolete. Banished by a wave of Dracula's sword.

Expensive forged documents represented me as a studious girl born in Rennes who had spent most of her (short) life in Martinique. If introduced to anyone who knew the Antilles, why – we lived on the other side of the island and seldom got into Fort-de-France. I couldn't recollect any notable people or places an amiable conversationalist might bring up. If pressed on my evasiveness, I sadly owned that my father was one of those gone-to-seed colonial drunks you'd steer clear of. Having painted pasteboard Papa as a useless (if kindly) sot, I callously killed him off – leaving me all alone in the world, and determined to put those sad years behind me. Oh, and thank you for noticing my unburnt complexion. Brown as a nut in the tropics, I faded on the voyage over. Complaining of the cold and damp, I managed a shiver that would register in the upper circle.

Remember, we vampires had to dissemble habitually, instinctively, without thinking of lies as lies. Those who now call me excessively blunt – and don't deny you're one of them, Charles – can't understand the relief of not having to go through such rigmarole every night of your life.

Yes, I have – in a roundabout way – said something good for Dracula.

I was used to telling lies within lies within lies. Sometimes, I was tripped by details. You'd not believe how many in Paris know Martinique as well as Montmartre and ache to share reminiscences. More rarely, I had the misfortune to run into someone with a nose for bad fish. Nurses, policemen and concierges cultivate a near-occult sense of when they're being told untruths. My stratagem was to be taken for an absconding daughter, mistress or wife. My unwomanly pursuit of medical education made it a likely story that I was disowned by a shocked provincial family. At least two of my fellow woman students were in exactly those circumstances. I reluctantly avoided their society, lest some notion of sisterhood prompt confidences I couldn't comfortably reciprocate.

If all this sounds complicated, consider that enrolling in the University of France without having to crop my hair and pose as a man was a refreshing nineteenth-century novelty. Last time round, I had to fight silly duels and bounce barmaids on my knee with the other young blades – trusting to spirit gum that my moustache didn't come off at an unfortunate moment.

My plan was to qualify as a doctor and become a *médecin légiste* in the coroner's office. For me, it always comes back to doctoring and crime. It is my impish reaction to what I am. Vampires are so often considered sick or criminal – or sick criminals – that it's in my interest to define those categories. The sick can be cured. Criminals should be punished. Neither solution will do for me. Both have been tried.

While other students attended the grumbling sick in charity wards and dreamed of specialising in the ailments of wealthy widows, I was a ghoul. Do not be appalled. I didn't sink to drinking the blood of the dead. That vile practice doesn't slake red thirst and turns the brain to rot. In Paris, *les goules* are students who work at the morgue on Île de la Cité. I assisted at autopsies and learned much about criminal investigation. Another science that has advanced in leaps and bounds in recent decades.

Captain of the ghouls was Nicolas Cerral, a humorous sport. He was forever sticking out severed arms (and legs) in the hope of duping civilians into 'shaking hands'. His other prize joke was to land me with the weightiest corpses to lug from slab to gurney and back. Maintaining my disguise as a warm and feeble woman, I had to make the task seem a titanic struggle. Cerral and my fellow ghouls (all men) had many fine chuckles out of me as I made a show of dropping a sewn-up indigent so stitches parted and innards spilled – then scooping moist organs up to pack back into body cavities. The ghouls *roared* at that. They'd not find me so amusing now.

It is also a relief, after centuries of pretending, to abandon such charades. I wish I could go back and play again all those games of tennis I contrived to lose with pluck and grace.

As a woman medical student, I was a novelty but not unique. As the sole girl ghoul, I was expected to be peculiar. Convenient distractions from strangenesses entailed by the Other Thing About Me.

If anyone asked, I said I was twenty-two. My tutors and other students all thought I was lying, which of course I was. Being considered a child was another innovation. Not so long ago, an unmarried sixteen-year-old was an old maid. I dressed severely to avoid being taken for a lost little girl by kindly passers-by or opportunist rogues. The ghoul uniform of mop cap, stained apron, hobnailed boots and scarf warded off those who would pet and pat and cluck and coo if I wore bonnet, pinafore and ribbons.

Everyone who visited the morgue complained of the cold, so I had to remember my fingers and toes were supposed to be frozen. All that stone, all that ice, all those dead. Even the ghoul Prince Cerral wrapped up in furs. The coroner only went mittenless when using a scalpel. I can't remember feeling cold or being blind in the dark. Walking barefoot in snow is no discomfort, but going outside on a sunny day is like being doused in fire ants. I amassed a collection of broad-brimmed hats, English umbrellas and smoked glasses.

Other students crammed into digs with comical

landladies or lodged with relatives. I impoverished myself buying a small house near the morgue, and of necessity lived alone in it. My reputation for standoffishness grew as I avoided receiving visitors. Vampires do not have homes. We have lairs, roosts, boltholes, coffins. I could not let anyone cross my threshold and wonder about the lack of mirrors, the peculiarly stocked larder or the seldom used (for any purpose) bed.

It was perhaps a ghost of a life. But it was mine, and I was prepared to live it.

In his castle in Transylvania, Count Dracula – as he then called himself – was poring over estate agents' brochures and travel timetables.

In his child-brain was a notion that it might be jolly fun to be an Englishman.

3

YŌKAI TOWN, DECEMBER 7, 1899

A mangy dog trotted down the middle of the cracked street, a severed human hand clamped between its jaws.

'Welcome to Yōkai Town,' said Christina.

She put her parasol between her and the unpleasant sight. The princess is a parasol-after-dark sort of woman.

A ragged, squawking fellow in a striped robe ran after the mongrel, bloody rag wound round his leaking wrist stump. He was *tengu*, a bloodline with avian traits – mouth and nose fused into a pushed-out beak, feathery hair clipped into a topknot. His sandals flapped against talons.

My red thirst rose. Even *tengu* blood draws my fangs. I must feed soon.

'Nice doggie,' said Drusilla. 'Can we keep him?'

'No dear,' said Christina. 'You don't know where he's been.'

Drusilla Zark is a friend of Christina's. A splash of deep purple to set off shining light. More pet than friend, really. The sort who sometimes give their owner nasty nips. Huge-eyed, black-haired and angular, she wears her corset outside her chemise – a fashion she might have invented. Other slender vampires copy her, cinching unneeded foundation garments as if whalebone were armour plate.

She also favours useless hats that have to be pinned to the hair – miniature replicas of what they were wearing in 1860. She might always have been doolally but earned a good living as a psychic medium before the Ascendancy. More like a music hall turn than an oracle. She goes cross-eyed when she has 'visions'. Her whispery accent is half-cockney, half-posh, all-witchy. Having hurt unimportant people in England, she boarded the *Macedonia* to evade the Commissioners in Lunacy. Her story changes every time it's told and she never gets to the end – though she's deathly afraid of a man called Becker who wants to lock her up in Bedlam.

The dog trotted into an alley, pursued by the mutilated bird-man. After a noisy fight, the *tengu* strode onto the street, bloody-beaked and triumphant. He screwed his hand back on and flexed empurpled horn-tipped fingers. The dog whined, cheated of a meat supper. The *tengu* noticed us – and was startled. He bowed, yapped and backed away. Then, with a gait like a flightless bird trying to take wing, he ran headlong into the fog.

Some of our party may be fearsome, but the local wasn't reacting to foreign devils. He turned tail feathers and hopped off the way he came because he caught sight of Lieutenant Majin. So he is more afraid of the blandly handsome, big-chinned officer than whoever cut off his hand and fed it to a dog. I don't have to be a psychic medium to interpret that as a terrible omen.

Majin isn't so much our native guide in Yōkai Town as our overseer. He conducts himself like chief warden of a prison camp – which might be uncomfortably close to the truth. We are guests of a ruler who insists no vampires number among his subjects. This district is where Tokyo keeps creatures which, by imperial decree, do not exist. Drusilla might have fared better in Bedlam.

We passed through an impressive gate to get here. A

thirty-foot-tall statue stands guard inside Yōkai Town. The snarling green-painted warrior isn't a decorative feature, but a man-shaped fortress. Its eyes and mouth – and the eyes and mouth of its demon-faced belt buckle – are rifle slits. Black Ocean banners and the Japanese flag fly from its shoulders. A poem inscribed at its base might read: 'Give me your poor, your tired, your huddled masses yearning to breathe free… and I will lock them up, and – if they dare to complain – rain fire and arrows upon them.'

The boundaries of Yōkai Town are marked by newly built walls topped with broken glass and sacred statues. These block old roads, cut parks in half and stand taller than most buildings. Non-anthropomorphic watchtowers, manned by riflemen, bristle with yellow parchments inscribed with red characters. *O-fuda* – spells of prohibition and confinement. Charms as potent as Van Helsing's wreaths of wolfsbane and garlic. Effective in conjunction with walls, towers, guns and silver.

Thick fog hangs perpetually over this shabby, desolate place. Not green-yellow London pea soup, but grey-white salty mist. Locals wade through the murk like fish in muddy water. Brute hulking whales leave obvious swirling wakes. Slim, sly eels slither without stirring eddies. I sensed curious things out there. Spying, circling, testing.

Twin bursts of fire, about the size of footballs, whooshed overhead, streaming flames like ribbons. Chortling with delight, Drusilla hopped like a *jiang shi* to try and catch one. Christina was also mesmerised by the fire elemental. She glowed like a gas lamp. In the fog, her light is sickly. Like many of us after the long voyage, she hasn't got her land legs back yet.

This is the old Edo waterfront, abandoned to monsters when the outward-looking Emperor opened Tokyo's deep-water docks to international commerce. Only ghost ships are welcome now. Yōkai Town extends into the Arakawa

River on platforms, forming an unsteady, expanding archipelago of artificial islands. Boats at permanent berth are homes, restaurants and government offices. Masts of sunken ships are telegraph poles. Some gambling hells, shebeens and bawdy houses have underwater entrances. Racks of flippers, snorkels and masks (some elaborately decorated) can be hired. Steel mesh submarine nets keep swimming creatures from reaching the open sea. The waters beyond are seeded with mines. The message is that we should stay put.

Ashore, buildings are ill-repaired and amenities meagre. Lanterns hang at irregular intervals. Few manage to stay lit. I swear I saw one lamp roll a large green eye.

Most of us are in coffins, stacked on carts. Kostaki awakened a few vampires to help remove our party from the *Macedonia* to Yōkai Town. Naturally, he picked Danny Dravot, a born non-commissioned officer, to get the job done. Not so long ago, a Carpathian Guardsman would have killed an agent of the Diogenes Club on sight. Dravot once shot Kostaki. The silver bullet was never properly extracted and the Captain limps slightly. Far from their old messes, the pair have become comrades-in-arms and brothers-in-blood. They enjoy masculine, soldiery gossip – talking easily of battles, horses, sport and barmaids – but go quiet if I catch them at it. Kostaki and Dravot have practical skills from archery to forgery, from mountaineering to map-making. They can 'pick up the lingo' and pass as a native. I'd rely on them in a sortie against the odds or an escape from deep dungeons. But they don't know how to talk to women who aren't serving beer or baring throats to be bled.

A paradox of looking the way I do and being the age I am is that I am simultaneously an elderly schoolmistress who wouldn't understand the joke if it were spelled out and a little girl who needs to be wrapped in cotton wool to protect her from the wicked world. Many women who aren't four hundred and eighty-three share this vexing experience.

You, Charles, are a man in several lifetimes. If I ever took you for granted, know that I regret it now.

I miss conversation, warmth and intimacy. Most of all, I miss blood freely given. As a vampire at large, I will not steal or coerce, so must buy or beg. Hunting rats is less wretched than grubby, guilt-making transactions.

The society of my own sex is no comfort. Christina insisted on uncrating Drusilla to have someone to talk to who isn't me. When not treating her as a lapdog or an errant child, the Princess uses Dru like miners use canaries. If her head explodes, we'll know we're in a bad place. Which we know already. We are always in a bad place. London is a bad place. The *Macedonia* is a bad place.

Yōkai Town is a home away from home.

After issuing the Emperor's qualified permission to come ashore, Higurashi abandoned us. A tug guided the *Macedonia* to a quay where Lieutenant Majin awaited. A crew of roughs were ready to pile coffins onto ox-carts. Their foreman – a lantern-jawed, pigtailed giant named Kannuki – might technically qualify as *yōkai*. Majin directed the dockworkers but wouldn't look any of us in the eye.

'That man's hands are alive,' said Dru, meaning the Lieutenant. 'More than the rest of him.'

'Yes, dear, I'm sure,' said Christina. 'You'll feel better after a nap.'

The Princess likes to have Drusilla around, but never listens to her. I've learned to pay more attention. Dru's piffle often makes horrible sense in retrospect. Perhaps she clearly foresees the future but suffers what Jack Seward called 'a mental block' and is incapable of saying straight out what disaster we should expect. The meaning of her topsy-turvy rambling only becomes apparent when it's too late.

If canaries could serve miners the same way, I bet they would.

'*O willow, tit-willow, tit-willow,*' she trilled.

Maybe she knew I was thinking of canaries. Maybe being in Japan reminded her of *The Mikado*. Or maybe she just couldn't get the tune out of her head.

Dru could mean something or nothing – trying to parse what she says is a waste of time, though people around her feel compelled to try. I think she isn't as mad as we take her for. She also has the trick of making people do what she wants, in a round-the-back-of-the-houses sort of way – not through force of will, but by tapping nerves with a mallet to elicit a reflex. Then she smiles to herself and changes the subject.

She had made me think about Lieutenant Majin's white gloves.

They make his hands seem huge. They shine, like Christina's skin when her blood is up. The five-pointed stars embroidered in red thread on the backs aren't standard Imperial Japanese Army uniform. These symbols (*seiman*) resemble European black magic pentagrams but relate to the Japanese occult discipline of *onmyōdō*. Traditionally, masters of the practice (*onmyoji*) can summon demons (*oni*) and bend them to their will. Proscribed as superstition by the Emperor, the craft still has followers. Evidently, the Lieutenant fancies himself a sorcerer.

Majin isn't a name but a title. Not a reassuring one. Demon Man.

Despite lowly official rank, Majin is a considerable person in Yōkai Town. I knew it even before he scared off the *tengu*. That Dru has blurry insights about him confirms his high standing.

His pristine sky-blue uniform cape – combined with the

gloves – give him the look of a stage conjurer. His gestures are precise, but forceful. He wears a shiny-peaked uniform cap low so his eyes glint in its shade. His boots are polished like leather mirrors. He is used to command. A true *onmyoji* commands more than men.

I mentioned the thing about him not looking at us.

'It's not that,' said Dru. 'He doesn't want *us* to look at *him*.'

Naturally, after that, Christina and I stared at Majin. If he noticed – and I'm sure he did – he didn't return the favour.

'That mousey girl should mind her Ps and Qs,' said Dru. 'Or she shan't have any jam for supper.'

There was no mousey girl. Christina and I exchanged shrugs.

'Just because you can't see her yet doesn't mean she's not important to the story,' said Dru. 'You should never forget the School Mouse.'

'Yes, dear,' said Christina.

Dru started humming 'Tit-Willow' again.

I appreciate that, in the context of comic opera, execution can have an amusing side – hence all those songs about heads being chopped off and punishments fitting the crime. '*That singular anomaly, the vampire bicyclist – I've got her on the list, I'm sure she'll not be missed.*' But why *The Mikado* includes a sentimental ditty about suicide is a mystery to me. I am told you have to be English to understand Gilbert and Sullivan, Punch and Judy, and cricket.

The Lieutenant walked ahead of the procession of ox-carts like the man with a red flag preceding an automobile. Higurashi had said accommodations would be found for our party in Yōkai Town. I trusted he didn't mean a cemetery.

While Majin's attention was on our coffins, Kostaki sent scouts into the fog with orders to whistle if we were being led into an ambush. Our spies are Mr Yam, as outlandish here as in London, and Marit Verlaine, an expressionless woman who keeps her cards close to her chest. Kostaki still

thinks like a soldier, which is just as well. He's a good judge
of character. Yam, an assassin, and Verlaine, a mercenary,
are about the only ones of our party I'd trust after a long
dry spell. Most of us would abandon the mission and hare
off in search of warm blood. Red thirst makes vampires
selfish, small-minded – and easy to gull, catch and kill. It's a
reason why, before Dracula, we never really accomplished
anything as a species. Too intent on our next feeding to
find common cause, we don't much care for each other's
company. Wolves are pack animals. Vampires are not.

Yam and Verlaine are as thirsty as the rest of us, but
are professionals. No one wants to hire an unreliable
mercenary. Like me, they earn their living by inflicting the
kind of harm on people that means I'll never be short of
work. Although I suspect their opponents need burying
more often than doctoring.

How many silvered swords are there in Tokyo? How
many cases of silver bullets?

Majin led us along a thoroughfare, broad enough so
the fog made buildings on both sides indistinct. We were
watched every step of the way. Shapes and eyes behind
screens and in shadows. Aside from the *tengu*, who had a
pressing reason to show himself, the streets were empty.
The inhabitants of Yōkai Town kept out of Majin's way
– and ours.

'What does *yōkai* mean?' asked Whelpdale, a newborn
vampire.

'Among other things, us,' I said. '*Yōkai* can be translated
as "monster", "ghost", "goblin" or "apparition".'

'And this is their town?'

'It's a polite Japanese way of saying ghetto.'

'I suspicioned as much, Miss Doodydunny,' said
Whelpdale. 'I knows a rookery when I sees one. Look at
this how's yer father. No life to it at all. We'll run the place
inside a week, mark my words and no mistake.'

In London, Whelpdale – a lesser light of the book trade – got on the wrong side of Special Branch by printing an obscene illustrated pamphlet entitled *The Private Memoirs of Prince Dracula*. He didn't write the smut himself. The author was his brother-in-law, a warm sharpie too slippery to be taken into custody. As publisher of record, Whelpdale was convicted of seditious libel – a capital offence if you libelled Dracula, seditiously or otherwise. Exercising newfound vampire flexibility, he squeezed between the bars of Pentonville Prison, breaking bones that healed within moments, and fled as far as he could. He was still floppy and stretched out of shape.

'Japanese prints are a popular item back home,' said Whelpdale.

I knew which type of prints he meant. Pillow books – exquisitely tasteful pictures of folk doing things in beds, or things traditionally done in beds done in other more stimulating locations. Unlike every other vampire on the *Macedonia*, Whelpdale thought to pack a trunk with books – exclusively his own publications. Thanks to a shortage of reading matter on board, Christina and I have been through all of them. Even Kostaki picked one up and looked at it. Amusement wears thin after a dozen or so pages. The author is another who should learn anatomy: many acts he describes would only be possible if – like Whelpdale – one were practically boneless.

Eventually, Majin signalled a halt in front of a *torii* gate – two orange-painted pillars with crossbars and a slate roof. The Lieutenant had the foreman Kannuki – whose long face looks like pulled dough, with raisins for eyes – tear a docker's hook through thick cobweb curtains hanging across the gate. Fat, fist-sized spiders scattered as the web shredded. The foreman took a mean, childish joy in stamping on them with spade-blade clogs. They squealed as they popped. The markings on their hairy backs resembled sketches of distressed human faces.

Beyond the gate was a large tiered building. Red wood, with flaking white and gold trim. A stack of projecting roofs like large square hats. Set in its own ill-kept grounds, with a shallow frozen pool in a front courtyard. The gardens were rimed with frost. Hard, dirty crusts remained from recent snowfall.

A banner bore red characters. SEN KWAI JI.

'What does that say?' asked Christina. '"No hawkers or circulars"?'

'Or "Beware of the dog"?' suggested Whelpdale.

Considering the specialised diet of dogs in this place, that wasn't a poor guess.

'So far as I can make out,' I said, 'Temple of One Thousand Monsters.'

'Sounds lovely,' said Christina.

'Poetic licence, ducks,' said Dru. 'There are only six hundred and ninety-eight monsters. Eight hundred and fifteen, if you include us. Eight hundred and *sixteen*, if you include the Demon Man with white hands. I'm reckoning the willow tree and the lady growing out of the willow tree as one singular monster, but you might disagree. Or not. Makes little difference.'

'Don't pay her attention,' said Christina, airily. 'She makes up numbers to sound impressive. When she says there are seven thousand, six hundred and twelve grains of millet spilled on the floor, no one ever counts them and contradicts her.'

'Seventy-six hours, fourteen minutes and three seconds,' said Dru. 'That's how long eternal life lasted for Prince Casamassima. Old black blood turned to charcoal and clogged his heart. Which went *sploosh*.'

Christina was cross with Dru for bringing this up. She shimmered.

But we had other concerns. A deputation of three

awaited us in the temple courtyard, on a raised stone platform by the iced-over pool.

A squat dwarf sat on his haunches, stunted body barely supporting a swollen head like a rotten green potato. Curly fangs stuck out of his slit mouth. He wore a coat of woven rushes and a circular straw hat a yard across.

A white-faced beautiful woman posed on a mat, playing a *samisen* – a long-necked musical instrument. Her kimono was decorated with a flight of cranes. She nodded with each plucked note.

A singular little fellow looked like a living folded umbrella. He had one bare, muscular, hairy human leg and a corrugated flesh cone body, sporting a single large eye and a smiling set of fleshy lips, and a topknot with a bow in it.

Whelpdale swore in astonishment.

'These are *yōkai*,' I said.

I'd known what to expect and was still rattled.

In woodcuts, the creatures look absurd and almost endearing. In the flesh, they exude *wrongness*. In the West, vampire shapeshifters are swimmers who stick close to the shore. They take on aspects of bats and wolves – or, in rarer cases, insects and reptiles – but retain basic human anatomy. They assume other forms for limited spells, often just a few minutes. With something like relief, they revert to walking on two legs and showing more skin than fur. At most, they have permanently sharper teeth.

In the East, traditions are different. Other practices, other shapes, have emerged.

Even with his bones crushed to paste, I doubt Whelpdale could turn himself inside out like an umbrella and can't conceive of circumstances whereby he'd *want* to.

Make no mistake: the *yōkai* of Japan are vampires, though distant cousins only to the *nosferatu* of Europe. The same goes for the *aswang* of the Philippines, the *penanggalan* of Malaya and the *pontianak* of Java. Not vampires Lord Ruthven would invite to Downing Street for a rubber of whist and a nibble on the maid… or that Prince Dracula would baptise with foeman's blood during a Carpathian Guard initiation. Dracula's get are shadows of their sire – so many seem impersonators or imitators, littler men trying to fill the Prince's armour or copying the cut of his cloak. Yuki-Onna, who reigns over the vampires of the East as Dracula has set himself up as the Wicked Warlock of the West, is a distant mother to her subjects, seldom deigning to walk among them and yet demanding reverence. Her cold rages are famous, but she's known for killing by slow freezing – the leaching of warmth is as much a part of her mode of feeding as the taking of blood – rather than avalanche. Withal, she encourages variety in her *yōkai* followers, not imitation. Is it for her chilly amusement or out of cold curiosity? How much shape can a shapeshifter shift? Perhaps only lack of imagination prevents General Iorga, say, from turning himself inside out and rearranging his bones into a living writing-desk. What appears grotesque to Western eyes may be decorative in the East.

Some *yōkai* vampires (*futakuchi*) have extra lamprey mouths on the backs of their heads or necks, hidden by long hair, used for feeding. Others (*krasue*) wear their lungs and entrails on the outsides of their bodies, and decorate their exposed innards with ribbons and bows. Many indulge in practices that would disgust von Orlok, the most repulsive vampire in Europe. *Jikininki* feed off carrion, skulking on battlefields to suck the spoiled blood of the slain – a practice as alien to European vampires as eating raw fish is to warm Westerners. The frog-faced pygmies of the *kappa* bloodline live in ponds, crawling out of the water to eat farmers' livers and rape their wives. They bleed horses and cows, fixing mouths over the animals' anuses while sticking tongue-tentacles into their bowels. The pale, perfume-and-powder murgatroyds who parade their ennui nightly in Mayfair and Park Lane wouldn't go in for *that*. Their frilly shirts and velvet britches would get filthy.

'At least the popsy with the sideways guitar looks halfway normal,' said Whelpdale. 'Though it sounds like she forgot to kill the cat before stringing its guts on that there plink-a-plonk affair. Is she one of them geisha girlies?'

The woman played and sang. Japanese music used to sound harsh and discordant to Western ears, but the *Mikado* craze gave London aesthetes a taste for it, along with fans and lanterns. As she plucked notes, the musician's neck elongated by six or eight feet; a trick of the *rokurokubi* bloodline. Christina was revolted and pained. Dru smiled, enraptured by the trick, and flapped the heels of her hands together. Whelpdale whistled, out of tune.

Majin walked up to the trio. The umbrella *yōkai* hopped behind the long-necked woman. The green-faced goblin rolled into a ball. The woman's neck undulated like a serpent. She was her own charmer, head swaying to the music of her hands. She smiled down on the Lieutenant, showing coal-black fangs.

Majin raised his hand and his glove throbbed with light. The threads of his pentagram sigil burned scarlet. It was a signal for us to come forward – or at least the most important of us: Kostaki and Christina. And me, to translate.

Majin stood back.

'I am Lady Oyotsu,' said the *rokurokubi* woman, voice ululating from distended vocal cords. 'Abbess of the temple. These are my attendants, Abura Sumashi and Kasa-obake.'

Abura Sumashi, the potato-head, rolled around so his grinning face was uppermost. His tongue poked out. I wouldn't trust him near the back ends of my livestock, if I had any. Kasa-obake the umbrella demon opened and closed. His struts were meat-sheathed ribs, fixed to a handle that was once a human spine. His long-lashed eye winked. Christina's Paris parasol has an admirer.

'My Lady Abbess, I am Geneviève Dieudonné, a physician,' I said in Japanese. 'This is Captain Kostaki, late of the Carpathian Guard, and Princess Casamassima, who you will find an enormous pain in the neck. We are *yōkai* from Europe. *Kyuketsuki*. In our language: *vampires*.'

Lady Oyotsu looked at each of us in turn, paying particular attention to Christina. Her head bobbed. Her neck was muscular and supple. At full extent, she was less like a giraffe than one of the prehistoric monster statues in Crystal Palace park. Her pallor was painted, as were the ash-smudge eyebrows in the middle of her forehead and the cherry-red bow of her lips.

'Vampires, you are welcome guests,' she said.

When she speaks, her mouth seems a dark cavity. Her teeth are artificially blackened. Whelpdale (the elasticated man) says the practice (*ohaguro*), once common among mature Japanese women, gives him 'the shuddering flesh-creeps' more than the Lady's extensible neck. I don't see the point either, but any continent that invented the bustle and the shrunken hat has no cause to take a superior attitude.

Majin made a signal and the ox-carts were unloaded. Kannuki and the workmen set the boxes down outside the gate, taking care not to step onto temple grounds. At a nod from Lady Oyotsu, several ogre-like *yōkai* – as big as Kannuki – shambled from the shadows to take over, hauling coffins into the courtyard.

'Eight hundred and fifteen again,' said Dru. 'One of us just died.'

Having spoken, the oracle dispensed no more wisdom. She looked at us cross-eyed for a moment. Then wandered off, distracted and skipping with every third step. When everyone pays attention, Dru loses interest.

Christina – as appalled as anyone else – tried to jog the conversation along with a 'be that as it may' but Lady Oyotsu politely asked me what the strange girl had said.

'Don't tell her anything upsetting, Geneviève,' said the Princess.

Lady Oyotsu's neck extended a foot or so. An unnerving ratcheting-stretching sound accompanied the process. Her bones must telescope. I had an idea it would be unwise to lie to her face.

'Our friend believes there has been a death,' I said. 'She has visions.'

The *yōkai* woman's features became a mask of sympathy.

Christina was annoyed with me, as usual. I had a clear flash of her thoughts – she was vowing to learn Japanese as soon as possible or find someone else fluent in the tongue, so she could dispense with my questionable services.

Good luck to her.

Kostaki looked at the stack of coffins. I knew what he was thinking. Had true death come to one of our sleepers?

My guess was also that – if Dru was reading the entrails properly, and not getting vampires mixed up with spiders – the unknown casualty was someone in a box. Vampires occasionally die in their sleep like anyone else. Since elders crumble to dust, autopsies have to be performed with a sieve.

'It'll be the better part of a night's work to open the boxes and count heads,' I said.

'We can't wake them all yet,' said Christina. 'It wouldn't be practical.'

Kostaki agreed with her. He was still unsure of the ground under us. I didn't argue with them. We can't let Dru direct our policy. Even if her mad witterings are a smokescreen for a deeper cleverness, she is wayward and wilful.

As our only doctor, responsibility for safely reviving the sleepers is mine. I'd prefer to take time over it, giving everyone proper examination. Vampires get aches and pains from extended periods of lassitude – especially if we overfeed before hibernation. Leech-bloat is a common ailment of vampire gluttons. Lying in blood-boltered coffins, greedy guts swell like overcooked sausages. Unsightly rents open in their skins. Even the tiniest prick from the business end of a stake or a silver scalpel makes leech-bloat patients burst like balloons filled with blood. Slayers used to get messy surprises when they destroyed them – they could be splattered head to foot with gouts of acidic gore and rotten flesh.

Until recently, vampire medicine wasn't a practical field of study. Too much of it is still folklore and quackery. Diseases peculiar to vampires don't even have Latin names yet. Leech-bloat might be *medici eruperunt*. We are too easily classified as simply sick. In some of its many forms, the vampire condition *is* barely distinguishable from disease. Christina becomes faint at times – almost ghostly, distracted and transparent. She flares if I enquire after her health. I have seen her take minutes to make her hands solid enough to pick up a cup. Many of us are ill and don't know it. Almost all of us are in some way mad.

Before organising mass uncoffining, Christina was keen to establish herself in Yōkai Town. Ignoring the potato person and the vampire umbrella as comic relief, she fixed on Lady Oyotsu, self-evidently a person of rank. Through me, the Princess wanted to quiz her about the Emperor. I know better than to ask any Japanese to express an opinion on the divine personage. A hint of impertinence and the Abbess wouldn't be the only one with a stretched neck.

I still get an occasional crick from when Mr Yam tried to kill me.

Happy days. Simpler times.

Which reminded me, where were Kostaki's scouts, Yam and Verlaine? Evidently, their mission hadn't ended with our arrival in Yōkai Town.

Dru floated off on another whimsy. She kept hanging her

head, as if trying to imitate Lady Oyotsu's flexible vertebrae, and looking at the temple through half-closed eyes.

'It's upsidesy-downsy,' she said. 'Cellars on the top, chimneys in the basement.' She did a limber handstand and said, 'That's the ticket.'

Christina, weary as a mother of three at the close of a very long bank holiday, told Dru to stop being silly and brush herself off.

'Their attic is deep, deep down,' said Dru. 'And their boot scrapers are above the front door.'

So far as I can tell, boot scrapers are unknown in Japan.

The Abbess turned her neck three-quarters of the way round – which was just for show – and looked at Dru.

'Your holy woman has the gift of prophecy?' she asked.

'She's not altogether holy,' I said. 'Her name is Drusilla Zark.'

Dru curtseyed gravely and Lady Oyotsu nodded.

Meanwhile, Kostaki had set off on a recce of the temple outbuildings and grounds. He never rests until he's surveyed weak spots in the defences. He wouldn't sit at his best friend's hearth for Christmas – should he have a best friend or celebrate Christmas – without first determining fallback positions in the event of a surprise attack down the chimney.

Abandoning Christina and Lady Oyotsu to smile and nod at each other while Dru got in the way, I caught up with Kostaki and asked about the scouts.

'When will they report?'

'When it's safe,' he said.

'So, by your lights, never…'

For a second or two, he grinned – showing little mirth, but revealing something of the live heart inside his dead skin. Kostaki is a conundrum but I trust him. He was the first vampire to show me anything like respect in this new age. And nearly the last.

We came to a shrine, one of several in the temple

48

grounds. The Japanese have more gods than they can keep track of. They rise or fall like earthly politicians. Whoever was god of this shrine was out of office. Awning slates were broken or missing; a bowl for offerings was cracked and full of rotten grass.

From this point, we looked back at the *torii* gate. Majin stood there, silhouetted by a green glow in the fog, motionless as a terracotta statue.

'Drusilla says the Lieutenant's hands are alive,' I said. 'More than the rest of him.'

'Majin doesn't stand like a lieutenant,' said Kostaki.

'He's young for a general.'

'You look young for a doctor.'

'We both know I'm not young. But Majin is warm.'

'He wouldn't be our keeper if he were an ordinary man,' said Kostaki. 'He's not afraid to be here, among monsters.'

Some ways of living past one's years while wearing a youthful face don't involve turning vampire. Blue flames. Pictures in the attic. Elixirs and potions. Not a few arcane longevity treatments come from the East. India, Tibet, China and… here.

'Majin doesn't stand like a general, either,' said Kostaki. 'He stands like a *prince*.'

'He dresses down, compared to most princes – and princesses – I've met.'

Kostaki scowled. 'Have you read that book? Stoker's?'

I nodded.

'Remember how Dracula is dressed when Harker meets him? As a coachman. That part, I believe. An old trick of princes. Wear the clothes of a servant or an ordinary soldier. It's like being invisible.'

The Carpathian was in the Prince's service for centuries. If Dracula weren't, at bottom, a damn fool, he'd keep Kostaki and get shot of ruthless, scheming toadies like Iorga, Ruthven and Croft.

'What do *you* think Dru meant?'

Kostaki turned to look at me. 'Bad news,' he said. 'That one only ever has bad news.'

'Are you worried about Yam and Verlaine?'

'The witch said one of us died. Not two.'

'And who knows what "dies" means to her?'

We continued our circuit. As we strolled, *yōkai* emerged to stare at the hideous foreigners. Timid at first, they grew bolder and skittered, slunk, lurched or loomed into our view.

A spindle-legged cook pot with eyes, cat-faced children with ears stuck up through white hair, a blue-skinned cyclops, a man-sized grasshopper with scales of rusty iron plate, giants and dwarves with matching *Noh* masks, moon-faced vampires with permanent snarls and frond-like eyebrows, a limbless torso floating on a cloud of fog, a crab-walking greybeard sage with hands for feet, a dragon-pattern kimono wrapped around a girl who wasn't there, mushrooms with human teeth, samurai with swords or saws for hands and razor-rimmed hats, a skeleton woman holding a fan painted with a lovely mouth and nose over her skull-grin, a crawling stomach with tube-like appendages and a cocked hat pinned to its plucked-chicken skin, a bespectacled heron in bamboo armour.

Kostaki strolled casually among the *yōkai*, submitting to a certain amount of pawing and prodding, but bristling enough to deter nonsense. He would fight no more duels – symbolic or genuine – on his first night ashore.

I let our hosts see me. I made small bows and returned greetings. A pea-green bald merchant with folds of flesh hanging over his eyes and mouth opined that Western vampire women were 'unmarriageably ugly'. Realising I understood him, he blushed scarlet and gabbled apologies.

The *yōkai* gathered and, like a living wave, swept us into

the temple. Some climbed the walls and nestled in the rafters.

Lady Oyotsu made provision for us. Attendants – not *yōkai* – were willing to be bled. We gratefully accepted the sacrament of blood in lacquer bowls. Kostaki, ever cautious, abstained from drinking. If we've been drugged, he'll be alert.

Vampire sailors have spread tales that the blood of Chinese and Japanese girls is laced with opium and jasmine, and has peculiarly delightful transportive effects. Would that it were so. The blood I drank, though welcome after so long a fast, was like that of any warm person. Through the veins of Europeans, Africans and Australian aborigines flows the same stuff – giving the lie to the pseudo-science of eugenics, which is gaining a vogue in the West. Under Dracula, even venerable British institutes of learning have to entertain any balderdash that crosses the Crown Prince's mind. Bombarding the editorial office with telegrams, he thoroughly critiqued the ninth edition of the *Encyclopaedia Britannica* – insisting the print run be pulped before distribution and entries on Turkish and Romanian history be completely rewritten to glorify his name.

After the feast, we listened to Lady Oyotsu play, accompanied by Abura Sumashi on a long flute made from a thigh bone. Two tiny porcelain *yōkai* princesses sang the lay of 'Hoichi the Earless'. Monks ink holy sutras all over the body of a blind storyteller to protect him when he is commanded to recite the Tale of the Battle of Dan-no-ura for an audience of angry ghosts from the Heike Clan, losers of the battle. The monks miss Hoichi's ears. With obvious results. The Japanese care little for mystery and suspense. The end of the story is given away in the title.

'I know this one,' Whelpdale whispered. 'In the version I heard, it's not his *ears* the monks forget to paint… jolly *ouch*, eh?'

Dru wanted to play with Kasa-obake. Since she's the sort who breaks kittens' necks with hugs, I tipped off Dravot. The Sergeant said he'd make sure Dru didn't get us in hot water by killing the umbrella *yōkai*.

'You don't want to be botherin' with the bloomin' brolly, Miss Zark,' he said. 'Try some rice wine.'

'An umbrella is always of use,' Dru said, in a governessy voice.

Looking at Kasa-obake, I thought you would have to be rain-shy indeed to get any use out of him. He was an astonishing, bizarre creature. His shapeshifting – organs flattened and twisted around rearranged bones – was extreme for such an absurd, trivial result. The fellow wanted to be an umbrella. Fine. Others might want to be fire engines, teapots or streetcars. *Yōkai* like that would come in handy in circumstances other than drizzle.

Christina interrupted my blood-reverie with a list.

She has decided on the order our comrades should be awakened. Some names are near the bottom of her list. Vampires she feels it best to leave where they are. If Dru hurts anyone, it'll be an accident. If Dravot breaks necks, he'll have good reason and – thinking practically – will cover his tracks. Even Yam wouldn't commit murder without being paid for it. But others among us have proven records of murder and rapine, and are malicious and cunning with it. Christina has a point about leaving them be until we turncloaks are settled more securely. However, the longer we put off opening our unwanted presents, the more unmanageable our troublemakers are liable to be. Indiscriminately preying on locals will undermine our case as refugees. We are only tolerated within the confines of Yōkai Town. Higurashi would be grateful for an excuse to rescind the provisional welcome and have Majin set about us with silver and fire.

For all my resentment of the Princess's high-handedness, I don't want to be in charge of this excursion. I'll step in with bandages and ointment if anyone gets hurt, but would prefer important decisions be made by others. I am done with politics and intrigue.

Politics and intrigue, of course, may not be done with me.

4

A KNIGHT TEMPLAR I

Pain was Kostaki's whetstone. It kept him from growing dull.

His knee stabbed if he walked, burned if he rested. It was like living with an animal; an old dog, grown sly and vicious. If he bound his injury, an ache settled in under the bandage. If he let the wound breathe, agony flowed like mercury – taking pincers to his toes, twisting a knifepoint in his hip.

He would have mended – but for the silver.

Because the metal is valuable – used in jewellery and coinage – making silver bullets used to seem a ridiculous extravagance. Effective in killing vampires, to be sure – but so was any length of sharpened wood. Enough spears to destroy a coven of *nosferatu* could be had for the price of a single silver shot. But the payment of Judas was favoured by modern vampire killers. Silver is a soft metal, softer than lead. All silver bullets are dum-dums. They burst, seeding wounds with poison shrapnel.

Kostaki had tried taking a scalpel to his own meat and muscle. He'd stripped his knee to the bone more than once, fishing for tiny razor pearls. Some bullet fragments were mere specks. He could never find them all. His accelerated healing process worked against him. Broken bones fixed and parted sinews knit swiftly, closing around atoms of deadly metal. His body swallowed minuscule hooks.

The bullet might still kill him.

Until then, he needed his pain.

Red thirst, unslaked for five years, raged in his heart, his throat, his hands, his teeth, his loins, his head. With every rising of the moon, that *need* grew keener. Pain gave him strength to resist. Unfed, he grew alarmingly lean. A skeleton, sheathed in cords of muscle, wrapped in papyrus skin. Without blood, he looked more obviously like a vampire – a ghost with a body, gums receding to emphasise fang teeth, colourless complexion. If he opened his veins, a clear, soupy fluid leaked. Tasteless as ectoplasm, it was not blood. He could not bestow the Dark Kiss or exercise a power of fascination. He was cut off from a world of sensation. That, he found calming. His feelings were his alone, not aftertastes of stolen blood. At last, he was alone in his head – as he had been before he turned. His will was stronger than what remained of his flesh. In pain was clarity, balance. He would not go mad. He would not become a wolf who walked upright.

Kostaki no longer thought about blood.

He had declined the Abbess's offer of drink. Blood donated by attendants, served in shallow bowls. He let others guess reasons for his abstinence, perhaps admiring his caution, grateful that someone else was keeping a cool head so they could indulge their red thirst. As on the ship, he kept the night watch.

He uncrossed his legs and stood, gritting his fangs as his knee burned. His sword clattered against the polished wooden floor. He had seen enough of the welcoming ceremony to grow restless. In theatres, Kostaki had an urge to poke about backstage. How were the illusions managed? Where was the switch that turned on the moon? If Juliet was older than the Nurse, what powders gave the semblance of a fresh fourteen?

In the Temple of One Thousand Monsters, he had the same impulse.

He excused himself, slid open a flimsy door, and stepped outside.

People who'd hardly noticed his presence wouldn't mind his absence.

Alone with his aches, he reflected on the duel of single strokes. Demonstrating control, not force. Baron Higurashi was swift, precise and dangerous, but not a soldier. In a battle, Kostaki wouldn't get within sword-reach of the man. He'd have archers – or, now, snipers – shoot him from a distance. Cut off the head, and the snake ties itself in knots. Kill the officers first, then take advantage of the confusion. He learned that from Dracula.

Once, commanders in the Carpathian Guard wore no insignia of rank so the enemy couldn't single them out. The regiment was a fighting force then. In London, the Guard turned into a show troupe. Toy soldiers trotted out for victory rallies and state occasions. The lists were clogged with officers who bought their commissions or secured promotion through patronage. The flabby Bulgar Iorga became commandant. A boudoir general who wore a breastplate to keep his stomach in – and because he was afraid of anarchists dashing out of crowds with wooden stakes.

Titled elders and their ambitious get wanted to look the part. They wore scarlet-lined capes, tunics weighted with braid, unearned decorations, fantastic helmets, and ever-tighter, ever-redder britches. Real soldiers mocked these new Guardsmen, calling them the Crimson Bums. The male impersonator Vesta Tilley put on a moustache and fangs to sing 'Ain't the Girlies Glad, I'm a Right Carpathian Cad' while a chorus paraded in red tights and gilt shakoes. Insurrectionists said they'd prefer to be hunted by the Bums. You didn't hear medals clinking from three streets away when Special Branch were coming for you. Not to mention the coos of passers-by at all those ripe red rears jogging like apples in sacks.

Now, Kostaki wore something like his original field uniform. A plain black coat and boots scuffed to take off the shine. He'd seen too many polished prizes pulled off dead men's feet by camp followers to wear anything else.

He walked across the courtyard to a fountain. A stone dragon, moustached like a catfish and scaled like a lizard, crouched over a shallow trough. In summer, water must trickle from its jaws. With the winter freeze, it slavered dirty icicles. Kostaki broke off a spar and idly whittled it with his long nails, making a usable knife. A row of ladles were frost-glued to a wooden beam. Too long-handled for drinking. Were the faithful supposed to purify themselves before entering the temple by pouring water over their heads? At present, they'd have to break a thick rind of ice to do it.

His mouth was dry. He shook a couple of aniseed balls out of a pill-box and sucked slowly. The tang was something – not blood, but *something*. He preferred aniseed to cigars. They weren't little lights in the dark that gave away your position. Dravot smoked so constantly a blind man could smell him creeping up, no matter which way the wind was blowing.

The Princess thought he had won the right to land. But Higurashi had his orders, no matter the outcome of their game of swords. It had already been decided, and the Baron had less say about the disposal of the foreign vampires than Majin. How would he fare in a duel with the Lieutenant? Kostaki had an idea Majin also knew the tactic of killing the senior officers. His lowly rank was as much a disguise as any matronly Juliet's wig and rouge.

The door scraped again and Danny Dravot ducked

through. He walked across to the dragon fountain. Wiping his lips with the back of his hand, he smeared dark red across his face.

Kostaki pointed to his own mouth. Dravot, befuddled, took moments to get the message. He pulled out a kerchief and dabbed his chin and nose. The Sergeant was not an abstainer. Blood served him as strong drink did in his warm days. It was a point of pride that a British soldier could empty every barrel in a pub but stand straight at roll call next sunrise and kill three Frenchmen before breakfast. With blood in him, Dravot was merry and a little clumsy. The English newborn's red thirst was a tiny thing, soon sated and put away.

Up close, Kostaki saw Dravot's face was still bloodied.

He picked a handful of cold, crackly grass from the base of the fountain and wiped Dravot's face like a mother cleaning a muddy child in the park.

Dravot burped thanks.

Kostaki looked at the earthy clump. He crumpled the bloodied grass into a ball and tossed it away. He scraped his fingers against the rim of the fountain, leaving scraps of dry, dead skin. He did not bleed.

Dravot chuckled, satisfied.

A condition of Kostaki's fast – a private compact, made with himself – was that he not boast of his pledge. He did not wish to be commended for temperance. Lady Geneviève had asked, several times, if he was properly fed. He always told her he had sufficient for his needs. In his mind, he meant sufficient aniseed balls. So he told a truth. Another condition of his vow was that he not lie about it. Even to himself.

In the Tower of London, unjustly accused of treason and conveniently forgotten, he quit blood. The yeoman warders noticed he wasn't feeding, but didn't care. Little enough was slopped into prisoners' troughs. Provision for officers in disgrace was not a priority. After his release – one of those gestures of magnanimity Dracula made whenever a jubilee came along – Kostaki simply refrained from drinking.

On his first attempt, he managed three dry months. Then, crazed and despairing, he rented a scabby neck in a courtyard off St Giles High Street. The blood tasted like dung. He spewed into the gutter. 'Never said I was no virgin, duck,' whined the fiftyish penny whore. He paid her tuppence to go away.

After that lapse, he learned to use the pain against red thirst. He kept his vow.

At Kostaki's discharge from the Guard, the officer corps turned their backs to him. Some were infuriated by his bitter laughter. Others had the decency to burn with shame. Colonel Brudah had Kostaki present an ungloved hand. A final month's pay was counted out in silver coins, each pressed into his skin like a hot coal. The money was then taken back to settle his stabling account. While he rotted in the Tower, his horse was looked after.

It was assumed that Kostaki could be goaded into a duel – which he had no doubt he would lose. He expected poisoned towels and silver blowgun darts. Kostaki was no longer willing to die to prove a point. A regiment with no honour was incapable of insulting him. Red thirst and silver pain were constants. Humiliations he could endure.

Everything he owned could be packed into a simple coffin. Once the box was half-filled with Moldavian dirt. It turned out he didn't need that comfort either. He hadn't slept for as long as he hadn't tasted blood. He believed he *couldn't* sleep.

Long ago, as a warm child, he was told he wouldn't grow strong if he didn't finish his turnips. As a vampire elder, he discovered he grew stronger through starvation. Dracula's get knew something they never talked of. They drank human blood not because they needed to, but because they wanted to. Needing was no shame. Wanting was weakness.

He was still a walking corpse, as his face made plain to all. Abjuring the act of vampirism did not make him warm again. The clock could not run backwards.

'Fancy a promenade round the park, Brother Taki?' asked the Sergeant. 'I'm not one for spooning in the shrubbery, but could do with a fellah to 'old me braces while I pee into the bushes. Unsteady on me pegs at present. Must 'ave been something in the bill of fare... seasoning 'erbs.'

Dravot exhaled. Dead air and rotten blood.

Kostaki agreed to the walk.

'Pippin,' said Dravot. 'Let's recce the turf proper.'

They didn't know enough about this place. Sanctuary was provisional. Yōkai Town could become a killing box at a clap of Lieutenant Majin's hands.

The soldiers left the temple grounds.

Kostaki knew Geneviève didn't understand how he could rub along with Dravot. In '88, the Sergeant put the bullet in his knee. If he hadn't served a purpose as a living scapegoat, the Sergeant would have shot him in the head.

...but Dravot was his brother Freemason.

The Sergeant wore the compasses on his watch chain. He had served the craft as tyler in lodges in London and Lahore. Ostensibly a door-keeper, a Masonic tyler was much more − agent, arranger, messenger, bodyguard, assassin and whatever else a Worshipful Master decreed. For the Diogenes Club, Dravot was still a tyler.

Kostaki was initiated into the Order of the Knights Templar in Sweden. As was Dracula, cementing a temporary alliance. The Prince quit as soon as it was expedient. In old English, 'warlock' first meant oath-breaker. Going back on his word was the Impaler's habit. Betrayal was Dracula's second nature before he learned necromancy at the Scholomance. He came back from that school as a newborn vampire. Scraps of coffin wood stuck to his grave-clothes like eggshell pieces in a hatchling's feathers. Dracula had turned, but he never *changed*...

When the Prince retreated with his women to sit and scheme in his Transylvanian castle, the Carpathian Guard disbanded. Kostaki spent the better part of two hundred years with the Templars in Portugal, guarding the tombs at Berzano, ascending the ranks by mastering rituals and mysteries.

When the rallying call came, the Old Guard reconvened to serve the Prince in London.

Fifteen years into the Ascendancy, too many elders of Kostaki's vintage were truly dead. Suaver officers took their places. Newborns whose crimson arses would never touch the dirt of their native lands. Victory in Britain came too easy, a conquest by marriage. The enemy did not understand they were defeated. The casualties came *after* Dracula's triumph. Under Iorga, the Guard turned into the Crimson Bums.

'You're broodin' again, Brother Taki,' said Dravot, lighting a cheroot. 'It don't do to brood.'

Kostaki shrugged.

If only thinking was as easy to give up as drinking.

Not all the locals were at the welcoming ceremony. This walled camp had its factions and the Abbess was not an undisputed authority. Off the temple grounds, Kostaki sensed watchful eyes in the fog. Sometimes, an odd number of eyes. In prisons, monasteries and outposts, new faces offer relief from boredom. Here, the exiles were more than a novelty. Assessment would be cold. If deemed a threat, they would be disposed of. That might be the intended stratagem.

'What a ruddy shower,' said Dravot, waving his cigar. 'The Mother Superior with an India rubber neck, the brolly bloke, the baked potato on legs... If that little lot is reckoned presentable enough to parade before the Princess, imagine the ones who *ain't*. I've seen rum coves in my time, but these yokey wallahs take the bleedin' biscuit... and the broken bits left in the barrel.'

'*Yōkai*,' said Kostaki.

'Yokey. That's what I said.'

'They're just vampires. Like us.'

'Speak for yourself, Brother Taki. They ain't like me. They is *natives*. Natives is the same all the world round. Smile to your face and a kris in your back as soon as you turns.'

'In England, few smiled at my face.'

Dravot chuckled and puffed. 'That says considerable much about your face.'

Sergeant Dravot hadn't appreciated the Carpathian Guard swanning around London like the new owners. For once, the English were treated as they treated natives. High-handed foreigners pushed to the front of queues, demanding service – peevish when shopkeepers spoke no Magyar or Romanian. They commandeered goods and services, which often included women, and occupied the best row at plays and concerts, pretending not to understand when patrons seated behind asked them to doff their plumed helmets.

Kostaki understood the kris in the back, as he understood the silver in his knee. But that treatment hadn't turned the Carpathian Guard into the Crimson Bums. Subtler traps were sprung, without the Diogenes Club even taking a hand. Eventually, the English took pity on the invader and condescended to issue invitations. Club membership was offered. Pews in churches set aside. More blood was freely given than could have been taken by force. It was put about in 'circles' that your Carpathian wasn't *necessarily* a rotter. Some were good sports. Respect was accorded Dracula's get as honorary, provisional Englishmen. *That* – not dynamite and silver – pulled the fangs. In the end, smiles were crueller than knives.

They had walked a distance from the temple.

Near the seafront were facilities of shipping companies, abandoned when the walls of Yōkai Town went up. Sturdy shells of buildings. Stone and plaster, rather than wood and paper. Defensible.

Squeezed between two dark warehouses was a thin building. Its arched windows were boarded over. Stone steps led to a stout front door. On the lintel was carved an ichthus – the sign of the fish. The first Christian emblem, used even before the crucifixion. Persecuted as apostate Jews and rebels against Rome, early Christians identified each other with the Galilean gesture – an oval monocle of thumb and forefinger. Templars still used the ichthus salute.

No one ever suggested vampires should shun the sign of the fish.

'That's a church,' Kostaki told Dravot.

'I thought we came from the temple,' said the Sergeant.

'No, a real church. A Christian church. Catholic.'

Dravot exhaled smoke. 'Them beggars gets everywhere, Brother Taki.'

Japanese characters were daubed on the door.

'Condemned by order of the Great Pooh-bah,' suggested Dravot.

'That's likely,' Kostaki agreed. 'The Black Ocean Society see the Holy Church as a foreign influence. They are against foreign influences.'

'Can't say as I blame 'em. Didn't much like chapel afore I sprouted fangs. And I've grown awful weary of 'aving crosses and crucifixes waved at me conk since.'

'I prefer crucifixes to crosses.'

'There's a difference?'

'You know as well as I, Brother Mason. A crucifix is an image of Christ crucified. A cross is empty. With the crucifix, you know where Jesus is. Pinned where he can't hurt you. The empty cross means He is risen.'

As a Templar, Kostaki was a warrior of God – but he had surrendered his own salvation. Holy wars were won by damned soldiers like him. The warm boyar Dracula styled himself defender of the faith, but cynically slaughtered Christian and infidel alike. As a vampire, the Prince sometimes swore allegiance to the Devil – an easy enough pledge to make (and break) if one thought to evade Hell by not dying. Berzano Templars were excommunicated, yet served Christ. Postulants must sin ritually, without pleasure, without pity. Initiation rites involved fornication, sodomy, blasphemy, idolatry (bowing before Baphomet) and a hundred other mortal sins. Including vampirism. Without hope of Heaven, a knight was free to do the Lord's dirty work. Even Jesus shouldn't have to know what Templars did in His name. Kostaki had done worse at the behest of popes than on the orders of Dracula.

'I smells a rat,' said Dravot.

A pile of rubbish by the church steps shifted, showed blinking eyes – just the two of them – and bolted. The startled specimen ran in a cringing crouch, as if used to being beaten with sticks. Dravot, vampire-swift, blocked the path. The ragman scuttled backwards and blundered into Kostaki. The smell of drink stung Kostaki's nostrils. Not bothering to draw his sword, he put his ice-blade to the man's throat.

'*Mestres, mestres… misericórdia, misericórdia!*'

The ragman was a warm Japanese, emaciated and unhealthy. Relatively young. His patchy beard and unkempt hair were black. His grubby skin was marred by gritted old scars and fresh raw sores. Scabs on his neck and limbs showed he'd been bitten often.

'*Mestres… misericórdia!*'

'That's not Jap jabber,' said Dravot.

'It's Portuguese,' Kostaki said. '*Português?*'

'*Sim, sim, eu sei,*' said the ragman. 'You are from Portugal.'

'What's the Chinaman saying?'

'That we're Portuguese.'

Dravot clucked. 'Tell 'im we bloody ain't.'

'To him, all Europeans are Portuguese... like some think all orientals Chinese.'

Dravot shrugged.

'Who taught you this language?' Kostaki asked.

'Father Rodrigues, many years ago. I serve Father Rodrigues. Serve his line.'

'A warm josser who won't quit the Yokey Pokey,' Dravot observed. 'Is 'e loony? Or just a blood-nancy? Look at the cankers on 'im. It'd take a long dry spell to make me draw from this well.'

Of course, it had been a long dry spell.

'He's not a madman, just afraid,' said Kostaki. 'In this place, I'd think him mad if he weren't afraid.'

'Stop further terrifyin' the poor basket with your ice-sticker then.'

Kostaki crumbled his makeshift blade and dropped the pieces. He stood back.

'What is your name?' Kostaki asked.

'Kichijiro,' said the ragman. 'I am good Christian.'

Kostaki raised his hand to his eye, making the ichthus. Kichijiro bowed low and looked up. His smile showed missing teeth.

'What is this place?'

'Their church, shelter, crypt. The disciples of Rodrigues. Those he make like him. Make like you.'

Kichijiro put his hands beside his mouth, kinking his forefingers like fangs.

'Like us?' Kostaki prompted. 'Vampires. Drinkers of blood. *Kyuketsuki.*'

The Japanese nodded vigorously. '*Vampiros Português*,' Kichijiro said. '*Nosferatu.*'

Dravot's ears pricked at that.

Kostaki looked up at the church door. While they were paying attention to Kichijiro, it had been pulled inward.

In ghost stories, doors creak. A door opening silently is more sinister.

Someone stood at the top of the steps, shadowed under the arch.

Kostaki's hand went to his sword-hilt. Dravot reached inside his coat for his revolver.

A lucifer flared and a candle flame grew, illuminating a face.

'Welcome, brothers,' said the vampire, in English.

He wore a black vestment and a long white silk scarf. His brick-red hair was cut and combed European-style, but his features were oriental. More Chinese than Japanese. His almond eyes were golden. Thin lips drew back from pearl fang-tips. In his hand was a brass candlestick.

Kichijiro shrank from the vampire – his *mestre*.

Kostaki knew what the ragman was. In English slang, a Renfield, named after Dracula's short-lived English minion, famous in a book no one was supposed to read. More than a servant, less than a lover. Watchdog, valet, messenger boy and day labourer. Bitten if needs must, but never turned – though many a Renfield nurtured the illusion that the Dark Kiss was promised. Some were kept alive beyond their allotted span, but only as working animals. Elders would butcher them without qualm if it became expedient. Masters grew blind to the commingling of love and hate in minions' eyes. Kostaki had heard of haughty elders spitted in their catafalques by Renfields who suffered one whipping or blood-rape more than the tatters of their pride could stand.

'I am Dorakuraya,' said the vampire. 'Enter freely and of your own will.' He held up his candle. Behind him was a black curtain. 'Come freely, go safely and leave some of the happiness you bring.'

Kostaki thought Kichijiro's *mestre* had learned that and was reciting.

'An invitation it would be churlish to refuse,' said Dravot, pulling his empty hand out of his coat. 'I'm Daniel Dravot, Esquire, late of the Queen's Own Right Royal Loyal Light Infantry. This corpse-faced specimen is Brother Kostaki, late of the Carpathian Guard – but 'e will swear on 'is solemn word as a foreigner that 'e has no more truck with those scoundrels. We is adventurers, come from a far land seeking our fortune. We meet on the level and trust to depart on the square.'

Dorakuraya bowed graciously.

Kostaki recognised his name – it was how the Japanese said 'Dracula'.

The curtain was lifted. Kostaki and Dravot followed Dorakuraya's candle flame. Kichijiro slunk after them like a shamed dog.

Lamps burned low and red. The church was desecrated. Behind the altar stood a man-sized upside-down cross. Ugly nails stuck out of stained wood, suggesting recent crucifixions. A tang of spilled blood made Kostaki's eyes water and his fangs prick. Scarlet cloth spotted with black wax draped the altar. A fouled Bible lay at the foot of the lectern, where it could readily be trampled.

Kostaki heard a scratching above.

In the vaulted ceiling roosted a colony of large bats. The flagstone floor was speckled with their guano. Rats and insects nested in the wreckage of smashed pews. Cobwebs hung over everything.

Amid this filth, Dorakuraya was immaculate.

Not so the other vampire in the church.

As Kostaki and Dravot stepped out of the vestibule, a disreputable Japanese rolled out of a hammock and landed like a cat. He ambled towards them with a peculiar gait – strutting and slouching at the same time. His topknot wasn't tied properly and he had a few days' growth of beard. A pair of sheathed swords were tucked into the belt of his kimono: a long *katana* and a short *wakizashi*.

Shrugging as if infested with itch-inducing bugs, he pulled his arms into his robe and scratched. Empty sleeves flapped like useless wings. He snarled lazily, showing cat fangs.

'My brother-in-darkness,' said Dorakuraya.

The shabby samurai looked dubious about this claim of kinship. He little resembled his 'brother'. Kostaki assumed they were related by bloodline not blood. Turned by the same father-in-darkness.

'This is Kostaki and this is Dravot,' said Dorakuraya.

The other vampire grunted and shrugged again, still wriggling in his clothes. He wasn't too concerned about formal introductions.

Finally, Dravot asked, 'What's your name, chum?'

'Sanjuro,' snapped back the vampire.

It was an odd name – Thirty.

'Thirty what?' Kostaki asked.

The vampire looked around the church, then up at the roost. 'Komori,' he said, sticking his arms out through his sleeves. 'Sanjuro Komori.'

A laugh cracked in Kostaki's throat.

'What's funny?' Dravot asked.

'His name means Thirty Bats.'

'Sounds like a Red Indian brave.'

'Or an alias.'

Komori had given them something to call him. That was as far as he felt obliged to go. Dorakuraya, however, gave the impression he wouldn't want *his* assumed name – and what it implied – called into question.

'You are *nosferatu*,' said Dorakuraya. 'Dracula's get.'

Kostaki admitted he was of the Dracula line. So did Dravot – whose blood was watered several times.

'We are cousins,' said Dorakuraya. 'We also carry the blessed blood. We have it from the Prince's disciple, Sebastian Rodrigues.'

Kostaki murmured noncommittally. Until Kichijiro mentioned the name, he'd not heard of Rodrigues. A Portuguese missionary, passing through Wallachia on his way to Japan centuries ago, could have received the Dark Kiss from Dracula or – more likely – one of his wives. The Prince wooed and turned his women personally, but had male get by proxy. This Rodrigues might have been a pawn in a scheme of Eastern conquest set aside when Dracula turned his attention to England. It was also possible that Dorakuraya's father-in-darkness was a liar. Claiming lineage from Dracula was like posing as rightful heir to the Hapsburg or Stuart thrones. A lot of ambitious bastards tried the trick. Few successfully.

'I am doubly the priest's get,' said Dorakuraya. 'A son of the Black Mass, conceived in blasphemy. On that altar.'

'Can't 'ave been comfy-cosy,' observed Dravot.

Dorakuraya's red hair must come from his father. The colouring wasn't common in Japan – or Portugal, either, come to that. It was a trait of some vampire bloodlines, like red eyes, hairy palms or sixth fingers. The mother must have been Japanese. A prostitute, most likely. The Black Mass requires veneration of a harlot in place of the Virgin. Latin chanted backwards. And blood that turns to wine – or, at least, is drunk like wine.

Could Father Rodrigues have been a Templar? Some lodges bowed to Satan rather than Baphomet. Doctrinally, a Christian goat-devil was indistinguishable from a pagan goat-god.

Dorakuraya made a reverse sign of blessing – bottom to top, left to right, with the left hand.

'In the name of the fucker, the spawn and the Holy Goat,' he blasphemed.

'God's 'oly trousers,' whispered Dravot, impressed.

As Dorakuraya turned to the altar, Kostaki realised why he stood so straight. A sword was sheathed against his spine.

'Him, he just found,' said Dorakuraya, indicating his brother-in-darkness, who grunted without complaint. 'The wretch Kichijiro wasn't a suitable bodyguard, so Father Rodrigues sought out this *ronin* and turned him. He is always Thirty Something. Thirty Dung Beetles, Thirty Peach Trees, Thirty Satisfied Courtesans, Thirty Bloody Graves. He was conscientious, putting his sword between our father and those who would stop him… until the European coin was spent. Then, Rodrigues was unprotected. From me.'

'Nemuri *beheaded* our father-in-darkness,' said the samurai, addressing Kostaki directly. 'A clean killing. Honourable vengeance. For crimes against us, and against all humanity. The priest murdered us both and raised us from death as slaves. And worse than slaves.'

Dorakuraya – Nemuri, his brother-in-darkness called him – flashed fangs.

'He betrayed this one's mother too,' continued Komori, jerking a thumb at Dorakuraya. 'And took it as his duty to commit many crimes. Before every sin, the Father would pause… to give Deus, the Christian god, an opportunity to speak out, to stop him. If God spoke to him, the Father would show the mercy of Abraham, reward those he had intended to harm, and devote his life to good works. Just a whispered word on the wind… and many would be spared, *saved*. Many he was about to outrage mistook his pause for a hesitation. Maybe, they thought, the monster would be moderate – would not burn, torture, ravage, drink blood. That hope was a sharper cruelty, I think, than he intended. Deus was always silent. The Father pressed on with his own pleasures – not that he got joy from them. He transgressed over and over again in a holy quest, seeking a sin so great that God was forced to talk to him. You would have liked the Father, I think.'

Kostaki doubted that. But he knew the silence of God.

'Father Rodrigues was a great man,' said Dorakuraya. 'The vessel that bore the sacred blood to the East. That was his true holy cause. He came not in the name of Deus, but of Dracula. Without him, this would be wilderness. The only vampires here would be poor, childish things… goblins such as you've seen in the Temple of Ice. But fathers must fall so sons may rise.'

At that, Komori spat blood.

Dorakuraya twitched with distaste.

The brothers-in-darkness were an odd pair. Their father had done more than make vampires of them. He had forged them into swords. One straight, one curved – both honed sharp. Perhaps he really was Dracula's get. In Kostaki's experience, the Prince didn't have to be present to cast a shadow over everything. Sebastian Rodrigues must have been truly dead for hundreds of years… but his little brood still clung together. They couldn't go two minutes without mentioning him.

'We are true vampires,' declared Dorakuraya. 'You are our kinsmen.'

Kostaki admitted Dorakuraya and Komori were what Europeans recognised as vampires. Not *yōkai*, but *nosferatu*. The bloodline was hardy indeed to take root in stony ground. Like Christianity, their vampirism had survived hundreds of years of persecution in the land of the rising sun.

For all Dorakuraya's prissiness and Komori's slovenliness, both were warriors. That martial aspect was another Dracula trait.

'Nemuri will try to enlist you in his crusade,' said Komori. 'If I were you, I'd keep out of it. You may prefer to keep your heads fixed to your shoulders.'

'My brother is fleshly,' said Dorakuraya. 'Obsessed with his comforts—'

'Which is why you find me wallowing in luxury.'

'Too lazy to fight for our cause.'

'When Nemuri says "our", he stretches the word. Later, once you're ashes, it shrinks again and he says "my". Causes make me itch.'

Kostaki suspected everything made Komori itch.

An idealist and a cynic. Or a fanatic and a realist. Had Kostaki and Dravot found a mirror in this church? If so, he was chilled to admit he preferred Dravot's reflection to his own. He trusted Komori, who was barely civil, over Dorakuraya, who greeted them as long-lost relatives.

Outside, things howled in pain and anger.

'Listen to them,' said Dorakuraya, eyes flashing green-gold. 'The children of the night – what music they make.'

'Sounds more like dogs fightin' to me,' said Dravot. 'I likes a tune you can march to, you know, or wring out of a squeeze box.'

'The only music Nemuri likes more than dogs fighting is dogs dying,' said Komori.

The commotion was near the church – on its doorstep. A knocking and rattling came. Kichijiro tried to hide in a confessional used as a privy. Dorakuraya lashed out with his scarf. Weighted in the Thuggee manner, it whip-snapped against the Renfield's head.

Whimpering, Kichijiro ducked under the black curtain.

Kostaki looked at Dravot. The Sergeant had his hand inside his coat again.

Komori fiddled with his belt. One of his blades slid a few shining inches out of its wooden sheath as if by accident. Dorakuraya wound his white scarf back around his neck, and gripped his sword.

Kostaki realised his hand also hovered near his carrack.

The racket outside turned to a piteous keening. Something not an animal, or not entirely an animal, was wailing. And making a concert of it.

The Renfield blundered out of the vestibule. He pulled the curtain behind him, clumsily tugging it off its rail.

Cold wind blew into the church.

The door was open. A small, white-faced − masked? − woman squatted on the step, swaddled in a padded robe. Her glossy hair was piled in an arrangement of spheres with needles stuck through them. Her eyes were glass buttons with horizontal slits for pupils. On her cheeks were scarlet dabs. Grooves cut into her skin from the corners of her mouth.

'Monster, give me my child,' someone screeched.

The high-pitched voice came not from the woman but from under a black blanket spread out behind her like a train. A small human shape lay on the steps, one arm buried in the woman's robe.

The woman's mouth clicked open. She was a doll.

The puppeteer made the figure crawl forwards. The chin hung idiotically, showing black wooden teeth. The eyes rolled on nails.

Porcelain hands clapped to the doll face.

'Monster… my child…'

Dorakuraya looked, with irritation, to Komori − who shrugged.

Like Dorakuraya, with his 'children of the night' speech, the doll − who spoke in accented English − was quoting. An extract from Jonathan Harker's Transylvania journal. This was a long way to come for a marionette travesty of Bram Stoker's suppressed book.

Terrified, Kichijiro threw the curtain over the doll. Muffled, it continued to bleat about its child.

The puppeteer stood, and the curtain hung over his blanket. He − if the sexless figure was a he − was a black version of the pantomime white-sheeted ghost.

The puppet head peeped out from a fold of cloth, mouth clicking in disapproval.

'Get you gone,' said Dorakuraya.

To emphasise the point, he drew his sword as if sliding it out of his spine. It came free in one smooth, easy move. The steel, slightly oiled, glistened in the firelight.

The puppet head craned, glassy eyes surveying the church. Kostaki had an urge to cut the doll's head off and the operator's hand with it.

Another puppet – on the puppeteer's other hand – emerged. This one wore a red-lined cape and was a European vampire, with widow's peak, spade beard and prominent fangs.

'I am… Dracula,' came a low, resonant voice. 'You think to baffle me, you – with your pale faces all in a row like sheep in a butcher's. You shall be sorry yet, each one of you!'

Kichijiro couldn't have been more frightened of the real Dracula.

Dravot was laughing, though he'd also drawn his revolver. Komori and Dorakuraya held their blades up. As did Kostaki.

This was not a door-to-door entertainment.

From behind the black-draped puppeteer peeped a small figure Kostaki knew at once wasn't another doll. A little vampire with many layers of ruffled skirts, a bodice embroidered with purple skulls, and sleeves of frill upon frill. He got an impression of huge coal-black eyes and a red bow in a mane of springy ringlets.

Dorakuraya also saw her – and hissed.

Kostaki had an uncomfortable sense of being in the middle of something he couldn't hope to understand.

The puppeteer, still draped head to foot, shambled into the church. Dolls bobbed along in front of the figure, heads turning eerily in unison. Ridiculous, but not amusing.

Both heads tilted back, like baby birds opening mouths wide to be fed. Broad knives extended from their bodies.

Dorakuraya planted his feet firmly and began to move his sword in a circle until it was raised above his head. Steel shimmered as the samurai cut through the air. The knife-head dolls jabbed and Dorakuraya sliced at the puppeteer's covered head, skipping past while whirling fast to slash. He should have cut through the unseen figure's windpipe and spine...

The dolls laughed.

The cloth parted where the sword's edge touched. The human hump collapsed, taking the puppets with it. The curtain and blanket flattened and wrinkled on the flagstones, as if no one had been there.

The bats in the eaves squeaked and flapped.

Dorakuraya lifted the curtain with the end of his sword and whipped it away. The puppets lay, abandoned. The vampire doll was cracked across the face. The grieving mother had choked on her knife.

'Nemuri makes enemies,' Komori observed. 'That's what comes of nominating yourself as the Dracula of Japan. Others take offence.'

'The child?' Kostaki prompted.

'Tsunako Shiki,' said Komori, 'a pet of Yuki-Onna, the Snow Queen. Tsunako loves toys, dolls and conjuring tricks.'

'An ungrateful whelp,' said Dorakuraya, with feeling.

'Little madam could do with a beltin',' said Dravot.

Komori nudged the mother puppet with his toe. A beetle crawled out of a cracked eyehole.

Lady Geneviève had mentioned Yuki-Onna. A Japanese elder – effectively queen of all *yōkai*, but absent. Evidently, she had loyalists and partisans.

Something hissed through the open door. Kichijiro yelped and held up his hand. Embedded in his palm was a sharp metal star shape.

Shadow men dropped from the ceiling, disturbing clouds of bats.

They moved vampire-fast and wore black wrappings. Hoods showed only their eyes. They were silent, but the bats made a lot of noise.

Dorakuraya spun again, making a circle with his blade. The shadow men danced about him as if he were a deadly maypole, staying beyond reach of his sword-tip.

Kostaki heard a child's laughter. Bats flapped against his face and flew out of the church. A shadow came at him, darting from side to side – or was it two shadows constantly exchanging places?

The church was full of shadow men.

Ninja. Geneviève had mentioned them too. A kind of warrior monk – Buddhist Templars? Known for quiet, skill and near-supernatural abilities. Like vanishing suddenly, appearing in puffs of smoke, mule kicks, steam piston thumps, snake-swift reflexes and – it seems – puppet theatre. If the troupe wanted a music hall career, the acrobat act was a better bet than the ugly ventriloquist dolls.

Dorakuraya scythed through encircling shadows. His sword slid across bleeding flesh. Shadows fell and tumbled out of his range.

Komori made ostensibly clumsy passes, but ninja dropped to their knees around him. He fought like an unpredictable drunkard. Very dangerous.

"'Ave you noticed?' said Dravot. 'These fellahs ain't botherin' us.'

Two shadows collided in front of Kostaki. He was pushed backwards by palm strikes. His chest was hammered. Geneviève had warned of the ninja vampire-slaying technique – a quick punch to break ribs, then a fond embrace. Sheared bones turned to heart-transfixing stakes.

'Sorry I spoke,' said Dravot, trying to find a target.

'Don't shoot,' Kostaki said. 'You'll hit someone.'

'That's the general idea of shootin', Brother Taki.'

'I mean you'll hit *me*.'

'Didn't do me much good the last time.'

'Didn't do me much good either.'

'I said before and I say again, if I'd known you was a Brother of the Craft, I'd 'ave let you be and shot the other fellah—'

The ninja leaped around them. Kostaki was half-right: they weren't attacking him and Dravot, but were trying to keep the Europeans separate from Komori and Dorakuraya.

Fed up with all this nonsense, Dravot got a grip on the barrel of his revolver and used the handle as a club. He connected solidly with a cowled head. A ninja tumbled face-first into a mess of kindling and cobweb.

His comrades paused in their activities and looked at the Englishman.

'What?' he asked. 'Not cricket?'

Something flashed across the church – another throwing star stuck in Dravot's cheek. It missed his eye, but his wound wept blood. Dravot was obviously too annoyed to feel the injury as more than a flea bite. He flipped his pistol and fired above their heads.

Ninja scrambled to get up and get back. Even the ones Dorakuraya had caught with his full moon cut were merely scratched. Their black tight-fitting clothes showed wounds and gashes. They didn't bleed.

The ninja didn't stay still long enough to be distinguished one from another. Fast as vampires and rapidly healing, they weren't undead – or even *yōkai*. This was some other trick.

The shadow warriors were another variety of puppet. And Kostaki knew who was out there in the fog, giggling as she tugged on the silk-thread strings.

Another cousin to the *nosferatu*. A nuisance and an

ungrateful whelp. There was a story here. Was Tsunako
Shiki another sprig of the Rodrigues' bloody family tree?
Or perhaps the once-pampered get of this pair of *ronin*?
Such parentage arrangements seldom lasted.

Dorakuraya and Komori stood, back to back, swords
raised, snarling like tigers.

Suddenly, the ninja were gone.

Dravot whistled and looked about. He holstered his gun.

'What was that all about?' he asked.

Kostaki shrugged.

Dorakuraya and Komori were gone too. They had their
own ninja tricks.

'It'd be an 'elp to 'ave a programme so we knew all the
players straight off,' said Dravot.

Kostaki sheathed his sword with a click.

Even Kichijiro had made himself scarce. Kostaki picked
up the bloodied star-knife he'd pulled out of his hand. It
was six-pointed.

'You ain't goin' to lick that,' said Dravot. 'You don't
know where the fellah's been.'

Kostaki flipped the star to Dravot, who caught it.

'It's called a shuriken,' Kostaki said.

'Been takin' lingo lessons with the fair mademoiselle?'
Dravot examined the thing, licking his lips.

'You already have one,' Kostaki said. 'On your face.'

Kostaki pointed to his own cheek. Dravot felt around
the star, his eye rolling to look at it.

'So I 'ave, Brother. Thanks for mentionin' it.' Dravot
plucked out the shuriken. His wound closed but his face
was still bloodied. 'Steel, not silver,' he said. 'There's a
lucky thing.'

'They'll be making them of silver soon enough.'

Dravot experimentally threw the stars one after another
at the vertical beam of the inverted cross. Both bounced
rather than stuck.

'There's a knack to this,' said the Sergeant. 'Years of practice. I could trounce 'em in any pub at a throw-the-darts tourney. And they could never 'ope to match my mastery of the ancient mystic art of shove 'a'penny.'

Kostaki wasn't convinced about that. Ninja probably shoved sharpened ha'pennies and played the game to the death.

The little girl's laugh sounded again. It was picked up and carried by the bats, which were clustering again in their roost. Not a real child, Tsunako was one of those poor, often vicious souls turned before they could grow up.

'Don't that give you the 'orrors?' Dravot commented.

Mirthless laughter was sad more than frightening. But Kostaki had concerns about the war they had just wandered into. It would not profit them to get involved in local disputes, especially before – as Dravot said – they knew who the players were. Komori mentioned Dorakuraya's crusade and Dorakuraya spoke of 'our cause'. Neither gave specifics.

As they looked up at the ceiling, a horsehair trunk abandoned among the broken pews popped open. Tsunako Shiki sprung up in a froth of petticoats and a cloud of paper butterflies, hands out like a conjurer expecting applause. She tilted her head to one side and then the other, and showed a fanged Cupid's bow smile.

Kostaki and Dravot looked at the vampire girl.

She tumbled out of the trunk and rolled across the flagstones, then scrabbled on her tiny hands and feet, moving swiftly towards them.

Kostaki flinched, expecting an attack. She put her arms around his legs and pressed her curls against his thigh.

'I think she likes you,' said Dravot. 'You always was a devil with the girlies, Brother Taki.'

Kostaki still expected a sting – teeth sunk into the meat of his leg, or snapping metal traps in her hair. But

Tsunako looked shyly up at him and blew a kiss.

Then, she let him go and flew backwards and upwards, disturbing the bats. The colony took flight and rushed at Kostaki and Dravot with scything wings. They waved their hands, sweeping the squeaking, flapping creatures away.

By the time the bats were out of their hair, Tsunako Shiki was nowhere to be seen.

On reflection, Kostaki was more worried by her hug than he would have been by a bite. Tsunako was a human doll. Kostaki did not play with dolls.

'Mercies that she's gone,' he breathed.

'Our 'osts have abandoned us too,' Dravot said.

'We should get back to the temple,' said Kostaki. 'We've left the others alone too long.'

'The ladies, eh, Brother Taki? I'm sure they can fend for themselves.'

'Maybe so.'

'One thing,' said Dravot. 'A piece of advice, from a spy to a soldier, as it were. Best not trouble the dear little things' pretty heads with talk of… well, of any of this. Bats and dolls and tumblers and steel stars. You know our Gené… and the Princess. They'd only worry. Worryin's not good for the delicate ones. We should keep this to ourselves, Worshipful Brother… An aspect of the craft, not to be discussed with the profane. Agreed?'

Kostaki thought of Geneviève a moment. And nodded.

'On the level, Brother Taki…'

'On the square, Brother Dravot.'

5

YŌKAI TOWN, DECEMBER 9, 1899

We have been made welcome in the Temple of One Thousand Monsters. We are fed and entertained. Our hosts are quietly courteous and deferential. But we are little better off than we were aboard ship. Awake or asleep, we are baggage. Christina drags me around so she can talk with important Japanese people, but has trouble finding any. It is becoming apparent that, though many have imposing titles, the residents of Yōkai Town are as powerless as we. *Yōkai* think of themselves as ghosts and, without complaint, haunt homes rather than live in them. There is no one within these walls we can make demands of, offer concessions to or come to arrangements with.

The occasional glint of a polished visor is a reminder that Lieutenant Majin spies on the compound. An observation platform is built into the helmet of the warrior statue by the gate. Majin is often there, pretending to doze on a striped deckchair with his cap over his face. Since delivering us, the Lieutenant has shown no special interest. If I mention his name, locals lapse into convenient deafness.

This morning, we obtained an audience with General Nurarihyon, whom we were gently misled into taking for the military leader of Yōkai Town. Christina suggested it would be best if Kostaki came with us; she thought the General would respond to a fellow soldier. Kostaki, lately even more closer-mouthed than usual, gave her no resistance. He had quiet words with Dravot before joining our little deputation. They are hatching something – something essentially *manly* – between them. They have made a more thorough survey of this enclave than Kostaki and I managed on our night walk in the temple gardens.

General Nurarihyon represents what is, on the face of things, the least threatening vampire bloodline I've ever come across. Whereas *nosferatu* are feared for entering houses while owners are at home and drinking their blood, the *nurarihyon* are resented for entering houses while owners are away and drinking their tea. Yes – a vampire who subsists on tea! With, on occasion, a few drops of blood added to the pot. The sting is that it has to be *someone else's* tea. The General's child-brain quirk is such that he can't just buy it. He must *steal* tea, or else it doesn't quicken him.

Abura Sumashi, the potato-headed courtier, was bored enough to tag along with our deputation. He pointed out a shack close to the General's hut. Lady Oyotsu makes sure a refreshed kettle always simmers on a stove there. In this community of oddities, Nurarihyon's kleptomania is indulged.

The Princess and I giggled like schoolgirls at this arrangement until Abura Sumashi further explained the General's potent power of fascination. Settled like a hermit crab in the place of an absent lord, he issued orders no one in the household had the strength to disobey. All in the pursuit of tea. That made Nurarihyon sound considerably less amusing and more unpleasant – though Christina always takes mention of others' powers as a challenge rather than a warning.

'Once settled in a residence,' Abura Sumashi chortled, 'it was not unknown for General Nurarihyon to whisper that retainers should kill themselves or each other for his amusement... or command a man's wives, daughters and concubines to lie with him. To rebuke Magistrate Shinbei of Otama, who displeased him by levying tax on his shrine, Nurarihyon had Shinbei's daughter Akino kneel before him – smiling and unblinking – while he slowly poured scalding tea into her eyes.'

Note that, in these stories, the antagonists are the General and the away-from-home masters. The women and the servants are property to be appropriated. Blinded Akino is less important than the bloody tea. No wonder so many Japanese *kyuketsuki* are angry, vengeful women. Many of them disfigured by men.

When not sneaking out to sip stolen tea, the General spends his time composing a letter to the Emperor, petitioning for full recognition of *yōkai* as loyal subjects and pledging service against his enemies. Abura Sumashi says that Nurarihyon, sometimes overcome by despair, is given to tantrums. Which explains the broken pots and snapped brushes strewn around his tatami mat and the dramatic ink stains splashed on his paper walls.

We found Nurarihyon in a placid mood, though faint and distant. Nestled amid coils of the paper, he was distracted by some point of epistolary etiquette. His swollen, hairless skull is almost transparent. I was fascinated by the pale, watery blood pulsing irregularly through his veins. At any teaching hospital, he could have earned his keep as a useful illustration in lectures on the circulatory system.

'These are vampires from the West – from England,' said Abura Sumashi.

We set sail from Plymouth, but are French, Italian-American and Moldavian.

'W.G. Grace, crumpets, "London Bridge is Falling Down",' said the General, in a high-pitched, drawn-out titter. 'Milk in tea,' he added, spitting disgust.

'Do I need to translate that?' I asked the Princess.

Christina shook her head. Her aura sparked.

Like the General, the Princess has distracted spells
– not *fainting* (though I believe she does that sometimes)
but *faint*. She becomes harder to see, like a fading stain.
Her substance bleeds into her light. You can make out
lamps through her and, sometimes, the walls behind her
– usually only for a moment. Her brows knit as if she is
fighting a terrible headache and she *coheres* through force
of will. How much effort does Christina expend on not
dissipating through boredom and frustration?

It took a minute for the Princess to write off the gourd-
headed General as a simpleton. His way of looking at us
while pretending not to made my fangs sharpen, but he is
a feeble remnant of whatever he once was.

Kostaki was imperturbable, as always. I suspect he has
mastered the soldier's trick of sleeping sat up straight with
his eyes open to fool superior officers into believing they
have his full attention.

The General has been working on his missive for many
years. The endless scroll loops around and in and out of
his dwelling. The Emperor he was addressing when he
took up his first brush is long dead.

Once, Nurarihyon – tea drinker or no – could walk
into a palace when the shogun was elsewhere and make
himself at home, swaying the destiny of the nation. All the
tea in Japan would no more slake his thirst than oceans
of blood satisfied other tyrants. That he could take it was
what mattered. At the zenith of his power, no one in this
country could own anything – or count on anyone – unless
he allowed it. Even Dracula would envy that. Now, he is
reduced to writing a letter no one will read. He cannot
have been easy to break.

'Who brought General Nurarihyon to Yōkai Town?' I
asked Abura Sumashi.

The *yōkai*'s puffy head throbbed as he looked up for a

moment at the statue by the gate. Then he straightened his hat and waddled off without answering me.

So, Majin is collector and keeper of this zoo. He has stocked the high-walled camp with *yōkai*. This is a cemetery for the living.

Our duties here are to lie down and rot.

6

BEFORE DRACULA (CONTINUED)

I was not the only vampire in Paris.

A nest of murgatroyds ran a macabre playhouse in the city for several seasons. They staged trivial operas – several about Lord Ruthven, who wasn't too flattered not to ask for a cut of the box office. Act One would find excuses for players to disport in elaborate, gorgeous costume, Act Two would find excuses for the ladies (and some gentlemen) of the cast to wear as little costume as possible and Act Three, for which the stage would be covered in oilskin and patrons in the front five rows advised to wear raincoats, would feature copious, unsimulated bloodletting. The Théâtre des Vampires went out of fashion, a worse fate by their impresario's lights than being impaled or burned at the stake. Some say Erik, the masked musician and murderer who lives under the Palais Garnier, is a vampire but he isn't. I met him once, in the morgue. A strange duck and liable to outlive us all if he stays away from politics... but warm.

Also – and this seems astonishing now – a band of French criminals call themselves Les Vampires. They are no more undead than apache ruffians are Red Indians. Last I heard, the gang were considering a name change. The point of wearing batwing cloaks and fanged masks while housebreaking and blackmailing is to evoke dread legend – not compete with everyday monsters. If vampires are normal, what's left to strike fear into the superstitious? Sea serpents, perhaps? Or giant armadillos?

Chandagnac, my father-in-darkness, was destroyed by the English in 1438, six years after he turned me – and, infuriatingly, before he could adequately explain why he chose to make the doctor's daughter, of all people, his get. Melissa d'Acques, *his* mother-in-darkness, is a strange, elusive little creature. The few times we met, she treated me like a newfound big sister or a soon-tired-of birthday present rather than the last of her line. I have no other blood connections. Melissa, I am told, was born the way she is – so rare a thing I doubt it's true. I have never bestowed the Dark Kiss – not even on you, dear Charles. I have no coven, colony or clan. Before the Ascendancy, I did not seek the society of my kind, for – as you once said – I really don't have any.

The other vampires of Paris were territorial, and – like me – preferred a quiet life. Six months could pass without me running into one, which, to be frank, was a blessing. As a traveller, you know how it is. You're in Sumatra or Tierra del Fuego and your host thinks it a kindness to introduce you to the only other Englishman in a thousand miles. He always turns out to be the most colossal bore, bounder or pill on earth. Imagine the same thing but instead of a dreary missionary with a passion for inflicting vegetarian pamphlets on the natives or a remittance man expelled from Rugby for roasting his fag, you're stuck with a periwigged fiend knee-deep in ragamuffin blood or a murdering trollop who never shuts up about the Saturnalian orgies of the Roman Empire.

Warm people always assume vampires have a bump of sensitivity that itches when we run into each other. When there were fewer of us about and folk generally didn't believe we existed, we'd see a pale, haunted face in a crowd and magically recognise another of our kind. As you know, that's not the case. Remember we *both* took the Daughter of the Dragon for a vampire when we met her in '88 because of her pearly teeth? Such mistakes are often fatal for either or both parties. Greetings, fellow night-walker! Die, bloodsucking vermin! Several *nosferatu* nitwits have taken me for a helpless warm wench and tried to play 'watch the watch' with me, salivating at the prospect of my fair, pulsing throat. That was less amusing to live through than write down.

Nevertheless, sometimes we do know each other on sight. A craze sprung up for visiting the morgue to view the unidentified bodies kept on ice. The original idea was that relatives of missing persons could put names to corpses and claim them for burial. But well-off wastrels started clamouring at our doors, intent on gawping – as if the dead were statues in an exhibition. This perversity spread to the *haut ton*. Society matrons and distinguished *seigneurs* took to ogling the frost-rimed remains of drowned pregnant shopgirls and throat-cut *boulevardiers*. After that, respectable *bourgeois* queued, as eager to tut-tut the callous connoisseurs of death as to cast an eye over cadavers. Finally, the Baedeker set caught up. The morgue became one of the places a tourist in Paris absolutely must tick off in the guidebook, along with museums, galleries, churches, cafés and buildings of architectural interest.

We medical students were cynical about the viewing parties, though in no position to sneer. We'd all volunteered and had our own reasons – many dubious – for toiling among the dead. Regular visitors became well known to the ghouls: the doleful priest who insisted on performing intimate examinations of young female corpses, on the grounds that he was looking for his long-lost sister (though he ranged far and wide among dead *demoiselles*, oddly unsure of the colour of his relation's hair – or even skin); the Belgian artist drawn to the dreadfully mangled or dismembered, who made exquisitely upsetting sketches of their fatal injuries and was once detained at the exit with a pair of delicate snipped-off ears pressed in his pocketbook; the retired army officer who brought his twin sons to view any bloated wretch fished out of the Seine so he could deliver illustrated lectures on the inevitable outcome of unmasculine vices.

And the tour guide.

Where there are tourists, there are inevitably professional guides. This fellow had the audacity to charge five francs a head for trips around the morgue. Holding a tiny lantern, he led groups through chilly galleries like the spieler in a waxworks – inventing fantastic stories about the unclaimed, uncared-for dead. Every one of his parties included a maiden aunt who broke out in tears at the sight of an unblemished, lifeless youth and a sticky-fingered lad who wanted to poke and prod to make sure none of the customers were being shammed. Attendants who were generally happy to oblige visitors thought the tour guide a pest. They were used to receiving 'considerations' from patrons. His customers felt they'd already paid for the show so didn't cross anyone's palms with further francs.

I was more often in the autopsy rooms than the viewing galleries, so I heard about the tour guide before I saw him. Cerral, who obviously wished he'd thought of the dodge first, told me about him.

'He's the most extraordinary specimen, Gené. Wears this stiff, tall horsehair wig. Looks like a startled prude in a comic engraving. His boots have six-inch wooden soles. Without the clogs and head-brush, he's a shrimp, not much taller than Toulouse-Lautrec. He's sick with something. His eyes bulge like someone has thumbs pressed into the back of his head. The classic symptom of Graves' disease, as I'm sure you'll recall from Charcot's lecture last year. Shouldn't be surprised if he comes to the morgue as a permanent resident. The oddest thing, though, is that in the icehouse his breath doesn't frost. Must have Eskimo blood.'

When I saw the tour guide, I knew him at once – and smelled the blood on him.

Worse, he saw straight off that he was like me. A vampire.

I was 'lunching' in a grassy court in front of the main building. The little park was ghoul territory, though I took the trouble to be between shifts when my fellows were less likely to be taking meal or cigarette breaks. The day was gloomy, but as usual I kept to the shade. I pretended to eat a slab of bread and cheese I was crumbling into tiny particles and feeding to pigeons.

Another practice I don't miss is feigning interest in food. All those chickens dissected and spread around on the plate while twittering about not having an appetite. All that wine tipped into flowerpots while burping extravagantly and humming tipsily. I am sure I overplayed it dreadfully. We all did. The vogue for the Théâtre des Vampires was brief because vampires are, on the whole, terrible actors. It's a wonder we weren't as often persecuted by critics as witchfinders. Remember Dracula promenading up and down Piccadilly in a straw boater and Jonathan Harker's tweeds, thinking himself perfectly disguised as an Englishman?

The tour guide and his latest party trooped out of the morgue. Beside the wig and elevator shoes, he wore a violently checked jacket and matching plus fours. The sensitive matron mused that life was fleeting and swooned, prompting a companion to produce smelling salts from her reticule. The sticky-fingered lad stamped and yelled, startling the pigeons. They rose in an angry flutter, leaving me with half a sandwich. I might have snarled at the boy, showing a glisten of fang.

That brought me unwanted attention.

The tour guide suddenly became brusque. With their money in his purse and the tour of the House of the Dead over, he was done with this party. They hastened off to Notre Dame, which loomed over every building on the island. Many tourists followed the chill thrills of the morgue with the spiritual uplift of the cathedral.

When they were gone, the guide approached me. His head oscillated. He wanted to look at me from several sides before coming to a decision. He circled as if I were a shtetl and he a detachment of Cossacks, eager to loot but expecting a trap.

'Can it be?' he exclaimed, standing in front of me. 'Surely not… no, I do not believe it. Yet, it is so. A pretty thing… exquisite, oh la! But definitely cold. A sister of the night.'

'I'm not a nun,' I said. 'Or nurse.'

He tittered and showed ratty brown front teeth.

'You mock me,' he said. 'Such a tease! I know what you are.'

Veins throbbed in his swelling forehead and around his prominent eyes. I saw why Cerral diagnosed Graves'.

He sat beside me on a stone bench not suitable for two people who hadn't been properly introduced. He was as cold as the customers I had been serving all day and, under the scent he drenched his clothes in, gave off the same whiff of decay.

He pinched my arm. He had rat nails too.

He touched his forefinger nail to a long tongue, tasting me.

'I fear I do not know your line but you are old, lady elder. Older by far than I, a mere stripling on our path through the dark.'

There was no point in me denying it.

There was no point in me giving anything away, either.

'I am Louis-Jean-Marie-Chrysostome, Marquis de Coulteray,' he said.

I counted to five in my head, hoping he'd take me for

an animated waxwork and go away… which, of course, didn't happen.

'Geneviève Dieudonné,' I admitted.

'Never heard of you,' he blurted out.

'I can't say the same of you,' I said.

He puffed up like a cockerel. I didn't elaborate.

What I had heard of de Coulteray was that he was a rare European of the *pishacha* bloodline, a strain usually native to India. He was the get of a dancer-priestess who had passed through France before the Revolution. She turned him in the hope he'd build her a temple but he didn't. He was one of those snobs who change their names every thirty years or so but insist on keeping the title, claiming to have inherited it from a previous identity.

It's a standing joke that a compulsion of vampires of this class is collecting pictures of themselves in different clothes and wigs. A vanity gallery was once a good way to get found out. Even the most inbred aristocratic family doesn't consist exclusively of lookalikes of the same sex who chose to have their portraits painted when they were the same age. At least the mob knew to tip their hats and address the screaming idiot as 'my lord' while hammering an ash branch through his gold brocade waistcoat.

'I have… a *reputation*!' exclaimed the Marquis, delighted. 'Don't believe any of it… or else, *do*. Please yourself. Tell me, what *do* they say about me? The elders. The ones that matter. Ruthven, Varney, Karnstein…'

He mouthed three syllables. You know the ones.

'I don't move in those circles,' I said. 'I knew Karnstein's daughter.'

'Oh, the flirty piece who was *destroyed*.'

'Yes, though that's not the whole story.'

'Do tell…'

This ancient was addicted to *gossip*. Another child-brain trait.

'I'm sworn to secrecy,' I lied. I didn't want to talk about Carmilla. You know why.

De Coulteray was pettish when I shut off the tap of tittle-tattle, but got over it quickly. He was mercurial. All over the place. Mostly repulsive, but with traces of charm…

Vampires sink their teeth into you in all manner of ways. De Coulteray's tactic was to be so ridiculous you laughed at him, then when you got tired of that you felt a pang of pity, and let him in.

There's a truth in the lore that victims invite vampires across their thresholds, but it's too often taken literally. When a spendthrift gambles away the deeds to the estate and no longer owns his front door, is the invitation unwisely extended to the sallow stranger with the hungry eyes revoked? If a property is rented, can a trembling tenant answer a scratching at an upper-storey window without consulting the landlord? It's seldom as simple as an engraved card entitling the bearer to call when convenient on Lady So-and-So at her town house and bleed her dry between the cucumber sandwiches and the string quartet. The undoing of a collar button can be an invitation. And tapping an empty teapot can be a dismissal.

Against my better judgement – no, against every instinct bred in me as a warm girl, compounded by centuries of experience as a vampire – I let the Marquis de Coulteray in. Not into my house, but my life. He made my acquaintance and that was enough. We were not friends. For a long time, I did not believe I could *have* friends, warm or vampire. But we knew each other.

And I could not get rid of him.

7

YŌKAI TOWN, DECEMBER 10, 1899

Christina chose to ignore Drusilla's announcement of a mystery death, brushing it under the carpet as she concentrated on more important things. Asking Dru to elucidate is always a frustrating endeavour. She won't even admit she remembers blurting out 'one of us just died' so it's no use hoping she'll revisit the topic and cough up something useful like a name.

Kostaki and I thought it worth taking a census and Danny Dravot was willing to take care of it, discreetly. The Sergeant made a survey of the warehouse where our sleepers are stored, examining coffins for signs of tampering. He found nothing except a few of the cheaper caskets (essentially crates packed with straw) have had holes gnawed in them by ship's rats. We picked the *Macedonia* clean of vermin – is this how vampire lords came to be hailed as Kings of the Cats? Rodents are entitled to chew a few boxes in reprisal.

At sea, I insisted on bed checks for medical reasons (not that I could do anything when a lid was prised open to disclose bone and dirt). Also to be sure none of our party were craftily preying on Larsen's crew. On the *Elizabeth Dane*, Yiorgos Jurek – arrogant even by the standards of vampire elders – enacted the fable of the frog and the scorpion by ripping out the throats of sailors carrying us across the sea. Kostaki tossed the *vrykolakas* over the side before he could bite a bosun. Christina had to work her magic on Captain Blake to persuade him not to consign us all to the deep. Jurek was subject to another of those vampire phobias – a fear of running water. The ocean maddened him, I suppose. It certainly swallowed him.

I was willing to let it drop, but Kostaki decided it couldn't hurt to be certain. He and Dravot set about lifting lids and peeping in. Some vampires stirred but stayed put. A few insisted on being let out. One or two showed no signs of life – which, in vampire terms, isn't the same as being dead. I determined they were just deep sleepers.

One oddity came to light. One of our problem passengers is Clare Mallinger, an English newborn. She looks innocuous – a blonde, spirited English rose – but is a vicious, amoral murderess. Something went awry in her turning. To examine her, I had to tear away a nest of gossamer-like secretion. She had spun a cocoon. Her eyes reacted to candlelight, though she didn't wake. Not the oddest quirk of a bloodline I've come across, but the webbing is new to me. Near Clare's head, the fine matter was studded with fragments of what felt like shell. Was she feeding on snails in her sleep? Her neck was stippled with pinprick dots – the stigmata of her father-in-darkness or a new variety of leech-bloat? Clare's was one of the shabbier boxes, a black paint splotch on the side.

Kostaki noticed I was giving her special attention.

'She's one of the ones foisted on us,' I said. 'The Mallingers are gentry or else she'd have been staked for what she did to the ploughboys in her village. The assizes gave her a choice between four hundred years' hard labour and transportation. We're a penal colony now.'

Kostaki looked at the placid face, surrounded by fuzzy white matter.

'She's not the worst of us.' He put her lid back on. Something squirmed in me and I suppressed a shudder. Kostaki looked at me, knowing I'd had a 'moment'.

'I have this powerful thought – an *urge*. Something not rational, which I don't understand. A child-brain thing. Like General Nurarihyon's mania for drinking someone else's tea or Dru's fixation on counting every blessed thing. I want to nail Clare Mallinger's coffin shut. And give her a good Christian burial.'

'Are you a good Christian?' He pointed at the plain gold cross I always wear.

'Not really. This was my father's. It's a keepsake. I've lost everything, over and over… except this.'

I kissed it – a gesture easy to mistake for religious devotion. And, before the Ascendancy, a good way to prove I couldn't possibly be what evidence suggested I was. That trick has worn out now.

'I thought it might be to keep the vampires away.'

I held it up at him. He looked at it, steadily.

'You are becoming droll, Captain Kostaki. Is that deliberate?'

'Not that I know, my lady elder.'

I slipped the cross back into my blouse.

A sighing hiss came from inside Clare Mallinger's box. It shook and settled. Had she turned over in her cocoon?

I know what cocoons are for. Changing. Clare was bad enough as a vampire. What would she be next?

'Should we do something about the state of her box?' I asked. 'Paint over the stain?'

Kostaki tapped the black splash with his boot.

'That's deliberate – look at it. That Japanese print of the wave…'

'By Hokusai.'

'Yes. Hokusai's wave.'

Looking at the blotch, I saw what Kostaki meant. It

96

wasn't an artless stain, but Hokusai's wave executed in black paint.

'Black Ocean,' I said.

Kostaki nodded. 'It's not the only time I've seen this mark. It's on the breastplates of the guards. The *yōkai* with the yards-across moonface has it etched into his forehead. That wasn't done by his choice.'

'We knew Baron Higurashi was with the Black Ocean Society. Lieutenant Majin too, probably.'

'They're not *yōkai*.'

'Not that I know of. Though there's something about Majin.'

Kostaki nodded agreement. 'I do not like this mark,' he said. 'It's as much a brand as a banner. It looks to me like a promise… a great wave, rearing up like a black dragon, poised to crash down, to sweep us away…'

'You know, Kostaki, sometimes you sound just like Dru. You should be her boyfriend. You could whisper apocalyptic omens to each other on the little bridge over the artificial stream and drop cherry blossoms into the water to be swept away like doomed souls offered up to the cruel gods of chance and chaos…'

Kostaki looked at me with eyes like red marbles – as if my attempted levity cut like a lash.

'Drusilla Zark. Is. Not. My. *Girlfriend!*'

He turned and walked away.

'What did I say?' I asked Dravot.

The Sergeant swallowed something like a laugh and didn't look at me. 'Nothing that I 'eard, miss,' he said.

I believe I understand lady loons like Dru better than I do the most sensible and straightforward of men.

8

A KNIGHT TEMPLAR II

He would not go mad. Not from pain. Not from red thirst.

Not from the unwanted, unneeded society of women.

Lady Geneviève and Princess Casamassima.

In different ways, each were capable. The elder was practised in surviving a world that might at any moment turn on her. The newborn believed she would live forever. Kostaki trusted Lady Geneviève and understood Christina Light. Sometimes, the other way round would have been more convenient.

Both were needed here. By the exiles.

And both, though they seemed not to notice, needed him.

Twice, since coming to Japan, Kostaki had experienced earthquakes. The ground lurched, bucking like a startled horse. The seconds-long events were trivial, he was told. Dust shaken from ceilings. Poles wobbling. Dogs barking. No damage worse than a shattered cup.

The *Macedonia* had steamed through storms that raised up and threw down four-hundred-foot, million-gallon cliffs of water. Captain Larsen steered between maelstroms that could suck a vessel under in seconds, tearing a ship's plate apart as if peeling an egg. Helpless against the elements, Kostaki had no choice but to hope the ship seaworthy and the crew competent. About that, he could be stoic. But the shifting, grinding and breaking Tokyo found so everyday as to be not worth mentioning disturbed him. When dry land was as treacherous as wild water, nothing was settled.

A twinge in his knee, as when weather was about to change, presaged the shocks. Then, a few unsteady moments and an impulse to run. Locals still as statues, paused in conversation or at work, silently counting between tremors, then carrying on blithely when they sensed – how? – that the quake had peaked and the danger was past. For now.

The Japanese lived with land maelstroms – the possibility that the ground might crack open and swallow them – as a soldier lived with the possibility of surprise attack. Troops couldn't sleep in armour or be always on watch. On a sunny day, no one avoided the shadows of tall buildings. But faults were there, red lines in the earth. At any moment, busy streets might fracture. Houses and temples could fall.

He felt it too. Ever-imminent catastrophe.

It wasn't unfamiliar.

In London he had been reminded that vampires were not true immortals. Dracula hadn't changed that. On the contrary, now everyone believed in vampires, dangers were more acute. Once, slayers were jeered at as crackpots or violent lunatics. With the Ascendancy, they were no longer ridiculous. Warm firebrands preached war to the death. In some countries, the heirs of Van Helsing were gathering political and popular support. More people had turned in the last ten years than in the previous ten thousand but more vampires had been destroyed also.

Jihads were declared. In the Sudan, under the sway

of the late Mahdi, *ifrits* were scourged to death in the desert. In the Ottoman Empire, where the name Dracula was forever reviled, giaours were beheaded on sight. In America, vampire hunts were a national pastime – even in states where there were no vampires. Suspects were burned alive by puritan sects, lynched by the Ku Klux Klan and shunned by neighbours.

Like an earthquake, it was never all at once. Small tremors presaged devastation.

In Japan, vampires were kept in their place. Concentrated in Yōkai Town.

There was no extermination order – yet.

Kostaki thought of the Black Ocean emblem. The Hokusai wave could fall on Yōkai Town like a steam hammer smashing a doll's house. Places could be subtracted from the world. All it would take was the will, and enough silver. For Dracula and the Templars, Kostaki had participated in such actions. Villages and towns – cities, even – could be obliterated. No one alive even remembered their names.

This was how they lived now. Waiting for the earthquake.

Would vampires be remembered for their works or their stories, like the Mayans or Trojans? Or would they pass completely from the world, leaving behind nothing but ghosts of memories, fables to frighten children into staying on the path or bad dreams consequent upon a surfeit of dressed crab?

Over and over, he patrolled Yōkai Town. He memorised names and faces. Kostaki knew the names of the gate guards and noted their tics and traits. Who was lazy, who was afraid, who was too confident and who was bored. He made an effort to pick up more of the language. He seldom let on how much of their hosts' talk he understood.

Another tactic learned from Dracula – a better linguist than scholar, and one to gain and press any advantage. The arrogant spoke freely around those they believed didn't understand what they were saying.

He had made little headway with written Japanese, but grasped an essential point. The kanji for rain looked like falling rain, seen through a window. 雨. In Japan, pictures – indeed, anything designed and made – were saying something. Building a watchtower in the form of a giant warrior was a message. Coded, yet obvious. The colossus of Yōkai Town. Eyes turned inward, not over the wall. So – a keeper, not a protector. An overseer. A giant sword hung from the statue's belt. Potentially, an executioner.

The snarling face of the statue was familiar. It resembled Lieutenant Majin. Again, a message. Kostaki knew who was watching.

When the scouts Yam and Verlaine reported back, they would help him make maps. Not just maps of the city – which could be had for pennies in any post office – but maps of power. Diagrams of how things worked. Japan, like many nations, was ancient as a vampire elder, slow and creaky and set in its ways but, like Dracula, tempted to embrace modernity and act like a ravenous newborn. All the throats of Asia were bared beneath its sharp new fangs. The country was riven by factions advocating tradition or change. Often, confusingly, both at the same time – tradition disguised as change, or change sold as tradition. The Black Ocean Society had resisted the Meiji reforms, but now embodied them – the new Japan was the very old one in a new hat. The Emperor was all-powerful in his palace, but as much a prisoner as any in Yōkai Town. Emperors and kings were all the same. Even Dracula, who conquered death *and* Britain, was coffined by his titles, the expectations of his subjects and a lassitude that set in after the victory fireworks burned out.

Kostaki walked by night and day. The perpetual fog of Yōkai Town meant even the most sensitive noctambulist could venture outdoors at noon, but Kostaki had taken to wearing a yard-across circular straw hat. It shaded his eyes from view but he could peep between loosely woven strands. It was like observing from cover.

The deconsecrated church was quiet, perhaps abandoned. Fresh snow on the steps was unmarred by boot prints. Dorakuraya and Komori were in hiding, though Kostaki had seen their Renfield scuttling about on errands. He was still mulling the business of the strange child and her puppet ninja theatre. As outside the walls, there were factions here: *kappa* and *tengu, yōkai* and *kyuketsuki*, disciples of Dracula and subjects of Yuki-Onna. In the short term, the newcomers must remain neutral. In the long, decisions about alliances must be made. He would need to share intelligence with Princess Casamassima. She was practical enough to know who to support, appease or oppose. Lady Geneviève did not need the distraction of the strife within Yōkai Town. She would ponder the moral course of action, then stick to it with certainty. Thinking like that was why she had been forced to flee country after country. She was admirable, but likely to get them all killed.

Dravot had posted guards on the warehouse where most of the exiles still lay in boxes. Even if it was just painting black waves on crates, no more tampering would be tolerated. Also, a few vampires had stirred and pushed up their own lids. It was a good idea to keep a tally of who was awake. The exiles had their factions too. Some were packed off for being too murderous even for Dracula; others, like himself, for being not murderous enough. It had already fallen to him to put down one mad dog among their party. Was this what Dracula intended when he let them set sail from Plymouth? That they slaughter each other to save the Prince the trouble?

Kostaki nodded his hat to the current sentry, Albert 'Smiler' Watson. Another old campaigner. A little too fidgety for the duty, prone to jump at every squeak. Dravot said Smiler had a Victoria Cross in his pack, awarded after an action on the North-West Frontier. Kostaki wasn't reassured. Some soldiers had only one fight in them. When turned, Watson sprouted permanent fangs, and his big ape teeth stretched his mouth into a permanent grin. With whiskers and bared teeth, Smiler looked like a jolly monkey… only monkeys weren't truly jolly, Kostaki remembered. The simian smile wasn't humorous, but a display of aggression – often to mask fear.

He called out a 'hello' so Smiler wouldn't shoot him.

The sentry had nothing to report. He was chewing on mouse meat.

Kostaki skirted the grounds of the Temple of One Thousand Monsters, where the Princess had set up shop. It was the spiritual centre of Yōkai Town – much more so than Dorakuraya's desecrated church.

His circuit complete, Kostaki came back to the gate. Snow fell from the peak of the giant statue's helm as a guard swept the observation platform. An icy, uncomfortable perch.

Lieutenant Majin wasn't up there, which didn't mean he wasn't inside.

Head bowed so his huge hat concealed him, Kostaki approached the statue. When he wandered too close, he was shouted at. He kept walking into the shadow of the giant until bayonets were raised, so the guards wouldn't realise he knew the Japanese for 'stop, demon' and 'stand back, foreign devil'.

He heard 'foreign devil' a lot.

He let the guards shout a while longer, then withdrew – as if the whims of his foreign, devilish mind had brought him here but changed like the wind and impelled him to wander somewhere else. He backed away, smiling as broadly as Albert Watson. The expression cracked his face.

After taunting Majin's statue, he passed the gate. It was easy to open the gate from the other side – not easy at all from here. It opened at set times, morning and evening, so workers and traders could come and go. Carts trundled to and from Mermaid Ancestor Place, the busy mercantile strip close to the gate. Produce brought in from outside the walls could be had at fluctuating prices. All the traders were thieves, each with their pet bribed guards and jealously guarded smuggling routes. A certain amount of black-marketeering was tolerated, even encouraged. Blood of doubtful provenance could be bought.

Consignments of philtres and blessings – mixed at the temple, under the direction of the Abbess – were sent out to merchants in the city. *Yōkai* medicine was admired, even by those who shunned its makers. Along with salves and tonics, the temple exported other valuable products. Lady Oyotsu was mistress of subtle poisons and curses. There was a market for *yōkai* magic and mischief too.

On the street, snow was trampled to discoloured, treacherous slush. On the grounds of the Temple of One Thousand Monsters, it settled thick and pure. Drusilla Zark knelt by the gate, scarecrow-black against white drifts, putting the finishing touches to a small, sinister snowman. The umbrella *yōkai* hovered over her, the handle of the Princess's parasol tethered to his rim. They looked like two mushrooms growing together on a tree trunk.

Kostaki slowed his pace. Miss Zark troubled him. She was mad – but, as the English poet had it, only north-north-west. When the wind was southerly, she knew a hawk from a handsaw – though he wouldn't be surprised if she used a hawk *as* a handsaw, or said one when she meant the other, or fed cut-in-half worms to a joinery tool, or did or said anything else which came to her mind.

Around her, his knee was on fire.

She might be what others called 'awa' wi' the fairies', but she *knew* things.

Miss Zark saw he wasn't drinking. On the *Macedonia*, when they first met, she had looked at him a moment, hunched her shoulders and pinched up her cheeks, and – in Romanian, *and* his mother's voice – said 'you won't grow strong if you don't finish your turnips'. Lady Geneviève looked at Miss Zark sideways, understanding what she'd said but not what it meant. The Princess frowned as if the woman had interrupted a perfectly reasonable conversation by flapping her arms and imitating the call of a yelkouan shearwater.

It was a mistake to think of Miss Zark as a child. Or an idiot. She was sly, thoughtful, sometimes sweet... and a killer. She finished her turnips.

She patted her snowman's cheeks, miming the application of powder. The figure was faceless, squat and strangely proportioned. At its base, child's shoes stuck out.

He waded through drifts and eased Miss Zark aside. The umbrella *yōkai* drifted off.

If Miss Zark had hurt anyone, there would be consequences. She smiled at him, lips rouged and sticky.

He broke apart the snowman's head and uncovered a doll's cracked face.

'Dolly wanted to be wrapped up cold,' said Miss Zark. 'Not wrapped up warm, but cold – rolled in a snow blanket fit for a queen. Snows fall but queens reign. Every flake is different but all fakes are the same. Are you a fake or a flake, Captain Kostaki?'

It ought to be a relief she hadn't snatched and bled some child. But the doll's dead face was disquieting. Why did they give such things to children? Fat faces, hard like polished bone. Big eyes, dead as glass. Dolls were ghosts. You grew bigger, but they didn't. They waited patiently. When you were lying in your last bed as a very old lady, they would creep on the counterpane – knowing you'd not forgotten their secret names. China hands like little knives. Teeth like needles. Spiteful and eager to pay you back for all the years put away in the wardrobe.

Those weren't his thoughts – as a boy, he hadn't had dolls, but wooden horses and carved ships.

The spiteful dolls were Drusilla Zark's.

Not this one, though. He recognised it. It was the doll Tsunako Shiki, the Japanese child-vampire, had hidden behind. He looked about, wondering if the Shiki girl was nearby. Did he see a dress slipping behind a tree? There were no little footprints in the snow.

'You mustn't mind her,' said Miss Zark. 'She's fresh as paint and twice as smelly.' She smashed another snowball into the doll's crusted shroud, burying that damned face. '*Up in a balloon, boys, up in a balloon,*' Miss Zark sang, '*won't we have a jolly time, sailing round the moon…*'

The umbrella *yōkai* danced back to them as Miss Zark sang, twirling the Princess's parasol.

In Moldavia, they burned witches. In Britain, they gave them a spot on the bill between Mr Memory and Little Tich. Show your appreciation with a big hand… for summoning the spirits of the departed to locate lost watches or foretell tall dark strangers.

Miss Zark had been right to repeat that message, though – everyone in Britain *had* fallen under the shadow of a tall dark stranger.

Kostaki turned on his heel.

'It looks like Geneviève… will need saving,' said Miss Zark, directly and sensibly. 'But you should think twice and not get tangled. It looks like Geneviève… will get broken. You should keep your weapon where it is. Not pull it and wave it about like some we could mention. Word to the wise, Captain Kostaki… *won't we have a jolly time, sailing round the moon…*'

He looked at Miss Zark. She was poking twigs into her snowman's head, humming to herself. She wasn't sensible and direct any more. Those moments were only ever fleeting. It was no use asking her to explain, any more than it had been any use pressing her on that 'one of us' dying nonsense that troubled Lady Geneviève. Miss Zark had said all she would on the subject and tripped on to her next fancy.

Where was Lady Geneviève?

Kostaki knew she was making her own surveys. While he looked at walls, buildings and guard positions, she introduced herself to many *yōkai*. She brought her medical bag and offered to treat ailments as best she could. She had the Abbess's blessing to set herself up as a doctor. Lady Oyotsu was professionally curious about Western medicine.

'It looks like Geneviève will need saving,' Miss Zark had said. 'It looks like Geneviève will get broken.'

He should think twice and not get tangled, eh? Keep his sword where it was?

Miss Drusilla Zark knew much about him – but she didn't know him.

He never finished his turnips, no matter what his mother said. He had chewed them to pulp and kept them in his cheeks till he was away from the table where mush could be spat into a stream or trodden in mud.

He had best go 'get tangled'.

When Kostaki intruded, Christina Light made an 'Oh, what is it *now*?' face. When he asked after Lady Geneviève, her disposition did not improve.

'I suppose she's gliding about somewhere,' said the Princess, 'inflicting help on some poor soul too polite to shoo her off. That's your lady's general habit. If she puts in an appearance, should I say you're looking for her?'

'That won't be necessary.'

'Can *I* be of any help? What a silly question. Of course I can't. I'm just a newborn and you wouldn't rely on anyone under four hundred years old. What is it the advertisements say – "accept no substitutes"? For your mysterious purposes, only *la Dieudonné veritable* will suffice.'

Princess Casamassima and the Abbess were taking tea in the temple, nodding at each other. The Princess, veins glowing, risked shaking her head clear off to compete with Lady Oyotsu's serpentine oscillation. Lady Oyotsu stretched to peer at Kostaki, as if peeping around a corner. She smiled, showing her blackened teeth.

Kostaki saluted and left the women to their tea.

He stepped into the gloom of the late afternoon. The lantern-lighter hadn't been round yet. The mist was thickening. In the distance, a tram *clickiticlicked* over tracks.

He sometimes had to remind himself that beyond the walls of this enclave was a city with trams, telephones, electric streetlamps, kinematograph exhibitions and the cakewalk. Yōkai Town was frozen in its comforting, chilling pool of no-time. Most *yōkai* were elders, like him. He'd stayed with the Guard and the Templars because those masculine orders afforded shelter from bewildering, uncontrollable changes, which were – only a few years on – already superseded, forgotten and replaced by even more dizzying, dazzling modernities. He should be comfortable in this preserve, but for the earthquakes… and the intimations that the place couldn't last much longer. A new century was imminent and tearing off a big calendar page was always a temptation to the young, the warm, the newborn. Time to throw out old curtains, burn dead wood and push great-grandfathers onto ice floes.

Miss Zark had wandered off, but her snowman was still here. Or was that her snowman? Kostaki could have sworn the doll's burial mound was on the *other* side of the temple fountain.

Knowing he was being ridiculous, he grasped his sword-hilt.

You should keep your weapon where it is.

He advanced steadily, in a wide circle rather than a direct line. He trod carefully, easing his carrack out of its scabbard by inches.

Not pull it and wave it about like some we could mention.

Hush, strega! he told the Miss Zark in his mind.

The snowman was bigger than it had been. Not the size of a full-grown person, but larger than a doll.

Was this some new *yōkai*? Kostaki had heard much about Yuki-Onna, the Snow Queen. Did she have snow courtiers? A Snow Queen's Guard?

He neared his quarry, sword raised. One stroke would sever its snowball head from its snow-boulder body. Shoes still stuck out from under the pebble-buttoned snow skirt. More bows and buttons showed than he remembered.

Miss Zark hadn't given her snow golem much of a face, but Kostaki made out a little bulb nose and the thin line of a mouth.

Two plugs of snow popped out as big black eyes opened. Nictitating membranes blinked sideways. Then the eyes focused on him.

Arms exploded out of the crust of snow and he was showered with pellets of ice. He tried to bat away the chunks with his sword. He stepped back.

The snowman's skeleton shook itself like a wet dog, scattering lumps of snow and shaking out many skirts.

It was Tsunako Shiki.

The vampire girl emerged from her snow shell, exaggerating with clutching hands and shaking shoulders, pantomiming a buried newborn's first crawl from the grave. She mewled like a thirsty baby, then tittered infuriatingly.

Kostaki didn't sheathe his sword.

No matter how girlish this one looked, she was tricky. Dangerous.

The Shiki girl's white dress had a superfluity of ruffles, pleats and ribbons – suitable for sitting in and being admired, not moving around in and getting mussed. Certainly not for being buried inside a snowman. A white band held back her unruly ringlets. She looked more like a doll than her doll did – and where was that thing now? If it crawled up his back, he'd hack it to flinders.

She wore whole white rabbits as mittens. Hollowed-out, stiff-furred skins sleeved her forearms to the elbows. Her quick hands worked the heads like puppets. She made the dead bunnies look at each other and at him, rolling red button eyes and sticking out stiff leather tongues.

Laughing again, she turned an agile cartwheel and scrambled off – bounding on all fours, kicking up divots. It was as if her mittens had quickened and run, dragging her behind. Rabbit outriders for a doll queen.

He let his sword click back into the scabbard. Another damned nuisance. He followed Tsunako's spoor. Tagged in a playground game, he was 'Sally It'. *Hell's breath!* Something else of Miss Zark's! He had caught her the way warm brats catch the measles. Spots of her childhood floated in the soup of his own memories. He hadn't played girls' games. He played war, as all boys do – and fought real wars when little more than a boy. Dracula broke his wooden sword and gave him a real one.

He hadn't officiated at funerals for dead dolls or pinched the silly Barley piece's fat arms until she cried, or piled mama's cloak, papa's ulster and the butler's havelock on her shoulders – topped off with two hats and a bonnet worn like tiers of a wedding cake – to make an entrance at a masquerade ball in costume as a coat stand.

Kostaki was still looking for Lady Geneviève. She

couldn't be far away. He also wondered where Miss Zark had got to — more out of an inclination to be somewhere else than concern for her safety. After an earthquake or deluge, Miss Zark would skip off, happy as ever. The mad and the incomprehensible were always unscathed when everyone else was crushed under rubble.

This susceptibility was what came from his long fasting. He was starved of blood, so he was feeding in other ways. He was taking on burdens that weren't his. Sustenance but not nourishment.

The rabbit tracks petered out at a crossroads.

The Shiki girl had stopped playing bunnies and moved on without leaving a trail. Swinging from tree to lantern-post to building like a spider monkey? Or had she sprouted frilly bat wings and flown to the moon? It didn't matter. She was just another distraction.

The smell of spilled blood made his fangs sharp. Red thirst clawed his gorge. His knee hurt. Something nearby bleated.

'*Mestre, mestre…*'

Kichijiro shivered against a covered well. Rags torn and bloodied. Missing one sandal. He'd been whipped recently. His head was bandaged. Weals on his back glistened with ointment.

'Who did this to you?' Kostaki asked, in Portuguese.

'I deserved it,' said the Renfield. 'I failed Mestre Dorakuraya. He was correct to chastise me and I bless his name. Flagellation mortifies the flesh but purifies the spirit.'

'Not the whipping,' said Kostaki, impatient. 'The treatment. The bandaging. Who did that?'

'An angel,' said the Renfield. 'A *mestra* with pale gold hair… and a black bag.'

'Lady Geneviève?'

Kichijiro nodded. He had scratches on his neck. Not from Lady Geneviève's — or anyone's — fangs. Dorakuraya's long, hard nail-barbs had stuck into the Renfield's throat.

111

Kostaki wanted to lick the weeping wounds as a cat licks milk... no, that was Drusilla Zark again. She was the lapper and licker. She popped blisters between her teeth. When no one was looking, she'd stick her finger in blood-spill – as she used to stick her finger in cake mixture – and suck it clean.

When Kostaki was drinking, he was an honest biter. He opened veins and drank deep.

The Renfield shrank from him.

Kostaki felt his own fang-teeth against his lower lip.

'Where is the Lady Geneviève?' he asked.

'The House of Broken Dolls. On Yokomori Street.'

Kostaki knew of the establishment. A brothel where worse than ordinary vice was practised. As Dravot drolly put it, a house of ill repute with a bad reputation.

If Lady Geneviève went to such a place, someone was hurt and needed treatment. There, getting hurt was likely.

It looks like Geneviève... will need saving. It looks like Geneviève... will get broken.

In the House of Broken Dolls?

Kostaki had a clear moment, and saw he was playing a game. The weird Miss Zark was part of it, also the weirder Tsunako Shiki. Sly, watchful Kichijiro too. He wasn't Renfield only to Dorakuraya. Too many vampires in Yōkai Town and not enough minions. Kichijiro was anybody's servant, anybody's whipping boy.

Kostaki was 'Sally It'. He was tagged and searching... and there would be a surprise at the end of the trail. A reward or a forfeit.

His worry was that Lady Geneviève didn't know this was a game.

On Yokomori Street, Kostaki bumped into the elastic-boned Whelpdale. The English vampire was backing away from a doorway, blowing kisses at three geisha who clung to the frame. Their kimonos slid artfully off pale, shapely shoulders. They had fluttery hands, hair done up in elaborate snail-shell spirals, pins and combs with falls of silk flowers attached, and smoothly convex, featureless faces. Whelpdale's chest was semi-inflated. He had the look of a satisfied customer.

He turned quickly and recognised Kostaki.

'Captain Kustardi,' he said, touching his hat. 'I, ah, was paying a business call… leaving samples of my new lines, as it were.'

His carpetbag was full of crude illustrated books: *Decadent Girls Who Sell Lingerie; My Nine Nights in a Harem.*

'I'd not have expectorated to come upon yourself in, ah, this knobbage patch, sir…'

Whelpdale swiftly got over being surprised in his vice. After all, Kostaki was in the red lantern district too. The publisher must suppose an equivalence of sin. Unembarrassed, he tapped an elongated finger to the side of his nose.

'I can thoroughly endorse the House of Silent Ease,' he said, intimately insinuating. 'Queer to the kiss, those blank fizzogs… but, all else is in working order. Who wouldn't apprecialise a wench who don't jawjaw at you after the pokery has been jiggeried? Yes, I shall award this hostelry four stars in the *Blue Baedeker*. That's a guide I publish, Captain. Hints for the discerning gentleman tourist in foreign parts. Parts here are foreign indeed, should you catch my meaning and I suspicion you do.'

Kostaki couldn't be bothered to explain anything. Let Whelpdale assume what he would. For he hadn't guessed Kostaki's real secret.

If it got about that Kostaki was visiting geisha houses, people would be less inclined to ask after his other appetites – whether he'd slaked his red thirst lately.

But he couldn't be detained.

'I am making an inspection,' he said.

'I thought nothing contradictory,' said Whelpdale, winking. His eye opened wide as a mouth, displacing the rest of his features, then shrank shut. The Englishman was practically a *yōkai*. 'I advise a most thorough inspection. Inside and out, if the mood takes. And an extra peek under the carpet afterwards, just to be on the safe side.'

The newborn sauntered away, limber knees bending like springs. Whelpdale prospered in Yōkai Town, making the best of his lot.

Kostaki looked at the faceless geisha. *Yōkai* of the *noppera-bō* bloodline. They nodded at him, heads like ostrich eggs with wigs. One had a portrait painted on her smooth flesh, but it was smudged. Suckers in their palms resembled pink pressed rose-flowers. Hidden in their intricate folds were thorns. The *noppera-bō* fed by fastening these hand-mouths on the necks of those who planted kisses where their lips should have been. What had transacted between them and Whelpdale?

Kostaki hurried on past the Teahouse of Blue Leaves, a rowdy saloon known more for fighting than fornication. In the garden, a microcephalic cyclops reeled under a blizzard of blows as the four-armed boxer he was trying to fight hopped about nimbly on a single leg. He hadn't lost a limb, but was a *yōkai* whose legs fused into a single muscular column. The monopod ended the bout by executing a devastating flying kick, which laid the other bruiser out in the bloody snow.

'Who else wants steamed dumplings?' said the winner, raising four defiant fists. Several volunteers piped up and came at the boxer with broken bottles and plates – and were smashed against tables or thrown through paper-and-wood walls. Builders must do a healthy trade around here. Their guild likely employed Major Four Arms to make damaging trouble every night.

Among the brawlers was Popejoy, the American Death Larsen nearly blinded on the *Macedonia*. He rolled up sleeves from massive forearms and piled in. Lady Geneviève had told her patient to avoid being punched in the head, but Popejoy wasn't one to abide by doctor's orders. Unlike Whelpdale's body, the warm sailor's face didn't snap back to its original shape after a pummelling. His jaw was swollen and half his mouth was mashed shut.

Major Four Arms punched the sailor, who slammed against Kannuki, Lieutenant Majin's pet. A full quart of beer splashed into the giant's long, puzzled face. Kannuki reached for a mallet with a head the size of a barrel...

The din of the fight faded as Kostaki walked on.

A miasma hung, mingled with the fog. A stench, like dead fish and ordure. Spoiled blood and sickness. He reached for his pill-box. One last aniseed ball rattled.

He paused. According to Lady Geneviève, Japanese star anise was poisonous, used for incense not flavour. The balls were made from Chinese aniseed. This would be his last taste until trade in confectionaries reached Japan. He popped the pill in his mouth and crushed it between his teeth.

At the farthest end of Yokomori Street, an abandoned-looking house was set well back from the pavement. Garden neglected, screens ragged, lantern burning low. A post outside was papered with yellow scraps – prayers or warnings or spells. Set on the front step were three half-life-size china figures of seated courtesans, with jagged holes where their faces had been knocked in.

This was the House of Broken Dolls.

From inside, on cue, came a high-pitched scream.

Carrack in hand, Kostaki sprinted towards the geisha house. Activity was projected on the paper walls by spreading fire. Shadow-puppet figures struggled amid what might have been agitated dangling ropes or flailing jellyfish tendrils.

The screen door was wrenched aside. A sobbing, cat-faced woman stumbled out of the house, panic in her slit-pupiled golden eyes. Her kimono was skinned down to her rump, hobbling her as she ran. Blundering against Kostaki, she pressed white-furred breasts against his chest and hooked claws into his coat. She was of the *bakeneko* bloodline. Usually prized and pampered. This one had been badly treated.

Something like a fleshy red tube whipped through the doorway, and wrapped around the cat-woman's ankles. She screamed as if stung by a Portuguese man o' war, and clung to Kostaki. Her fur stood up and her docked tail twitched.

He steadied her but she was pulled away. The red rope was reeled in.

It was a tentacle, more squidlike than octopussy. Strong as ship's cable, it pulsated with rich blood. Its underside was coated with a thousand nasty little barbs, which fixed in the cat-girl's skin.

She twisted and clawed the ground – and almost got purchase on one of the broken-face statues. Then another tentacle uncoiled from the house, almost lazily. It lashed her across the face and coiled around her head, shutting her mouth, stopping her eyes.

Kostaki slashed at the tentacle. It was pliable and gave easily – but the tough hide would not break. Like a gaffed fish, the cat-geisha was dragged into the house.

Through the torn screen, Kostaki saw a huge wet eye and a horny, bird-like beak. With a dragging sound, whatever it was shambled away.

Blood was smeared on the steps. *Bakeneko* blood.

He sheathed his sword and drew the revolver he'd

checked out of Dravot's travelling armoury. He had six silver bullets.

He entered the House of Broken Dolls.

The antechamber was a wreck – shattered screens and smashed pottery. Blood and other discharges splashed across the floor matting in curls and strokes like Japanese characters.

He passed through to the central room of the house. There, he found a broad-shouldered man in a samurai helmet and partial armour, lying on a strew of pillows. His helmet mask looked like the face of Majin's statue. Ink serpents coiled round his biceps and real snake heads stuck out of his shoulders like angry epaulettes, hissing and spitting. His arms ended in sucker-covered flippers. He was dwarfed by a living thing that grew from him as a tree grows out of a mossy riverbank. His exposed torso was covered with a tattoo of the Hokusai wave – from out of this sea surged a kraken, source of the red tentacles. Around its central eye were many more glinting segments.

The cat-girl screeched, trapped inside a constricting jacket of living ropes. Others lay around the room, twisted in broken-backed shapes, eyes dull.

Where was Lady Geneviève?

Kostaki levelled his gun but didn't know where to shoot.

Laughter came from all corners of the room. Looking about, he saw the walls were covered with wax-leafed tendrils, which grew out of the squid samurai. On the vines hung head-like flesh bulbs with many mouths.

Looking down, he saw the samurai's legs were planted like roots, sunk through the matting. Prominent veins throbbed in the tentacles. Each cat-girl was penetrated in some natural or new-made orifice by a wicked, spike-ended tendril. Kostaki thought that, as blood was drawn, foulness was pumped into them – some narcotic, rotting poison. He hoped the slime wasn't spawn, for he could imagine what might grow from this thing's eggs if hatched inside vampire hosts. Some of the geisha moaned, dimly aware of what was being done to them.

This *yōkai* – if *yōkai* it was, and not a true demon – was at once animal, vegetable and mineral. The chimera, burst out of the samurai, had made a nest of this building, and was digesting the food it found within.

He had walked in through its open jaws.

He shot at the mask, which broke apart. A green cabbagey face showed – a smoking hole punched through its middle. The wound chewed like a mouth and spat out the silver bullet.

Kostaki put his gun away and drew his sword again.

Trees could be cut down. Squid could be sliced for food. Paper would tear.

And even whatever this thing was would bleed.

He hacked at a tentacle, closer to the main body. It parted like a rubber pipe, squirting red liquid.

Kostaki's fangs ached. To his eyes, the blood spurts were a sparkling scarlet fountain.

He made a decapitation pass, and the samurai's main head came off.

Like the hydra, he had plenty more.

A purple warty bulb sprouted off-centre on his shoulders. Its leaves peeled away to show a pea-green babyish face covered in ropy, milky fluid. It blinked in the light and drew breath. Kostaki sliced it in two, cleaving the crown of the not-yet-formed skull. His blade cut into the body as if through lard – only to snag on bone. He wrenched his shoulder pulling his carrack free. The cleft healed as he watched.

The new head fit itself back together. The sundered face reformed. The green skin was infused with blood and became pinkish. Eyebrows and hair grew.

The samurai had a blandly handsome Japanese face.

It was Lieutenant Majin. Or it wanted to look like Majin.

Oily water spouted from buds on the walls. The mat under Kostaki's boots got slick. The Black Ocean wave had come.

'Captain, oh my captain,' shouted someone in the next room.

Lady Geneviève!

The Majin face smiled. The bulk of the *yōkai* was between Kostaki and the wall. Its tentacles stretched and flexed.

Kostaki charged, slicing through flesh. Tiny mouths sighed and screamed as he scythed away limbs and organs.

He felt disgusting wetness on his face. Not blood, not water.

Firmly, he shut his eyes and his mouth. He cut up and down. Left and right. He got past the *yōkai* and ploughed straight through the wall into a bathing room, and fell into shallow hot water. The water was rancid with congealed blood. Scummy oil floated on the surface. Braziers burned and steam rose. His clothes were sodden and heavy as he stood up.

He saw Lady Geneviève.

A crustacean *yōkai* − ten feet across − gripped her head and ankles with unwieldy lobster claws. A huge, stiff human face was etched into its bright red carapace. A crablike arrangement of mouth-claspers and a thicket of eyes on stalks peeped out from under the bony rim of its shell.

The room stank of sulphur and saltwater.

With her free hands, Lady Geneviève pounded the pincer that encircled her head. She had cracked the shell. Ichor trickled. The carapace rose, split and spread, like a beetle's wing casings. It displayed the carved face − the mask of Majin.

Did the Demon Man manifest himself in multiple

bodies? Was he snug in his statue, playing with the squid samurai and the shrimp behemoth as Tsunako Shiki played with her ninja puppets?

If Lady Geneviève were harmed, Kostaki would execute every last one of Majin's monstrous forms – no matter that it meant going to war with the Emperor of Japan.

Corpses floated in the pool.

At a glance, Kostaki saw the *yōkai*'s weakness: where the skin attached to the shell, the soft, mushy regions around the eyestalks. When eating crab, he knew where to stick his fork to get to the tastiest scoops. He thrust his sword – his crab sword, *hah!* – into the cluster of eyestalks, penetrating deep, and *twisted*.

He pulled the sword out. Yellow stuff – bright and tart as mustard – gouted from the wound. A shrilling whine came from inside the creature. Its claspers gnashed and shook.

Kostaki used the sword tip on the joint of the cracked claw. Inside the exoskeleton, muscle tore. He sheathed his blade, prised the pincers apart with his hands…

…and looked at the face of a broken doll.

What he'd thought was Lady Geneviève was a limp, life-sized puppet.

Laughter came from above, and he looked up to see Tsunako Shiki in the eaves of the bathing room, cradled by wires and pulleys. She sat in what looked like a dissected church organ, little stockinged legs dangling. Her hands played over keyboards, turned clockwork control wheels and squeezed rubber bulbs. Unearthly sounds issued from trumpets, drums and bells. It was a ridiculous contraption. But it had gulled him.

Tsunako worked levers and made the bulky crab monster rear up and dance. Water poured from its sundered shell. Its wood legs came off and danced separately, then collapsed in a tangle, joints bobbing independently on fine wires.

She simpered, pleased with herself, as if expecting

applause. To her, this was all a game, an amusement. She was another bloody music hall turn.

More laughter, from behind him.

Kostaki, soaked with bathwater and repulsive oils, turned.

A litter of *bakeneko* sat on the edge of the baths, furry feet dipped in the water. The stray cats hissed and chortled, mewed and stretched. Some peeled off the red linen patches that had looked like wounds. Some hiked up kimonos to cover painted scars. None were in the least hurt. One wore the squid-samurai puppet's helmet. It was too big and heavy for her, and the cheek-guards cramped her whiskers.

The corpses in the water were stuffed dolls with crude painted faces, like the *noppera-bō* geisha. The blood in the water was foul. Not *bakeneko*, not human either. True cat blood, perhaps.

He had been right. It *was* all a puppet show.

'It-looks-like-Geneviève will need saving,' Miss Zark had said. 'It-looks-like-Geneviève will get broken.'

In his arms was a life-size doll with a shattered face. It had needed saving and was broken.

Miss Zark had told him exactly what would happen. She had even told him to 'think twice and not get tangled'. He hadn't listened properly.

It-looks-like-Geneviève did not mean Geneviève.

He had thought *once* – of Lady Geneviève – and now he was tangled.

'You are a delight to play with, Captain,' said Tsunako Shiki. 'Much more fun than the others. They are poor companions.'

Splendid! Kostaki had left his homeland, been betrayed by his father-in-darkness and voyaged to this far country of the insane just to become playmate to a monster child, the clown in her grotesque harlequinade.

Couldn't she have singled out Danny Dravot? Or the Princess? No, it could only be him. He was *fun*.

Again, she blew him a kiss.

Tsunako slipped up through a trapdoor, leaving him with the geisha. They were more like cats – amoral, wicked, pretty, petty – than women. They hauled him out of the baths, wrinkling their noses at his smell. What had Tsunako used for ichor? Something repulsive. Mewing insincerely, the *bakeneko* darted long tongues at his face. They rubbed the smooth-furred backs of their hands on his cheeks. Meiko, the girl who'd lured him in, offered the usual hospitalities. He was too proud and annoyed to be further insulted.

As he stepped out of the cat-house, his hot wet clothes frosted. They crackled as he walked away.

If he ran into Kichijiro, he'd give the Renfield a clouting for his part in the sham.

He skulked in shadows, coat collar up around his shamed face. He didn't want to be seen on Yokomori Street and have to explain the state he was in.

9

YŌKAI TOWN, DECEMBER 11, 1899

Princess Casamassima has appropriated the best-appointed rooms in the Temple of One Thousand Monsters for her own use. Yuki-Onna herself could not expect such a welcome. Lady Oyotsu has retreated with her *samisen* to practise self-elongation behind a screen upon which her distinctive silhouette – more disturbing even than her distinctive person – is thrown by well-placed lanterns. Christina takes such preferment as her due, but the Abbess's hospitality is suspiciously generous. The famous Japanese ideals of welcome and self-sacrifice are seldom practised without self-interest. Christina should be warier of obligations that come with accepted courtesies.

'Read Japanese history,' I told her. 'You'll find dozens of stories about retainers who dutifully disembowel themselves to honour a commitment to their *daimyō*. That a top dog might be an unworthy rogue is unthinkable. Even while looking into a pool of his own entrails, a lesser person daren't question the rectitude of the noble lord who told him to open his stomach.'

The concept of *giri* is impossible to translate. It's especially impossible to explain to Christina. For someone who says she wants to overturn European social order, she navigates it with something like genius. However, she mistakes Japan for Titipu, the imaginary place in *The Mikado*. To prosper here, she must learn that this is just another country with codes of conduct and ways of getting things done. We have not voyaged to a fairy-tale realm – though it often looks that way. Christina is literally a sparkling princess and Yōkai Town throngs with living umbrellas, cat-eared beldames, blood-drinking frogs and bird-people with detachable hands. I shouldn't be surprised to find wheels that spin gold coins in a temple anteroom or tinderboxes that summon demon dogs with unusual eyes on a market stall in Mermaid Ancestor Place.

While Christina plays high priestess in the temple, I'm quartered in a women's dormitory, along with Drusilla Zark and Francesca Brysse. Daffy Dru has acquired a cricket in a wicker cage and claims it talks to her in scissoring chirrups. I suspect Brysse, a just-woken crony of Christina's, is spying for the Princess. Her long, excessively curled fringe is supposed to stop people noticing her persistent peeping. She has sharp ears too. To confuse the minx, I'm coaxing Dru into making gnomic pronouncements she must waste time committing to memory and sharing with her mistress.

We vampire women share a large, one-storey building – something between a sturdy tent and a flimsy bungalow – with many female *yōkai*. I am learning names and histories. The most welcoming of our hosts is Topazia Suzuki, a vampire of the *yamachichi* bloodline. She looks like a blue-haired, human-sized monkey, as if she once shifted shape and Yuki-Onna breathed tiny ice-diamonds on her, fixing her in her present form. It looks well on her, and she is very handy with the prehensile tail that pokes out of the back of her robe and functions as a third arm. A refined, intelligent woman who speaks excellent French, Topazia is au fait with the latest Paris fashions in couture and philosophy. A confirmed gossip addict, she has filled me in on the others in the dormitory.

Rui Wakasagi, Lady Oyotsu's music teacher, wears a striped scarf over a third of her face to cover a swollen bruise. She was murdered with a disfiguring poison generations ago and has spent centuries as a *yūrei* – a vengeful vampire stalking, bothering and killing descendants of the villain who wronged her. All her instruments are disguised weapons – the neck of her *biwa* cancels a poisoned blade and the strings of her *koto* are strangling loops. She doesn't take kindly to requests for 'Elsie from Chelsea'.

The invisible girl is Suzan Arashi, who claims she faded from men's sight after bathing in the glow of a fallen star. For someone who can only be seen just after she's drunk enough blood to make her veins visible, she spends an extraordinary amount of time on her hair. She is a real geisha – a calling she equates with being a nun – and has mastered seven disciplines of sacred hospitality. She scorns the soiled doves of Yokomori Street, who call themselves geisha but don't know a teapot from a chamber pot.

The quietest resident is an elegant older woman known as the Mantis. Her party trick is undoing her obi to tie the hands of fellows she's cuddling so they can't fight back when she sticks a needle-tooth hair comb in their jugular veins. She isn't even a vampire, but a homicidal madwoman confined to Yōkai Town because her shamed family think she can't do any harm here.

I took the phantasm flames (*ona-bi*) that caught our attention on the road to the temple for a mindless meteorological phenomenon. That was wrong. The fireballs are the spirit form (*shito-dama*) of the venerable O-Same. I wonder if she might be a shapeshifter like Christina, further along in an evolution from flesh to light. O-Same is held in high regard in Yōkai Town as the spark who set the Great Fire of Meireki in 1657. Getting even is prized by Japanese vampires. Compared with their grudges, Italian blood vendettas and Kentucky mountain shootin' feuds are drawing-room spats over whether cook should cut the crusts off sandwiches. Rui was seduced, betrayed and murdered before setting out on the path of bloody vengeance but O-Same devastated Edo – at the cost of 100,000 lives – because an exorcist tried to burn her favourite kimono. To be fair, it was no ordinary garment, but a long-sleeved silk *furisode*, watered with the tears of hopeless love. Still… as the sage has it, learn to forgive and try to forget.

When I told Kostaki the story of O-Same, he immediately saw what I hadn't.

'How can someone – *something* – as powerful as her be kept where she doesn't want to be? Walls and guards can't stop living fire, any more than they can imprison an invisible woman or a general whose orders can't be disobeyed. There's an army of *yōkai* here. They could take Tokyo and rule the way Dracula rules London. What makes them stay put and keep quiet? What shackles have we not yet seen?'

It's a good point. Has Yuki-Onna decreed her people hold themselves apart from earthly affairs? The Snow Queen is revered, but no one I've asked is forthcoming about what she's been up to lately. Or where she is. Perhaps she has withdrawn from the world. If she were to deign to take a player's seat in the Great Game, she might displace the Black Ocean Society and hold sway over the Emperor. If Dracula can ascend to a throne in the West, Yuki-Onna should be the rising vampire power of the East. But she isn't. It's midwinter – the height of her social season, when she traditionally takes a husband or two (often not her own). Yet the only sign of her is the snow that falls most nights and gets kicked to slush in the streets.

When Yuki-Onna is mentioned, Lady Oyotsu – her most loyal retainer – hangs her head. I've pointed that out to Kostaki.

'Women of snow, women of fire,' he said. 'What's wrong with women of flesh and blood, I'd like to know.'

'Don't forget women of light,' I prompted.

He bared his teeth at that.

'Vampires and light do not go together,' he said. 'Not where I come from.'

Kostaki is in a mood. I worry that he keeps bad news to himself. He has also been sulking since I made that thoughtless remark about him and Drusilla. He is very wary of the poor girl. He now thinks she has designs on him. That's unlikely. Dru treats us all as figures in a lazy dream she drifts through after falling asleep in a poppy patch. Dravot teases Kostaki about being a dashing ladies' man, but the Sergeant is another expert at keeping quiet about things he thinks women don't need to know. With his spectre face, Kostaki can't blush – but he can look more like death than usual.

My trunk is in the dorm, but I haven't curled up in it since I came here. I was asleep long enough on the *Macedonia* and won't be overcome by lassitude for weeks. I don't want to go in the box at the moment. Day-to-day routine in Yōkai Town is dull but I wouldn't want to miss startling developments and wake to find some *ronin* shoving a pike through me in the purge Kostaki and Dravot obviously expect.

We are an informal council: the Princess, myself, Kostaki, Dravot. We meet in the Casamassima quarters at the temple. There are lists to be compiled, argued about, ticked off and thrown away. Sometimes Dru attends as observer and interjects non sequiturs to derail business. Often petitioners drop by to ask for something impractical.

Because her dress isn't compatible with squatting on cushions, Christina has hired carpenters to make Western-style upright chairs and a table-desk. Broken packing cases, fallen shrines and abandoned houses provide wood – even nails – for the furniture. In the joinery, dwarves with big hands and giants with small heads turn scavenged materials into useful things. Shut away from the rest of the city, *yōkai* must make or make do.

I've learned my way around Yōkai Town. It's more like an enclosed, fortified camp than a district or a village. Fortified to keep us in, not enemies out. No one except Kostaki calls it a prison out loud – despite the towers, the guards and the fact that we're prohibited from leaving. Higurashi made it clear the vampires of the *Macedonia* are not to be found outside the walls for our own safety. You always hear that when they aren't ready to massacre you yet.

Something is strange about the temple – even by Yōkai Town standards. While we waited for Christina to finish looking over a list, I noticed Kostaki flexing his fingers. I've been doing the same thing. Only in this building. My toes twitch as well. It's involuntary.

'I do that too,' I said to him, showing my hands. We both wore gloves.

He was affronted – as if I'd said his shirt tail were hanging out. 'It's strange,' he said. 'That... *tingling*.'

Dravot laughed out loud. He was rubbing his hands together too.

'Vampire elders!' he snorted. 'You've actually forgot what it feels like.'

'What *what* feels like?' I asked, rattled.

'Cold,' he said. 'It's ruddy *freezin'* in here.'

Kostaki made fists to stop the shakes.

'You're right,' I said to the Sergeant. 'Cold... how *odd*.'

'That's one way of puttin' it. Odd.'

Like most vampires, I don't feel hot or cold. With turning, some senses dull as others become keener. We have to relearn the instinct not to play with fire. I'm used to not minding extremes of temperature. On Napoleon's retreat from Moscow, I was comfortable while everyone else was skinning dead horses and live dogs to patch together thicker coats. The naked sun hurts my eyes and blisters my skin, but candle flames, gaslight and electric incandescents don't bother me. There's supposedly an explanation in Moriarty's *On Tithonic Rays*, but he couches his theory in such infernal jargon I can't make head or tail of it.

I strained to recall feeling cold. Nothing came. It was lost to me, like the taste of bloodless foods. I loved strawberries as a warm girl, I think. If I try to summon the flavour of ripe strawberries squishing, my vampire mind translates the taste memory into juice-squirt from rare steak.

The prickling in my fingers was a novelty. Not a pleasant one.

'Yes, it's chilly in here,' said Christina. 'Such flimsy walls let in draughts.'

Kostaki's eyes rolled. The Princess was a relative newborn too. Not yet used to her new senses. The *wrongness* didn't strike her.

'How cold does it have to be that we feel it?' the Moldavian asked me.

'Colder than frozen-over Hell?'

'A witch's tit,' put in Dravot, grinning.

Christina frowned. Did she want to call for a vote of censure on the Sergeant's barracks language? Bloodthirsty revolutionaries who would put whole classes up against walls and shoot them can be surprisingly prissy. A ruthless member of Robespierre's Committee of Public Safety told me off for wearing an immodest gown to my own hanging.

'Yōkai Town is where they put unnatural things,' I said. 'Us included. The temple is the heart of the place. It's why this is the quarter of the city the Emperor cared so little for that he allowed it to be turned into a reservation for *yōkai*. The ghetto was built around it. Put this cold spot on your list of Things to Look Into.'

'Yam and Verlaine have yet to report,' Kostaki reminded us.

'If Majin caught 'em, we'd know of it,' Dravot said.

I'd like to see Mr Yam fight Lieutenant Majin.

'We need to know what goes on outside the stockade,' said Kostaki. 'I smell powder. And I hear gun carriages rattling. I'm sure there are mortar emplacements.'

'For our protection,' said Christina. 'I asked Lady Oyotsu—'

'Who could set our minds at rest by just looking over the wall,' I put in.

'Yes, what's stoppin' 'er sticking 'er neck out?' said Dravot.

The Sergeant lit a cheroot as the Princess glared at him.

'Don't try to be funny,' she said. 'The Abbess has been hospitality itself. She extends us every courtesy and asks for nothing in return.'

'Yet,' said Dravot, exhaling plumes of smoke.

The Sergeant goes through cheroots, cigars and cigarettes like a fiend. It's because he's a newborn. He hasn't got used to not tasting something that used to be a pleasure. The next smoke – that'll do the trick! It'll all come back and tobacco will be what it used to be! Not just smoke in the lungs, but a *rapture*. For years, did I suck watery strawberries and spit out tasteless pulp? If so, I can't even remember that.

'I'll bet those mortars are pointed the wrong way for our protection,' I said.

All of us find ways to pass time and gain small advantages in our polite prison. I set bones and patch scrapes, though *yōkai* medicine is new to me. I offered to put ointment on Rui's giant purple bruise, but she was offended. She insists nothing is wrong with her head. It's best I confine my practice to patients with approximate human shape. Dr Charcot's lectures were wide-ranging, but didn't address the issue of how to treat a cut suffered by Ittan-Momen, a *yōkai* who manifests as a living roll of cotton with embroidered eyes. How do you bandage a bandage?

A sewing kit might be more use than my medical bag.

And we all have red thirst.

After the initial feast of welcome, it's been scarce. Dru eats insects and gives leftover legs to her cannibal cricket. The rest of us chew the insides of our cheeks – a bad habit few vampires can resist. How do the *yōkai* sustain themselves? They aren't all tea-drinkers or cow-suckers. There can't be enough willing attendants to go round. How many sordid blood transactions take place on the gambling barges? Or in crowded, ramshackle stews close to the walls? Even in Yōkai Town, there are chasms between respectable and vile, between the calm temple and the seedy Yokomori Street.

Francesca Brysse is rosy-complexioned. I suspect she's tapped extra rations. That's one thing she'll keep to herself.

Dravot reports that – despite language difficulties – trade has begun between our group and the locals. I've seen *yōkai* proudly wearing gloves and bonnets – even shoes – from our travelling wardrobes. My patients press coins, fans or combs on me. If you have needs unmet by our hosts, Whelpdale is the fellow to ask. He accepts payment in small items of value and has amassed a trove of watches, rings, jewels and – perhaps most valuable of all – IOUs to be redeemed with favours or labour.

Whelpdale is always on the move, a spring in his rubbery step. He carries messages and delivers goods. He knows *everyone*, including creatures I have no idea how to approach. I've seen him strike lucifers and write in the air with flame while O-Same bobs in agreement. I daren't think about what they might want from each other.

Whelpdale wasted no time discovering the covered barges where unending Go tournaments are held. Under emerald lanterns, fortunes rise and fall with the clicking of white and black stones placed on or removed from boards. Whelpdale doesn't play, but takes side bets. He cleaned up backing Drusilla, a novice against Hon'inbō Kokingo, the faceless monk who is – *was* – champion of Yōkai Town. The audience laughed as Dru made a series of criminally stupid moves, but shut up when she won the game. You wouldn't think a man with no features could frown furiously, but Kokingo managed it as he dropped his death stones on the board. 'What's the matter, chummy?' Whelpdale asked. 'Lost face?' That trick won't work twice. I'm astonished it worked once. I expected *yōkai* gamblers to be cannier. If someone as slippery as Whelpdale entered a donkey in a contest to recite Shakespeare, I'd bet on the ass to beat Henry Irving.

Within a month, Whelpdale will be fixing matches and splitting his take with corrupted Go masters. And he hasn't even discovered mah-jong yet.

Kostaki thinks we should shut down Whelpdale's enterprises. 'There's one in every regiment,' he says. 'Sells the men their own kit and rations. Deals cards and wins most of the time. Organises "dances" to make introductions to the local girls. While you're skirmishing in the streets, he's looting the wine cellars. Sees a campaign as a series of business opportunities. Ends up shot for treason or promoted to general staff. We should kill the cur now, lest we be strung up either side of him down the line.'

Dravot – who, in happier times, might have been Kostaki's 'one in every regiment' to the letter – argued for letting the newborn stay in business. If our man's trading is curtailed, who knows what sort of robber baron manqué will crawl out of a coffin to take over his dodge. The pliable pornographer is a busy, enterprising, mostly harmless thief we might need in the future. It's no accident he's up and about and enterprising – even forging trade and diplomatic ties our council can't – while others snooze in their caskets.

Also, I've met the local girls. Any fellow who thinks he'll

make time with Rui or the Mantis is due a disappointment. Kasa-obake has a better chance with Christina's parasol than any of our fine bucks have with the almond-eyed does of Yōkai Town.

Whelpdale's illustrated publications are gaining a Japanese vogue. This morning, I saw Abura Sumashi paging backwards through *Erica Littleby-Little or: A Harlot's Progress*. To him, the story must be about a slut who rises from a pauper's grave to be cured of the pox, has back-to-front liaisons with low persons, takes on a fresher-faced appearance, foreswears gin, doles out coins from her purse to gentlemen who retreat while she puts her clothes on, rebuffs the kisses of her employer's rakish son and reforms to become a priggish maid-servant and devout Sunday school attendee.

Christina asked about the head count. I mentioned Clare Mallinger's cocoon.

'Mallinger? Which one is she again?'

'The murderess.'

'Thank you, Geneviève, but that doesn't narrow it down much.'

'The mad murderess.'

'Now *you're* being facetious.'

'If you don't know, it doesn't matter. Who she is isn't as important as what she's doing inside her web.'

'She may not be doing it,' said Kostaki. 'It may be being done to her. Her box had the Black Ocean wave painted on it.'

'You think she's been… tampered with?' asked Christina.

Kostaki shrugged. 'We've posted guards on the building,' he said. 'If something was done to her, it won't be done to anyone else.'

Christina was pleased. She liked to be told things were being done.

'So, if the tampering was fatal… we've lost a spare

murderess. If something else was intended, she'll bear watching.'

'I'm her doctor,' I said. 'Murderess or no, I have responsibility for her wellbeing.'

'Don't mistake my meaning. Clare Milliner matters to me.'

'*Mallinger*.'

'Milliner, Mallinger, Mulliner – she's one of us, and we need all of us. We are too few.'

'Too few for what, Princess?'

'To matter, my dear.'

I shrugged at that. Christina seesaws between callous disregard and neurotic concern. She can't decide whether she's our Boadicea or Mother Hen. She took the shipboard losses personally, though none of Death Larsen's victims were her intimates. She was even curt with Kostaki after he jettisoned Jurek, which kept the rest of us alive. She has a mosaic in her mind. Each of us is a tile with an allotted position. Losing any of us means a white space in the picture.

I don't want to be Princess Casamassima's puzzle piece.

10

BEFORE DRACULA (CONTINUED)

Whenever de Coulteray came to the morgue, he sought me out. At first, he didn't believe I was really studying medicine. He was convinced I'd devised a subtle scheme to bleed living patients. He knew I couldn't be draining customers on the slabs.

Real ghouls (another Indian bloodline) do feed on corpses, but the black blood of the dead is to European vampires what seawater is to humans – drunk only in desperation, always with ill effects. The squeezed juice of the lowest live rodent is more appetising than the cooled blood of a two-hours-dead princess royal. I know this from experience and wish I didn't.

De Coulteray was one of those corkscrew souls who can't imagine anyone being different from themselves. He kept trying to surprise me, to catch me in my grand swindle – and cut himself in on fabulous imaginary profits. He proposed joint enterprises, offering a share of his tour earnings in return for my secret. He admitted he liked to pinch fat children until drops of blood welled. He would lick the wounds while cooing and patting, in the pretence of 'kissing it better'. When I frowned, he swore he selected only the vilest of brats – the ones who stamped and frightened birds, or poked the corpses. After his 'treatments', he was sure they mended their ways. Probably, they became little angels, singing in choirs and making charitable visits to the poor. I'd have been readier to accept his rationale if he hadn't giggled while advancing it.

He also took advantage of swooning matrons, tapping thin veins with his rat-teeth. He favoured children and short women as prey. Even with clogs on, he couldn't look a full-grown man in the eye, let alone bite his neck. In his way, he was accomplished. He could nip a person without them noticing. If most *nosferatu* are wolves, de Coulteray was a mosquito. Insects are blood-drinkers too. As much nature's vampires as the Peruvian bat or the phalaenophis orchid. It was an amusing dance to watch, with a sting and an apology at the end of it... and the blush of blood on his lips.

He pressed me for my stories, but more often he told me his own. His favourite topic was himself, and the unjust treatment he had received. Estranged from Dorga, his mother-in-darkness, he had not had an easy time of it since the Revolution.

'The wretched trouserless ones would have to invent a *decapitation machine*,' he said, as if the guillotine were designed expressly for his neck. 'When they cut throats or shoot us, it's merely a question of lying there till they've got drunk and left you to rot... then springing up and running in the other direction. But there's no coming back from the head basket. If I hadn't been fast on my feet and quick with my tongue, the de Coulteray line would have ended with so many others – a very curt, curtailing sort of end. Inglorious, you might say. No sooner was that over but who should come along? Bonaparte! He wanted me in the army, would you credit it! It was all I could do to stay out of the path of half the cannonballs of Europe. La, but what a dreadful time! Nothing will ever be worse than that.'

Nicolas Cerral noticed me with the tour guide and took to calling him my fiancé. At first, the captain of the ghouls meant it as a joke. Then, he thought he'd hit on the truth and stopped endeavouring to be amusing and shocking in conversation with me. I had a sense Cerral was aggrieved at the trespass on his turf. As the sole girl ghoul, I was his preferred confidante and he resented the loss. It's also possible Cerral liked my looks and was shamed and frustrated at being cut out by such a ridiculous rival. A mistake I have made time and again over the years is assuming people with faces as young as mine are as experienced as me – not just a few years (*months*, really) beyond toy trains and dress-up dolls. Dracula may have a child-brain, but I am cursed – I see your lip curling, Charles! – with a child-face. It misleads many, and in turn they surprise me.

Lecturers and physicians also noticed that de Coulteray turned up wherever I happened to be. That didn't help my cause. The Marquis was more unwanted pet than admirer – the sort of dog you idly give a spare bone, only to find it yapping at your skirts forever afterwards. What made it worse was that he couldn't be inconspicuous if he tried. My habit was to pass unnoticed. His was to be such an enormous tent show that no one took him seriously.

The Marquis followed me from the morgue to Pitié-Salpêtrière, the teaching hospital attached to the university. He sat in on lectures, asking impertinent, humorous questions, which Professor Charcot did not appreciate. Pets, he pointedly said, were not welcome in classes. De Coulteray trailed me to student haunts and tried to persuade me to hunt with him. He offered to beguile comely barmaids or drunken bucks and share the spoils. He robbed those he bled – another practice he laughed at me for being shocked by. I thought it a foolish risk. He was more often sought by the police for the robberies than the attacks. People don't notice fleabites but know when their pokes have been pinched.

What a strange freedom it was not to be believed in. The Devil's greatest trick, it is said. Those who don't believe in ghosts do not see them. Those who didn't believe in vampires didn't notice us, even as they put cotton wool on the fang punctures.

My studies proceeded well, but I was marked harshly. I knew from other women on the course that some professors were still set against us. A well connected, near illiterate male lackwit could pass exams by sending a crate of wine to an assessor's house, but any excuse would be found to deduct points from a woman's score. Categories were invented which we alone could fail – deportment, nerve, constitution, associations.

Thanks to de Coulteray, the last was a problem. The Marquis encouraged the spread of fantastic untruths about him as a distraction from the fantastic truth. People suggested that he was a disciple of Victor Frankenstein, seeking perfect body parts to sew together a Future Eve, or else a canny lust-murderer, who would guide victims to obscure corners of the morgue, leaving their stripped corpses among the other dead. Whenever we did a stock-take and checked slabs against the register, surplus stiffs were discovered – thanks to poor bookkeeping on the part of overworked servants – and boosted the myth of the tour guide as a homicidal lunatic.

In all his rumoured depravities, I was now his known associate.

I had several uncomfortable interviews with tutors and one with Inspector Daubert of the Sûreté. I found myself led into unnecessary lies – claiming the Marquis as a relative on my mother's side, a family embarrassment I was obliged to bear for her sake. So that was the reputation of my imaginary parents blackened. De Coulteray thought it hilarious and invented amusing stories about my precocious girlhood.

He would not be deterred. I believe he was simply unromantically lonely. And I sympathised. Who would not?

I had little gossip for him about our kind, but he had plenty for me. At that time, by most reckonings, there were fewer than five hundred vampires in Europe. The Marquis de Coulteray knew something scandalous (if unverifiable) about every one of them. He put it about that Sir Francis Varney had unnatural congress with a pig's severed head as a rite of initiation into the Order of Palladium – a nonsense invented on the spot by Lord Ruthven to make his fellow British elder look foolish before their peers. Come to think of it, that might well be true. I was less convinced by de Coulteray's other yarns. That Baron Meinster indulged a predilection for dressing up in his late mother's ballgown and dancing alone in his empty Transylvanian chateau, sweeping her train over dusty stone floors. That Countess Ranevskaya uses her uncanny trick of seeing into men's hearts and minds to cheat at Écarté. That Barnabas Collins writes sickeningly sentimental three-volume novels under the pen name 'Maud-Lynne Drivelle'.

Less amusingly, the Marquis would bring up the name of some formidable elder, then bluntly tell me he or she had just been destroyed. He quivered with terror when recounting tales of burned-down castles and dug-up graves, of heads severed by silver and hearts pierced with oak but couldn't suppress gloating relief. In his mind, he had escaped yet again while someone more magnificent than he – of all the vampires roaming free, he was by far the least magnificent – was pinned down, done away with and gone to red dirt.

Much tosh is written about vampires being romantic, devil-may-care outlaws. The truth is we were always afraid. We could be found out and killed at any time. Being constantly terrified leads to strange fancies. You know the myths about us. What you won't find, even in the secret files of the Diogenes Club, are all our myths about you.

De Coulteray had it in his head that something called the Congregation of the Doctrine of the Faith – a secret society funded by the Vatican and the House of Rothschild – was hunting vampires to extinction. So far as he was concerned, their ultimate purpose was the ruin and destruction of the Marquis de Coulteray. He detected agents of the conspiracy in every shadow. Any elder who turned to dust in his coffin had been throttled with a papally-blessed rosary. This or that politician was in the pocket of the Congregation. A final purge was coming. He had a notion of fleeing to northern latitudes where nights last for months and making a last redoubt of the undead. In visions, he was told to build a tower. It was never clear who was telling him this. He claimed regular congress with the goddess Kali. Of course, he wanted me to come to the Arctic. He urged me to abandon medicine and study architecture. He didn't know how to build a tower and thought I'd be better at the practicalities. Having failed to put up a modest temple – no more than a pavilion, in truth – in two hundred years, even he doubted his suitability for ambitious construction projects. After a while, I just heard the chattering – not the words. De Coulteray was being de Coulteray, and I had other things to be getting on with. Like not being expelled from the University of France.

Where were you when you heard about Dracula?

That's a question everyone can answer – not just vampires.

Most didn't believe it when they first heard that vampires were real. That a 450-year-old creature was marrying the widowed Queen of England. That other *nosferatu* were rallying to his standard, as it flew over Buckingham Palace; that many more vampires were turned – a rising generation of newborns, washing across Britain and its empire, threatening to swamp Europe with the undead. That the world was changed.

This will surprise you – I didn't believe it either.

But, consider the source.

The first item de Coulteray had from England was unusually easy to confirm. The Paris papers carried accounts of the sensational case. A foreigner in London survived attempted assassination – presumably an anarchist plot against a titled plutocrat. A distinguished Dutch professor and a mad American cowboy were killed in self-defence by a Romanian prince. Dracula had already promoted himself from nobility to royalty in his press releases. I knew of Professor Abraham Van Helsing as 'a specialist in obscure diseases' but not that he had an interest in vampires. When Charcot made us read Van Helsing's book on hysterical symptoms, students joked that his author biography must have been mistranslated – he was really 'an obscure specialist in diseases'. De Coulteray said Van Helsing and 'this Quimby Maurice' were hired stooges of the Congregation. He took poor mad Jack Seward for a sinister Jesuit and swore Mina Harker was a secret Jew.

Dracula would be destroyed within the month, he was sure. I thought that quite likely.

Before everything changed, vampires who got their names in papers tended not to live long enough to enjoy celebrity. De Coulteray's *feuilleton* fantasy of a secret crusade masterminded by the Wandering Jew, the galvanised corpse of Tomás de Torquemada and Comte de Saint-Germain, was ludicrous. However, a few grim crusaders knew we were real and made careers of killing us. A vampire had actually to murder warm people to attract the attention of Captain Kronos, but few of his rivals were as fastidious about exact measures of guilt or innocence. If the vampire-slayers Dr Gänsflügel and Xander Anderson hadn't chosen victims who weren't legally dead to torture and dismember, they would be reviled among the worst murderers in history.

A long-standing myth among vampires posits a cabal of lofty, remote elders called the Number. People who talked them up said the Seven, the Nine, the Thirteen and so on – either the number of the Number varied or no one could get the made-up story settled. The primary purpose of the Number was keeping the existence of vampires quiet. Guarding the Secret or the Covenant or the Pact or the Shadows or the Whatever We Called It. The Number liked capital letters, obviously. You won't be surprised to learn that chief among the Number was an elder called the Master. Before Dracula took the title King of the Cats, this Master – who may be a conflation of several different elders – was ruler of our kind. He was also known as the Ancient One, the Anointed One and – among the more cynical – the Annoying One. So at the head of the table of the Number sits a One. We've heard nothing from the One or the Number since the Ascendancy, which suggests I was right to be sceptical about them even existing.

If de Coulteray was afraid of the Congregation, he was terrified of the Number – who sent silent killers to evaporate vampires who imperilled the Secret. The Marquis prophesied that the impudent rascal Dracula would be impaled by a falling lightning rod or garrotted with a hawthorn noose before he could make more noise on the world stage. I didn't believe that, but I presumed Ruthven, Varney and other British elders would see Dracula's presence in England as hunting on their preserve. They must have gamekeepers to see off the poacher. I still don't understand why that didn't happen. Does Lord Ruthven, for all his jack-in-office status as Prime Minister, ruefully reflect that he could

142

have stopped all this after Van Helsing missed his shot?

It was just gossip. And fanciful theory.

Until it wasn't.

I was taking notes at a dissection performed by Dr Petre Gheria, my least favourite lecturer.

Anatomy specimens were drawn from the morgue's unclaimed. Their symptoms told as much about their lives as their deaths. Having hooked a ripe female corpse for his table, Gheria took every incision as an excuse for superfluous observations on the immorality of the sex – as if male Parisian down-and-outs didn't have livers pickled like tumorous sponges or generative organs eaten away by syphilis. Gheria liked to style himself as a 'scientific misogynist and anti-Semite'. His published papers argued that women, Jews, Negroes and – to be blunt – anyone not a middle-aged European man were physical and moral inferiors who should be subject to strict hygiene laws. It might have been significant that Gheria's much younger wife – a former dancer, often persuaded out of retirement for charitable causes – was a popular figure with the wealthy students of the university branch of the Jockey Club.

Gheria exposed the uterus, hoping to find twins – a Jew and a girl, preferably – strangling each other with the umbilical cord. He would take that as an example of hereditary degeneracy.

There was a disturbance in the viewing room. Grieving relatives, perhaps.

I heard the shrill, trilling cry, like some sort of bird – a pigeon, perhaps.

'Gené, Gené…'

Students got out of de Coulteray's way as he crawled over the benches to get to me. Some yelped, others swiped at him with their notebooks. His wig was off-centre and that scent of his inescapable.

Gheria paused, scalpel hovering. He was unhappy with this interruption. I hissed furiously and – again – hoped this would all go away. Then the Marquis was next to me. His talons hooked into my sleeve.

'Gené, Gené, we have to go to London, now! La, it's a marvel, you'll not credit it – I can hardly believe it myself. But it's over.'

'What's over?' asked Cerral, who was sat in front of me. 'What's over, you fathead ponce?'

'The hiding,' de Coulteray said, showing his teeth.

The bloodline of Dorga takes after the cobra. His fangs were curved needles. His jaw dislocated to show their full length. Venom sacs pulsed in his wattles.

Cerral shrank away, in surprised terror.

'Yes, peasant scum,' said de Coulteray, climbing up on the bench, mouth open. 'You should cringe! Fear me, fear all that I am… for I am a vampire!'

I tugged at his coat, trying to calm him down.

'A *vampire*?' said Gheria, scalpel still in hand. 'There are *no such things*.'

De Coulteray hissed. He flicked out his long, forked purple tongue.

'Yes, there are,' insisted de Coulteray, slurring his words. 'And I'm not the only one here.'

Everyone looked at me.

Everyone *thought* about me, remembering things: my habits, my diet, my looks, my character. That time the kitten was found dead in my locker. My odd scraps of historical knowledge. My preference for dark nights over sunny days.

I saw it all on Cerral's face – in his look of horror. I could hear the tickertape running through his head. The transparent lies brought to mind. The evidence.

The proof. The truth – no longer unbelievable.

Insights I had shared on types of blood astounded specialists. Conventional haematology lagged behind vampire understanding. I hotly regretted the vanity that had prompted me to show off. I could easily have kept quiet.

So could de Coulteray... only, being him, he couldn't.

'Dracula, Gené... of all the elders, Count Dracula. Not the Master, not one of those Karnsteins, not Dorga. *Dracula*. He has delivered us. London is our sanctuary. It's what I foresaw, but didn't understand. The tower and the temple were the same place, and I didn't have to build it because it was already there: the Tower of London. At last, we shall be what we were meant to be. Lords of the earth, Gené. And ladies. We must go now. There are trains from Gare du Nord. You speak English, don't you? I don't, but you'll interpret for us. Should we need new coats? Or British umbrellas? I've heard about the rains and fogs of London. But Dracula will end that. There'll be no rain, no fog, no sunny days, just moonlight, and velvet night and the stars. They are ours, Gené – the stars.'

His arms flapped as he spoke. I wondered if he was trying to turn into a bat. Or a flying snake.

Nicolas Cerral, the ghoul, produced a small cross and held it up at me.

I tugged at the chain around my neck and showed him my father's gold cross – the one I've worn all these years. I pointed at it.

'Doesn't burn,' I said. 'Doesn't hurt.'

Cerral wasn't listening. He stood up and backed away. He wasn't the only one. Students fell over themselves to give me a bench to myself.

'Dieudonné's a vampire?' someone asked.

'Dieudonné's a vampire,' Cerral confirmed.

My own fangs were sharp against my lower lip.

'She can bite me any time she likes,' said some rake.

No one laughed. The tour guide wasn't ridiculous any more.

Dr Gheria's lecture was abandoned. It was as if the lamps that directed light onto the cadaver were adjusted to illuminate me. I was picked out like a special turn in the follies, hemmed in by a circle of light.

I half expected students to break furniture to make stakes and torches.

We vampires had our own fears and prejudices, Charles. That's why the myth of the Number and the Secret took root. Once, it was almost all we thought about, talked of when we were together. Passing among the warm, passing *for* warm. Maintaining the fiction that, in another of Gheria's ignorant pronouncements, *there are no such things as vampires*. We lived in dread of exposure. A public accusation, even by a child or the village idiot, was enough to make an elder abandon name, rank and property and depart for a distant land.

No one made a move. But they all stared.

It wasn't as if I'd been accused of crimes – that came later. It was more like a cry of plague in the room, a virulent infection, which spread by touch.

Gheria held his scalpel up like a silver crucifix. The head of the anatomy specimen flopped to one side. Even its dead fish eyes were fixed on me.

Eventually, someone else came into the lecture hall.

'You'll never believe what rot the papers are printing about England,' said the newcomer. 'The *rosbifs* are having a laugh at our expense.'

'No,' shrieked de Coulteray. 'It's all *true!*'

11

YŌKAI TOWN, DECEMBER 15, 1899

Just before sunset, I was in the gardens. It's no more wintery on the grounds than inside the temple. The building might as well be constructed like an igloo, from carved blocks of ice. Yuki-Onna must feel cosy here when she's in residence.

With spring thaw a distant prospect, the novelty of feeling the cold wore off quickly. Kostaki and Dravot keep bonfires lit. Christina and I wrap ourselves like Egyptian mummies. I've bought fur-lined boots, a padded jacket, a scarf and a cap with earflaps. All the best people are wearing them this year, and shall continue to do so until Edison's patent electric hat reaches the Far East market. If we had a tea dance, O-Same would have the fullest card.

The temple pool is frozen solid, trapping big-eyed, red-tailed fish. The spiderwebs are frosted. The courtyard gravel is iron-hard, and threaded with ice. White grass crackles when walked on.

A public Go table is set up under a weeping willow. An emerald lantern hangs from a low branch, casting light on the grid. Gambling is forbidden on temple grounds. Here, Go is a form of prayer. The black and white patterns that form and break and form again on the board offer spiritual lessons. If you look hard enough.

Abura Sumashi, unexpectedly a Go master, is teaching me the game. I can't say it does much for my spirit... or my spirits. He cedes me the advantage of the first move, but his white stones always swarm around my struggling black. It's a mistake to think the timid, sweet-natured *yōkai* childish or silly. Inside that swollen sponge head, his brain is enlarged too.

Kasa-obake hovered over us, opening and closing whenever a move was made, jogging the lantern. Higo Yanagi, a slender reed of woman, also sits and watches the Go games. At first, I didn't even notice that her feet are sunk into the ground. Her ankles are knotted, like roots. Higo is an aspect of the tree, or the tree is an aspect of her. True weeping willows are dioecious and deciduous, but Higo is female and evergreen. She lives by trapping birds. She shapes nests in her branches, each containing sweet purple berries. When unwary warblers settle on these lures, she closes twiggy fists, crushing with vegetable mercilessness. Yet she simpers sweetly.

Dravot calls Higo 'Tit-Willow' and whistles that damn song when he passes her. I can tell he likes her looks and would be tempted to risk it if she were to construct a bigger, cosier nest – a bower, say – and invite him in. He has a rival, though. I've seen Popejoy, the sailor with the pushed-in eye, making time with Higo, sitting next to her and smoking his clay pipe. Though warm, my old patient has stayed with us rather than returning to the *Macedonia* and risking Death Larsen poking his other eye.

The game turned decisively against me. Opportunities I thought I saw were traps. The umbrella *yōkai* spun with delight at my downfall. Higo shook her branches, tinkling bells of approval. I am the ugly, wicked foreigner – a villain for this moral story. Abura Sumashi attempted a modest shrug, which is physically difficult. He is pleased with his victories.

'When they call you big head, it means something different in English,' I told him.

He offered to let me resign and call it a draw, but I wanted to play on. Sometimes, you learn more from losing than winning. At least you do in Go. The principle doesn't apply to duelling. At the finish, the loser puts death stones on the board. I was noting stratagems Abura Sumashi favoured, clever moves he couldn't resist. Such intelligence could be used against him.

Not in the next game. Or the one after that. But…

A true master shouldn't be so ostentatious in his mastery. Perhaps a lesson my teacher needed to learn.

Christina swept through the gardens. She wore a hooded floor-length cloak of pristine white *mi-go* fur – a gift from one of her six or seven suitors. *This* is diplomacy she understands. She plays *yōkai* admirers against each other to extort maximum tribute from each, with no intention of settling laurels on any one swain. The war for her favour already has casualties. The *kappa* Lord Kawataro's head-plate is cracked and the heron samurai Aosagibi has his arm in a sling. Being bound with the Mantis's obi or settling in one of Higo's false nests are less certain paths to doom than courting Princess Casamassima.

'Just the person I was looking for,' she announced.

'I am about to secure a famous victory,' I said.

'No you're not,' she said, glancing at the board. You don't have to know the rules to see which colour is winning.

'True,' I admitted. 'I am nearly vanquished.'

'Knock over your king or give up your forfeit, Gené. I need you.'

'I pledged your hand to the umbrella goblin,' I said. 'He is prepared to marry beneath him.'

Christina smiled viciously.

I gave in and put my death stones on the board. Abura Sumashi began sorting the stones into leather bags.

'Have you seen my parasol?' she asked Kasa-obake, in English. I didn't think an umbrella *could* look guilty, but he did – and darted around Higo to hide in her dangling fronds.

The Princess humphed.

'What do you need me for?' I asked her.

'Lieutenant Majin has come down from the tower. He is in that park with the little bridge over the winding stream.'

I knew the place. A typical Japanese public garden, as painted on fans displayed in the homes of British couples who've seen *The Mikado* more than twice. The new-built wall cruelly cut across the park, ruining the harmonious design. A loop of stream sluiced through grilles set in stone dams to prevent underwater egress. A Black Ocean wave cautioned eel-boned *yōkai* (or our own Mr Whelpdale) against trying to squeeze between the bars. Lovers separated by the wall could float messages on paper boats, I supposed. Stunted, bare trees pined for fellows on the other side. Neglected or abandoned, the park was overrun by hardy weeds and creepy-crawlies. Tough winter-flowering flora and venomous fauna. Poisonous species. Anything else would be exsanguinated.

On my visit, I had noticed a curious, unique feature: an iron door in the wall. With no handle or keyhole on this side, set so smoothly into brickwork it couldn't be prised open with fingers or tools. Another way in to Yōkai Town, but not out.

'I wish to speak with the Lieutenant,' the Princess told me.

I didn't doubt her.

That first night ashore, Christina treated Majin like a junior subaltern – irritated by this bland nonentity, looking past him for a superior officer. Surely she deserved more than a bureaucrat in uniform! Where was the Emperor? Lords and ladies of the court should have turned out. Reporters and photographers. A police cordon to keep back admiring crowds and a full military escort to convey her to the finest hotel in Tokyo. The Lieutenant and his crew of cart-haulers were less than her due. She was even piqued Higurashi beetled off when she wasn't looking.

Only after being told by Kostaki and me – and having it pointed out that everyone in Yōkai Town was terrified of the man – did she accept what we realised at once: Majin is in charge. He is the horseshoe-jawed face of the Black Ocean Society, the quiet voice of the Emperor. Despite his modest official rank, he is Baron Higurashi's superior. So far as the *yōkai* are concerned, Majin outranks God.

I've asked what the Lieutenant's real name might be. Everyone has a different answer. Yasunori Kamo, Jubei Kato, Master Baison, Wizard Washizaki. The *onmyoji* is treated with respect born of fear. I am told the *seiman* sigils on his gloves command demons. Some *yōkai* think themselves demons.

Princess Casamassima was now of a mind to dazzle Majin properly. She was not content to collect furs, compile lists and sit in an icehouse. She had demands to make and propositions to put forward. She wanted to get on with her conquest of Asia. The next recruit to her campaign must be Majin.

If I didn't go with her, she'd go by herself.

An annoyed Majin might slice her open with a sword swipe or lay her out with a slap from his demon-summoning hand. I had an inkling we survived only on his sufferance.

He might signal the mortars.

That he hasn't rained fire and silver on us all is a puzzle Kostaki, Dravot and I have chewed over. Yōkai Town is technically in violation of imperial edict. There must be a reason Black Ocean permits us to exist. I hope it isn't that sufficient silver shrapnel shells haven't yet arrived from Sheffield. Maybe a meeting with Majin would offer some clue. So I went with Christina.

The Princess pooh-poohed my suggestion we dragoon Kostaki and Dravot into the mission. This was to be a feminine expedition. She wouldn't share her expected triumph. Except with me as interpreter, and I didn't count. If she ever sits down, stops scheming and looks at her life, I've a feeling Christina might be unhappy with how it has turned out. She's so *alone*, even surrounded by moonstruck johnnies offering flowers, jewels and furs.

As we walked to the park, I saw *yōkai* hurrying in the same direction. O-Same flew above us. Her fire eyes zoomed through the air, ahead of her transparent heat-haze body. Her famous *furisode* trailed like a gorgeous flag. A doddery, cat-eared crone was assisted along the path by a wrestler whose rolls of blubber were circled with spiral snake tattoos.

It was as if the circus were in town. Or a concert planned. Christina glittered, irritated by the gathering crowd of gooseberries.

'I should have known,' she said. 'The poor lieutenant will be overwhelmed by petitioners. What a nuisance. Really, time should be set aside for *important* concerns.'

'Yes, Princess,' I said.

Electricity sparked around her. 'Do not be facetious, Mademoiselle Geneviève.'

'It's *Doctor* Geneviève,' I said.

'I don't believe in titles. As I think I've mentioned.'

'Yes—'

'If you say "Princess" again, I shall tell Kostaki you love a man in uniform… especially when the buttons are torn off.'

'*Touché.*'

I reconsidered feeling sorry for the Princess. At the end of the world, when the red sun sets for the last time, the only living things on the face of the earth will be giant cockroaches and Christina Light.

We came to the park.

Ryomen leant on his stick by the entrance, exhausted by the effort of dragging himself here. The serene, shaven-pated monk wears a loose, low-necked robe to accommodate the angry, bearded face thrust out of his doughy chest. I don't know whether he is one man in two minds or two men in one body. Both his foreheads bear tattoos of the sign of *in* and *yo* – the symbol of balance the Chinese call yin and yang, a black and a white comma fit perfectly into a circle of harmony.

'What's this place called?' I asked him.

'Jisatsu No Niwa,' he replied, talking out of his chest.

I shivered. Nothing to do with the cold. Away from the temple, the chill didn't bite as badly. I wished I'd not come along on this jaunt.

'What did he say?' Christina asked.

'The name of the park, it's—'

'Oh, hush now. There's Majin. Lieutenant, Lieu-*ten*-ant!'

She waved at him. I tugged her shoulder but she ignored me. She hopped up and down, trying to draw attention.

Majin posed on the ornamental bridge, cloak folded back like wings. A scabbarded ancient sword and a holstered modern automatic pistol hung from his Sam Browne belt. His tunic collar pressed into the skin of his throat. That made him look priestly, but not holy. Again, I noticed the theatrical figure he cut. His uniform is so sharp! The planes of his face are so perfect. Does he use powder and paint? The domino-mask shadow of his cap peak set off his shining eyes.

No one dared approach the bridge. Majin stood in the centre of an unmarked circle. Everyone knew where the line was. Nevertheless, *yōkai* filed into the little park.

Five *bakeneko* from Yokomori Street arrived on bicycles, and cleared *yōkai* from a prime lawn they marked as their territory by hissing and baring fangs at anyone who dared trespass. They stretched as if basking in the sun. They lit cigarettes and said funny things to men who pretended not to hear them.

I noticed Francesca Brysse in the crowd, folded *kasa* hat angled to hide her face. What was the sly chit up to?

I nudged Christina, who shot Brysse a deadly look. Whelpdale was here too, along with some of his Go chums.

'Our invitation must have got lost in the post,' I said.

Christina hissed. The fur on her cloak bristled. I suspected that if I touched it, I'd get an electric sting.

'I wouldn't worry about it,' I said. 'Trust me, we don't want to be at this party. It's not a tea ceremony.'

'What *are* you talking about?'

'The name of the park—'

She shushed me again. 'Something is happening…'

Majin drew his sword with a dramatic, steely rasp. Lanterns flared all round Jisatsu No Niwa – hung from the trees, the bridge and the wall, floating on the stream in little barges. The *bakeneko* caterwauled in unison.

'That's a Muramasa sword,' said lower Ryomen.

'Once drawn, it cannot be sheathed unless it has tasted blood,' commented upper Ryomen.

'Much like us,' I said.

'If the sword's thirst is not slaked,' continued upper Ryomen, 'demons will savage the disrespectful custodian of the blade.'

'Demons, pah!' said lower Ryomen. 'What does the Demon Man fear from demons?'

The chest-face had a point.

As custodians of Muramasa swords go, Majin was no traditionalist. The fifteenth-century treasure was sacrilegiously electroplated silver. A vampire-killing blade. *Yōkai* were fearful. Even O-Same backpedalled in the air like a frightened kite.

A lowly *kappa* rushed onto the bridge and bowed at the

Lieutenant's feet, like a supplicant begging favour. With a casual, contemptuous flick, Majin scraped the edge of his blade on the *kappa*'s cheek. Blood splashed across the wooden struts of the bridge. Drops fell into the stream.

So, that was the curse of the sword assuaged.

Majin kicked the *kappa*'s turtle shell back with his polished boot. The *yōkai* scuttled back to the crowd, trailing spots of greenish blood.

Oiled hinges creaked. The iron door was pushed open from the other side. It took several men with stout poles to do the job. The door was weighted so it would shut of its own accord once the poles were taken away.

People walked through the doorway. Some with pained dignity, some whimpering and stumbling. An army officer, epaulettes torn and buttons missing. A sobbing woman, head pressed into her hands. A composed young man in black robes. A paunchy official, shaking from his natty spats to his straw-coloured hair. A gaunt, nervous merchant with circles under his eyes. A naval cadet with bruises on his face and boot prints on his uniform. A girl in a cheap, bright kimono. Others. All, so far as I could make out, warm. Soldiers prodded stragglers with bayonets.

Once the whole group was in the park, the soldiers withdrew and the door clanged shut. The noise shook branches and rattled teeth.

My fangs were sharp.

Lieutenant Majin recited names that meant nothing to me.

Each newcomer was required to make a short statement.

'I have failed in my duty…'

'I stand here as substitute for the son of my *daimyō*, who forced himself on my sister. By my blood will his honour be restored.'

'I let it be believed that if a plebiscite favoured my cause, I would endow a clinic in my district but the money was

needed for household expenses. I made no promise I could
be held to, but hid behind a smoke of assumption for
political gain. Once I was held in public affection for my
wit and erudition... now I am vilified by all.'

'Curse you, monsters! Curse you for seven incarnations!'

'I am a woman of low morals and the shame of my
parents.'

'All my class took part in the disgraceful activity, but it is
my lot to be here.'

'I throw myself on your mercy. I have a wife and five
children. I am respected... a useful subject of the Emperor.'

'I intended to restore the funds at the end of the month,
but my superior in his wisdom instituted an audit.'

And so it went on.

Christina did not follow. The *yōkai* reacted to each
statement, nodding approval at those who owned up to
their sins, jeering those they found evasive, throwing
accusations ('usurer!') at the defiant, howling in sympathy
with sad stories. The *bakeneko* girls found everything funny.

'On your knees,' commanded Majin.

The wretched warm people knelt. Not visitors to Yōkai
Town, for visitors go home afterwards. The Lieutenant
descended from the bridge and inspected them. One or
two had to be encouraged into line by a kick. A rough,
scarred samurai – a self-confessed bandit and murderer
– was defiant until Majin pressed the flat of his sword
against the backs of his calves. He grunted as he crouched,
robe falling open to show a sunken, hairy belly.

A *tengu* – not the fellow with the chopped off and stuck
back on hand, but an older specimen with grey feathers –
passed along the line of kneeling folk with a sack, handing
out short, wood-sheathed knives (*tanto*).

'Those look too blunt to do much damage,' said
Christina.

'The point's sharp,' I said. 'It goes in easily, but it's

156

supposed to be difficult – agony, in fact – to draw across the stomach to commit suicide.'

'This is *hara-kiri*?'

One of the Japanese words everyone knows.

'More politely *seppuku*,' I said. 'Though there's nothing polite about it. Let's leave, Christina. We don't need to see this.'

'What's this place called?'

'Jisatsu No Niwa. Suicide Garden.'

No wonder only poisonous things lived in this park.

'I shall stay,' said the Princess, hugging herself under her furs.

'You can't *want* to watch this.'

'Not want. *Need*, Gené. Duty. Perhaps *you* wouldn't understand.'

'I didn't mean you *couldn't* understand Japan, but that it'll take time. This... this shouldn't be understood. This should be stopped.'

Yet I made no move to intervene. It wasn't just the prospect of mass execution-by-suicide – though I can't say it ranked high on my list of Unmissable Wonders of the Orient. What worried me was an inkling of why the ceremony was held here. This suicide club drew members from around the city, from all classes of people.

An ice-bud of terror bloomed in my heart. I did not want this spiritual lesson.

The disgraced army officer slid the knife into his stomach, made the sideways cut, and fell over into the cascading mess of his insides.

The smell made my eyes bleed. Heightened senses can be a curse. I've been a doctor long enough to know the stenches too well: on the battlefield, in the hospital ward, at the scene of the crime. Every single time, it's a struggle. For the beast inside, spilled blood is the spell of Circe. We vampires love to claim kinship with noble wolves or mysterious bats but when there's gore in the trough, we're just *swine*.

The samurai threw his blunt knife at the *tengu*. It bounced off his beak. Majin pricked the unrepentant brigand's neck from behind. A red geyser rose, splashing the *tengu* and the next suicide in line.

An empty kimono dashed from the crowd and knelt before the samurai. His wound rained blood on the invisible geisha. Suzan Arashi's head appeared – face a scarlet mask, elaborate hairdo a gory hood. Even her eyes showed up – as red lamps.

Knives were stuck into stomachs, tentatively or decisively. To cheers or jeers. The job was done perfectly or botched terribly. The embezzler couldn't bring himself to do the deed so Majin chopped off his head. Something small and many-armed seized the head and scuttled away with the prize. Chittering, shrieking creatures gulped at spilled, spoiled blood.

My fangs cut my lips. Red thirst tore at my chest, my stomach, my brain.

Fangs *hurt*, by the way. In anticipation of feeding, my teeth sharpen and cut through the gums like ivory needles. I've seen cases where a vampire's entire skull liquefies and flows into a new shape, reforming as a knotty tangle of impossible teeth strung together by exposed nerves. Imagine that coming at you, with panicked eyes and an exposed brain.

The servant who took the place of his *daimyō*'s son neatly ended himself. At that moment, if I could have reached him, I'd have dripped my blood onto his lips while sucking him empty, so he could rise and seek revenge on the vile, pampered bastard who put him here while striding off to a life of prestige, position and other servants' sisters. But Brysse got to him first. She sprang over the crowd with athletic grace, clashed claws with the cat-granny, and sank fangs into the servant's still-pulsing throat.

My sharpening nails cut my own fingers.

Whelpdale was also in the melee with the *yōkai*, as much blood on his face and clothes as in his mouth. Even aristocratic monsters waded into the horror to get their portion. O-Same swooped, setting light to fur and feathers, and swept the adulterous wife up into the air. The woman burst into flames as the *shito-dama* absorbed her essence. Cinders and soot fell into the stream and a kimono burned like a twist of paper. The cat-girls played with their prey, the cadet singled out from his class, letting him run between them, holding his arms across his sundered stomach. They put scratches in his clothes and face until, overcome by pain and exhaustion, he collapsed. Then they *pounced* – tail stubs up in the air, whiskered faces in his open wounds. A silent, shamed army officer was caught in the coils of Lady Oyotsu's neck, a goat trapped by a boa constrictor. She darted at his throat from several angles, biting over and over. Her rice-powder make-up was smeared off in lumps by spurts of blood. The Mantis – a warm woman! – pricked an inefficient clerk's neck for the bitter joy of it, then pushed the bleeding, dying man into the arms of true vampires. She was avenging some long ago wrong, over and over. No matter how many died, it would never be enough.

The only thing that stopped me joining the carnage was Christina's hand on my shoulder. I *know* she is as bloodthirsty as the rest of us... but she has *control*. An iron will I hadn't appreciated.

'We can't,' she said to me. 'This is beneath us.'

I agreed with her, but finer feelings were asleep, like the upper head of Ryomen. The conscienceless, appetite-driven monster in my chest took charge. Open a vein in the next room and I cease to be Dr Dieudonné. I am Grendel, I am Cronus. I am a berserker.

I am – hateful to think it – *Dracula*.

I fought Christina but she was strong. She *shone* now – light pulsed under her skin, poured through her eyes and mouth. Her bones showed, like coals in a fire.

She had fangs but also a halo – a sparking circle of electricity.

'Are you a vampire or an angel?' I asked.

'I am Light,' she said. 'Remember.'

Her rays were calming. She made me look at the Suicide Garden.

The park was strewn with corpses, intestines, puddles of blood with *yōkai* lapping at them. A dead girl, face down in the stream, driven against the grille by the current. Feeding took place – a rhythmic, gentle sucking on the dying and a savage rending of the dead. Some *yōkai* were killed too – torn apart in the frenzy, or exploded by their own gluttony.

The westernised official who preferred not to endow a clinic was bent over the bridge wall, pinstripes and drawers around his ankles. A crouching *kappa* extended a barbed tongue deep into his bowel. The official screamed for mercy. Lieutenant Majin smartly chopped off his head.

I didn't want to see any more.

I am a monster. A vampire. I know this. But this is not how it has to be. This is not how I have been. This is not what I want. This is not the only truth.

Striding through the abattoir, smiling like a nasty child, the Lieutenant was every inch the Demon Man. He had not a speck of blood on him, except his boots and his sword. Even his gloves remained unnaturally white.

But he was *feeding*. The way vampires feed.

He drank pain and terror. From the spoiled blood, from the ozone in the air, from the vileness pulled out of the guilty and the innocent. He primped like a peacock.

Was this how he survived? Drawing sustenance from horror.

He looked at the vampires – faces in meat and muck and blood – and laughed. At that moment, he was as far above them – above *us* – as any emperor. How could such a creature bow to any earthly power?

'That's it,' said Christina. 'He doesn't.'

I hadn't spoken aloud. I had been shouting with my mind.

'He's in here, with us,' said Christina. 'Only we are witnesses. Look, no one on the walls. His troops behind the gate, his masters nowhere to be seen: the Emperor, Black Ocean, generals, admirals. They don't know about this… or don't want to know. Majin *has* no masters. He dares to think he can look down on all the world. We can *use* this, Gené. It's pride… and I know a thing or two about that. A weakness that looks like strength. Dracula has it too and it'll be the end of him. I'll bet Majin polishes his boots himself. Has a batman to do it for him, but is never satisfied. The same with his bloody sword. He burnishes it like a mirror and contemplates his lovely, lovely eyes. Have you ever seen a fellow who cares so much for his looks? He is swollen to bursting with self-regard… ready to be pricked?'

Her light was calming. My fangs retracted. I swallowed bloody spittle. I drew in my nails.

Some of the feeders slunk or crawled away, ashamed or hotly self-deluded. Replete and sluggish or unsatisfied and jittery. Brysse washed her bloody hands in the stream, splashing like Ellen Terry as Lady Macbeth. Whelpdale, bent out of shape, struggled to get his arms and legs to work so he could stand up. Both Ryomen's mouths were dripping. The *bakeneko* twisted their heads around and licked blood off their own fur and each other's faces.

Finally, Majin looked at us. For the first time, noticed us. Noticed *Christina*.

I was wrung out, on my knees. Christina stood, shining. Majin sheathed his sword and touched his cap – a salute. Christina had what she wanted. His attention.

He lowered himself into a crouch, like the stance of a sumo wrestler, cape around him like owl wings. Carefully, finger by finger, he took off his gloves. The *seiman* sigils were tattooed on his hands. His nails were polished blue. He pressed fingertips to the springy earth... all the while looking at Princess Casamassima.

I heard – no, I *felt* – a rumble, deep underground. A shifting of rocks and dirt.

Those who could fled Jisatsu No Niwa. Only the dead and the insensible remained – and Majin and Christina.

I counted myself insensible.

Rifts appeared, radiating from Majin's hands. His sigils burned red, like hot wires under his skin. He poured something of himself into the earth, as if warming buried dragon eggs. Much of what he had drawn from the blood orgy was given away, purged into the ground. Those eggs cracked. Dirt was breathed in, then expelled as subterranean fire. The bridge fell apart and tumbled down. A small red-leafed scuttling tree – a *yōkai* bonsai! – fell, smoke belching from mouths among its exposed roots.

The quake struck.

I've been in earthquakes before, but only natural ones. All Saints' Day, Lisbon, 1755. The Rann of Kutch, 1819. They weren't like this. The world – not just the physical world, but *everything* – seemed torn in half, like a sheet of paper. It took seconds, but I can *feel* it now, hours later. We all have a connection to the earth. Perhaps vampires, who have escaped being buried in it, more than most. We owe the grave a debt we are defaulting on. It's why some elders sleep on a layer of their native soil. A quake is a sharp reminder of that tie. Earthquakes spur philosophers to deep thought. In the immediate aftermath, men with spades or buckets of water are of more use.

A chasm gaped in Suicide Park. The stream poured into the new abyss. Corpses slid to the edges, then rolled over them. A few *yōkai*, lost in blood-dreams, were swallowed too.

A fluttering cloud rose from the crack. Butterflies!

Christina still defied Majin. She rose inches off the ground, partially insubstantial. As painful to look at as a furnace, wavering inside her shimmer. What Kate Reed told me was true – the Princess could turn into animated light.

A living star.

The butterflies whirled around her, streaming like ribbons, blotting out her light. The ribbons tied and for a moment she was enveloped in blue beating wings. A light burst scattered them like chaff. Wings turned to flickers of flame.

Christina wiped her face. Tiny wounds healed.

Majin stood and put his gloves on. He gestured like an orchestra conductor who has volunteered to command the firing squad at the execution of his most hated critic.

A dead tree broke apart, roots erupting, branches cracking. The largest branch fell like an axe, shearing through Christina's right arm, severing it from her shoulder.

She was flesh again, screaming and bleeding. Her cries cut through my lull of fascination. I blinked away the light-spots burned into my vision. The tang of vampire blood quickened me. I was sober.

I had to be a doctor again.

I examined Christina. Her arm wasn't completely detached – thread-like golden veins connected it to her shoulder. Glowing discharge oozed from both stumps. I pushed the head of the humerus against the glenoid cavity and twisted the bone until it set, trusting the muscles to swarm around the rotator cuff. I could tell by the piercing quality of Christina's yelp that everything in her shoulder was in its proper configuration. Her shapeshifter body should do the rest. Her clothes were ruined, though. Gold blood soaked into – and ate through – her beautiful fur cloak.

Lieutenant Majin walked over to where I was working on Christina and observed, taking a student's interest in my efforts. He could have cut us both down with his silver sword but let us continue. Another gesture of contempt. I glimpsed the blurry, distorted fudge of my not-quite-a-reflection in his shiny boots.

Christina was a poor patient.

She was badly injured a few years ago in an act of defiance at the Tower of London – her own damn fault, according to the reliable Kate Reed – and I believe never properly healed. However, she has been reluctant to submit to even cursory medical examination. If I went near her with a stethoscope, she reacted like a superstitious Carpathian elder confronted with a peasant girl holding a blessed crucifix. The strange, glittering Oblensky bloodline makes diagnosis thorny – but something is wrong with her. The Princess finds it difficult to retain the semblance of human form.

In pain even after I'd set her arm, she wavered. Her inner light was furious. A fire-shape like O-Same's demanded to be born from her body – seeking the freedom of the air, leaving behind the corporeal, transcending personality. I was worried Christina might turn into a scatter of stars. More poetic than crumbling to red dust, but still true death. I had no idea how to treat her condition. Beef tea and Carter's Little Liver Pills were likely to have a limited effect.

Christina gripped my blouse with her left hand and pulled me close to her.

'Don't let me fall apart, Geneviève,' she said.

I understood her fear. Shapeshifting – not a trait of my bloodline – is dangerous, often fatal. Newborns whose turning doesn't take, dissipate into grave dirt or transform into perfectly formed but dead wolves or bats. I've seen that too often. At the other end of unlife, senile elders forget what it's like *not* to be a pool of fog or a swarm of rats and never come back from a shift. I think Christina is haunted by what happened to her husband. She bridles whenever Drusilla brings it up.

'Just keep me awake and I can fix myself.'

I looked around, as if expecting my medical bag – back in my trunk in the dorm – to be magically there. I doubted Majin would dash off on an errand of mercy to fetch my kit.

Christina convulsed, as if shocked. Her right arm was limp. I talked to her, asking her to pay attention. I apologised for being cold to her and laughing at her plans. I insulted her for being a bore and a snob and a princess. I promised loyalty to the Revolution – *any* revolution! – and swore to be her friend, if only on the condition she didn't close her eyes and go away inside herself.

I hadn't changed my opinion, really. Maybe I saw her courage for the first time – it was usually masked by ruthlessness. She had kept me out of the bloody trough, saved me from debasing myself. She was still infuriating, but wasn't simple – not a *Punch* cartoon of a hypocritical radical prig.

She was my patient.

I'll do a lot for my patients.

Her eyes closed. They glowed through shut lids. The convulsions stopped, stilling like the quake. She was receding. I worried that her light would go out.

Something waved near my head. I looked at it.

Lieutenant Majin dangled a scorpion. He had pinched its head flat between his thumb and forefinger, but its tail still thrashed.

I bared my fangs at him, but he smiled, almost sweetly, and nodded.

'Medicine,' he said – in English.

I realised what he meant me to do. Gingerly, I took the scorpion – vampires are resistant to natural poisons, but not completely immune – and jabbed the tail-sting into Christina's chest.

The venom struck like lightning. Violet fire lit up the veins of Christina's neck and face. Her eyes and mouth snapped open. She sucked in a great breath.

Sitting up, she knocked me backwards. Her right hand lay dead as a fish in her lap but she grasped the air with her left.

She struggled against the poison. Half her head swelled like a puffball and she bled purple from her right eye.

She needed *something* to fight, to bring all of her back, to focus herself, the way a magnifying glass turns a shaft of sunlight into a burning beam.

Then she let out breath, exhaling a long string of Italian words she hadn't learned at the Palazzo Casamassima – unless it was in the stables.

She said things about my mother, my preferences and my person. Then she stopped and said, 'Thank you, *Dottore*.'

I was about to give credit to Majin – but when I turned, he was gone.

12

A KNIGHT TEMPLAR III

'Tonight's a rum 'un, Brother Taki,' said Dravot. 'Deathly 'ush all over. Too deathly, to my way of thought. The usual 'aunts is abandoned. Yokomori Street deserted. No tarts, no staff, no punters. The gamblin' flotilla lies derelict. You can hear an 'ummingbird fart in the marketplace. If I knew no better, I'd say our yokey pals was convenin' a chinwag on the sly. No foreign devils invited. First order of business up for discussion – the cuttin' of our *gaijin* throats and the reportin' of our demises as a sad inevitability.'

Kostaki had also noted the scarcity of *yōkai* on the streets. But vampires of their own party were in short supply too. Which troubled him more.

When people weren't where they should be, his knee hurt.

At the warehouse, Albert Watson grumbled at his post. His watch should have ended an hour ago. Francesca Brysse, a vampire Kostaki didn't trust, was supposed to relieve him. She hadn't reported for duty.

They were forced to rely too much on civilians.

Watson was given to shifting his weight and looking in odd directions. To his ever-twitching bat ears, small sounds were like rifle shots. He was always saying 'Did you hear that?' Tonight, there weren't even small sounds. Not this side of Yōkai Town.

'Run along, Smiler,' said Dravot. 'We'll keep your spot warm till the Brysse piece turns up. If you bump into 'er, kick 'er up the jacksie and inform 'er she's to wend her way 'ere sharpish, or we'll want to know the reason why. Now, 'op to… *lef'-right, lef'-right…*'

Watson saluted and jogged off.

Kostaki opened the warehouse door.

'We should check the sleepers,' he said.

The temporary mausoleum was utilitarian. Stacks of crates under tarpaulins. Trunks of the sleepers' belongings stored in a locked room, protected from pilferage. Larcenous dockworkers and sailors had been a problem since Plymouth. By the rules Kostaki laid down, guards were to take a turn of inspection around the warehouse at the beginning of every watch.

'The snoozers can wait,' said Dravot. 'I've a thirst on.'

He swigged from a hip flask. His eyes glinted red. He wiped his dripping moustache with his hand. He offered Kostaki the flask. 'Finest wild boar, fresh-bled on Mermaid Ancestor Place not an hour ago,' he said. 'With a pinch of pepper. It's the stuff, Worshipful Brother. The stuff indeed.'

Kostaki thanked him and refused.

Dravot shrugged. 'More for me, then. You know not of what you're missin'. Savin' the palate for more refined fare, are we? 'Ave you requisitioned a nutritious, nibblesome Nipponese?'

Kostaki didn't answer.

Dravot swallowed again and screwed the cap back. He sloshed the flask as a last temptation. 'Billy Bottle's stuck close through many a campaign,' he said, patting the flask. 'Seen me from brandy to blood. A better friend than a Bible is Billy Bottle. 'E'd stop a bullet for me.'

This morning, an elder – Arcueid Moonstar – woke

in her box and pushed off the lid. She was disoriented after lassitude. Lady Geneviève had to give her salts. She remembered her name, but was patchy on how she came to be aboard the *Macedonia*. She'd gone to sleep in a long jersey, wool skirt and knit cap. She looked like a serious girl – a student or governess. She refused blood. Which was odd, but Kostaki didn't draw attention to his own abstinence by asking about hers.

'I dream of other stars,' she said. 'Cold stars.'

'Another mouth to feed,' commented Dravot. Except she wasn't. 'Another princess too, a princess from the moon,' Dravot went on. 'We've one too many as it is. Want to bet Tina Sparkles 'as the Moon Maid put down? What kind of a name is "Arkwayd" anyway? Anagrammatical or somesuch. 'Ave you heard of anyone else called that?'

'I can't think of anyone else named "Dravot" either.'

Dravot chuckled. 'Not many to the pound, I admit. As your Scotchman says "'Ere's tae us wha's like us... damn few and they're a' deid."'

'"*We're* a' deid", you mean.'

''Appen so, Brother Taki. 'Appen so.'

In London, Kostaki had known a Scotchman. A *Scotsman*, he would have said. Inspector Mackenzie. A warm man; an honourable officer. Danny Dravot killed him and arranged it so Kostaki was arrested for the murder. The Diogenes Club set out to damage the reputation of the Regiment. The Crimson Bums had a reputation worth damaging then.

In the Tower, Kostaki vowed to settle the debt but circumstances changed. He was released into a new world. The vampire who shot him in the knee and knifed Mackenzie in the back was his Lodge Brother. Kostaki discerned traces of Mackenzie in Dravot. Some vampires downed a jigger of soul alongside a pint pot of blood. In Dravot, somewhere, was the Scotsman's fading ghost.

If circumstances changed again, Kostaki and Dravot might return to opposing lines. One could kill the other. Most likely, a duel would leave both truly dead. But any murdering would be professional. Execution, without rancour. Masonic loyalty superseded other allegiances.

Kostaki had told Dravot about the House of Broken Dolls, leaving out Miss Zark's prediction and the mannequin Lady Geneviève.

He was warily on watch for the vampire doll and her puppet shows.

They walked past the statue by the gate. Guards inside hustled to point rifles at them.

Kostaki couldn't see Lieutenant Majin. 'I prefer it when Majin is there,' he said. 'In his place.'

'That's the cove we should mark closely, Brother Taki,' Dravot said. ''E's like a boy watchin' red and black ants go to war. When 'e gets bored, 'e'll empty a kettle of boilin' water on the 'ole bloody lot of us.'

'It'll be black water… that wave of theirs. It's daubed everywhere.'

'The Lieutenant likes to splash it about. Bad 'abit, that. Ownin' up when 'e doesn't have to.'

'He wants us to know it's him, Dravot. That no one can stop him, that no one outside *wants* to stop him. He has his plans for this anthill.'

In Whitechapel, the Diogenes Club stung vampires and vampire haters alike. A tense situation was exacerbated. Fires were started. Inspector Mackenzie had seen through it.

'To a copper, it's the oldest game in town,' the Scotsman said. 'You stir up both sides, set them at each other like dogs. Then sit back and watch the fireworks.'

Was that stratagem being repeated in Yōkai Town?

Mackenzie had educated Kostaki in new ways of thinking – as, in a different way, had Danny Dravot. Neither would have been as easily fooled by Tsunako Shiki.

'We should have heard from our spies,' said Kostaki.

Dravot shrugged. 'A slow sport, Brother Taki. Soldierin' is football. Charge and ruck, 'ack and blast, boot the Spaniard's 'ead into the back of the net. Cripple as many of the other lot as you can before the ref sees red. Then in the pub or down the bawdy house. 'Ooray, we've won! Now for a pie, a pint and a poke. All clear and above board and out in the open. Like you, Worshipful Brother. On the square, on the level. Espionage is cricket. The Great Game, they calls it. You falls asleep waitin' your turn at bat... or stands about on the off-chance the ball will bonk you where you are. Scorin' is arse-around-frontwise. Someone has to write it down in a notebook or else they lose track of 'oo's winnin'. No one 'as to do that at a soccer match. It wears you down with its sluggardliness. Bop and run, bop and run... And it stretches out till sunset. Nothin' ever settled. Bloody awful game, cricket. Played by gentlemen – which is to say, the worst pills and bounders turned out of Eton and Oxford and set loose to plague the four corners of the earth.'

In Moldavia, the accepted sport was fighting. Not boxing, wrestling or fencing – just fighting. Blow for blow, kick for kick, stab for stab, until the winner was standing, blooded. The loser was in the dirt, one way or the other. Kostaki excelled at that game – until Dracula told him he should not be content to fight other Moldavians. Turks were easier to put in the dirt and could be robbed of prizes. Moldavian losers had nothing worth taking. Even fighting was a poor sport, Dracula said, next to the proper pursuits of the Carpathian Guard – hunting... and killing.

Much rested on the Chinese assassin and the vampire mercenary. Within the walls of Yōkai Town, they risked stagnation at best... extermination at worst. Kostaki didn't think the Princess was taking tea with the right people. Lady Oyotsu was polite and charming (if unnerving), but said little and gave away less. Conversation with her might be as useless as their visit to the feeble General who would never finish his letter. Kostaki had shared his worry with Lady Geneviève. Creatures powerful enough to face Dracula himself meekly accepted being penned like cattle. There was no lid to this cage – why didn't the birds fly? Plenty here had wings. Once, these *yōkai* were formidable. They all trailed legends of their doings – revenges, murders, conquests, devastations. In the shadow of Majin's statue, their fangs were sheathed.

His inclination was to take Lady Geneviève, at least, into their confidence. Dravot was against it. 'The more in on the screw, the more likely it is to go awry.'

Kostaki couldn't argue with that. But he was wary of more deceptions. They would not hold.

Someone scuttled towards them, disturbing the fog.

''Oo goes there?' said Dravot, aiming his revolver. 'Identify yourself, friend or foe, or be plugged through the noodle!'

Swirls and eddies. Hands stuck up and waved.

'*Mestres, mestres.*'

Kichijiro threw himself at their feet.

'This bastard again, eh,' said Dravot, holstering his gun. ''Aven't you a bone to pick with Mr Kitchikoko, Brother Taki? Somethin' to do with a bagful of flirty pusses and a shabby trick played on Yokomori Street?'

The Renfield held his hands over his face and gabbled. '*Misericórdia, misericórdia!*' He wailed and touched his head to the ground.

'Mercy my eye,' said Dravot. 'Would you care to apply your size eleven to this bleeder's bonce, Brother Taki? Or don't you want the bother of scrapin' him off after?'

The Renfield pleaded incoherently.

Kostaki was leery of the man. Once bitten…

But Kichijiro was never top of the bill. He was the warm-up act, the scene-setter. The Baptist, not the Redeemer. The bird who picked the crocodile's teeth in return for not being eaten.

Kostaki looked into the fog. Golden eyes gleamed through murk. Cat's eyes.

Dorakuraya.

While they were distracted by his Renfield, the Japanese vampire *manifested*.

Kostaki would severely discipline a sentry who let anyone get so close to a position without challenge.

The sleek silhouette coalesced from mist and darkness. Fog boiled out from under his cloak, pooling around his feet. His white scarf was a cold flame in the night.

And his eyes shone.

Dorakuraya came nearer, seeming to float on a cushion of mist, back straight and stiff as a ramrod. 'My friends,' he said.

'Evenin', squire,' said Dravot.

'My servant's life is yours,' said Dorakuraya. 'Bleed him as you like. Drain him and toss him away.'

'Not too peckish at the moment, thank you very much,' said Dravot, patting the flask in his pocket. 'Supped my fill tonight.'

Kostaki's red thirst was keen as a sickle. Dorakuraya's golden eyes – small full moons – affected him. Even a scrap as meagre as the Renfield was a sore temptation, for the blood was the life, and the life was *delicious*.

It had been so *long* without feeding.

He was mad to think he could hold to the pledge. A vampire who did not drink blood was not a vampire. Not a man, not even a ghost… *nothing*.

He tried to look away from Dorakuraya's eyes.

'Can we assist you?' Dravot asked. 'Brother Taki and me are always disposed to be of the 'elpful persuasion.'

'I come to offer succour,' said Dorakuraya, 'and a

prospect of eternal prosperity. As is fitting for such as we.'

'Most generous, I'm sure, sir—'

Dorakuraya's hand emerged from his cloak. He stretched his long fingers and held up his lightly furred palm in a gesture of command. The Sergeant stopped talking. Dorakuraya wasn't looking at Dravot – just at Kostaki.

In a finger-snap, Dorakuraya moved closer still. The fog was agitated. A damp, intangible whirlpool. He stood between Kostaki and the silenced Dravot. Hair red as copper, golden eyes shining bright... chilling, calming, *fascinating*.

Kostaki remembered Dracula in the village square. His first sight of the Prince. A general, acting as his own recruiting sergeant. A pile of bloodied, chipped enemy swords at his feet. He fixed his gaze on first one youth, then another, then on Kostaki. He kicked a curved sword up in the air. Kostaki caught it. The hilt slapped into his hand with a sting. The blade completed him. Later, turning vampire was nothing compared to that moment, when Kostaki the fighter became Kostaki the soldier. Already, though he didn't know the word, he was a Templar.

In his memory, the face of Dracula – moustached, pockmarked, gaunt – faded. The clean-shaven, paler, rounder Dorakuraya formed in its place. The Japanese vampire – get of a red-headed Jesuit, son of the Black Mass – stood in that Moldavian square. Before his arrival, Kostaki's course was set and inevitable. A few years' ruinous toil in field or forest, a bony wife and more stillbirths than sons, a drunkard's death in a stream or a neighbour's dirk in the back. The Impaler took him away from that.

Now, transfixed, he believed Dorakuraya carried the Dracula bloodline.

Kostaki remembered his first moments as a newborn, get of none, looking up, with changed eyes, at the proud Prince. Dracula had a grip on his own sword blade, cutting his heavy glove and slicing into his hand. He squeezed vampire blood onto the battlefield like a farmer watering crops. Kostaki had never admitted it until now, even to himself, but he was the Impaler's bastard, turned in the shambles of war, recruited from one army into another.

Others too were blessed – or cursed – like him. It was no honour. Dracula was profligate and wasteful. Many of his get did not survive their first night. Even those who fought well and drank the foeman's blood might combust at the first rays of dawn. The Prince sent wave after wave of mayfly berserker *nosferatu* against his enemies, never shy of adding to the butcher's bill. Kostaki lasted that first night. A spark of caution, battle-won wisdom, and perhaps something more – something he owed his father-in-darkness – fit him for his new condition. After all, he was still here.

Over Dorakuraya's shoulder, Kostaki saw Dravot's mouth open and close. No words issued that he could hear.

Kostaki's impulse was to draw his sword.

But he could not. He was held by Dorakuraya's eyes.

Dorakuraya's cloak parted like theatre curtains. He tossed his scarf over his shoulder and pulled open his shirt, diamond-shaped nails deftly popping buttons out of holes to reveal his bare, muscular chest. His flesh was the white of old tomb marble. Sparse black hairs sprouted from his chest. Red veins threaded through slabs of muscle. On one breast was tattooed a gold-eyed red bat, a ragged wing extended like a Hokusai wave.

With a long, sharp thumbnail, Dorakuraya pricked his flesh. Blood trickled, gold as his eyes. A shining river.

Kostaki *tasted* the blood, just by looking at it. It flowed over his tongue, down his throat, into his belly.

Warmth, rapture, wonder.

'Drink deep, my friend,' said Dorakuraya. 'Drink… and behold…'

* * *

In the castle, he was visited by the Master's three wives.

Mouths he knew well. They had kisses for him. Pearl white teeth, voluptuous ruby lips. Ladies, by their dress and manner. Wantons, under the velvet.

Tina, Drusey... Gené.

Light, dark... and blonde.

A sane woman, a mad child... and a lady elder.

Calm, wild... and *delicious*.

Kostaki's knee didn't trouble him. His mind was clear. His red thirst was slaked.

The Master was pleased with his good and faithful service. Dracula.

No, the Master was something more than Dracula.

The Master was a golden-eyed vampire saint.

He was in a vaulted space, flagstones swept clean, vermin banished. Moonlight shone through tall mullioned windows. Pure, clear Templar voices sang the *Ave Satani* in the Black Chapel.

He sat on a plush divan. He was divested of his sword-belt, but it hung within his reach. The jewel on his pommel shone like a star.

The pale women plied him with warm blood from golden goblets. They took turns on his lap. Their bodies had warmth, but no weight. They wound slim fingers in his moustaches, traced his scars with pointed tongues, pressed cool lips to his. They tasted like sweet wine.

They laughed, like little bells. They stretched, like Persian cats. Their touch was gentle, fangs and claws sheathed.

Three faces became one. A six-armed Kali folded into a single body.

The woman in his arms was not the Master's. But his own. Kostaki's wife.

Cat's eyes. Golden irises. Black velvet pupils.

Lady Geneviève's eyes... and her face, mostly. Her lips, her nose, her chin.

But Drusilla Zark's cheekbones. Christina Light's complexion. Arcueid Moonstar's near-white hair. Francesca Brysse's long legs and arched shoulders. Carmilla Karnstein's hourglass shape, waist cinched in the fashion of the late eighteenth century. Elizabeth Báthory's slender hands, nails polished scarlet. Clare Mallinger's strange sleeping smile, the web-mesh of her cocoon laid over her mouth like fine lace. The infinite nape of Lady Oyotsu's neck. The rumps of the girls of his village, finest in Moldavia. The wickedness of the *bakeneko* of the House of Broken Dolls. The wit of the women of the salons of London and Paris. The devotion of the nuns of Arcangelo, the compassion of the nurses of Sebastopol. The warmth of his mother, the sinew of his sisters, the spirit of daughters he'd not had and other men's daughters he'd wished were his own. The love of all.

His vampire wife.

'Kostaki,' she breathed.

There was honour, reward and satisfaction. He was a worshipful Brother of the Order of the Knights Templar, he was a Commandant of the Carpathian Guard, he was high in the councils of the King of the Cats.

He was the heart's blood, the brains, the sword of the Draculas. His father-in-darkness acknowledged him. For was not Dracula a generous master?

'Are you satisfied, my lord?' asked his wife.

He answered her without words.

A forest of stakes was raised within sight of the castle, tall and straight as the trees cut down and stripped to make them. The Master's enemies hung twenty feet or more above bloody earth. Bodies twisted, pressed onto impaling stakes by their own weight, insides displaced. Ravens

177

pecked eyes. Dogs lapped the pooling blood. Oaths and prayers coughed out of throats too torn for screaming. The enemy suffered, but did not die. Their lot was an eternity of well-earned pain.

Turks, first and always. Turbans nailed to their heads, pig parts stuffed in their mouths to mock their faith, cuts in their flanks dribbling thin blood.

Monks, priests, witchfinders.

Stretched on their own racks of inquisition, spikes thrust through their chests, hung upside down so their heads dunked in buckets of holy water replenished by the Renfield's piss.

Slayers, professors, doctors. Broken in combat, shot or stabbed with silver, necks snapped, veins opened with long scalpel cuts. Dictagraphs smashed and wax cylinder fragments pressed into staring eyes.

Strews of red ash, exposed to the day star and trodden into pine needles. Rotting, fanged heads piled up like balls beside cannons. Wraiths in oubliettes, red thirst rising to intolerable torment.

Kostaki's stomach roiled; not at the sights, sounds and smells of execution by torture but at the sacrilege, the affront, the temerity of those who dared defy Dracula.

Whatever they suffered wasn't enough. He contemplated the sea of pain.

The Master was beside him, armoured gauntlet resting on Kostaki's shoulder. No words passed between them.

Dracula was pleased with him. Honour enough.

Victory followed upon victory. Nations knelt before Dracula.

The warm were herded onto reservations, pampered and fed through the year, culled come Hallowe'en. Blood flowed to the Master, and from the Master to his disciples. From the Arctic wastes to the Australian outback, the standard of Dracula flew.

History drew to a close.

But for one small scattering of islands.

From the castle, everything could be seen. In the eastern sea, a nation cowered behind walls of ice and mist.

Dracula convened his court.

Kostaki stood with the Templars.

'There is my final foe,' said the Master, pointing at Japan.

'I shall bring you the head of the Emperor,' volunteered Kostaki.

Dracula looked at him.

'Your resolve does you credit, son-in-darkness, but a warm emperor is less than a village headman. Always, the living are our livestock, servants, possessions. Now we ride against those who think themselves our equals. Our ships and machines will swarm over the shores and skies of the Rising Sun. The vampires of the East will bow to us. As once we broke the Turk and made him our vassal, so now we will conquer the Woman of the Snow, the Night Queen. She is cold and she is haughty. Her breath is frost and her touch the chill of true death. She commands armies of monsters. Yet, she will be brought down. She will be less than a maidservant to our wives and all that is hers will be ours. Dracula shall reign in the East as in the West.'

The shadow of Dracula's wings spread. He turned to the Templars, singling out Kostaki.

'This is my command,' he said, 'that you, Captain Kostaki, seek out the Yuki-Onna. Break through her defences, slay her protectors, penetrate her lair. In a cave of ice deep under her palace is a coffin. There you will find the Winter Witch. She has the face of Medusa, but you must look upon it without turning to stone. Strike her breast with iron so that her body shatters like ice in the spring. Then pull out her heart and bring me that so I may drink from it.'

As he spoke, Dracula's eyes burned brighter than suns.

A red film passed over the gold.

In Kostaki's heart, fire caught.

His wife was beside him, her mouth close to his ear, her hands under his cloak.

His Lodge Brothers and mess comrades were assembled. They toasted him in fresh blood poured from enemies already vanquished, in anticipation of glorious banquets to follow the greatest victory of all.

He drew his carrack – the blade with no name. It glistened in the firelight as he held it up in salute.

'So you have spoken, my father,' he said. 'So shall it be done!'

The ground moved under him, shockingly.

His knee exploded. Had he been shot again?

No. It was just pain, coming back like the tide.

'God's 'oly trousers, I felt that in my water,' said Dravot. 'The worst quaverin' yet.'

The fog of fancy was shredded. What had been so vivid – imaginings sharp as life – unravelled like an ancient tapestry hauled from a tomb. Exposed to light, it rotted like some vampires at dawn. Threads came apart, colours faded to grey. The picture was gone.

Music had played – stirring, martial, inspiring, devotional. Now he heard only the bark of distant dogs…

He was looking at Dorakuraya's bleeding chest. He didn't know why.

The blood-trickle zigged and zagged as the vampire swayed, shifting this way and that. He knew how to roll with the tremors.

Inside the warehouse, coffins toppled. Someone

groaned and swore – suffering sudden, uncomfortable awakening. A lantern crashed and broke near Dravot's boots. He stamped out the fire.

Jarred from a dream, Kostaki tried to recapture details. It was a sketch on pond water. He thought he remembered Lady Geneviève's face. It melted.

'Like ice in the spring...'

Where had he heard that before? Recently?

No – it was lost, all gone. He had forgotten something as important as his own name. He felt the absence like a missing limb or a lost eye.

He scratched his moustaches – then remembered they were gone. He patted his shaven pate. It felt wrong, again.

He leaned back to steady himself. The wall he touched was shaking. Nothing could be trusted. This was worse than the worst storm at sea.

'You've popped your dicky buttons, chum,' Dravot told Dorakuraya.

The Japanese vampire refastened his clothes. Blood rivulets – dull red, not shining gold – soaked into cotton.

'Brother Taki, are you with us?'

Kostaki couldn't speak, but saluted. What was it? What couldn't he remember? Moments ago, it was clear and bright in his mind. Or was it long since gone? What was it? A woman, perhaps? And Dracula – always Dracula.

The world lived under Dracula as once it lived under God.

The ground stopped shaking. Water was gushing somewhere near – a broken pipe? In the warehouse, a newly awakened sleeper complained in Low German.

Dorakuraya was gone. A patch of bare earth, a hole in ground mist, showed where he had stood.

'There's a fellah with a predisposition to mystification,' said Dravot. 'Not 'ot on the 'ow d'you dos and fare thee wells... pops up and pops off like a surprise attack. And what's all that standin' to attention and givin' the dead-

181

eye stare about? Tell you what, Brother Taki, I'll bet 'e's a shrimp who uses stilts to look down on us. Notice you never sees 'is feet for fog. Much mischief is concealable under a cape. But 'e's left 'is rubbish behind.'

Kichijiro lay face down. He had fainted with terror.

'What do you suppose that oogle-eyes malarkey was about?' asked Dravot.

Kostaki shook his head. He had no idea.

'A queer quacker,' said Dravot, 'our Mr Dorakuraya Nemuri or whateversuch 'e calls 'imself. A strange duck.'

Kostaki still tried to remember the dream.

It couldn't be important, but…

13

YŌKAI TOWN, DECEMBER 16, 1899

After Suicide Garden, I knew I'd be no good to anyone until I quenched my red thirst. What happens to vampires who go blood simple is ugly. What happens to anyone within reach of them is worse. Unless I fed soon, I'd be chewing my own wrists.

It didn't take long to find the mongrel.

The scavenger was in the foggy alley where it had fought for the *tengu*'s hand, curled in a lair of chewed bones and shredded lanterns. A meagre, mean scrap of an animal – but warm-blooded. It panted in its sleep, glistening threads trailing from its jaws. Scratches on its flanks. One leg kinked the wrong way. I told myself it was dying.

I was scrupulous enough to make certain the dog was not a shapeshifted *yōkai* before pressing my barbed nail into its carotid artery.

I did not stop drinking until my prey was limp.

It wasn't just the blood, it was the *death*.

When vampires kill, blood is richer, more satisfying, more intoxicating. Even a cur is a tonic. It's why so many of us become murderers. Some justify themselves by hunting the worst of humanity – assassins and criminals. Others kill for king, country or cause. Drinking the blood of a defeated foe is a tradition of warrior races –

183

though, before the Ascendancy, few admitted to *liking* the stuff. Even Genghis Khan washed the taste away with fermented yoghurt. Drink death's blood often and nothing else will do. The definition of criminal or foe becomes elastic. In time, the noblest will take to slaughter the way an opium fiend sucks on a pipe. And it's never enough, never as good as it was – so they become monsters who kill just to keep their eyes open. Some need no slope, slippery or otherwise. Those who like killing before they turn like it all the more after.

I had to fight lassitude. The ground under me felt spongy. I heard running water far away. I couldn't keep my eyes open. Dreams waited in the dark. The temptation was to lie beside the dead dog and pull scraps of alley debris over myself, a funnel-web against the sun.

I allowed myself to be lulled…

…then came the mad magic lantern slides. Unwelcome sights and sounds spurted into my mind. Tastes too. I convulsed, knocking my head against a wall. I was the dog. Tearing into stringy meat, barking at the moon, rutting with bitches, rooting in corpse guts. The mongrel fought harder in my head after it was dead than in the alley when I was killing it. There's less to rat lives. Their deaths flare briefly. A dog knows the difference between cruel and kind. A dog can be disappointed in you. A dog can hate and fear its killer.

Once, doctors spent lifetimes dissecting dead men's eyes. Shining candlelight through disembodied eyeballs suspended on wires to test the folk belief that the last thing seen in life is imprinted. It's a fallacy. The eye is not a camera. But, as vampires always knew, something salts the dregs of death's blood. For long moments, you see what your victim last saw, feel the shock of their death. You are together with what you kill at its finish. You share a dwindling, a draining into darkness, panic and dull pain, a glimpse perhaps of something bright. Then they're gone and you're alone.

It left me shuddering, sickened and desolate.

I tried not to hold on to what the animal had seen but there's no shutter for the mind's eye.

A monster creeping out of the fog. Long-haired, long-limbed, crafty. Fang-rimmed remora maw, huge ochre eyes, talons like tapered razors.

And the sound of it – wetly whispering, almost singing, cruelly soothing. A lying sound. *I'm not going to hurt you...*

My fur prickling, my insides knotting.

La monstre c'est moi.

How much worse – how much better! – to see myself not with the limited colour palette of a dog but the complex vision of a human being.

Three times – unwittingly, unwillingly, I tell myself – I have tasted human death's blood.

So I *know*. I know how precious, how desirable, how *dangerous* it is.

Some vampires are addicted to that moment of seeing themselves through their victims' eyes. Denied mirrors, they kill to contemplate their own radiant beauty. They collect final memories, stored away and polished. Some shapeshift to take the faces – even personalities – of people they drain to death, shucking a human shell and forming another with each murder, forgetting their original names, obliterating whoever they were, spending lives at such a pace they become nobodies. The field of vampire medicine is in its infancy. The field of vampire psychiatry is a continent yet to be mapped, an Antarctica of the mind.

I trotted out of the alley on all fours, dragging my left hind leg. Then forced myself to stand and look at my paws until they were hands again.

I found a public well and emptied a bucket of water over myself.

The dog was gone. I missed him – then I didn't. My head was clear. No red thirst. My tongue ran over even teeth. My nails were trim.

I hauled up another bucketful and cleaned myself as best I could. I scraped sticky blood and dirt from my face and hands. I dried my face with my hair.

I went back to the dorm to change clothes. I resisted the urge to throw away what I had been wearing. No telling when I'll next get to a couturier.

Drusilla and Topazia Suzuki were plaiting each other's hair.

'You've been to a party,' Dru said.

Suzan Arashi sat in a tub, washing off dried blood, making herself invisible again.

Not every *yōkai* went to the Suicide Garden. That is encouraging. Some here are fastidious, will not feed off the condemned. The canny might be warier of being beholden to Majin than of going hungry. Dru, who knows *everything*, skipped the *seppuku* party. Francesca Brysse, Christina's tame spy, went to supper without telling her mistress. Brysse wasn't home yet. She might still be huddled under the bridge, sucking marrow from ripped-out bones.

'The Handyman made the ground shake,' said Dru. 'He shouldn't have done that. It's rude to rattle people when they're snoozing.'

Topazia's tail twisted. 'Taira no Masakado lies under the city,' said the monkey woman. 'If his shrines are neglected, he will turn over in his sleep and Edo will fall.'

I know that legend. In life, Taira was a rebel sorcerer. In death, he turned into a demigod. A considerable presence in the city. His daughter, the witch Takiyasha-Hime, is not to be trifled with either. King Arthur reputedly slumbers in Avalon until England's hour of greatest need – which, to this French woman's reckoning, was fifteen years ago. The old gentleman has overslept. Taira rests in the earth only

186

until he gets annoyed enough to destroy Edo. Changing the name to Tokyo isn't likely to fool him. If Majin is a disciple of Taira, that would explain his trick of summoning tremors. Taira no Masakado is god of earthquakes.

Each emperor is supposed to make a pilgrimage to the shrine built over Taira's grave at Ōtemachi, on the hillside overlooking Tokyo Bay, to placate him and ensure a reign uninterrupted by natural disaster. The tradition has been revived under the Black Ocean Society. It can't have helped the earthquake god's disposition that his original shrine was burned down in O-Same's inferno. If he ever does wake, he'll have words with her. After all, devastating the city is his *pièce de résistance* and he's not the deity to be upstaged by a flying bonfire in a posh frock.

'Don't wake up the fluttery-bye man,' said Dru, making wings of her hands and flitting about, flinging herself from one side of the room to the other like a very modern dancer. '*Buttery fluttery uttery bye-bye fly-by flies,*' she sang, '*bittery bottery buttery boo-hoo itchery hatchery fleas…*'

Clouds of blue and gold butterflies appeared before Taira no Masakado's battles, in anticipation of him winning most of them. In 940, the butterflies were black and red and – betrayed by a cousin – he was killed at the Battle of Kojima. His shrines, maintained by the superstitious or the fearful, are supposed to swarm with crickets, beetles and butterflies. So, besides looking after earthquakes, he's the god of creepy-crawlies. Suicide Garden, with its medicinal scorpions and murderous butterflies, is probably sacred to him.

Butterflies had assailed Christina Light with myriad little nip-bites. We think of butterflies as pretty, poetic and short-lived, but rarely see more than a few at a time. A million butterflies are aerial piranha. They can strip a crop from a field in moments. Their wings are beautiful but they're just better dressed locusts.

'You've eaten,' said Dru. 'Woof woof.'

She made dog ears with her fingers and sang the refrain 'Daddy Wouldn't Buy Me a Bow-Wow'. Topazia laughed – a monkey laugh, not a human's.

'I've got a little cat and I'm very fond of that but I'd rather have a bow-wow-wow…'

I left them to their amusements and delved into my trunk. I dug out a navy-blue pea coat and green knit cap – originally Dr Doskil's deck gear – to wear over my fresh dress. Not very modish, but refugees are seldom exemplars of fashion.

I also found my medical bag, with its University of France student identification tag still tied to the handle. For the ten-thousandth time, it crossed my mind that I ought to cut it off but left the faded label where it was. Who was living in my house in Île de la Cité now? Or was it abandoned and shunned?

Could everything go back to the way it was before Dracula?

Now I come to think of it, life in the frying pan hadn't been so bad. We should never have complained.

Though someone must be enjoying the fire.

I quit the dorm and walked to the Temple of One Thousand Monsters. Fog was thick today, so dawn light wasn't a bother.

I tasted spoiled blood in the air. How often did Lieutenant Majin convene the Suicide Club? I could see it served a purpose. Where better for those required to kill themselves than Yōkai Town? Self-slaughter is respected in Japan. Death is another spin on the wheel of reincarnation and *seppuku* wipes the slate clean of bad karma. I'm used to the warm tempering fear of vampires with envy of our long lives. In the East, some who see me for what I am express pity. By their lights, I have been cheated out of future existences. The wheel of karma spins. Turning vampire – becoming *yōkai* – puts a bamboo stick in the spokes. I was detained on the upwards path, prevented from climbing the mountain to be with Lord Buddha.

If anything, Majin has found a way to make suicide horrible again. What I'd seen in the park can't help anyone's karma — not those who died, those who feed off them, or those who watch in horror. Only the Demon Man comes out ahead, and I doubt he gives a fig for Lord Buddha.

What is Lieutenant Majin's connection with Taira no Masakado? Is he a worshipper? Or perhaps a lineal descendant? There's the question of the curse. Rui Wakasagi is expected to carry out revenge unto the seventh generation. Higo's leaves can be brewed as a tea delicious to all — but deadly poison to the family of Toba, who once decreed she be cut down and her wood used to make a bridge. Is Majin obliged to avenge the betrayal and defeat of Kojima? That would explain what Christina and Kostaki both believe — that he doesn't answer to the Emperor or the Black Ocean Society. His true master *might* be Taira no Masakado.

It is said that Taira will return as a giant dragon. Note that — not just a dragon, but a *giant* dragon. A reptile as tall as a volcano wading through the city. Majin might want earthquakes, fire and deaths in the hundreds of thousands. Not a comforting prospect.

We fled Dracula and came halfway round the world for this.

I had to lift successive layers of mosquito netting to reach my patient. The mesh curtains should be packed away for winter, but the butterflies and scorpions of Jisatsu No Niwa don't mind the snow. Yuki-Onna is still in eclipse. The nets were brittle with rime and stung my bare fingers. Stoves burned throughout the building, but the temple was colder than ever.

189

Christina was propped up on pillows in a day-bed. She wore a lovely pale-blue *furisode*. Her reattached arm was in a black silk sling. Her face was no longer bruised, but her right eye looked like red glass.

Incense sticks burned, sweetening the air. Lady Oyotsu – face perfectly white, teeth perfectly black – sat quietly by the patient. Her neck extended a mere nine inches from her collar. Unobtrusive attendants saw to their needs. One young monk had an angry weal on his neck and bleached white patches on his saffron robe. Christina had seen to her own red thirst without lowering herself to alley dogs.

I asked her to look at my finger as I passed it in front of her face.

'I see perfectly,' she said. 'I'm sure my eye will go back to normal soon.'

'Thank you for your diagnosis, doctor,' I said. 'Do you want a second opinion?'

She was impatient. 'Very amusing,' she said, not meaning it.

Her eye wasn't just bloodshot. It was *coloured*, with faint difference between scarlet iris, crimson pupil and pinkish 'white'.

'Are you seeing red?'

'Not literally,' she said.

I looked at her arm and asked her to wiggle her fingers. She couldn't. I eased off the sling and *furisode* and examined her shoulder. There wasn't even a scar. Her skin, which needed no powder, was unblemished. The bone was set and in its socket. I squeezed and prodded... but got no reaction.

'It can't be helped,' said Christina.

'Are you sure you're American and Italian?' I asked. 'That sounds English.'

She smiled, weakly. A martyr's simper. 'I have spent too much time in London. I have got into bad habits.'

'I'll say. Do you mind if I stick pins in you?'

'What on earth good will that do?'

'It might make me feel better.'

'Stick away, then.'

I probed her shoulder with a lancet. The tiny hole healed at once. 'Nothing wrong there. Have you any feeling at all in your arm?'

'What's feeling?'

'Are you enjoying this?'

'You tell me,' she said.

She slipped her left hand into my hair and took the back of my neck in a firm grip. She forced me to look into her red eye. I remembered how strong she was. I had cause to be thankful for her strength. Last night, she prevented me from abasing myself. Today, she just made me uncomfortable.

After making her point, she let go.

'You should have healed completely,' I said. 'Even after what happened. I don't know the Oblensky line well.'

'It's very fine. I shopped around.'

'Wonderful. Perhaps I should have pulled the arm right off and let you grow a new one. Like a lizard.'

Christina was thoughtful.

'No, that wouldn't have worked.'

'I grew new toes once,' I said. 'That's my d'Acques blood. I've seen vampires recover from worse.'

'Five years ago, I turned to light and couldn't change back when I wanted to. Your friend Kate Reed was there. She thought it amusing. She's not laughing much now, I fancy. It took *weeks* to pull myself together. And I'm not sure I should have. It might have been better to accept the change. Since then, I've not been the same person – not entirely. I don't know if everything came back from the light or if it's in the proper place. I don't *feel* as much as before, not while I'm just flesh and blood. The arm is just the latest loss. I can't feel my face. It might as well be marble. My heart doesn't beat at all. I can't be sure, but I think I might be immune to things that kill other vampires. When I'm light, my essence – whatever it is that's *me* – is scattered. I still think like myself, but the body is gone. There's no heart to stick a stake through. No skin to cut with silver. I'm not what I was, not the vampire I turned into. I've never stopped turning. Even after feeding, there's just… a distant memory of what feeling was. Only when I'm light do I *feel*, and then it's like I have liquid lightning in me.'

'How much shape can a shapeshifter shift?'.

'I beg your pardon?'

'It's something we say. Vampire doctors. A question we can't answer. For so long there weren't enough vampires for us to study. Now there are too many and things change too fast for us to keep up. It doesn't help that for all of human history before 1885 the chief concern of specialists in the study of vampirism was how to kill us. I suppose you should be thankful your flesh didn't decide to mangle itself into the semblance of an umbrella, a potato or a burning bush.'

She thought about that for a moment. Lady Oyotsu's head swayed.

'Christina, I'm not sure I can help,' I said. 'I'm sorry.'

'Don't apologise. It makes you sound like Kate Reed.'

I put my lancet back in the bag. At the moment, laid out in comfort, Christina seemed fine. She radiated a little light. Not enough to read a newspaper by.

'Thank you for looking after me,' she said. 'I believe in thanks, not apologies.'

'It's my profession, Princess. I'll send you a bill.'

She smiled, not weakly now. 'You don't love me, do you?'

'This isn't the time…'

'It's always the time. We should be friends, Geneviève.'

'I don't think – with respect, Princess – you have friends.'

She was thoughtful. 'Maybe not, but you do. Kate is

your friend. Kostaki is your friend, though he wants to be more − even Drusilla follows you about like a lamb and tries to get your attention. The *yōkai* women copy your hair and wonder what they'd look like in your dresses.'

I doubted my current look − girl run off to sea, disguised as a cabin boy − would catch on. 'Why don't you move out of the temple?' I suggested. 'We can find you a room in the dorm. It'd be easier to treat you. And you'd be away from this bloody *cold*.'

She shook her head. 'I am proving you wrong. *Giri*. Obligation. I understand it. I always have, I think. Duty. It comes with position and privilege—'

'Which you want to tear down.'

'Yes, but I'm not fool enough to think I don't have them. You have friends, Gené. Lovers, if you can find them. I will have followers. I will be worshipped. I will be loved. I don't say this from pride or because it's what I want, but because it's what must be… so I may carry out my duty.'

I found I was frightened of Christina Light again.

Kostaki had said it. Light was not kind to vampires.

'One thing, though,' she said. 'You don't have to love me; you don't have to *like* me. It's easier for us both if you don't. Because I have to stay and you have to leave. Dru told me that − in so many words, and you know that's rare for her. I must continue my journey by staying in one place − this place. Soon, this won't be Yōkai Town. This will be a mountain. My mountain, not yours. You are tied to too much else in the world. People and causes and your own whims. But, Gené, sometime you'll have to learn to love us.'

'Us?'

'Vampires. You don't love vampires, do you?'

I was taken aback.

'What's to love?' I said.

'*Exactly*.'

She *seized* me − not with her free hand, but something

like the light she had shone in the Suicide Garden. An unbreakable grip, many degrees of magnitude greater than an ordinary power of fascination. I could not look away. Her skin shimmered, luminous oil on water. I saw the pillows through her head as she became transparent. A vampire ghost, or a vampire's ghost; an apparition, or an angel.

'You don't see the worth in us,' she said. 'The beauty. The potential. You see only red thirst. And you hate that. It's a dishonourable obligation and you feed in shame. You don't have a reflection because you don't need one. You see Dracula and think you're the same as him. A monster. A repentant, abstinent, holier-than-mere-bloodthirsty-immortals monster, but a monster for all that. You love the warm in the abstract and the particular. Your Charles – Mr Beauregard of the Diogenes Club – you love him. That's part of your story. Everyone knows it. Kate loves him too, of course. That must be a trial for you both. I should like to meet this extraordinary man, though I'd better not, to avoid disappointment. There have been and will be others. All warm, living, not vampires. You couldn't love Kostaki, though he would die for you. You don't even look at him and wonder – the way men and women look at each other and wonder – how it would be. Why can't you love a vampire, Gené? Is it because you can't love yourself?'

She let go of me, and ducked out of further conversation by falling into deep lassitude.

At that moment, if my Gladstone bag contained a wooden stake or silver knife I'd have tested her theory that she was immune to such things. She was *blinding*.

14

BEFORE DRACULA (CONTINUED)

The French newspapers all dismissed their London correspondents by cablegram, then had to rehire them at increased rates. Each boat train brought further confirmation. Vampires were real. A vampire ruled Britain.

You are an insider, Charles, a habitué of the corridors of power. You were given briefings from the first. The Diogenes Club knew – and *know* – much the general public would scarcely credit. And they didn't see Dracula coming. Imagine what it was like for those who read the news in the papers or heard it in a café. Suddenly, without precedent, an unbelievable thing had incontrovertibly happened. A blood-drinking monster was Britain's new Prince Regent. The worst person in the world commanded the greatest empire on earth. What would he do? What would he *not* do?

All hotels in Paris were booked out by English parties. Gentlemen who could not secure their usual discreet rooms for liaisons were put out by this British invasion. Society doctors were summoned to treat real or imagined bite wounds. A rumour went around that anyone bitten would inevitably turn and be compelled to spread the infection. Hoteliers reminded of this old wives' tale were less happy to have Londoners in residence, and began presenting bills to urge the now-settled English to quit.

Many refused, though faces were slapped and bellboys kicked down stairs.

Ambassadors were recalled. Did this mean war? If so, between whom? Should British administration of the Suez Canal be contested? Alarmist journals imagined Dracula's Britain might ally with Bismarck's Germany and split helpless France between them. It was said French women fetched prices above £25 in Piccadilly Circus, for their blood was especially piquant to elder vampires (this is nonsense). Sinister procurers – Jewish, naturally – were reputedly at large in Paris, with chloroform pads in their pockets, harvesting fair tributes for the leech-lords of London. Vendors of crucifixes, icons, statues of the Madonna and other portable religious knick-knacks enjoyed a boom. Pilferers stripped churches of sacred objects. The franc was strong against the pound. The price of silver rose and rose again. Chefs complained of speculators trying to get a monopoly on garlic – and withholding it from the catering trade, because matrons afraid of vampires under their beds paid a higher price for a bulb than a restaurant would for a bushel. Take garlic out of a Frenchman's soup and you might as well light the fuse to another revolution.

The character of those fleeing Britain changed. The first arrivals were rich enough to charter a special train or wire ahead for the best suites. The next wave were less well off. Gare du Nord was overwhelmed with terrified folks who had gathered up all they could carry and run for their lives. Some were escaping newly turned family members. Demons prowled the streets of London. A vampire plague was running like scarlet fever through households, districts, professions, towns – the whole country.

Then the British closed the ports. That meant an increase in small boat traffic across the Channel, and the establishment of camps around Calais and Dunkirk –

and Le Havre and Bruges – for *les anglais*. You know how wretched conditions became after a few weeks. Fifteen years on, despite all that's happened, the tents and shacks are still there. A few of the original refugees remain, queuing for their monthly tea ration and waiting till it's safe to go home. They were the first displaced people of the Anni Draculae, just as we in Yōkai Town are the latest.

The British government suspended the Continental telegraph service – or cut the wires. The London correspondents stopped filing. With the public hungry for news of this greatest story of the day, the press were driven to interview British exiles. Some started demanding money to spin fanciful, picturesque tales. Many of which, of course, were true.

I had my own concerns.

A black cross was burned into the front door of my house. A live bat was crucified to it. I nursed the animal for a while, dripping milk into its mouth with a pipette, but it died. I was being stubborn. Bats are rodents. I've literally bled more of those than you've had hot dinners. I'm not even *nosferatu*, so I feel no kinship with the vermin. Even when it's rubbed in my face that all right-thinking Christians would put poison down if they thought it'd get me out of their house... or country.

Garlic – by now, ruinously expensive – was smeared around my windows and on my doorstep. The *jeannot*-come-lately vampire hater who did that didn't even get his folklore straight. It's the odourless flowers, not the smelly bulbs, which traditionally deter vampires. A belt and braces measure. Superstitious vampires who shrink from flowers also wouldn't cross a threshold without an invitation. Besides, it was *my* house... I lived there and nothing was going to shut me out of it.

Someone set a fire in the unused outdoor privy a week later. It didn't spread to the house. I reported the burned-down jakes to the police and was assured they took such things seriously. All citizens were protected by French law, for the moment. A trifling legal matter was yet to be settled – whether the dead could hold citizenship. I grew weary of repeating, to warm and vampire alike, that we of the d'Acques line turn *without dying*. I am long-lived, not back from the grave. If you want a reanimated corpse, look to those mouldy *nosferatu*, *wurdalak*, *strigoi*, *vrykolakas* and *upiorski* bloodlines. The gendarmes spent more time confirming that the implied accusation (vampirism) made against me by the lout with the tinderbox was true than poking around the charred patch for evidence.

Every few days, a policeman – not always the same one – paid a call. Not to say the bat abuser or arsonist (I presumed they were separate *salauds*) had been apprehended, but with questions about other matters. I was required to prove my innocence in a number of petty assault cases. A vampire panic caught on. When the Sûreté needed someone to take blame, vampires vaulted over Jews and Arabs to win the uncoveted Most Convenient Culprit Award. To avoid prosecution, surviving duellists claimed sword wounds were vampire bites. If the till was empty, vampires were behind it! If the girl was pregnant, why – look at the bruises on her neck! – she was the innocent victim of a vampire's powers of fascination!

The Great Vampire, hooded head of Les Vampires, called a press conference in the Jardin du Luxembourg at high noon on a sunny day to insist he *wasn't* a vampire… and none of his confederates were either. It was a matter of policy that vampires were not admitted to Les Vampires, so there. Parisians could be reassured that those robbing, murdering and swindling them were one hundred per cent not undead. I'm sure that came as a huge relief. The mysterious Irma Vep, long-serving lieutenant to a succession of Great Vampires, did not attend the conference. We've always had suspicions about her. As you know, the mask and body-stocking conceal a multitude of sins – including ours. When reporters asked the Great Vampire to doff his hood to show an unfanged face, he vanished in a cloud of crimson smoke. An impressive feat – which undercut his stated purpose of convincing the public he was not a supernatural creature.

The next day, a detailed, tetchy letter from the Great Vampire appeared in *Le Figaro* explaining that he had made his exit under the cover of cleverly applied stage magic. He included a recipe for smoke bombs, which the paper refrained from printing, lest its junior readers make mischief. Had I the ear of the Sûreté – rather than presenting a lingering smell in its oversensitive nose – I would have advised the inspector who held the criminal conspiracies portfolio to look among Paris's active or just-retired conjurers for the true identity of the Great Vampire. Maybe that worthy flic had more important things on his desk. For instance, a list of all the cats reported missing near my house. Oh, and reopening the dossier on that rash of pick-pocketings where victims robbed of wallets and watches felt light-headed and had unexplained pinprick wounds.

I kept working my shifts at the morgue and going to lectures.

Before, I had been a novelty – and ignored, patronised, picked on or joked about – as a woman. Being exposed as a vampire was, at first, more of the same. Fellows who formerly flirted with me transferred their attentions to other female students. A few eager new faces popped up with a 'scientific' interest in my condition. Professor Cataflaque, one of the dustier lecturers, was eager to do a paper on my 'disease', and tempted me with an offer of co-authorship. His ice-blue eyes and wet mouth deterred me from the collaboration. I had no desire to be a talking specimen.

I assumed Nicolas Cerral was responsible for writing

my name on a tag and leaving it on an empty slab at the morgue. 'Vampires sleep here,' someone added – as if the audience might miss the joke.

Cerral kept his distance for a few days, but started talking to me again, which at least got me back into the marginal fraternity of the ghouls. He'd played the toe-tag joke on others before me.

Plainly, the reasoning went, it was silly to be terrified of poor clever Gené or that ponce of a Marquis. If they were vampires, then vampires must not be so terrible after all. So, the ghouls pestered me with questions. Medical student questions. Drinking blood – what does it *taste* like? How can you live off it? Do you need the *pissoir*? Powers of fascination – could one prevail on a tutor to alter grades? They were disappointed by my answer to that. Rapid healing – a revelation. Students gawped as penknife cuts on my arm closed in seconds and I wiped away blood to show unscarred skin – though I didn't like to take that trick too far. Vampire blood is dangerous stuff. I didn't want to expose anyone to its transformative, quickening effects. Fangs – how can dentine serve as erectile tissue? Aversion to direct sunlight – ah, yes, that explained the smoked glasses! Could I fly? Or float? Shapeshifting – had I been the Beast of Gévaudan?

After the shock that I was what I was came slow realisation of all the other things I was.

Etiquette about enquiring after a woman's age was suspended. Over and over, I was asked how old I was. I know, Charles, that you have reached that age when you have to think for a moment before answering that question and quite often are a year – or two! – out in your response. You can't believe you are nearly fifty, poor love. Methuselah is put in the shade. Think what it's like for me – after so many years of trying to keep ever-changing supposed birthdates and ages and names in my head – when asked flat out to tell the truth.

I was born in 1416. That's what I took to saying. Boldly.
Which famous people had I met?

Jeanne d'Arc? No, but I saw her several times from the
back of crowds, including at her execution by the vile
English (*spit!*). I hacked off my hair like hers when I first
took to doctoring. Marshal de Rais? Yes, but I don't want
to talk about that, *ever*. Cyrano de Bergerac? It was the
same size as everyone else's, so far as I could tell. Kings
and queens? No, I didn't move in those circles, and I wasn't
an intimate of Napoleon either, for all that I cut off legs,
dug out shot and sewed up wounds in his army. I didn't
imagine then that I'd be invited to Buckingham Palace
within a few eventful years. Or how that would turn out.

Other vampires? Dracula? Once, but in the company
of other elders, many more distinguished, most now
destroyed. Ruthven? Yes – funny story, though he wouldn't
remember it. The Devil? Not so far as I knew. I hadn't
signed any pacts in blood to become what I was. Where
had I travelled? What had I seen? Was I really from
Martinique? Did I have any living relatives... or dead
relatives still among the living? How old were you when
you died? When did you die? Where are you buried? Yes,
some poor fool actually asked that to my face. Over and
over, I said I wasn't dead but no one took it in. I was the
first vampire any of them had met... so far as they knew.

Was Sarah Bernhardt a vampire? Not then. Oscar
Wilde? I said not, but he might have been newborn
already. He was first in any fashion, they said... and first
out, too. That was another thing they asked. Was there a
cure? Could I go back? Would I want to? Would anyone?

Did I want to bite them?

If I didn't answer, they were suddenly afraid again.
Maybe I wasn't just poor clever Gené... maybe I was
the diabolically cunning, unendingly deceptive Vampire

Dieudonné. If I said no, that I had supped enough already, they pressed for details I was no more willing to give than if they'd asked me who I'd slept with last. If I said yes, then it was a provocation and a threat.

These were medical students – young, bright, curious, mostly open-minded. Not all were men. And they already knew me well enough to accept me as part of the scenery – not a harpy siren come from Hell intent on blood-raping the lot of them and making them my undead slaves. The ghouls knew death and were unsqueamish about its most grotesque aspects. This, without me especially seeking it, was the best possible human society I could have in a city where vampires were known about, but not numerous.

And it took them two hours to get to the question they most wanted answered.

'How many have you killed?'

I've been in battles, wars. I've been attacked and fought back. I have killed, and I have also saved lives, shown mercy. Yes, but… how many people have you killed – and fed off? Killed with your teeth?

You, Charles, are the only person I've ever volunteered the answer to that question – which, pointedly, you did not ask.

Three.

Not a day goes by that I don't think of each one of them. So many names and faces I have forgotten.

But not those.

Dafydd le Gallois, Sergei Bukharin, Annie Marriner.

Names not remembered by history. Faces remembered only by me.

The ones who died of me. Who invited me in, let me bite and were too weak, too willing. Or met me when I had less control of myself, when red thirst ruled, when something in me which I will not disown made me the monster vampires are popularly supposed to be.

202

Three.

I didn't answer, and that was answer enough for the ghouls.

Cerral changed the subject, but the evening was over and the long night begun.

Within a fortnight, the vampire-slayers came for me.

Captain Kronos laid in wait outside the morgue, leading a band of torch-bearing hirelings of the Congregation of the Doctrine of the Faith. They pursued me to the steps of Notre Dame – where the mediaeval doors were slammed in my face. Kronos slipped inside my guard with an elegant move and slid his sword gently between my ribs, piercing my newly broken heart. I saw a glint of regret and pity in his beautiful blue eyes as I turned to dust floating on the first rays of dawn.

Except it wasn't like that.

I had worked a long night's shift among the dead. Waiting for me at daybreak was a liveried lad with a *billet-doux* from Hippolyte Modéran, assistant clerk in the university's Department of Admissions. I was invited to call at his office to review discrepancies in my filed documents. I knew at once that I couldn't get away with ignoring the casual summons. The next liveried lad would be taller and armed. I tipped the message-bearer a sou, as was customary. I remembered how kind Jeanne was to the workman who made a mess of tying her to the stake at her burning. When he dropped the rope, she held one end of it to make his job easier. I wondered then why she didn't spit in his face. Now I know. Force of habit. It is harder than you think to stop being kind.

So, to make things easier for everyone (else), I walked to the Latin Quarter and presented myself at the edifice in Place de la Sorbonne. I was directed to a less imposing building across the square from the old college. Inside was the domain of M. Modéran. Here were kept the records of past and present students.

I sat all day in a waiting room, missing lectures. Students came and went. Pressing matters were addressed – misfiled documents, changes of address, bills to be settled, refunds to be issued. The assistant clerk's assistant regularly told me I would be seen in turn, but didn't look me in the eye. I wished I'd brought something to read.

I'd almost slipped into a state of lassitude when my name was called.

It was the end of the working day. Outside the windows, a new night had begun. The city of lights began to sparkle. Paris is never truly dark.

In his office, Hippolyte Modéran was in shirt-sleeves, sat on a chair away from his neat desk, being shaved by his valet. His tailcoat and top hat adorned a dressmaker's dummy with a wickerwork head. Another servant brushed his opera cloak. A grand fellow for an assistant clerk, then – but the University of France is a grand institution. Its functionaries put up a front.

M. Modéran apologised as profusely as was possible without moving his mouth. The keen blade scraped foam from his cheeks.

There were minute spots of blood.

Was this a deliberate provocation? Or just thoughtlessness?

I touched my tongue to the points of my fangs.

'Regrettably, this meeting must be brief, Mademoiselle Dieudonné,' he told me. 'Madame Modéran and I have a box tonight. De Boscherville's *Don Juan Triumphant*. Have you seen it?'

'I don't get time for the opera. My studies are demanding, and there's my work at the morgue.'

'Ah, yes, well,' he said, expression changing with each

word, foam dripping on the towel round his neck. 'That need not be the situation from now on. A bright side, *hein*? All the things you will have time for.'

'When I am expelled?'

'Oh no, Mademoiselle Dieudonné,' he responded. 'You are not expelled, for you were never here.'

'I don't see—'

'You could not have been here for you – the student who gave these references – do not exist. You were not born where these papers say you were. You did not attend the schools listed. The referees who attested to such things were, shall we say, in error. In fact, the documents are in such a sorry state it would be best if you withdrew them altogether, then there would be no question of fraud or forgery, or taking a place which should have gone to a candidate who is—'

'Is what, sir?'

'You know very well.'

'A man?'

'Not necessarily.'

At that point, I might as well have converted to Judaism to complete the trifecta of checks against me in the ledger of unacceptability.

'Are you not, Madame, a trifle *old* to be a student?'

I had slipped from Mademoiselle to Madame, I noticed.

'For the sake of argument—' I began.

'More tiresome words never were spoken. Whenever anyone says "for the sake of argument", one knows nothing good will come of it.'

'*For the sake of argument*,' I insisted, 'what would be my position should I *not* withdraw my documents?'

'Out of my hands, I'm afraid.'

Newly shaved, M. Modéran sprang up and peered into a hand-mirror, giving his moustache and chin-thatch minute examination. He caught sight of a blurry shadow and shook with undisguisable disgust.

Then he was fascinated.

I was his first vampire. The mirror brought that home.

Had he arranged for two servants – broad-shouldered fellows, not at all like the dainty prisses you think of when valets are mentioned – to be in the room during our meeting? Was that why the wait had been so long? The barber cleaned his razor but did not put it away, or even close it. He folded it back, so the blade rested across his knuckles sharp-side out. An apache trick, not unknown to the High Rip gangs of Whitechapel.

'Fraud and forgery are serious crimes,' said M. Modéran, fussing with his white tie. 'And a police investigation would be thorough. I should not care to be subject to such scrutiny. Who knows what might turn up?'

M. Modéran set mirror and towel down on his desk. The other valet had his tailcoat ready for him to shrug into. It was a little tight around the shoulders.

'Skeletons are often found in cupboards, I understand,' he went on. 'Or placed there in medical student jests with unfortunate consequences. You see the reasoning? You are an intelligent… person.'

'I have degrees from this and other universities.'

He barked a humourless laugh at that. 'Yes, we know. We keep records. No one thought to look back to see if you had been here before. I should address you as Dr Dieudonné – though if that title were obtained under false pretences, we shall have to see about getting you struck off. What with this English tribulation, we shall have to institute measures against other impostures. An additional clerk will have to be engaged to go over all the books.'

The cloak and hat were handed to him.

'I appear to be in want of a position,' I said.

'I should not advise applying for this one,' he said, popping his hat on. 'Hiring policies are being settled upstairs.

ds were sprouting. However, the violation of his person presents an enormous loss of face. I found forceps in my ag and got a grip on the nail stuck in Yam's forehead. It idn't come free without a struggle. I dressed the wound ith a pad and bandage. Blood seeped through. The stain esembled a third eye. A weeping third eye.

I looked up at Majin. He did not look at me. He was nterested only in the Princess.

Does he think he has surrounded our stones? By breaking Yam, he has countered Kostaki's first move. Another message is sent. Yōkai Town is his to rule or wreck. He plays five or six games at once. He must believe those of us who were at Suicide Garden appreciate the rewards of bowing to him and the risks of remaining defiant.

At the gate, Whelpdale had a conversation with Kannuki, handing over a book-shaped parcel and receiving a sack of goods. Black Ocean, meet Black Market.

Kostaki stepped over the bullet divot and joined me. 'Whatever Yam saw out there, he won't tell us about it till his tongue grows back,' I said.

'We aren't learning,' said Kostaki. 'We are being taught.'

I agreed with him.

Majin waved his gloved hand and disappeared inside e giant's head. I assumed he could still see us.

Kostaki knows all about Jisatsu No Niwa. He wonders hy he was not invited to the Suicide Garden. I think the play was for Christina's benefit and Yam is for Kostaki's. afterthought.

Kostaki is keeping something from me. Maybe from lness, maybe from shame. I have not the patience to get to share his worry; I have enough of my own. But he become uncommonly thoughtful. On the voyage here, as a man of action. He did what had to be done, swiftly directly. Now he mulls things over and keeps quiet. people act out of character, it is seldom good news.

Employment of the dead is a nettle unlikely to be grasped for a few years yet. Still, I suppose you've learned patience. You have had more than enough time. Good evening.'

I was given the fat folder of documents, relieved of my student identification papers and escorted from the building.

I hear *Don Juan Triumphant* has one or two stirring tunes but is otherwise a dreary evening's wallow in self-pity.

I hope it gave M. Modéran a splitting headache.

15

YŌKAI TOWN, DECEMBER 19, 1899

This evening, a gong rang inside the statue by the gate. The clanging reverberated in its chest and boomed out of its snarling mouth.

I went to see what the fuss was about. A small group gathered. Kostaki and Dravot were there, a head taller than the *yōkai* around them. Whelpdale hurried past, bright-eyed as if he had a notion of something to his advantage.

Lieutenant Majin stood alone on the observation platform, arms folded, cape stirred slightly by the wind. He looked down on us over the rim of the giant's helmet. I fancied he was searching the crowd for a particular face he did not find. Christina is still asleep. If the summons was for her, it was wasted.

With a grinding, the gate opened. Soldiers roughly escorted a coffle of prisoners into Yōkai Town. At the head of the line hopped Mr Yam, an *o-fuda* nailed to his forehead. In case the binding spell was ineffective, weights hung from his chains. His hair was unbound. His chin was blackish red with congealed blood, though his sucked-in cheeks and shining eyes suggested he hadn't fed.

How had he been caught? Did a posse of samurai cowboys rope him? Or could Majin bring the Chinese

elder down with magic gestures? Seeing Yam and yoked did not give me comfort.

Shackled to him were others. A woman in a kimono with a shapeless sack over her he extraordinary ball of glossy black hair surroundir girlish face. A young Japanese man in a white Eu in-the-tropics suit. He had a pulsing rift in his fo and the bridge of his nose. A hatchet might on been sunk in his face and pulled out again.

The soldiers kept a wary distance from the day's Our old friend Kannuki was sergeant of the deta uniform must be custom-made. A Black Ocean b stretched between poles stuck up from his tunic. huge hands, a rifle looked like a child's toy.

Kostaki walked to greet his spy. A bullet – a plain slug, for show – kicked into packed snow at his feet stopped and looked up. A rifle poked out of the stat left eye.

Kannuki took a set of keys from his foot-wide le belt and unfastened chains. The *yōkai* I didn't stamped, trying to get feeling back in their leg swayed but stood in place. Kannuki tore the pa from his forehead and threw it away. He steppe biting range and aimed his rifle at the *jiang shi*.

Yam's mouth sagged open and greasy blood s

Majin tossed an object from the platform. I Kostaki's feet – a wriggling, slithering thing centipede. Yam's tongue.

I assumed our intelligence mission was cor

If Verlaine wasn't here, she was most likel

Yam sank to his knees. I went to him wi bag. No one shot me.

I wiped the elder's chin and mouth w Besides having his tongue ripped out, h The *jiang shi* was already healing, phys

Dravot – who at least is still himself – arranged for a cart to take Yam to the men's dormitory. The other newcomers were received by Abura Sumashi and Kasa-obake. The hairball *yōkai* shut her eyes and her locks curled and spiralled, like fast-growing water-weeds or a tangle of black snakes. She seemed asleep, held upright by living hair. Her captors had bound her with ribbons, combs and pins, which now shook loose and scattered. The cleft-headed man – can we call him hatchet-faced? – helped her get steady on her unseen feet. He took a pair of dark glasses out of his top pocket and fit them onto his head as if to prevent it falling apart. In his raw gash, small teeth glistened. His apparent wound is a vertical mouth. How wide can it gape?

The woman with the sack on her head blundered against soldiers – who backed away from her – and the wall. No one made any effort to help *her*. Even other *yōkai* edged out of her range. Her hands were unbound. She tried to get free of the sack by shaking her head or scraping it against the wall. She threw herself about spasmodically. Recognising the early stages of a fit, I had concerns for her condition.

The sack came loose and she staggered our way. Kostaki nodded to me.

'Here, let me,' I said, taking off the makeshift hood.

Her face was a sight. Unsurgical cuts through her cheeks gave her an ear-to-ear grin. The inside of her mouth was vivid red velvet. Her chin virtually detached as she smiled, showing rows of yellow shark teeth and a slither of black tongue.

'Do you think I'm pretty?' she asked.

16

YŌKAI TOWN, DECEMBER 20, 1899

Our new dorm sisters, the slit-mouthed woman and the long-haired girl, are Kuchisake and Zhang Fa. The dapper gent they arrived with is Gokemidoro. He has gone to the men's dorm. He doesn't know it yet, but Goké is the man the sleeping Princess has been looking for. He speaks English, Portuguese and Spanish. Before the mouth in his forehead opened – rendering him unfit for government service – he was a translator in trade negotiations. Another *yōkai* with fabled powers of persuasion. He claims modestly that he wears dark glasses because otherwise everyone who looks at his eyes falls into a daze. He runs himself ragged because those he fascinates can't move, breathe, eat, walk or sleep without his say-so. Pull the other one, I suggested – it's got bells on. After all, he got netted and poured into this pond.

Kuchisake is fairly famous and completely insane. Even the Mantis thinks she's unreasonably vicious. Like many *yōkai*, she sings a sad song about how she came to be the way she is – which in no way excuses her predilection for mutilation. Japanese vampires are often not turned so much as *twisted* – permanently disfigured by fathers-in-darkness who leave makers' marks on their get. On no account is Kuchisake to be allowed scissors. Her compulsion is to slit faces to make others look like her and she has an *idée fixe* about scissors. She scorns knives, swords or other blades, because she loves the snipping-scything sound. To limit her exposure to temptation, I've removed the surgical scissors from my instrument wallet and hidden them in my coat pocket.

Zhang Fa, originally from China, is sweeter natured but has to be jogged or jostled so she stays awake. If she falls into a deep sleep, her hair becomes bad-tempered and tries to choke her. She is of the *kejōrō* bloodline, who are traditionally prostitutes though she works as a server in teahouses. She can hold six separate cups in tendrils of her hair, which would be more impressive if someone hadn't invented the tray.

What interests me most is how they got here. Someone is keeping lists and ticking off names. *Yōkai* are being collected. It fell to me to get more intelligence by the surprisingly little-used espionage technique of just coming out and asking.

The least-mad *yōkai* in the dorm is Topazia Suzuki, so I picked her. As she warmed blood-threaded sake for us, I asked her how she came to be in Yōkai Town. Her tail stood up straight and she looked away for a moment before deciding to talk.

'Some of us can pass outside,' she said. 'Kuchisake stayed free for so long because she can wind a scarf around her mouth.'

Not because she's ashamed of the way she looks, by the way. She's proud of her grin. No, she wears scarves and masks because she likes to get close before unveiling. She *loves* the fear and revulsion in people's eyes as she asks her question. To which there is no right answer. She slashes with scissors whatever you say.

Topazia looked across the room. Kuchisake, wearing a surgical mask I've given her, was playing a version of

Go with Drusilla. They use living or dead insects instead of stones. The living ones add a random element by not staying where they're put on the grid. I've told Dru to be careful with scorpions but they are pieces of superior power – like chess queens – so venomous pests scuttle around the place.

'Others of us look like trees, mushrooms or monkeys,' Topazia continued. 'We cannot hide in a crowd. We were brought here first. For our protection, they said. The grounds of the temple are sanctuary for *yōkai*. Like your cathedrals.'

Topazia reads European books in the original languages and translation. She particularly admires French writers – Émile Zola, Eugène Sue, Victor Hugo.

'I came of my own accord,' she said, sadly. 'Imprisonment was presented to me as salvation. I *knew* we were being lied to but I still came. The alternative is unpleasant. Most of us have died once and changed into what we are. Few of us wish to die again, even to be with Lord Buddha. Majin knows ways to end any of us, even those who are hard to kill. Behind the temple is a shrine where Lady Oyotsu keeps markers for *yōkai* who are done away with. The ones who fought hardest, the most powerful – they are gone now. Majin sometimes just brings the heads.'

So, that was why *yōkai* stayed put. As ever, it was fear. Even the fearsome fear something. Here, it was the Demon Man.

'The Lieutenant,' I asked, 'is he *yōkai*?'

Topazia spat sake on the floor and chittered – an animal sound. 'Something else, something old,' she said. 'And bitter. Anyone who puts trust in him is a fool.'

'None of us exactly trust him,' I said.

'Not in here, not *yōkai*. We know him for what he is. The way he chooses to feed us is a reminder of how contemptible we are. He bathes in our hatred, for we cannot tell it in the world of men and women. Out there, they trust him but should not. He doesn't serve their cause – not the Emperor, not the knights of the Black Ocean.'

'Is he a follower of Taira no Masakado?'

Topazia flinched at the name, turned her head round in a near full circle to see who might be listening, and continued. 'Taira is an excuse. A paper banner. Majin's only master is Enma Daio, ruler of Hell. Even to him, he is no loyal retainer.'

Lights reflected in Topazia's watery, beautiful eyes. I glanced up. O-Same was rolling across the low ceiling. Her two fireballs are like eyes. She listens too.

Topazia shivered, rippling her neck fur. She said no more about Majin and his master in Hell. She gave me sake.

We sent spies out there. It follows that Majin has spies in here. Kostaki wondered how someone like O-Same could be imprisoned. Perhaps she can't. Fire – even more than air and water – must eventually run free. The questions Kostaki didn't ask nag me. What can living fire want? What are her dreams?

O-Same's fire-eyes slid slowly between beams. I smelled heated sap, sweet and rancid. The walls and ceilings of the dorm are scorched where she has touched. The sliding doors (*shoji*) which she has no hands to open have burned-through corners. A type of *yōkai* – *mokumokuren* – can disguise itself as a door or a mat or a wall and wrap an unwary visitor in reed-like strips which sting like jellyfish fronds and draw blood. Is O-Same a natural enemy to such creatures?

'Those who came after you, were they arrested?' I asked Topazia. 'Brought here in chains like Kuchisake and Zhang Fa?'

Topazia got out of answering by dropping a sake dish, which broke on the floor.

'Another dead soldier,' said Dru.

Topazia looked puzzled. I began explaining the European superstition to her.

'No, poppet,' said Dru. 'I mean what I say. Not cracked crockery – that's plain for all to see and need not be mentioned. No, listen. It's just happened. A soldier. A real one, with musket and medals. Done down, and truly dead.'

A paper rope was tied to the steps of our dormitory. It was strung through Yōkai Town, looped around trees, posts and statues.

Kostaki untwisted a stretch, which tore in his hands. It was a long scroll covered with *kanji*.

'General Nurarihyon's letter,' I said.

'In writing to emperors, it's best to be brief,' the Captain commented. 'Such persons dislike reading and always seek excuses to kill you. The more words you set down, the more likely you'll end up strangled with them.'

I didn't disagree.

Dravot shouldered his way through fog to join us. I told him what Dru had said about another dead soldier. He rolled his eyes and shrugged. He's firmly of the ignore-the-ninny party.

Kostaki was already following the scroll. He has taken to listening more closely to Dru – a sign of oncoming dementia or visionary genius. Abura Sumashi and Kasa-obake were ahead of him, the potato-head and living umbrella playing the game as if the rope were hung with lanterns and bells and a feast of sweetmeats awaited them at the end of it.

Under a streetlamp, peering at a tangle of the scroll, we found Kawataro, the *kappa* lord who is paying court to Christina, and four of his retainers. The green-faced, child-sized creatures look like frogs clamped into turtle shells. Reputedly adepts of ninjutsu, they are noisier than any shadow masters I've met. You don't notice real ninja even after they've beaten you up. Lord Kawataro

216

is a power in Yōkai Town, a rival of Lady Oyotsu and somewhat pompous, especially for a pint-sized amphibian with disgusting feeding habits. His castle island is half-sunk, lopsided thanks to collapsing foundations. Topazia tells me he was vehemently against taking in foreign vampires, though he modified his opinion slightly when he saw the Princess. If he had his way, he'd exclude Topazia too – she's from Hokkaido, an island he deems insufficiently Japanese. His household guard is the closest Yōkai Town has to a militia or police force.

'Stay back, *gaijin*,' Kawataro ordered.

His *kappa* ninja snapped to, raising weapons. Each posed with his speciality slicer, thumper, basher or stabber – *katana* (sword), *bo* (quarter-staff), *nunchaku* (chain-sticks), *sai* (twin three-pronged knives).

Kostaki warded them off with a flash of silvered steel, quarter-drawing his carrack. All the brows-knit posing and fancy metal in the world doesn't make up for having the reach of an eight-year-old. Kostaki could fell all four of them with one pass. And, if that didn't take, Dravot had a revolver in his greatcoat pocket.

The *kappa* with the *sai* snarled.

Dravot laughed and sang 'A Frog He Would A-Wooing Go'.

'*With a rowley, powley, gammon and spinach, "Heigh ho!" says Anthony Rowley.*'

Kawataro's retainers circled us, angry at our foreign jabber.

'Yours is the one with the two bits of wood,' said Dravot.

I could take the *nunchaku* from the mean-eyed perisher, but would get a broken arm out of it. Even healing quickly hurts.

'You're French,' Dravot went on. ''E thinks you're goin' to eat 'is legs with butter and parsley.'

'Most chefs would recommend butter and garlic,' I said. 'But we don't talk about that, eh?'

No matter how they decorate their shells like armour or strap on fearsomely crested *suibachi* helmets, the *kappa* militia look like mean-eyed children playing soldiers. Treating them as funny is a mistake, though. The tips of their tongues slither like snakes, poking out of lipless mouths, suckers pulsing greedily. By nature, the riverbed-dwelling trash vampires are crafty, libidinous, cruel and none-too-fastidious. The apt term is 'bottom feeder'. Dravot hadn't seen what a *kappa* did to the dishonourable official in Suicide Garden.

O-Same flared overhead, following the scroll-rope as a bird in flight follows a road or river. We all looked up.

'Let's avoid a needless fight, my lord,' I suggested. 'Impress Princess Casamassima by acting firmly after giving the matter due consideration.'

That was the right name to drop. Lord Kawataro raised his stubby green fist and opened it, stretching the webbing between his fingers. His retainers stood down, sheathing or putting away their accessories.

I was relieved not to have a broken arm.

Dravot needs to appreciate our uncertain situation. His soldiering was done in the British Empire. He could sneer at native customs and trample on idols because the Great White Queen's army and navy would back him up. A bully knowing his bigger bully of a father will finish any fight he starts. It's not like that now. If the Sergeant is decapitated or boiled in Japan, Lord Ruthven won't send a gunboat. And Gilbert and Sullivan got one thing right – here, chopping off your head is considered a mercy.

We trudged through the snow. O-Same lit the way ahead for us. As we had all guessed, the scroll led to General Nurarihyon's hut. Green fog hung about the marshy place. Reeds were broken all around. The scroll wrapped a stone idol then lay on the steps like a carpet. *Kanji* were blurred where the paper was soaked.

Abura Sumashi and Kasa-obake were already there, refraining from entering. They weren't the only amateur investigators on the case. Gokemidoro and Kuchisake followed us, drawn by all the activity. As new arrivals in Yōkai Town, they're still more curious than wary. They were in the same coffle. Perhaps they're walking out together. The idea of them spooning – her ear-to-ear mouth locked onto his tongueless head gash – made me giggle and feel queasy at the same time. Was Kuchisake so taken by Goké's extra mouth she hadn't tried to expand it with scissors? Or did she just not see how to cut?

Goké took out a cigarette case. He stuck two in his (regular) mouth and lit them with one match, then gave one to Kuchisake. She poked it into one cheek slit and smoke puffed out of the other. Goké offered the case around. The *kappa* with the *katana* took one. He choked on the first lungful of smoke. Dravot chuckled and nearly started another showdown.

We all looked warily at the General's hut.

A curtain of silky cobweb hung over the entrance. I remembered the face-backed goblin spiders of the temple grounds. This web was thicker, whiter, more like rope than string. And somehow foul.

Lord Kawataro croaked an order.

The *kappa* with the *bo* tore through the web. Deliquescing strands stuck to the pole. The samurai hopped and screeched, trying to scrape the mess off. Instead, he smeared it over his shell. His comrades had to duck as he swung the staff around.

'Careful, Sonny Jim, you'll 'ave someone's eye out,' said Dravot.

'He is impressed with your martial skills,' I interpreted.

Goké was about to correct my translation but I gave him a warning look. He signalled acquiescence with his cigarette.

Kuchisake fumed, smoke seeping from the full length of her mouth. Now the *yōkai* woman was jealous of *me*.

Considering what she did to people she had nothing against, an unwelcome development.

I felt in my coat pocket. My scissors were still there.

We couldn't all get into the small hut at once. Kawataro and Kostaki entered, shoulder to hip. Kostaki took one look and ducked out again, summoning me. I hurried up the steps and into the low-ceilinged space. I had to wade through knee-high webs. It was dark until O-Same floated overhead. She cast firelight through a lattice canopy.

Under frosted layers of web was the General.

I needn't have brought my medical bag. There was no question of him not being dead. Dru had, for once, spoken simple truth. Even a stopped clock is right twice a day. I can't help thinking of her flash of candour as more misdirection. It'll be back to fairy talk and riddles next time.

Nurarihyon was shrunken and dry, cracked skin wrapped around a skeleton. He had four puckered holes in his neck and chest, bigger than usual fang-punctures. His skull was caved in like a rotten melon. All his blood was gone, and most of his flesh. A honey smell with a rancid aftertaste hung in the air.

'Are his eyes moving?' Kostaki asked.

'He has no eyes,' I said. 'It's her up there…'

As O-Same hovered, fire shadows shifted in Nurarihyon's empty orbits.

All his soft tissue was gone. I should say he'd been injected with potent acid that turned his insides to a gruel that could be sucked through tubes. Some spiders or wasps do that to smaller creatures. No *yōkai* I knew had the habit, but it wouldn't surprise me to learn of some new species. Something fearsome, which could ignore Nurarihyon's demands to desist. Surely, at the last, the venerable soldier would have summoned his powers and tried to compel his murderer to leave him alone.

The General's hut was desecrated. His tea-bowls were

scattered fragments. His low writing-desk was smashed as if by a blow from a giant's hand. That made me think of Kannuki, but the clumsy oaf wasn't a likely karate master. Silky, sticky discharge lay over everything like the sperm of a dozen candles.

'Look,' said Kostaki, holding up the dead *yōkai*'s sticks of fingers.

Kawataro shouted to us not to touch the honoured General. He called us barbarian defilers of corpses.

'Remember, he sucks cows' arses,' I told Kostaki.

Kostaki signalled to Kawataro to look closely at the dead man's hand. The General's fingers were black with ink. Kawataro looked from the hand to a broken screen that was within Nurarihyon's reach. He scraped away a swath of web to show scrawled *kanji*. A dying testament in any militia's book. The vital clue that closes the tricky case, better than distinctive cigar ash no fool would scatter on the body of his inheritance-withholding uncle or the smashed watch that establishes what the alibi-shielded murderer would like you to think was the time of death. A clear accusation from beyond the grave.

'What does it say?' Kostaki asked.

It was hard to make out.

'*Kaban wo motta kawaii on'nanoko*,' I ventured. 'Pretty girl with a… purse, or bag. Something like that.'

Kawataro took a Colt Peacemaker out of the waistband of his *hakama* and aimed at me. Not a traditional samurai weapon, but he's noticed their shortcomings on the eve of the twentieth century and has decided to keep up with the times. I assumed the single-action revolver was loaded with silver bullets.

'What now?' I said.

Kostaki pointed to my medical kit.

'"Pretty girl with a bag",' he said. 'It's what they call *you*, Geneviève.'

17

YŌKAI TOWN, DECEMBER 21, 1899

I was impressed by the respect shown me while I was being unjustly arrested. Seldom have I been so politely accused of a murder I didn't commit.

I stepped out of General Nurarihyon's hut ahead of Lord Kawataro's Colt. Kostaki stopped Dravot pulling his Webley and facing off against the *kappa*. Turning Yōkai Town into Tombstone would help no one. Least of all me.

Being caught in the crossfire during the gunfight at the O.K. Corral was enough of the romance and excitement of the Wild West to last a long lifetime. When I let him dig a bullet out of my head, I didn't know John Holliday was only a *dentist*. My wound healing over while 'Doc' had hot tongs in it made the procedure extremely painful. I told him all French girls mended quickly and got out of town before sun-up. Arizona Territory is full of silver mines.

I asked Gokemidoro to translate for our party while I was unavailable. Lines of communication must be kept open. Kostaki wasn't ready to trust the split-faced *kyuketsuki*, but interpreters were in short supply. The lips of Goké's head-cleft pursed as he nodded, accepting the job.

Kostaki tried to explain to Kawataro that I couldn't have killed the General. He held up his forefingers like my tiny fangs and wiggled them around, then made fearsome tusks

222

of his bunched fingers and jabbed them viciously. I saw his point, but the *kappa* lord was in no mood to consider suspects beyond the obvious. Marshal Morgan Earp of Tombstone had been just the same – though he had the excuse of the shaman Misquamacus gestating in his goitre and whispering in his mind. Kostaki grunted terse sentences, which Goké translated into well-argued paragraphs. If I needed a lawyer, he was my man – especially if he took his dark glasses off to address the magistrate.

The four militiamen escorted me away from the shrine. Kuchisake smiled at my removal. Her chin dropped to her sternum, exposing alarming mauve tonsils. Can she swallow a watermelon whole?

This was my fault for playing sleuth. I should have had enough of the game in Whitechapel. I worked in the office next to Jack Seward's for months without realising he was the Silver Knife. This time, I had proudly pointed out the clue that made me look guilty. Inspector Lestrade would snort through his whiskers at that.

That scroll wound straight from the dorm to the shrine – a lure into a trap? I had skipped along the bloody trail.

Who gained from making trouble for me?

Conceivably, almost everyone. It was awfully convenient that Drusilla suddenly took it into her head to say something easy to understand. Majin might have marked me down as a useful scapegoat; another scrap to toss to the sharks to whip up a feeding frenzy. Christina had made an effort to woo me over, which could be like petting the dog you're about to shoot. If Dravot had sealed orders to have me indicted for murder, he'd do it in a wink and not ask questions. And arresting me let Lord Kawataro crow over Lady Oyotsu that he had been right about the foreign devils, boosting his position in Yōkai Town.

At that, I doubtless had enemies I'd not met yet. The Black Ocean Society. Could one of us be a sham refugee like the Americans were afraid of − acting as the long-distance Renfield of Dracula or Lord Ruthven? Kostaki and I had chewed that over and not come to reassuring conclusions.

Whoever was behind this could do to a *yōkai* whatever had been done to General Nurarihyon. And prevail on a dying man to accuse me.

I was encouraged into a shallow boat and ferried out to Castle Kawataro. The *kappa* with the *bo* stood at the stern and poled us away from the waterfront, then the others took up oars. They rowed the boat between walkways and under low bridges. The sounds of clicking stones, laughs and cries and arguments, and raucous music − Japanese and Western − spilled across fog-shrouded water from gambling halls.

Though the mass of junks, lean-tos and artificial islands extends well away from the shore, a stretch of clear water separates it from the castle. The roisterers and reprobates of the emerald lantern district dare not encroach on Lord Kawataro's domain.

We slid through a gateway into an enclosed harbour. More *kappa* militia lined the jetty, aiming muskets and pikes at the dangerous vampire woman. Prodded with the blunt end of a *sai*, I got out of the boat.

A dog-headed turnkey of the *inugami* bloodline hauled open a heavy iron door. I stepped into a cave-like hall lit by torches in sconces. A wide ledge ran around a saltwater pool. A rattling and splashing of excitement greeted me. Bamboo cages were suspended on chains dangling from crossbeams; some were completely submerged, others half out of the water. A few held wretched *yōkai*. The *tengu* we had met on our arrival at Yōkai Town was a caged bird − wrist bandaged, feathers sodden, beaky countenance miserable. *Kappa* and *tengu* do not get along.

The *inugami* cranked a handle and a cage rose from the pool, a larger version of the box Dru keeps her cricket in. Eels flapped in the bottom, then slithered between bamboo poles and slipped into the water. Winding ripples broke up reflected firelight. Murals of sea battles painted around the room seemed to flicker into life. The *kappa* with the *nunchaku* helped me swing out from the ledge to stand on top of the cage. The *kappa* with the *bo* used it to open a trapdoor at my feet. My escorts made gestures, indicating I should drop into my cage like a good little birdie.

Didn't they know I understood Japanese? Or were they under orders not to talk to me? Kawataro might believe I could exercise siren-like power over lesser *yōkai* – as was claimed for Nurarihyon or Gokemidoro. Of course, he also thought I could suck someone empty. The militiamen must be *terrified*.

I lowered myself into the cage and got my boots full of water. The trapdoor was flapped shut and fastened with a rusty padlock. I held the bamboo bars and looked out at my captors. The turnkey worked the pulley and the cage sank until I was up to my chest in brine. My escorts were happier now I was put away and clashed their weapons together musketeer-all-for-one style. Then they executed a strange shell-wiggling dance step while flapping free flippers at each other in handshakes sillier than Kostaki and Dravot's Masonic *pas de deux*. The *inugami* barked approval of their antics and tittered in a rassin-frassin-grassin dialect pitched so high only other dogs – and, as it happens, vampires – could hear him.

Eels swam between the bars, scraping me with skin like wet sandpaper.

So, it had come to this. Jugged, like a hare.

My medical bag was confiscated. I supposed the militia were looking in it for the fearsome murder weapon I used on General Nurarihyon. Lord Kawataro – a parade soldier, not a policeman – didn't think to have me searched. Even Lestrade would have made me turn out my pockets. I still had the scissors I was carrying so Kuchisake couldn't steal them for use in her campaign to put big smiles on everyone's faces. Underwater, out of sight of the guards, I experimentally snipped one of the waxed string knots holding the poles of my cage together. I could get free if I wanted to. With seawater lapping my chin, it was a temptation – but escaping would make me look even more guilty.

My best bet was to sit – or float – quietly until the murderer struck again. A position as uncomfortable morally as my cell was physically. I didn't want anyone else to get killed, but I was stuck here until they did. I imagined pleasant, if unlikely outcomes. The murderer caught red-fanged before his (or her) next victim was much harmed. If an innocent being merely *assaulted* led to my freedom, I could square it with my conscience. However, a trail of ravaged corpses was more likely. Even that might not lead to my release. The Pope and the Emperor of Japan aren't the only temporal powers who subscribe to a doctrine of infallibility. Most authorities literally can't be proved wrong. Justice for all is more trouble than it's worth. Convicts proved innocent of the original charges in the morning are found guilty of a raft of other offences in the afternoon. Innocence is no guarantee of release and reunion with loved ones and thanks to the campaigners who've overturned the case. All too often, the result is a longer sentence, fewer rations and a closer acquaintance with the wheel.

I would soon be thirsty enough to bite eels.

At least they hadn't put an iron mask on me.

My nearest neighbour was the *tengu*. I tried to start a conversation. He squawked in panic and flapped to the other side of his cage, terrified to be so near a monster.

I whiled away the hours compiling mental alphabets.

Usually, the lists are easy, except for Q, X and Z, so I start by filling in those letters, and often skip the rest.

> *Places I've Visited: Quebec, Xochimilcho and Zinj.*
>
> *Languages I've Learned (and Mostly Forgotten): Quiripi, Xârâcùù and Zulu.*
>
> *Dances I've Failed to Master: quickstep, xibelani and zwiefacher.*
>
> *Authors I've Read: de Quincey, Xenophon and Israel Zangwill (Zola is too obvious).*
>
> *Vampires I Like (tricky): no, nothing and nope.*
>
> *Vampires I Hate (easier): Quinn, Xanhast and Zargo.*
>
> *Old Lovers: now that's just depressing, though a lawyer I bled in Massachusetts might have been called Quincy Something.*
>
> *People I Would Consider or Have Considered Possible Lovers, Even*
>
> *When There Is or Was No Likelihood of Anything Coming of It: Arturo Quire, James Xavier and – despite not earning a place in the Vampires I Like alphabet above – Zepia Oberon.*
>
> *Adjectives Which Have Been Applied to Me: quixotic, xenophilic and zany.*
>
> *Adjectives Which Have Not Been Applied to Me: quartzy, xanthic and zaftig.*
>
> *Prisons In Which I've Been Unjustly Incarcerated: Stonehaven Tollbooth, Yuma Penitentiary and Castle Zenda.*

What does it say about my life that it's easier to list prisons than lovers?

Time passed. I thought about slipping underwater and sleeping. I didn't think I'd drown.

Without falling into lassitude, I lulled into a state of non-thinking.

18

BEFORE DRACULA (CONCLUDED)

Nicolas Cerral got up a petition to have me reinstated. Most of the ghouls signed, and about half the other medical students. Several of the women knew better than to put their names to it, realising what Cerral didn't – any excuse would be found to get rid of them too. All our lecturers were asked to support me, but only Charcot and Cataflaque did. Some deemed it beneath their station to get involved with administrative affairs. The conservatives airily implied those pestering reformers should have expected this. Let a woman through the front door, and all manner of fantastical creatures will flood in after. Why, we'll be giving doctorates to performing seals next!

The petition was politely set aside on a technicality. The university couldn't reinstate someone who didn't exist and therefore had never been instated *or* dismissed. If the matter were pressed, Assistant Clerk M. Modéran would reluctantly be obliged to refer it to an office more inclined to involve the police in matters of fraud and forgery – and skeletons in cupboards. I had to ask Cerral to stop agitating on my behalf. He was incensed, but I saw he was the alone. Fellows initially willing to stand up were uncomfortable with how far he had taken things. They had to think of their as-yet-unearned degrees. All they wanted was to let the matter drop and get on with their future brilliant careers, unencumbered by vampire associations.

That Hallowe'en, police raids on several Paris addresses revealed the authorities had taken steps to address 'the vampire question'. My evening passed without incident. I was not piqued to be left out. I assumed I had been investigated and determined to be relatively harmless. Eva Van Meerhaegue, a vampire I'd never heard of, was arrested in Montmartre and accused of several murders. She had a lair in the shell of the old Théâtre des Vampires and was mixed up with the decadent Des Esseintes set. Styling herself *la Papesse Rouge*, she demanded blood tribute from besotted worshippers. Rituals of sacrifice were mentioned at her sensational trial. She may well have been guilty. Guillotined at dawn, she turned to dust. Her acolytes, all warm, were convicted of lesser crimes, except the one who informed on her, who went free. Several were killed in prison; guilty of vampirism by association.

The fate of Eva Van Meerhaegue put the Marquis de Coulteray into a panic. The Vampire Ascendancy wasn't ascendant enough for him. After his first gush of enthusiasm, he found it a disappointment. Not least because, for all his efforts, he couldn't ride Dracula's coat-tails to the position he deserved. Where was his castle? His treasure? His willing acolytes?

De Coulteray's attempts to get to London were thwarted. British ports remained closed. The boat train was not running. Navies lined up against each other in the Channel. Sunburned soldiers withdrawn from North Africa were sent on manoeuvres in rainy Brittany, as if the Hundred Years' War were about to resume. You'll love this: by virtue of not dying since 1812, I was still listed (under the name of Guillaume Dieudonné) as an army reservist. Somehow, I was tracked down and served notice that, in the event of hostilities, I would be called up to serve as a military surgeon by the Conseil de Santé des Armées. The military were prepared to accept my qualifications and address me as 'Doctor'. Thanks to seniority, I would be mustered in at the rank of major.

More than ever, the Marquis was convinced that the Vatican/Rothschild-funded Congregation of the Doctrine of the Faith was coming for him. He changed addresses and gave out false ones, moving from bolthole to bolthole, but still intermittently bombarded me with dire warnings, predictions and worries. His elation at the rise of Dracula dissipated. He was sick with fear he would perish in the period of terror before establishment of the worldwide vampire utopia where we would be lords of all and the warm kept like cattle. To wait so long in shadow only to be staked or decapitated when the promised land was so close was a frustration that could not be borne.

As de Coulteray dashed about the city, I was in limbo. With my documents refused, I was an unperson – an undead unperson. Unless war was declared, my military status was as a secret weapon. Kept in an icehouse while governments denied its existence. Accustomed to shifts at the morgue and a full programme of lectures at Pitié-Salpêtrière, I found idleness not to my taste. I missed my studies, my work. I no longer had the company of the dead and my fellow ghouls. I just had ghosts.

I was even sorry to lose my benighted imaginary parents.

I thought about the Number – not the imaginary High Table of Vampire Elders. My Number. The Three.

Dafydd, Sergei, Annie.

Being known for what I was meant my victims were with me constantly. The quizzing of the ghouls would be repeated. It was not avoidable.

I have seen you kill a man, Charles. An unarmed man. Oh, I recognised an act of mercy. Like all doctors, I understand sometimes swift death is the only medicine.

I have never asked you how many others you have killed.

You understand what it is to be asked the question, though. Everyone who meets you and has a sense of your service to the Crown has an impulse – a child-brain urge – to ask.

I spent time in my own house. Neighbours crossed the road to avoid walking past my front door. Children were told to play in other streets away from the haunted house and the monster with the face of a girl. At Christmas, presents were thrown through my windows at odd hours.

A new year came: 1886.

A clearer picture of what was happening in England formed, as more news became available. Overseas post resumed. The new British stamps – printed in two colours! – excited almost as much comment as the letters that bore them. The Queen's profile was minutely examined. Some claimed a tiny mark at the corner of Victoria's mouth was a fang. British newspapers and publications again reached Paris. Fleet Street, obviously subject to official censorship, learned how to fit real stories between the lines of bland items about court affairs, parliamentary sub-committees and royal romances. The jingo papers turned virulently vampirish. 'Shame the Nay-Sayers', 'Hang All Traitors' and 'Smash the Shoe-Throwers' headlines ran above illustrations of Dracula looking grim, cruel and smug.

The boat train was reinstated for government officials and a very few journalists and dignitaries. De Coulteray couldn't raise the exorbitant bribe that would have got him a seat though he told me other elders – the well-connected Countess Báthory and the snob Count von Krolock, for instance – secured first-class carriages and cabins for themselves and their entourages. They prospered under Dracula, ensconced in the finest London addresses, the Elephant's Castle and the Earl's Court. The Marquis believed he was snubbed because of his *pishacha* bloodline.

Dorga was venerated in India by princes when Transylvania was populated by cavemen and no Roman had set sandal in what would become Romania, but Carpathians were intolerant of 'muddied' Asian bloodlines.

After the royal marriage, the Liberal Gladstone resigned – or was made to resign – as prime minister. A snap election (with a very low turnout) was won by the Conservative Lord Salisbury, who immediately stood down and was replaced (controversially) by Lord Ruthven. An elder vampire, but a newborn Tory. *His* documents wouldn't be scrutinised for fraud or forgery, despite a reputation as a rogue among rogues. Until he attained high office, other vampires wanted little to do with the eternal cad. If you let him visit your castle, he'd have the brass handles off your coffin while you were resting and couldn't be trusted around your mistress, stableboy or a locked desk with your cheque book in it. Now he was Dracula's Grand Vizier. Following unrest on the streets, Ruthven found it expedient to beseech the Prince Regent to step in. No sane person would appeal to Dracula for 'calming measures'. The Carpathian Guard were deployed to support (then supplant) police forces and home regiments of the British armed forces. The French press noted the Guard were initially charged with protecting citizens from anarchists and crusaders, but took a broader view of their mission and conducted themselves like a conquering army. Parallels were drawn with Prussian behaviour in the late war. This was the crackdown.

After only a few months, there were new norms... and many new vampires. London theatres and pubs reopened. Vampires were everywhere, setting styles in costume and deportment. Famous faces disappeared briefly from the public eye to return as newborn vampires and were presented at court. There were drolleries about these debutantes and, yes, Oscar Wilde was mentioned often.

Punch caricatured him crawling head-first down a wall and tangled in ivy. Famous beauties like Lillie Langtry were hailed as 'preserved for the nation' in the rotogravure while death notices in small print listed those whose turning 'did not take'. Serious journals noted other famous names who disappeared and did *not* show up again in black velvet with sharper teeth and a red glint in their eye. Where was Adam Adamant? Friedrich Engels? Sherlock Holmes?

The first mention I saw of the concentration camp at Devil's Dyke was in a smuggled anti-Dracula pamphlet, *Red Sunset*. That included a list of the casualties of the Ascendancy. At the head of the roll were Abraham Van Helsing, Quincey Morris and Lucy Westenra – though, technically, newborn Lucy was murdered by Van Helsing's crew of light before she could do anything wicked enough to earn impalement and decapitation. Had Dracula or her warm suitors cared enough for Lucy to look after her on her first nights as a vampire, things might have gone very differently for the world. She became a martyr for both sides: Dracula's first victim, Van Helsing's last. The habit of distortion for propaganda purposes is not confined to the Prince.

And yet…

The British Empire did not explode in flames. Lightning did not destroy London.

Dracula was Prince Regent, but Victoria still reigned. And was restored to the pink of health and youth.

She photographed, unlike her new husband. And glowed, almost as Christina does.

Viscount Lyons, the British Ambassador, was recalled. Lord Drewe Bennett, his replacement, arrived in a coffin.

At this, I was assailed by yet another liveried messenger. I thought my call-up papers had come, but it was an invitation from the office of President Jules Grévy. The pleasure of my company was requested at a reception for Lord Drewe. I might be a non-person so far as the university was concerned but the Third Republic needed me to demonstrate a lack of prejudice. With Eva Van Meerhaegue and her like tidied away, rocks were turned over to find presentable French vampires who could be produced to greet our brother-in-darkness from perfidious Albion. The messenger circumvented my instinct to decline on the grounds that I didn't have anything to wear by handing me a parcel containing an organdie evening gown. It was a perfect fit, quashing any notion that I wasn't being closely watched.

The reception was held in the cupola ballroom of the Paris Opera House. Bennett, reputedly, was keen on the *entr'acte* ballets. Were strong-hearted, supple-limbed dancers made available for his amusement? He wouldn't be the first diplomat to make that demand in Paris though he would be first to be more interested in bleeding than bedding the *corps de ballet*.

I saw torn-down posters for *Don Juan Triumphant*.

After being directed to the appallingly gold-encrusted ballroom, I was commandeered by a fellow who turned out to be the President's son-in-law, Daniel Wilson. He was my escort for the evening – which meant he was to ensure I didn't bite anyone in public. Later, Wilson was caught trafficking offices of the Légion d'Honneur, a scandal that brought down the Grévy government. He didn't strike me as any shiftier than anyone else at the reception. Government ministers and civil servants strutted, sporting all their medals and decorations, whether earned or bought, accompanied by wives whose dresses were more spectacular than mine and mistresses whose figures were more spectacular than anyone's. The opera lover Hippolyte Modéran was there, with his homely wife. He ignored me for, after all, I did not exist.

Also gathered were the respectable – or semi-respectable, or as-yet-unarrested – vampires of Paris, each with their personal attentive escort. Princess Addhema, famous for a faddist diet of 'aetheric spirit', was squired by Grévy. It did look as if she drained something vital out of him. An extremely pretty ancient youth whose suit cost more than my house required several policemen in tailcoats to keep him on a leash. He tittered at everything, made eyes at the boys and girls of the ballet, and kept wiping cherry-red smudges from his beestung lips with a frilly yard-square handkerchief.

I was presented to the Ambassador – who showed no interest at all. Elder vampires often complain – at length – of dreadful ennui. Lord Drewe was the most impossible example of the breed I've ever come across. He sighed at my curtsey and flapped his wet fish of a hand at me. He might have been embalmed before turning. Every movement was great effort and his face was frozen like a statue's. If a diplomatic ploy, it was ill-judged. It just made the French even less interested in talking with him.

'Only England could produce such a sport,' wrote the tittering dandy in his later-published diary, 'a *boring* vampire.' You'll remember the acute observation comes just before twenty-five pages describing (accurately) the clothes he wore that evening and a lengthy aside about how sad and lonely he was in that crowd as in all crowds on every night throughout eternity. The dapper diarist *doesn't* mention the twin blonde girls I saw him spooning with on a divan in the powder room or the handsome gendarme he lured behind a potted palm tree in the lobby for some activity that involved twanging braces and strenuous gurgling.

After an agonisingly protracted minute or so, my audience with Bennett was at an end. The next French vampire – Comte Hubert de Sinestre, soon to become the

Third Republic's unofficial Minister for Undead Affairs – was brought forward to replace me. He was received with just as much enthusiasm. I predicted a declaration of war before the carriages arrived. What would I look like in a major's uniform?

A resentful string quartet played English tunes they couldn't have heard before rehearsal. Selections from *H.M.S. Pinafore* and *The Pirates of Penzance*. Country airs and 'D'ye Ken John Peel'. The performers were contemptuously note-perfect, but rigid, strident and in a seethe about abandoning real music for the evening.

Lord Drewe might well be tone deaf.

It goes without saying that he didn't drink wine. Or care for cakes. He'd seen everything in the Louvre and wouldn't give any of it space on the walls of his town house. The Seine was very inferior to the Thames. Haussmann's boulevards were too straight and the wheels at the casinos too crooked. And these vaunted French beauties could all do with a good wash behind their ears and between their toes.

I wasn't above being bitterly amused at the efforts of *la belle France* to make the British boor welcome.

Diplomatic duty discharged, Wilson abandoned me. He might have been sent off to find dancers willing to be bled. With so many starved predators about, there was likely to be a shortage.

None of the *hors d'oeuvres* presented on gold platters were vampire fare. Most involved nougat, which gets caught in my gums. I drifted, pondering architectural features of the Palais Garnier. An outrageous amount of gold was stuck to the walls, the ceiling and the furniture. Even the mirrors I didn't reflect in were backed with gold not silver. I felt more at home with the penniless, nameless dead on bare slabs in the cold, dark morgue than in this riot of overdecoration.

A fellow in a skull mask, feathered hat and red pantaloons made a grand entrance under the impression that this was a costume party. He was barred by attendants and skulked off, swearing revenge on the prankster who so misinformed him. 'Write an opera about *this*, ha ha!' shouted someone from the crowd. Comte Philippe de Chagny. The booby in the fancy dress was my acquaintance, Erik de Boscherville – composer of *Don Juan Triumphant*, voice trainer to notorious adventuresses, and a famous grudge-holder. The waggish Comte would do well not to walk under chandeliers.

I was hissed at from a golden alcove.

It was de Coulteray, in a taller wig and shoes with wooden bricks for soles. 'His wife's the coldest creature in Europe,' he said, nodding at Ambassador Bennett. 'Marie Sanglante. His virile member went flop on his wedding night and no amount of blood will bring it to attention again.'

I hadn't known whether the liveried messengers would trawl so widely as to haul in the Marquis. Or if he would poke his head out of his hole to attend.

'They found you, then?' I said.

He looked this way and that. His wig tottered.

'It's a trap,' he said. 'We are to be rounded up and herded into the sub-cellars. They did it before, in the commune. We are dancing on the tombs of tortured men, Gené. There's a secret guillotine down below, with a silver blade. We are to be got rid of. I shan't be taken.'

Since I'd last seen him, the Marquis had contracted a fungus condition. Blotches on his face were inexpertly powdered over. Damp patches on his white gloves betokened weeping sores. He was missing several teeth.

'I have a plan to get to England – with the apples,' he said. 'Trade is resumed, and I have found a boat which will take us as cargo. But we shall need money. Much of it.'

I had some savings left, but decided not to mention them. I might want to buy myself a ribbon *d'honneur*. It should be protection enough from the guillotine.

I noticed Hippolyte Modéran loitering within earshot.

I thought of telling de Coulteray that the assistant clerk of admissions was an agent of the Congregation – but I worried he'd believe me. The way the world was, I worried *I'd* believe me.

At the end of the evening, it was made clear that vampire guests should leave. There were seven or eight of us, including several unknown to me. I half-expected Grandmère Melissa to be among us, but she had gone to ground. The dandy diarist pinched my organdie shoulder ruffle as we were descending the stairs, and rubbed the material between his fingers – then sneezed as if the gown were impregnated with garlic. Up close, I saw he was much older when turned than he claims. His boyishness is as preserved and brittle as a glacé cherry. He is another gentleman of modest stature, too. As Dravot would say, 'a shirty short-arse'.

'They're not taking us to the sub-cellars,' I said to the Marquis, trying to be kind.

We were escorted out through a side door.

Three gendarmes awaited in Rue Gluck: two with drawn silver swords, one with a warrant made out for the arrest of Louis-Jean-Marie-Chrysostome, Marquis de Coulteray. He was accused of sundry offences under the Code Pénal – including eight counts of common assault, three of indecency in a public place and seventeen of theft of objects from the person. De Coulteray shrieked and tried to run but two more sword-wielding gendarmes sprang from hiding places either side of the door. The four policemen held sword-points to the Marquis' tubby torso, pricking his brocade. He couldn't move without being skewered from one direction or another.

De Coulteray whimpered, hemmed in by four points of silver.

All other vampires decided to vanish and did so. Last out of the Palais Garnier was a tall, beautiful brown woman in a silk sari and shimmering cloak. She had a blood-red dot on her forehead and a necklace of jewel-eyed gold skulls. She looked with something like disgust at the Marquis. He made a pitiful, imploring face as she walked into the night.

He should have built her bloody temple!

I was the only vampire to stay.

Out from under an awning came another old acquaintance, Inspector Daubert of the Sûreté. He was on the Marquis' case well before the fool owned up to being a vampire. When de Coulteray declared himself a blood-drinking monster, he essentially signed a blank confession.

Daubert had lit a cigar to signal his men to pounce. He threw it away.

'Mademoiselle Dieudonné,' he acknowledged.

'*Doctor* Dieudonné,' I insisted. Since we were being open about what we were, I was getting insistent about the title I'd earned several times over. 'Where are you taking the Marquis? La Santé? When will he be up before an examining magistrate?'

'He won't be, *Doctor*. This man died in 1745. We cannot put a *corpse* on trial…'

M. Modéran, *sans* madame, poked his head out of the door. I'd suspected he held a wider brief than assistant clerk of admissions.

'You can't arrest him, then,' I said.

'He isn't being arrested, Dr Dieudonné,' said Modéran. 'We are picking up a body. You should know who has claim on the corpses of criminals with no living relatives.'

Two other men stood by an unmarked coach. Professor Cataflaque and Dr Gheria. Professional ghouls.

'For the advancement of science, such remains are at the disposal of the School of Anatomy,' said the Inspector.

De Coulteray fainted.

* * *

I dug up the last of my savings, which were buried in my tiny garden. A chest once filled with *Louis d'ors* now held barely enough coins to stuff a purse. I stung my fingers on an écu – a *Louis d'argent* – which had got in among the gold. Degradation of coinage means modern money doesn't have enough silver in it to give me an itch.

I spent a frantic day trying to find a lawyer to act for the Marquis – and, by extension, other vampires potentially in the same situation (including me). I was turned away from many offices – one firm had a secretary brandish a crucifix in my face and threaten me with a spittoon supposedly blessed by a priest.

Invading a café near the Palais de Justice, I descended on startled groups of lunching jurists. I made an appeal to the contrarian vanity of the profession. Surely, someone saw a percentage in arguing for the rights of the most downtrodden of all clients, the living dead? Vampires were an accepted fact. Changes in legislation must come. Inheritance law would be up for revision. Wealthy newborns would rise invigorated from the grave and sink their sharp fangs into lengthy lawsuits over property prematurely claimed by grasping heirs. The definition of homicide would have to be altered. Risen murder victims might testify against fathers-in-darkness. Judges would set precedents. Famous rulings would be made. Ramifications would earn fees for generations to come.

I reminded my audience that the first thing Dracula did when executing his plan to conquer Britain was engage a firm of solicitors.

No one was tempted to sign up for a doomed crusade, though a sharp court reporter suggested Émile Zola might be prevailed on to write an editorial – even a pamphlet – on the vampire issue. I would have appealed to the author directly, but there wasn't time to start a debate and wait for public opinion to change. The Marquis de

Coulteray was already on a slab, awaiting dissection.

At sunset, I returned to the morgue. I wore a hooded cloak and hoped to be mistaken for a bereaved relative but instead was hailed cheerfully by the doorkeeper, who said he'd missed my cheerful face lately and I best hurry because the lecture had already begun. So, my non-existence hadn't been impressed on everyone attached to university, hospital and morgue.

I thanked the doorkeeper and made my way to the dissecting theatre.

That I didn't hear screams as I neared the room gave me a spasm of hope – dashed as soon as I slipped in at the back.

The Marquis de Coulteray – wigless and stripped bare – was tethered to the table, showing his patchy scalp, withered legs and swollen stomach. A contraption like a scold's bridle was fitted over his head. His mouth was filled by an iron flange that pressed his tongue far back into his gullet. Talking was impossible. No lecturer of anatomy liked to be interrupted in full flow – especially if heckling came from the specimen not a student. De Coulteray could make only small, shrill sounds. His watery, wide, panicked eyes were exposed by the muzzle's straps.

The device was newly made. Shiny metal and supple leather. That appalled me almost more than the torture. Someone – I suspected the practical Cataflaque rather than the pompous Gheria – saw a need for such a thing and commissioned an artisan to manufacture a usable prototype. Was a patent pending for the vampire gag? Would many more of the vile instruments be needed?

Gheria wielded the post-mortem knife, while Cataflaque lectured.

A deep incision in de Coulteray's torso – the Y-cut favoured by all autopsy surgeons – was made, but healed over before the chest flaps could be pulled back to lay the ribs bare. Cataflaque talked about the process of accelerated (if not instant) healing. A desirable aspect of the vampire condition, he conceded.

The doctors' audience wasn't just ghouls and medical students. Taller, silkier hats outnumbered student caps on the writing ledges. Greyer heads were present. The first public dissection of the common vampire – though *pishacha* was not that common a bloodline – drew a crowd of medical men, academics, priests, politicians and interested parties. Inspector Daubert was there, representing the Sûreté, and M. Modéran, representing whomever he represented. A masked man and woman – the Great Vampire and Irma Vep – made a showing for respectable, decent, non-blood-drinking criminals. Comte de Sinestre sat alone at the back, resolute in his lack of empathy for the man on the table. It wasn't his blood in the runnels.

I was gladder than ever to have refused Professor Cataflaque's offer of collaboration. I knew, without question, that I would be on the next available train, apple boat, hot air balloon or pneumatic tube out of the country. London, the most dangerous city in the world, was currently the safest place for a vampire. We could shelter behind the cloak of Dracula and the skirts of Victoria.

Having repeated the incision three times, exciting gasps with each magic-seeming closure, the Professor produced more new-made implements: a silver scalpel – the first I ever saw, but sadly not the last – and a set of custom surgical retractors. With some effort, Gheria made a serious Y-incision. Cataflaque fit the retractor into the wound, exposing the thoracic cavity. Flaps of flesh tried to knit together, but shrank from silver like slugs from salt.

Even with the gag in his mouth, the Marquis de Coulteray keened in agony.

A gentleman pushed past me to leave the theatre, hand clamped over his mouth. The ghouls hissed. Gheria looked furiously at the audience. His black gloves were slick with vampire blood. It rolled and balled like mercury, trying to flow back into the open wound.

With bone shears – tempered steel, plated with silver, he explained – Cataflaque cut through the subject's ribs. With his hands, he bent the bones upwards to expose a beating heart. The organ did not look healthy.

Gheria touched the point of his silver knife to the heart.

'A simple puncture and the processes of pseudo-life will end,' he said. 'At least, this is what tradition tells us. Eventually, that theory must be put to the test. For the moment, many more avenues remain to be explored with this subject. In the second stage of the lecture, we shall examine the mouth, assessing the unusual formation of the throat, investigating these sacs of unknown purpose, laying bare the bones of the jaw and skull. And, of course, the famous teeth.'

De Coulteray kicked against his restraints.

'For shame,' shouted someone. Cerral, the ghoul captain.

'For shame, for shame,' repeated other students, and even a few of the guests.

Comte de Sinestre was silent. Modéran and Daubert looked around, as if ready to write down names. They both saw me. Neither could look me in the eye.

For shame, indeed.

'This is a necessary study,' insisted Cataflaque. 'We must learn what we can… and quickly. The extinction of the human race as we understand the term is a possibility. The future of France will be decided by what we discover here.'

The 'for shame' cries were drowned out by the 'here here' crowd.

I walked down the aisle and up to the dissecting table. De Coulteray's eyes rolled. He would not recover from this outrage.

Gheria saw me and waved his scalpel. I thumped his

chest with as much force as I could muster. Pushed off his feet, he flew backwards. His head cracked the blackboard and left a chalky, sticky smudge.

I bared my fangs.

'*Et, bien sûr, les dents,*' I said.

Some of the audience hissed. Cerral, unwisely, applauded.

Cataflaque stood away from me. I knew I was proving his point for him.

Even those who had been appalled by the dissection now saw a vampire – me! – as a dangerous creature. Not a Frenchwoman who worked in a hospital, paid her taxes and stood up for 'La Marseillaise', but a panther loose in a kindergarten. See her fangs! Muzzle the hellcat! Sharpen a stake!

I looked a question at the Marquis. He nodded a response.

I took out my purse. Cataflaque was astonished. He must have thought I was going to offer a bribe. I felt in the purse for the coin that hurt and pulled it out.

I pressed the silver écu into de Coulteray's heart. It burst like an overripe tomato. Vampire blood squirted on my cloak and into the Professor's face.

Uproar in the audience. Interested parties scrambled and fought, missing a perfect chance to observe the accelerated process of decay. The Marquis bubbled and dwindled to red sludge, draining off the table. That ghastly gag was all that was left of his head. I took it up – ignoring the silver shock – and brandished it at Cataflaque. How would he like it strapped in his damned mouth?

I turned and marched out of the room.

Nicolas Cerral held the door open for me. I paused, looked back at the academicians of France, and kissed the captain of ghouls on the lips, spreading blood all over his jacket.

I left the morgue, running. I did not stop until I reached Whitechapel – where you, Charles, found me, and our adventures began.

19

YŌKAI TOWN, DECEMBER 22, 1899

Something large was moving through the pool, displacing water but not breaking the surface. Gentle waves pushed through my cage.

Chains creaked. A prisoner complained.

The *inugami* barked at him to shut up.

There was a little excitement. Guarding me in a cage must be as boring as being me in a cage. Any distraction was welcome. The *kappa* looked about, checking prisoners. The *bo*-wielder prodded me through the bars. I showed my hands above water.

If I weren't behind bamboo, I'd have taken his blessed stick away from him and thwacked his silly helmet with it.

Weapons I Could Injure a *Kappa* With… quarterstaff, xiphos and zhanmadao.

I looked across at the *tengu*. His parrot eyes were fixed on me. Then, quickly and quietly, he was gone. He hadn't held his beak and ducked under water of his own accord. It looked to me as if he had been tugged from below.

Feathers floated in his cage. I tasted blood in the water. Spoiled, brackish. I spat it out.

Then a wave rolled over me. The *tengu* bobbed up, face down. Trapped air tented his robe over his back.

Slowly, he twisted. His face came out of the water. Half of it gone.

The *kappa* gathered to prod the corpse. My cage was clattered.

I was swimming in blood. My fangs sprouted.

Orders were given. The *inugami* turned the crank handle. My cage rose from the water. My soaked clothes weighted me down. I left my scissors in my pocket. It was best no one notice I had a weapon – no matter how small.

The *tengu*'s wounds were severe. Whatever killed him did it quickly. He hadn't even splashed.

The *kappa* argued. A difference of opinion arose about who to alarm with the news. No one was overly concerned about the dead prisoner. And, foolishly, they were more worried about the wrath of Lord Kawataro than the possibility that their own scaly hides were in danger.

While the guards argued, I noticed more floating things. Flimsy ropes I first took for seaweed. One got snagged on my cage. It was an exsanguinated eel. A tube of ropy muscle rendered into a brittle streamer. A patch of skin came away, exposing little white bones. No flesh at all.

Something screamed at the other side of the room. Another prisoner.

Two *kappa* rushed to investigate. The others kept watch on me.

I showed my hands and opened my mouth.

I wanted to signal *no blood, no fangs, no claws*.

But blood in the water sharpened my teeth and nails.

The *katana kappa* called me a disgusting witch.

Another shout, and a splashing-thrashing from another cage! A *tenjoname* – a long-tongued, muscular *yōkai* – put up more of a fight than the *tengu*, dripping venom and hovering as something speared from below. Seized by his tongue, he was pulled under. He bobbed out of the frothing water and I saw his face shrivel. He turned into a husk, like General

Nurarihyon. Leached of all substance, his body surfaced. His skin floated like a suit of empty clothes.

The other prisoners – all awake now – started screaming.

The *inugami* got tangled in chains trying to hoist all the cages, before the *katana kappa* ordered him not to.

The room was too dark to see clearly.

I heard more prisoners die... and saw blood threads in the water, along with scraps of dead eels and strands of white foam. Whatever was picking meals out of the bamboo boxes grew less stealthy.

It didn't escape my notice that I had been spared so far.

Was I saved – or saved for last?

The *kappa* stood on the ledge and waved their precious weapons at the roiling pool. For all their ninja mastery of cutting, stabbing, thumping and bashing, their toys were no use against anything that didn't come at them directly. Upon sober reflection, they needed a fifth frog-turtle musketeer who specialised in *kyudo* – archery. Kawataro's American gun might also have been handy. Only now, when I had more immediate concerns, did it occur to me that the *kappa* would have a struggle *using* his Peacemaker. With child-sized hands and webbed fingers, he probably couldn't outdraw Wyatt, the Earp family idiot.

The *inugami* whined. That set my fangs on edge.

Whoever killed General Nurarihyon was here, tearing through *yōkai* like a fox in a henhouse. At least it wasn't me. I hadn't entirely rejected the possibility I might be guilty and not remember doing the deed.

The room quieted and the water stilled.

Finally, the *katana kappa* ordered the *inugami* to sound the alarm. The castle was under attack. The turnkey tried to open the door but it wouldn't shift.

Kappa shouted at him.

'Death stones on the board, dog-man,' yelped the *sai kappa*. 'Death stones on the board!'

The *kappa* competed for turns at the door. No-hope knights jostling for a chance to dislocate shoulders trying to pull the sword from the stone.

My cage hung in the air. Close to me, distorted by water, a face loomed.

A white oval, with round eyes… a European face. A woman.

A head broke the surface and rose slowly, without making ripples. Her sleek hair smoothed over her ears and against her shoulders like a sealskin hood.

She was a vampire.

Her arms and chest were above the water. She was steady… not treading water but standing on the bottom. Either the pool wasn't as deep as I'd thought or her legs were twenty feet long.

Was this some siren loosed from our stack of coffins?

This woman was distantly familiar. I had seen her recently, I thought, and before, but a long, long, *long* time ago.

Only when she smiled and showed little fangs did I realise where and how I'd seen that face – distorted, and through the eyes of a dying dog.

I knew why the General accused me.

The vampire wore my face.

'Enjoy it,' she whispered, in English. 'A reflection, like a looking-glass. Don't have one usually, do you, my lover?'

The voice wasn't mine. She had a Wessex accent.

She shook her hair out. Dark wet blonde.

The face rippled and a hairy, moth-eyed, mosquito-proboscis horror broke through my flesh portrait, then another woman's face, like mine but not me. Rounder and rosier-cheeked. Pretty, if narrow-eyed. Lighter blonde hair.

Clare Mallinger. Daughter of gentry. Murderess.

Something shifted under her hair and a bulb inflated from the back of her neck. Clare turned away, neck twisting like a wrung-out wet sheet. Eight round black eyes sprouted from a fist-sized lump. Another head. Not remotely human.

I remembered the odd rash on Clare's neck. And the hole in her crate. And the detritus – eggshell fragments, I realised – in the straw. And the Black Ocean wave daub.

This wasn't just Clare Mallinger.

She would be bad enough, but something else inhabited her. Clare looked at me, face screwed up in pain, eyes red and pleading, but the new head, the imp bug homunculus, was in charge. It swelled and Clare's face crumpled. Eight eyes focused. Jaws cracked open and mouth parts tumbled out. Rows of jointed mandibles. Venom-injecting needle-fangs. A maw rimmed with clasping tentacles.

On the whole, I preferred to look at my face. Already, again, I couldn't remember what I looked like.

The guards noticed the Clare creature. The huge, swollen lower body – mostly spider-like, with sturdy armoured legs and a bloated puffball abdomen – lifted out of the pool. Spurts of congealing silk trailed from her spinnerets.

Clare was commingled with a *jorōgumo* – an arachnid vampire, the 'entangling bride' or 'whore spider'. Once, a creature like this dared challenge Yuki-Onna as queen of *yōkai*. It was a close thing. The Woman of the Snow vanquished the upstart by bringing winter in July. The freeze, with its attendant famine, lasted a human generation.

Stupidly brave, the militiamen attacked.

The spider-woman killed all four at once – juggling the screeching *kappa* and slicing through shells with bone scimitars. They stabbed and pounded valiantly, but wielded pins and needles against a threshing machine. When they slashed Clare's human arms and chest, red wounds healed over as soon as they were made. Someone got a torch and shoved it in one of her faces. Angry, she took it away and lobbed it across the room. It smashed against the wall and fell into a basket of rags. The quality of the screaming changed, as the aggressive yells of would-not-be-told nursery tyrants gave way to the terrified shrieks of tots stretched on the rack by a governess gone mad.

The *nunchaku kappa*'s head and limbs withdrew into his shell, leaving one of the silly sticks flapping out of the neck-hole. The *jorōgumo* extended a skewer-proboscis into the fore-aperture as if sticking a straw into a coconut. She sucked fluid and lumps of meat, throat expanding to swallow until loose bones rattled in the shell. With powerful mandibles, she cracked the *katana kappa*'s carapace and emptied a torrent of green blood over her faces, arms and breasts. She bit with multiple mouths and he came apart. Greedily, she tore into the *bo kappa* and the *sai kappa* with separate heads, simultaneously draining the last of the turtle musketeers. She dropped her leftovers into the water. A single *sai* stuck out of Clare's face. A white well-shaped arm slipped out of the hairy jumble of arachnid and human parts and plucked the trident like a splinter. After wiping Clare's mouth with the back of its hand, the arm was reabsorbed into the *yōkai*'s constantly shifting shape.

I had my scissors out and cut strings. I kicked bamboo poles loose.

The *inugami* cringed against the webbed-shut door and fouled himself.

Clare's head was its regular size again, but with feathery antennae. She turned to the dog-man and shot out an elastic tongue. He was speared through the throat, impaled to the door. The *inugami* weakly pawed the tubular tongue as his head expanded, eyes swelling, mouth forced open by something coming up in his throat. His face cracked like a hatching egg, then came apart like a jigsaw portrait on a pool of spreading gruel. For an instant, the turnkey's eyes stared in horror at each other... then his skull exploded. A thousand black spiders scuttled out from his severed windpipe, poured down his limp body and spread across walls and ceiling, leaving trails of criss-crossing web.

Death stones on the board!

Either Clare was going to kill me last – a palate cleanser after this gluttons' feast – or leave me here, covered in blood and webbing, looking guilty.

This wasn't just Clare gorging herself silly after a long sea voyage, surrendering to the base instincts which got her transported. She had been grievously violated and who knew what was left of her inside. Enough to still talk like a Casterbridge lass, but not enough to control the *jorōgumo*.

'Clare, can you hear me?' I called.

I kicked the front of my cage open.

Clare sucked in her tentacle tongue and gulped it back into her mouth. Her lips were scarlet with dog blood. Her eyes were compound – lots of little irises and pupils swirling in the whites. What must the world look like through them?

'Clare, it's Geneviève – Dr Dieudonné. From the ship. Remember me? Can you fight it? The spider. Can you change back?'

She laughed – out of her own mouth and the spider's, and a dozen others that ringed her neck and thorax.

'My lover, why would I want to?'

20

YŌKAI TOWN, DECEMBER 22, 1899 (CONTINUED)

Clare left me alive for Lord Kawataro. He'd believe a prisoner who could tear guards apart like soggy origami figures and bleed out every mother-loving *yōkai* in the room would then sit in an open cage waiting for an unkissable, four-foot-tall frog prince to dispense justice. The *kappa* magistrate would assume his sheer amphibian authority would put me in such a state of reverential awe I would meekly bare my neck for the executioner.

'*Heigh ho! says Anthony Rowley*,' I hummed.

I sounded hysterical, even to myself. Being found giggling and mad wouldn't help my case.

I considered escape options. The spider-woman – wider round the abdomen than is fashionable this season – got into the prison without using the obvious door. I leaned out of my dangling cage and plunged my head into cold, filthy water. I kept my mouth firmly shut but salt blood got in my eyes.

Through murk, I saw a new-made tunnel mouth. Rocks pushed out from the wall were strewn on the pool bed. The egress must lead to the open sea.

I climbed back into my cage and tried to dry my face with my wet sleeve. I rubbed my eyes and blinked away blood.

Body parts floated about. Webbing dripped from chains.

I could leave the castle. But I'd look even more like a murderer. The frame was obvious, but still subtler than I'd expect from Clare Mallinger. So, she had little say in the grand scheme of things. Her other head did the heavy thinking. The *jorōgumo* hatchling was a creature of Black Ocean. When Dru said one of us had died, she meant Clare – killed and eaten while she slept in her cocoon. What had spoken to me was an undigested lump – a parasite ghost. Majin must have had the egg slipped into Clare's crate. He had even signed his work, with the daubed wave – a sigil of ownership.

How long till anyone came to relieve the guards?

The torches went out one by one.

In the dark, I rehearsed arguments. Being sarcastic in a language you've not spoken in three hundred years is a challenge. Yes, My Lord Frogface, I assassinated everyone here without getting more than a few smears of blood on my person... then webbed the door shut from the outside with silk *pulled out of my ear*... and got back into the room by becoming intangible as autumn mist... Since then, I have sat quietly in my cage, digesting my supper, composing my last will and testament in anticipation of your righteous vengeance. I should like the orchestra to play *anything but* selections from *The Mikado* as I climb the scaffold... awaiting the sensation of a short, sharp shock from a cheap and chippy chopper on a big black block.

Stop being a goose, Gené, came a voice, *and pull your socks up.*

There was a light in the room. No, there was a light – and a *voice* – in my mind.

A funnel of gold fog whirled, lit from within. It did not make shadows. It did not illuminate the walls. I shut my eyes and still saw it.

This is something I can do, said Christina. *It's like astral projection... or the telephone. You can 'talk' back to me, if you like. Speak aloud. Or imagine you are speaking; that works best. If I concentrate, I 'hear' what you think. I can know what you know.*

I was alarmed.

Yes, you're alarmed. I know it's an imposition. Peeping at your most precious secret thoughts is like reading your diary.

The golden fog assumed the shape of Princess Casamassima. She was a sketch of herself – as if she were too impatient to fill in the details. Her eyes were wrong. One was red and dead, reproducing the injury suffered by her non-astral body. The other was a star, focal point of the illusion. She was…

Pepper's ghost, yes. The theatrical illusion. I know the principle. But that's your choice of how to see, how to interpret. Everyone sees me differently, and I see their ideas of me in their minds. You are about to think of looking-glasses and be wistful about your lost reflection – you've used that chestnut to fish for compliments for four hundred and sixty years. Just like Little Miss Big Mouth: 'Do you think I'm pretty, do you think I'm pretty, do you think I'm pretty?' Snip, snip, snip! Oh, and you've rediscovered death's blood and want to indulge your fondness for putting the knout across your own back by seeing yourself through the eyes of your 'victims'. Are you so presumptuous as to assume the cowl of the Grim Reaper and usurp the throne of Death? Geneviève, dear, you must grow up. I know you were sixteen and unkissed – nearly unkissed – when you turned, but just now we need you to be less of a mope. While you've been cooped up like a laying chicken, some of us have been busy with useful work.

I remembered Christina falling into lassitude to end a conversation.

You are overly sensitive. I awoke when needed, when Kostaki had to tell me about General Tea Leaf. And your mad murderess, Clare Mallinger…

The name sounded strange – if voiceless communication can have a sound or be any stranger. This works both ways, I realised with a frisson. While Christina hovered in my mind, I knew what *she* was thinking. Or at least the surface of what she was thinking. It was like a connection of death's blood.

You were going to say *Milliner* again, I told her. But I know better, so you *can't*. With this wonderful new ability, you can't tell people what they know not to be true. Ha. A telegraph wire that won't carry lies. I'm astounded, Christina. This will change the world…

I can't tell people what they believe *not to be true. A vital difference. But thank you for the insight. This is fresh for me too, a talent for the new century. I need you, people like you, to see what I can do.*

Because you can't.

That was a small, mean, cruel thought.

I'm sorry.

Don't apologise. You couldn't help it. People can't.

You hear the first thing people think of saying – the things they think better of?

That's not the worst of it, though it's sometimes embarrassing or revealing. It's when the first impulse is generous, but the considered response is uncharitable, cold or cruel. I see hearts harden, good intentions set aside.

I tried to suppress what I felt.

That's a fudge. You're trying to be calm and quiet in your head, not putting your emotions into words. It's vain to hang a mosquito net against me. Like not thinking about an elephant. The effort sounds a trumpet.

I imagined an elephant – standing on his hind legs, wearing a green suit of clothes and a bowtie, tipping his bowler hat with his trunk. When Charles realised our blood connection meant me knowing his thoughts, he devised mental exercises to cloak them. He'd remember the dullest afternoons, the most boring places (Basingstoke!), sermons and algebra.

Him again. Thinking of Mr Beauregard, are you? And a dressed-up elephant. I have no earthly idea what that's about.

I imagined myself shrugging.

That's a strange taste. It's your pawky French sense of humour, isn't it? I think I understand it now, but understanding doesn't help. What's funny?

Not you, Christina. Not now. Perhaps never.

You misunderstand the question. Funny? *What is it? I've never known. Quite a few people laugh at me. Women, mostly. Your friend Kate thought I was hilarious, until she didn't. And certain types of men. Homosexuals, often. They think I'm a scream. But I still don't see it. If I do this with more people—*

Do this *to* more people?

I'll get to the bottom of it. And your sense that this is a violation is noted. I shall take your perspective into account. Gené, from now on I won't do this uninvited. Not with you, not with anyone. I shall be a proper nosferatu. You will have to unlatch a window and bid me come in. This should be a miracle, not a new crime.

Christina's ability isn't a new form of wireless telegraphy. It's a new form of vampirism.

I could see her light. Her body was indistinct, like a candle flame. She clad herself in the impression of clothes. Her hair flowed into a dress. A shroud-like, vaguely Grecian gown.

We're both vampires.

I know, I'm sorry.

Please stop apologising. I have heard too many apologies. What I want now is for you to be someone with nothing to be sorry for.

I felt a buzzing-sparking behind my eyes. My hair crackled as if combed too often. Christina wasn't just light. In this form, she was *electricity*. Rather than shapeshift into a bat, she turned into lightning… no, into something more like a Marconi wave or a magnetic field. She really was the Vampire of the Future.

All very interesting, but I know already.

'Just thinking out loud,' I said, silently.

There you go again – humour. *You say something conventional, but in this context it's extraordinarily apt. I see how the pieces fit together… but not how it's supposed to be funny.*

It's not supposed to be anything. It's how I think.

Untidily? But with sparks, points of inspiration. Zig-zagging all over the board. You'll beat Mr Potato Head within the month. If you stick with Go, and don't — as is your wont — swan off to some other fancy.

Abura Sumashi.

You have troubled to learn his name. Interesting. I see now that you won't beat Mr Head Potato. You'll improve, rise to his level, then stop… he takes pride in Go mastery. In this place and with his shape, he has little else to be proud of. You won't strip him of that. It's a kindness, but also a stratagem. Losing a game that doesn't matter to you but matters to him. You're playing a larger game.

No I'm not! That's you looking into your own heart — not mine. I'm not *playing*, Christina, I'm just trying to live, as I've had to do for a very long time. Ah, I'm arguing with a fairy in my head. I've finally gone mad.

Dru. Does Christina do this to her? Is that why…

No. Drusilla is unreachable this way. Some people are. Not many, not if I know them well enough.

But she had tried.

Of course.

And who else do you 'speak' with?

Marit Verlaine. The spy.

I saw Verlaine in my mind because Christina put her there.

She's not a spy. She's an envoy. *Briefed by me, not your faithful Captain Kostaki and the stalwart Sergeant Dravot. I knew we needed someone to establish connections outside the walls. We need them more than intelligence, which is to be found everywhere if you know how to look. She—*

Speaks Japanese, I gathered. But hadn't let on — as Baron Higurashi didn't admit his English.

You were right about Majin. He conceals things from his superiors.

He doesn't believe he *has* superiors.

Your insights are on the mark, Gené. You saw him for what he is, which is why he picked you as scapegoat. For his purposes, Clare would do just as well on her own. I daresay that was the original idea. All he needs is that one of us, a Western vampire, take the blame for General Tea Leaf and these others, and more to come. He trusts the yōkai will turn on us. They are to be our executioners, and – why – if some of us are formidable enough to kill many of them before we're cut down, Majin will have no objections to that. Who dies doesn't matter, so long as plenty do. Just as in Suicide Garden. He wants this walled town, this vampire refuge, watered with blood. Immortal blood, even. He thinks it's magic.

I think it's magic.

No you don't, Gené. You can't believe in anything. Over centuries, you have seen too much and become an incurable agnostic. Lord Ruthven is the same. Majin is old too, like a vampire elder, but has climbed the other mountain – he believes in everything. As Dracula does. They both value blood sacrifice. The Lieutenant is feeding a dragon in the earth.

She had that image from me. I'd thought of hatching dragon eggs when Majin made the ground tremble.

She didn't even quibble at that.

Could she even know what was her own mind and what came from outside her head? *I* couldn't tell what was the Princess and what was me filling in the gaps for her. I had been worried about everyone else in a world with her in it. Might it be worse for her? Could she remain Christina Light with a tickertape in her skull feeding her scraps of other people's thoughts?

That's easy. I can turn it down or off. Like a gas-jet... no, before you think it, like an electric light.

She got distracted. New toys.

You distract me.

Sorry. No, *sorry.* Majin.

He thinks he's a sorcerer. I know he's a fool. I can stop him.

With my help?

With all of your help: Kostaki, Dravot, Verlaine, Drusilla, the

Monkey Minx, Mother Longneck, the Queen under the temple.

What?

She's why it's so cold there. You knew that. I got it from you.

Yuki-Onna?

Yes. Vampire Queen. The Witch of Winter. Lady Iceblood. Not seen much, but a presence. You thought of her – I couldn't. Unnatural cold is her aura, like my light. You wondered where she was – I'd never heard of her. You have it all in your head but, I understand now, you didn't put it together. *I had to. Maybe some of the puzzle tiles I needed came from others. Kostaki reads signs like a big game hunter. And Mother Longneck knew all along. The stretch between head and heart makes her hard to read. Anyway, your Woman of the Snow sleeps in a crypt under the temple. In her own block of ice. She is why Yōkai Town exists. Why Majin found it easy to bring and bind so many others. Subjects are drawn to the sleeping queen.*

This was why Christina was so impatient. She raced ahead all the time, peeved that it took so long for the rest of us to catch up.

I'd have realised eventually why the temple was so cold... just as I would – will? – improve at Go. But now I didn't have to. Christina had told me how the game would come out, so was it worth playing on?

Another thing she had told me before I realised it on my own is that I do not love, cannot love, Christina Light.

Are you finished? Do you want to apologise for hurting my feelings?

You have feelings?

The angel shimmered – a form of shrugging?

I couldn't tell how far away or near she was in the room. She had no size the way she had no substance. She was just there. A picture on fog.

We must have words with Lieutenant Majin. Through Verlaine, I have made new arrangements for us and he must be informed of them. Indeed, it is a condition of the treaty I have drawn up with Imperial Japan that we present the situation to Majin ourselves and ensure he abandons his own ambitions. Which are to level Tokyo with an enormous earthquake, by the way. That's what all the blood is about. And the magic. He is a bringer of catastrophe. It's to do with some old sorcerer.

Taira no Masakado.

That's the fellow. Tarara No Mascara. I say, is that funny? Is there a play on words there?

Almost.

Hah. Humour. 'Must try harder.' My governesses said that a lot.

They would be proud now.

When I turned vampire, I invited them all to a party to present my new self... and killed them. I don't believe I meant to share that. I am being indiscreet.

You will have to cultivate ways of holding things back.

So I shall. Thank you, Gené. I know you don't think I mean that, but I do.

The golden image flickered as she learned to communicate without it. She was getting round her limitations. The ones she seldom considered. Must I get round mine? Magic – really? I'd rather believe in Marconi waves.

Majin wants us to kill each other, but he's grown impatient. If we won't do the job for him, he'll send in his followers. He's not the only worshipper of his sleeping sorcerer.

I had a sense of great upheavals.

Come at once. To the temple. I need you.

She was gone. Drat. I had a lot of things to say to her. But I had more still to think about to myself. With Christina's light withdrawn from my darkness, I had the privacy and freedom to make a start.

The new Christina was blinding. She believed she couldn't be killed. She could flag down people's trains of thought. I didn't believe for a moment she'd honour her promise not to creep uninvited into open minds. Promises are limitations too. She'd abide by a treaty, but never keep a promise that didn't serve her interests. A princess cannot be held to the standards of lesser mortals. Lesser immortals, too.

Christina had never played Go or chess or any other game of strategy. As an electric ghost, she could best any master by leeching his thoughts. She should never be let near a card table. She could outdraw Doc Holliday at stud poker or in a gunfight.

The door was noisily battered in.

A scruffy vampire *ronin* I'd not seen before stepped through, swords in both hands. I tensed, wondering how I could fight this executioner with only teeth and claws.

Captain Kostaki followed the samurai, and laid a hand on his shoulder. He relaxed.

'My lady, this is Mr Bats,' said Kostaki. 'He is with us.'

I was relieved.

Behind the Captain and the *ronin*, Mr Yam held a chain attached to a yoke around Lord Kawataro's neck. The crack-plated *kappa* was aggrieved at this reversal. I was petty enough to be pleased. Three burly *tengu* accompanied the rescue party. They hauled my cage to the ledge and I jumped out.

'I've brought dry clothes,' said Kostaki.

Christina, in this one instance, was wrong. I could love Kostaki, if only for this moment.

21

YŌKAI TOWN, DECEMBER 22, 1899 (CONTINUED)

Kostaki wanted to give me Kawataro's Peacemaker but I picked up the *kappa* musketeer's *katana* instead. I held the sword one-handed to get used to its weight. I looked along its blooded, silvered blade.

A *tengu* snickered. I sliced through his topknot. Three feathers drifted downwards. I made a triple pass. Six smaller feathers danced apart in the air. I learned the Z-formation stroke from a Spanish *kitsune* in Old California. Then, Los Angeles was a pueblo bothered by slavers, bandits and Jesuits. *It's all in the wrist*, Diego taught me. A *flowing*, not a chopping. The *tengu* had the decency to nod nervous apology.

From my showing-off, Mr Bats got the measure of me. This is why I'm no soldier, gunfighter or card player. I give too much away. Professionals take notice. If I'd not let the parrot *yōkai*'s mockery sting me into childish display, my proficiency at arms might later have come as a surprise. As it was, everyone here knew I could do blade tricks. At least I'd kept my knowledge of anatomy quiet. Last time I was in Japan, I studied acupuncture. I know points on a human (or *yōkai*) body where the prod of a sword-tip can paralyse.

I sheathed the *katana* in its wooden *saya* and tucked it into the belt of Kostaki's old greatcoat, which I wore over the divided skirt (*umanori hakama*) and thigh-length jacket (*haori*) he had brought me. I kept my good boots, though they squelched with each step.

Kostaki pocketed the gun, though he was no firearms enthusiast. After centuries of honing close-combat skills, he wasn't best pleased that any idiot with ironmongery thought they could stop him from fifty feet away and get home for breakfast.

Kawataro reluctantly conducted us to a private jetty where his personal motor launch was tied. Kostaki had commandeered the boat and brought the *kappa* lord along to ensure safe passage. At the wheel was Popejoy, the Sailor Formerly Known as Hawk-Eye, my old patient from the *Macedonia*. He saluted me with his pipe.

From the jetty, we saw all Yōkai Town – the floating district and the notionally firmer ground. On dry land, buildings shook. Dust clouds spread. Flame spouted. Waves – radiating the wrong way, from the shore out to sea – disturbed boats, platforms and gambling barges.

'Earthquake?' I asked. 'Majin?'

Kostaki nodded. 'He's on top of his statue waving his hands like a sorcerer. A display of power. The ground is moving; not breaking, but *rolling*. Enough to cause panic, start fires, bring down paper houses. There are Black Ocean troops inside the walls, too – not helping. Majin is showing the *yōkai* they live only because he lets them. *If* he lets them. The Princess sent a deputation of *respectable* vampires to reason with the Lieutenant. All this is him telling her he's not to be reasoned with. She should have sent Dravot with a tiger rifle.'

Sitting in my big birdcage thinking up alphabets, I had missed several instalments of the serial. From Christina's mind telegraph, I knew she was less naïve about Majin than Kostaki thought. She was playing her own game, as usual. Stones on the board. And Dru's scorpions.

We all crowded into the launch. Kawataro instinctively sat in his highchair of command, but Yam dragged him to a hard bench. Mr Bats shouldered him into an uncomfortable corner.

'*Ak ak ak ak ak ak,*' said Popejoy.

I was worried the sailor had a lump in his throat I'd have to cut out. It was just his way of laughing.

As the launch headed for the shore, I asked questions. Had they seen the *jorōgumo* Clare? Did they know she'd killed General Nurarihyon?

'We found her box smashed open *from the inside*,' said Kostaki. 'And two more *yōkai* turned up dead. Both like the General, empty husks covered in sticky webs. One of ours was served the same way. Josef Cervenka, a Wallach supposedly cashiered from the Guard. No loss – he was Dracula's spy in our party.'

'Dracula had a spy in our party?'

'Not any more…'

'So everyone knows I didn't kill the General?'

'What people know and what they say are seldom the same. Kawataro insisted you were responsible for all the murders, including the ones committed while you were in his jail. He said you were conspiring with Mallinger. A good officer abandons a position if new intelligence is presented; Kawataro is a poor officer and prejudiced against anyone taller than him with a skin that isn't green. When his accusations were contradicted by facts, he took to screeching all foreign vampires should be beheaded. Except the Princess. As a gesture of mercy, he would take her for a concubine. She told him she'd rather be beheaded.'

'Good for her.'

'I've never said she lacked spirit.'

The *kappa* lord knew we were talking about him. He glared at us, sulking, tongue darting. Mr Yam and Mr Bats squeezed either side of him and he sat uncomfortably with his hands in his lap.

'Kawataro might itch to add a porcelain doll to his collection, but he has no use for the rest of us.'

'He keeps saying *gaijin* as if he's bitten a lemon.'

The first expression you learn in any language is their insult for everyone else. G-words: *gringo, goy, gweilo, giaour, gentile, gadje.*

'Kawataro had to be *reasoned* with,' said Kostaki.

The *kappa* rubbed his cracked head-plate. Mr Yam smiled threateningly at him. His mouth was crowded with sharp new teeth. Kawataro shrank even smaller and adjusted his yoke like a too-starched collar.

'Christina talked to me in my mind,' I admitted.

Kostaki shuddered. 'She worries me. Always has.'

'But she's our leader.'

'No one else will take the baton. I served under Dracula. I know what it is to have a monster on the horse at the head of the charge. Victory is assured, but so's the next battle and the one after that, and so on forever. A shining path in front and mass graves behind.'

'If we *don't* line up behind our fairy princess, what happens?'

Kostaki shrugged. The Captain understood the situation and was awaiting orders. From someone. He was a soldier, not a natural member of a steering committee. He'd do what had to be done and not chew it over till he got bellyache in his head.

'Where's Dravot?' I asked.

'Opening crates. The Princess said it was better to die awake. What she means is that she needs minions who understand what she's telling them to do.'

'That might upset the *yōkai*. So many of us – *kyuketsuki gaijin* – up and about.'

'The *yōkai* are *already* upset by the tremors, the sunken

266

boats, the spreading fires, the sucked-empty corpses, the giant webs—'

'The icebergs?' I suggested.

Kostaki looked away from me to see what I saw.

Jagged peaks rose from the land and sea. The water was turning to ice. Crested breakers curled and stiffened, becoming sculpted Hokusai waves. Hulls cracked as boats were caught by the sudden freeze. Sails frosted and became brittle. Lanterns went out. The ice spread rapidly, as whole sections of the sea became solid. With a wrench of the wheel, Popejoy turned the launch away from an advancing ice shelf. He sought a channel through the expanding floes. We zig-zagged, blocked at every turn. Kawataro, not appreciating he was no longer in command of his boat, gave the helmsman a tongue-lashing. Fortunately, Popejoy didn't understand threats of keel-hauling and yardarm-hanging in Japanese. Mr Bats elbowed the *kappa* to keep him quiet.

'Where did you find the samurai?' I asked Kostaki.

'He keeps his head down, usually, but was compelled to volunteer. A good one to have at your side. He grunts like a hired sword, but he's a man of honour. Watch out for his brother-in-darkness, though. A red-headed devil in black. He has his own ambitions. A priest of Satan, he calls himself Dorakuraya. He sees himself as the Dracula of the East.'

'I haven't kept up with Who's Who,' I said.

'Another to be wary of is Tsunako Shiki. A child-thing, and a little pest. She plays silly games at the worst possible time. Majin might have turned her loose, or she might be stirring up trouble for her own amusement.'

Kostaki was rattled. If we'd had more leisure time, that would have disturbed me. It took a lot to get under his skin. I committed the names to memory. Dorakuraya. Tsunako Shiki.

I looked back at Castle Kawataro. Ice swarmed over my former prison like white-clawed ivy. We were trapped by winter whatever course we took. We circled in a dwindling patch of sea.

'Never seen an iceberk ashores afore,' said Popejoy. 'Musk be me squinky eye.'

I looked landward and was astonished.

'There's that,' said Kostaki. 'It just appeared.'

A mountain sprouted on the site of the Temple of One Thousand Monsters, perhaps five hundred feet from base to tip. Christina had said this would happen, I remembered. Had she got it from Drusilla? The snow-dusted slopes glistened with reflected firelight, but it also had an inner glow. Steady, greenish light, like the bioluminescence of cavern fungus or deep-sea fish. A monument to pure cold. I imagined a frost-lashed eye near the summit. Yuki-Onna looking down on us all.

'Someone is waking up,' I told Kostaki. 'Not one of us.'

'The Ice Queen,' he said. 'I know.'

His inflexion was curious. Flat. Not himself. With his dead face, he was difficult to read. I had been relieved that he'd come to my rescue. Now I saw how all this affected him. He was out of his depth. If *he* was worried, only the profoundly ignorant could presume not to be. Everyone was changing. Clare. Christina. Kostaki. Except me. I was still stuck with who I was – though now I had a sword.

The ice mountain radiated cold the way a forest fire radiates heat. As water froze under our bow, the launch lifted out of the sea. We skidded across the ice, rudder snapped, motor choking. The propeller finally stuck and held like an anchor. The jolting halt flung us forwards in a jumble. *Tengu* squawked and Popejoy muttered nautical expressions. The boat tipped to one side. Only Mr Bats stayed upright. He had a cat's agility.

At first impression, I was taken with the *ronin*. A touch

of Captain Kronos in his deft swagger. With a shave and some pomade, he'd be a handsome devil, too.

We sorted ourselves out. I patted my belt to make sure I still had the *katana*.

It was no longer possible to say where the shore had been. The frozen sea and the frozen land were all one.

'We walk,' said Kostaki.

'Is the ice thick enough to support our weight?' asked Kawataro.

Yam tossed the *kappa* lord over the side. He landed with a thump. The ice cracked but did not break. Kawataro scrabbled to his webbed feet and made a run for it, forgetting the yoke. His chain stretched to its limit with a gallows crack. He fell, croaking and spluttering. *Tengu* laughed at their hated rival. I'd lost any desire to get my own back, even though the fool had treated me badly.

Yam smiled cruelly again. He had demonstrated the ice would hold us up. At least those of us who weighed as much as children. Which, mercifully, included me.

I swung out of the launch and dropped in a crouch, making the mistake of landing on all fours. My palms stung as I pushed my hands against naked ice. Bloody prints were left behind when I stood and steadied myself. I healed quickly but my skin tingled.

'Careful about that,' I said, as Kostaki climbed down beside me. 'It's what they call "black ice". It bites. You usually find it only in Arctic waters. It shouldn't be this cold here, even in winter.'

One of the *tengu* muttered about Yuki-Onna.

Obviously, the Queen of Unnatural Cold was making her presence known.

Yam hopped out of the boat and bounded away, dragging Kawataro as if the *kappa* were a fat dog reluctant to be walked by an energetic master. Wherever Yam landed, star-shaped cracks radiated. Water welled and froze instantly in flower-snowflake patterns. The air itself was icy. If I breathed in, beads formed in my mouth.

Kostaki wasn't happy on the frozen sea.

'Are you worried about crossing running water?' I asked.

'That's superstition. I don't like fighting on ice.'

'You're not elder enough to have fought with Alexander Nevsky in 1242.'

'No, *I* fought with Carl Gustav of Sweden in 1658. Transylvania was ill-used in that war. A monk with a rifle fired at Dracula's feet, ice cracked under his boots and the Prince took a chilly dunking.'

'What happened to the monk?'

Kostaki raised his forefinger in an impaling gesture.

'Kawataro's wrong,' I said. 'The cold would kill a warm body, but not a vampire. We'd just sleep until spring thaw.'

'I've been asleep. I didn't like it. Clare Mallinger was asleep. Look what happened to her.'

'I take your point.'

I also had my doubts about spring thaw. This wasn't natural winter. This was Yuki-Onna, doing what she'd done to see off that first *jorōgumo* challenger and damn the folks who had to scrabble through seventy years of famine.

Mr Bats slouch-walked across the ice, shifting his weight. He wore two swords, crossed on his back.

Kostaki caught me watching the *ronin* and shook his head. 'Mr *Bats*?' I asked Kostaki.

'When we asked him his name, he said "Sanjuro Komori". Thirty Bats. He was looking at a colony of bats. When the Princess asked him his name, he said "Sanjuro Tsurara". Thirty Icicles.'

'He was looking at icicles?'

'Yes. I prefer bats to icicles.'

'So, Mr Bats?'

'He answers to it.'

'It'll have to do then.'

Out on the ice, sound was muted. We saw fires raging ashore. Yuki-Onna's glacier tomb was swelling. We felt great movements in the ground, rippling through the sea like a tide. But we heard only small sounds. Seabirds cawing. Ice cracking and creaking. *Tengu* clucking. Kawataro's chain rattling. It was easy to think of Yōkai Town as a toy theatre. With each step, we got closer to the play.

Japanese Noh dramas seldom have happy endings. Suicide Garden was a light comedy compared to what lay ahead. Christina had convinced me of that. And, in a different way, so had Kostaki.

What was *wrong* with him?

We walked until we had frozen earth rather than frozen water under our boots. The ground shifted and ruptured. Everyone was wobbly on their legs, except Mr Bats – he leaned this way and that, deftly avoiding falling bricks and sidestepping upheavals. Yuki-Onna's cold struggled with the heat of Majin's dragon eggs. Creepers of ice bound dirt, stone and ghosts together against the forces straining to tear the town apart.

At a crossroads, a collapsed shrine was wreathed in cobwebs. A dead *abumi-guchi* priest, eyes popped and fur bloody, was stickily roped to the ruins. At the sight of this, the *tengu* and Popejoy made similar *ak ak ak ak ak ak* noises. They understood each other.

Clare had passed this way.

Rockets fired over the wall and exploded in the sky above Yōkai Town. Streamers and stars. Coloured streaks and fireballs. Delightful shapes. Fireworks (*hana-bi*) and artillery. The Imperial Army was providing lighting effects.

We saw the silhouette of the statue by the gate. I noticed its two faces – the one on its head and the one on its belt buckle – were not just rictus-grinning *oni*, but classical Greek masks of tragedy and comedy. That must be deliberate.

On top of the statue's helmet stood the man with the flapping military cape and the white hands. The sigils on his gloves burned scarlet.

Lieutenant Majin. The Demon Man.

22

YŌKAI TOWN, DECEMBER 22, 1899 (CONTINUED)

A robed giant – snaggle-toothed *oni* mask held in place by a Black Ocean headband – strode through a flock of *tengu*, swinging an implement that might have been Gargantua's croquet mallet. The flock scattered. The barrel-sized hammer flattened a head against the town wall. A *tengu*'s big dead eyes and broken beak stuck out of a smear of blood, bone and feathers.

I recognised the lesser demon as Kannuki.

The hulking imbecile was enjoying himself. He pounded the already-dead *tengu*'s chest, breaking ribs, bursting organs.

Kostaki pulled out Kawataro's Peacemaker and aimed at the red mask. The gun misfired and burst. Kostaki's sleeve caught light. Prejudice against firearms confirmed, the Carpathian threw the hot pieces away and patted out flames. The *kappa* lord didn't have anyone in his service to properly clean and maintain his American toy.

Kannuki stuck a real tongue through wood lips.

He raised the mallet above his head.

Mr Yam jumped out of shadows, pigtail streaming, robe flapping. He hopped back and forth around the giant – Kannuki's mean little eyes registered incomprehension – then sprung away again. The *jiang shi* had looped Kawataro's chain around the thug's neck. Kannuki would have to put his hammer down to disentangle himself. He didn't want to let go of his favourite killing tool.

Mr Yam crouched, embroidered robes trailing in the snow… then his thighs pumped like grasshopper legs, and the spring-heeled *jiang shi* launched into the air. The chain snapped tight. Kawataro was pulled off his feet, scream stopped short by his tugging yoke. Kannuki was lifted from the ground. His hammer fell from his grip. Hoisted on the chain, he hung – tense, and then limp. Blood trickled from his mask's mouth.

Tengu raised a racket of applause.

Kannuki wasn't finished. Slowly, he brought his hands up to the chain. His big, blunt fingers scrabbled against links that bit into his throat. Kawataro, gulping for air, was dragged towards him.

The chain parted. Kannuki dropped to the street…

Popejoy gave the giant a tremendous punch in the mask. Kannuki was felled. Bird-men danced around his head. His mask fell away in pieces. His nose was mashed, his teeth broken.

'Not so funny when it's *your* face getting flattened,' I said.

'I hates all palookas what ain't on the up and square,' explained Popejoy.

Kannuki grinned through blood. The *tengu* fell on him.

Since someone had to, I knelt by the dead giant, driving away the *tengu*. I untangled the chain before Kawataro choked to death. Furious at the unwanted kindness, he tried to spit-lash me with his tongue. I held up the *katana* and his extended member scraped across it. His eyes bulged with panic, until he realised the sword was sheathed. He'd licked the wood scabbard not the whisper-sharp silver blade.

Smaller *oni*-masked marauders patrolled Yōkai Town, stabbing, burning and shooting anyone or anything. They had licence. They counted bloody *coup* until they ran into *yōkai* who could defend themselves. Though many fell, dozens more poured through the gate.

Christina had said Majin wasn't the only worshipper of Taira no Masakado. This must be his congregation – drawn from the ranks of the Black Ocean Society, but devotees of older beliefs, committed not to empire but apocalypse. A Hokusai wave of black fire.

I saw Mr Bats surrounded and drew my *katana* to rush to his assistance. But before I had my sword fully unsheathed, the *ronin* put down eight men. With a sword in each hand, he made clean, simple, breathtaking passes. He sliced spines, stomachs, necks and legs. Heads flew free and lopped limbs fell twitching. The masked men died before they could yelp. The *ronin* stepped aside casually to evade clumsy counter-chops and fountains of warm blood.

Black Ocean assassins must chew something to hop themselves up before going into battle. When punctured, their veins spurted like firehoses. Arterial spray *can* decorate a room, but generally warm bodies don't function like fountains. The soldiers' blood pressure and heart rates must be dangerously elevated. Samurai berserkers who survived the fray – admittedly, none who got within a sword-length of Mr Bats would be on that list – were likely to succumb to seizures and strokes. Majin cared as little for their lives as ours.

My fangs were as sharp as the *katana*. So much blood spilled. Wasted.

The tremors grew in frequency and severity. With each jolt, my knees went watery. My sense of balance was thrown out of true. Crossing a street in the quake zone was like dancing over rolling logs in a raging torrent.

It was snowing – or else sheets calving off the ice mountain above Yuki-Onna's cold grave were becoming tiny wind-propelled splinters. My face stung but not just with snowflakes. I wiped my cheeks and looked into my hands to see a mess of blood and crushed blue butterflies. The air was full of avatars of Taira no Masakado. Kostaki waved his carrack, which just attracted attention. Individual butterflies could be cut apart. A swarm couldn't be stopped by any number of swords.

Kawataro caught butterflies with his tongue. More landed on his broad green face, covering his leaking plate, his eyes, his wide mouth, stopping up his ears, his mouth. He chewed and spat and choked.

I scraped butterflies out of my hair. They were inside my clothes, wings cutting like wafer-thin razors. Being killed by vampire butterflies sounds poetic. It feels less romantic.

One of the *tengu* stumbled and was buried in a drift of beating wings, which writhed and heaved and flew apart, leaving a picked-clean strew of delicate bird bones.

A blanket of intense heat fell on us from above.

For an instant, we were surrounded by tiny scraps of flame. Then the butterflies were a scatter of ashes on the snow.

The heat passed.

Above us flew O-Same. The woman of fire, with a *furisode* of exquisite overlapping flames. Wherever she flew, butterflies died.

I looked to Kostaki. He wiped blood and ash out of his eyes.

Now we could feel foolish. But what was left of the *tengu* was testimony to the cruel power of Taira no Masakado's tiniest followers.

'Hullo, chums,' said Drusilla, happening along as if out for a stroll. 'Lovely weather we're having, I *don't* think.'

She twirled a parasol with a painted eye – not Kasa-obake, but a paper imitation. Its spiked ferrule was bloodied.

'Have you met the Ice Lady?' Dru asked. 'She's ever-so ever-so. Christina found her in the basement. A cold customer.'

'Yuki-Onna?' I said.

'A chill wind,' Dru responded. 'Winter draws on... and so winter drawers on.' She lifted her skirt above her ankles to show woolly stockings.

An *oni*-soldier ran past, hands pressed to his neck. Blood streamers trailed from his bite wounds. He was yanked to a halt – like Kawataro at the end of his chain – and contorted, spine curving like a longbow. His bites were worried at by teeth I couldn't see. Flaps of skin tore. His eyes looked in terror through his mask and then went dull. Threads of blood spurted from his wound with each pulse. A woman-bubble glistened in firelight.

Suzan Arashi, the glass geisha.

For tantalising seconds, it was possible to appreciate the sculptured perfection of her nude form outlined by rivulets of fresh blood. Her face bloomed out of nowhere, an eyeless, beautiful mask of red gauze. When the soldier died, Suzan faded away. Fire behind her was distorted as if seen through a flawed window.

She padded on, leaving shallow prints of tiny feet.

'Does it ever bother you that you can't *do* anything?' Dru asked me, and perhaps also Kostaki. 'Turn to pudding or wake up shrubbery or see through walls? Weep tears of gold or breathe out steam? Memorise railway timetables before they're published? Play at being a big spider or a hive of bees?'

'Staying alive is enough of a talent for me,' I said.

'It's as well to be satisfied... but not too satisfied.'

Kostaki walked on, not wanting to be detained by conversation. As ever, I had a sense Dru was saying something important if only I troubled to listen and work out hidden clues.

Popejoy caught up with us. His striped shirt was stretched over his brawny torso.

'Hello, sailor,' said Dru, with naked interest.

Bashfully, he took off his hat and went *ak ak ak ak ak ak.*

Dru tittered at whatever he'd said with sly, flirty encouragement. 'I'll wager you've a sweetheart in every porthole,' she said.

'I loves to go swimmin' with all of the wimmin,' he admitted, bashfully.

Popejoy blushed, shifted his weight from one foot to the other and put his hat back on. His pipe-bowl glowed and smoke seeped out of his mangled mouth. Death Larsen's rope-end twisted his face like putty. I'd not been able to make him pretty. I trusted he wouldn't find a clean mirror and sue me for malpractice. At sea, before Larsen decided to take him down a peg or two, he was often assigned extra watch duty because of his horizon-scanning vision. He'd have to find something else to be known for. Thumping 'palookas' and making goo-goo eyes at weird thin women?

A rift opened nearby and a row of warehouses fell into it.

A few long-limbed *yōkai* tried to crawl out of the crack. Black Ocean soldiers kicked them back in again. The edge crumbled and collapsed, and masked men tumbled into the chasm too. Any dragon hatchling under Yōkai Town wouldn't go short of snacks.

'It's getting worse,' I told Kostaki. 'As you said it would. Everything here is trying to kill us.'

23

A KNIGHT TEMPLAR IV

Kostaki walked through a dream of battle.

Lady Geneviève was fetched. Not rescued – she would have been safer where she was. But fetched. The Princess needed her. And so did…

Kostaki could not remember who else needed the lady elder.

'Ten thousand years!'

A pikeman charged out of drifting smoke, yelling. Kostaki stepped aside and slashed the backs of the soldier's legs, cutting deeply into meat and muscle. His battle cry ascended sharply in pitch. He staggered on like a drunk, blood spurting through rush-matting puttees. His pike angled down and stuck into a pile of bricks. He slumped to his knees, the fight cut out of him.

'Ten thousand years,' he repeated.

Someone else killed the soldier. Goblin *yōkai* gathered to drink from his still-bleeding legs.

Kostaki's instinct was to kick the jackals away. There was no discipline here. No chain of command. Even without earthquakes and icebergs, the whole camp was the Teahouse of Blue Leaves at chucking-out time. Every man for himself and God against all. East against West, *yōkai* against vampires, Christian against Buddhist, bird-head against frog-face. If the Black Ocean murder party fell, the prisoners would obligingly kill each other. His job done for him, Majin only need step onto the field when the smoke cleared to finish off the wounded and execute the survivors.

Kostaki was ashamed to be part of such a leaderless rabble. Dracula would not have allowed this.

Had the enemy taken their queen? Cut off the guiding light?

Princess Casamassima was under ice. But not yet a ghost, for all her insubstantiality. She survived. She was not an ornamental vampire.

In Panama City, Kostaki had seen her *feed*.

On a busy street, just after moonrise, a sunburned *muchacho* approached, doffing a big gold hat and showing a big gold grin, humbly recommending a cantina where the lovely *señora* would be well served. Christina tried to step around the pavement pest, but Gold Hat jabbed a pistol into her back and shoved her into an alley. He pushed her face to a wall and tore a brooch from her lapel. Then he pressed his pelvis against her rump, reaching into her blouse. She hissed. '*Ay, Chihuahua*, Carlos,' exclaimed the bandit, 'the *gringa* is a spitfire! I *love* it when they bite!' Carlos – a pockmarked, tattooed brigand – held a razor to Kostaki's throat. Christina, slippery as a wet mink, twisted in Gold Hat's grip and slid long teeth into his jugular vein. Gulping his blood as if drinking from a fountain, she wound herself around her assailant. Kostaki heard his ribs pop in her python embrace. Razor Carlos scraped his useless blade across Kostaki's neck. Christina glowed as Gold Hat blanched. His skin, hair and moustache – even his eyes! – turned the colour of milk. The shining Princess didn't just blanch his flesh. His colourful patterned serape became white enough to be used as a flag of surrender. Kostaki spat blood in Razor Carlos's face. The cur ran off, calling to all the saints and the Virgin herself for protection. The Princess rose from her impromptu feast, and pinned her brooch back on. Briefly, through a film of blood, her front teeth flashed gold.

'I *love* it when they die,' she said. Death's blood turned her aura into a rainbow. They left the corpse in the alley for the dogs and the police. He had to talk the Princess out of visiting the recommended cantina. One bled-white cutpurse was of no consequence, but a roomful of albino dead would be ostentatious.

Since Panama, Christina Light had only become more formidable. In their first battle, Majin gave the Princess a red eye and a dead arm. That wouldn't deter her from a rematch. She got stronger and stranger with each passing night. Most shapeshifters were there and back but she was on and on and on.

He imagined her smiling with Lieutenant Majin's mouth. Wearing his cape, cap and gloves.

It could happen. A vampire like that was dangerous enough to respect.

She would be hard to break, but worth the effort. The Master would make Lady Light First among Three. With Geneviève and Miss Zark.

That hit Kostaki like a bullet. Not his thoughts – not a thing he would *ever* think – not as he was now.

But soon.

A cloaked bat-shadow fell on him. Not on the ground around him. But on his mind.

A human-headed pig trotted at speed down the road, panicked and grunting, a deep cut across his face and sword-slashes on his flanks.

The blood was *gold.*

No, red!

Gold.

He remembered Dorakuraya bleeding gold.

He remembered something else… something more.

A vision and a reward. Justice done, and a restitution.

Dracula had spoken with him. Had given him his orders.

He was a Templar, and he had his quest. By the square, by the level, by the plumb rule, by the compasses, by the all-seeing eye. A monster to be slain! A witch to be brought to heel. A master to serve. An empire to be won.

Was that real? He no longer knew. It might have come to him in delirium. After so long a fast, dreams were death's blood to him. An intoxicant, sustenance, a necessity.

Until further orders, this was his command – even if he commanded only himself.

More pikemen charged at him – screaming, clumsy, maddened. He executed them with precision, cutting so lightly it took moments for them to realise they were dead. Blood blossomed from arterial wounds, spurted from pricked veins, leaked from deep stabs. His fangs, sharp as his carrack, were unblooded – aching ivory, unsheathed and deadly. Still more masked enemies came. Samurai with swords, riflemen with fixed bayonets, knife-fighters. More skilled, just as easy to kill.

He shrugged off arrows. This was his old life again! His face was flecked with blood. His bald pate, his eyes, his nose, his mouth. His fangs sliced into his lips. He spat at the foe.

Beneath the fearsome demon masks were frightened men. Many turned and ran, but that did not save them. He cut spines as easily as throats.

As he fought, Kostaki sang one of Danny Dravot's songs:

> 'The Dragon's Son goes forth to war
> A golden crown to gain;
> His blood-red banner streams afar—
> Who follows in his train?
> To meet the tyrant's brandished steel

The lion's gory mane;
Who'll bow their heads the death to feel
To follow in his train.'

Others fell in behind him. Popejoy, sleeves rolled up, delighted to be in a real roughhouse fight at last. Miss Zark, twirling her dagger-topped umbrella. Invisible Suzan, a sensual *absence* in drifting smoke, triple-pronged *sai* floating at arm's length. Smiler Watson, grinning in terror, swearing at Pathans, not knowing Tokyo from the Khyber Pass. Arcueid Moonstar, with a slingshot and a drawstring bag of marbles. The defrocked priest Rikard Moritz, whirling a chain with the skill of a dock-front rowdy. Two parrot warriors, with trumpet-barrelled rifles. Meiko, his least favourite *bakeneko*, claws out, lasciviously eyeing him sideways. *Yōkai* Kostaki didn't know, vampires he did. An arrowhead formation, with him at the tip. Black Ocean marauders fell before them – tossed aside, stabbed or torn, unmasked, trampled underfoot, their 'ten thousand years' cut short.

His comrades sang their own battle songs, joining their voices with his.

'*I am what I am, and that's all that I am,*' sang Popejoy – cracking masks with punches to faces. Moritz sang the '*Dies Irae*'. Smiler knew Danny's song, with different words. Miss Zark counterpointed with a music hall song:

"Wotcher", all the neighbours cried—
"Who yer gonna meet, Bill,
Have yer bought the street, Bill?"
Laugh – I thought I should 'ave died…
Knock'd 'em in the Old Kent Road.'

Then the tip was separated from the arrow.

Kostaki was too far out in front. A rift cracked across the

street, cutting him off from the others. Meiko hissed and pointed in warning.

Kostaki turned to look, just as something slammed into his chest. He went down on his bad knee, momentarily blind from pain.

He looked up at a samurai in filthy patchwork robes. His mask was made from human faces – several men and at least one woman. A striped mane streamed from a skullcap of stitched-together scalps. His weapon was a slaughterhouse hammer.

Kostaki parried the next blow with the flat of his carrack, feeling the impact in his whole arm. He let the hammer's handle slide down the blade to get pinched in one of the hilt's crab-claws. With a practised wrist-twist, he yanked the sledgehammer from the samurai's hands.

The slaughterman produced two long skewers and aimed them at Kostaki's chest.

Then… the samurai toppled, felled like a tree.

Smoke and dust cleared. Kostaki saw a vampire standing over him, sword in hand.

Grinning, Komori stuck out his free paw and pulled Kostaki up.

Mr Bats had saved his life – or, at least, his face. The slaughterman wouldn't wear any of his skin.

Men and monsters fought all about him – which was he?

The earth bucked and more buildings fell.

He tasted blood on his lips – his own, and the men he'd killed. After so dry a season, even the merest pinch of blood was lightning behind his eyes.

He felt himself to be invincible. Here, at last, he admitted it. He was what he was.

A vampire. That was all.

He *thirsted*.

24

YŌKAI TOWN, DECEMBER 22, 1899 (CONTINUED)

The gate was open, but no one escaped through it. *Oni*-soldiers, more disciplined than the first wave, marched in with rifles. The wounded tried to crawl away, over the dead. They were crushed under boots or jabbed with pikes.

From the head of the statue, Lieutenant Majin conducted carnage. Phantom flames poured from his *seiman* sigils.

I was close enough to see his face. As smug and calm as at the Suicide Garden. He was *feeding* off this explosion of hatred, death and terror. He was just another vampire. Butterflies whirled about his cloak. Bullets evaporated before they reached him.

Skirmishes raged through the streets of Yōkai Town.

On Mermaid Ancestor Place, amid overturned carts and strews of trampled produce, I ran into an unmasked Black Ocean soldier bleeding so profusely my fangs pricked like nails. His hands pressed folds of flesh that used to be his cheeks.

Someone had given Kuchisake a pair of shears.

The soldier went down on his knees, pale from loss of blood, and hung his head. His traditional coiffure – shaven pate and tightly folded queue – came undone. Mr Yam bit into his hackles and sucked, chewing thick neck and shoulder muscles. The Black Ocean man dropped his hands away from his face and his jaw fell off.

Had he thought Kuchisake pretty or not?

Soused on death's blood, the *jiang shi* detached his mouth from the corpse and kicked it aside.

I got back on my feet and ran onwards.

I found Kostaki fighting, back to back with Mr Bats. Sabre and *katana*, against the Black Ocean. Vampires and *yōkai* alike rallied to their lead. Dancing *sai* − wielded by unseen hands − speared the breastbones of masked men, lifting them in the air then throwing them aside. We gained ground step by step, even as it buckled and shook under us. I parried sword strokes and tried to slip through the battle without getting hurt or hurting anyone.

Most of our party pressed towards the statue. I scouted back towards the temple. I assumed Christina would be there. She had, after all, sent for me. Dru came along, dragging her new beau. As she hung from his swollen arm, Popejoy punched *oni*-soldiers off their feet. We reached the lower slopes of the new-formed ice mountain. Higo Yanagi − woman and tree − were rooted, drifts piling up around them.

Popejoy thumped a big-bellied, fierce-bearded bruiser who was going after Higo with an axe. The willow woman sighed. The sailor had made another conquest. It must be the tight striped sleeveless shirt. Would Dru be jealous? Both ladies cosied up to their protector as he stood his ground. Popejoy squared off against the amateur lumberjack. He made fists the size of medicine balls. Sumo wrestling versus bare-knuckles pugilism. They traded mighty blows and fearsome holds. Popejoy got as good as he gave.

Higo watched the fight, hands knitted, eyes wide with adoration. Dru, distracted again, sat cross-legged on a drift and drew nursery pictures in the snow with a twig.

A happy cat. A house with a curl of smoke. A mouse with a sword. An angel, radiating lines like a picture-book sun. A big clock, nearing midnight. A dragon. Only Drusilla could discover a new craze in the middle of a war.

An unmasked, flushed *oni*-soldier came at her, swinging the bearded grappler's axe. She put up her hand in a halt gesture. Willow branches wrapped around the impudent art critic, hauling him off his feet. The axe fell from his grip. Higo's tendrils grew inside the soldier like cancerous weeds and poked out through his eyes. Dru used his blood to colour in her pictures.

'In the song about the Ice Lady, the most important person has no name,' said Dru.

I paid attention, which is what she wanted.

Dru used blood to dot the eyes of her mouse. 'The School Mouse,' she said. 'One of the ten tiny tots… and not here yet.'

She'd said something about a mousey girl once. Was this that again?

'Christina will have her to tea… or have her *for* tea. I can't quite make it out.'

I was suddenly surrounded by thin wooden-faced fellows with sticks. They looked like Mr Punches stretched out on a rack, long-featured as Easter Island statues, with spikes in their shoulders and nails through their hands. They danced on a web of wires. I glanced up, expecting a *jorōgumo* and saw a black-eyed little girl squatting in Higo's branches, just above the dangling dead man. Her dress was purple velvet and bright little buttons sparkled on her boots. Many layers of gauzy veil were wired into her explosion of ringlets.

Tsunako Shiki. Kostaki's little pest.

I cut wires, but not the right ones. Tsunako laughed as I was ensnared and strung up by her apparatus, a reluctant addition to her cast of puppets. My arms and legs jerked as she twitched wires. Using a throat-swizzle, she squawked, 'That's the way to do it!' and laughed – like merry hell clearing its throat – as her toys repeatedly hit me with batons. The blows weren't strong, but I hated this game. Kostaki was right about Tsunako. Dru saw my antics and, clapping with unhelpful delight, sang, '*Wiv a ladder and some glarses, you could see the 'Ackney Marshes, if it wasn't for the 'owses in between!*' Wires bit my wrists and ankles and I nearly dropped the *katana*. Then Tsunako lost interest and let me go. Puppets fell on the snow, unstrung and cracked. I crawled out of a tangle of wire.

What was that child playing at?

A roar went up near the statue. I was caught in a crowd of combatants, surging away from the ice mountain. I fought against the tide for a moment, but gave in and was swept towards the gate. Over the heads of angry *yōkai*, I saw Majin, outlined by red smoke – still in command.

Francesca Brysse and a cadre of bleary, just-out-of-the-coffin vampires tore through a guard post at the foot of the statue-tower, glutting themselves on Black Ocean blood. Sava Savanović's severed head was kicked out of the scrum, still wearing his knit cap. Few of our newly awakened refugees were armed with anything but teeth and nails. They had not expected to be hauled out of lassitude and tossed into a pitched battle. Some – our complement of murderers and barbarians – thrived on a chance to let loose the wolf in their hearts. They killed without conscience, fed without a second thought. Others – out of favour with Dracula because they strived to live as civilised men and women – would be crippled by shame if they survived the night. They had no choice but to act like monsters.

What had Christina told the awakened? If she'd told them anything.

Where *was* the Princess? I couldn't hear her in my head. We pushed *oni*-soldiers almost to the gate. Brysse rallied the vampires behind her. A mass break-out was possible until Majin decreed the lid be clamped on the kettle. Wheels turned and chains pulled the heavy gate shut. Masked men now trapped in Yōkai Town had a moment to panic before they were overwhelmed, disarmed and killed. Brysse howled in savage frustration, blood thick on her face like war paint.

I held back from murdering anyone not actively trying to kill me, but we were not all so fastidious and I made no great effort to stop anyone from slaughtering the fallen.

Lieutenant Majin watched, as happy to see his own troops killed as his enemies. All blood was an offering to Taira no Masakado.

Spears thrown at Majin turned aside. Even O-Same, who swooped from above, was repelled, bouncing off an unseen barrier like a rubber cannonball. Majin's palm-out halt gesture projected the *seiman* sign in the air in a puff of purple counter-flame. He was snug inside a protective sphere – invisible ectoplasmic armour.

Inside the head of the statue, Black Ocean soldiers were busy. The hinged green jaw ratcheted open. Boiling oil spewed.

I saw a mass of liquid pouring at me then it was blotted out and deflected. Oil rained all around me, hissing and steaming in the snow, but I didn't get gallons of fire full in the face.

I looked up and saw Kasa-obake hovering – umbrella stretched out in a perfect circle, exposing the flesh frills and bone struts of his underside. Oil spattered as he spun like a pinwheel. I would have to apologise to the *yōkai* for thinking him trivial.

Damn – Dru had been right again. 'An umbrella is always of use.'

Kasa-obake couldn't protect all of us. Bearing the brunt of the oil raised blisters on his corrugated hide.

I saluted him.

Someone with a rifle fired into the statue's head – *crack! crack! crack!* Majin's minions weren't shielded by his mystic barrier. Soldiers were dropped by sniper fire. The last of the oil dribbled from the mouth.

I looked back towards the ice mountain and saw Lady Oyotsu sitting demurely on an open palanquin, ornamental kimono arranged around her like a vast silk water lily. Her neck was extended to its fullest. High up on the white muscle tube – gripping with his knees and a loop of one arm, as if he'd shinned up a tree – was Sergeant Dravot, a high-powered hunting rifle steadied against his shoulder. He called out clipped instructions. The *yōkai* craned to give him sniper's vantage points. He fired through the eyeholes of the statue's demon-mask belt buckle. More minions were potted.

It was hard to tell from below, but I think the Abbess was smiling. She manages the expression by pinching her mouth into a circle and widening her eyes. This covers her blackened teeth. She has become self-conscious since noticing Westerners take her for a toothless crone. She craned and arched her neck like a rearing serpent to get a panoramic view of the battle. From his position, Dravot kept firing. Like Kasa-obake, Lady Oyotsu must have been grateful for a chance to demonstrate that her unique abilities were actually useful. Being patronised as harmless and amusing (if slightly disturbing) must pall after centuries.

An agile, barefoot vampire child in a white shift – someone I didn't know, lank-haired and of indeterminate sex, fresh out of the coffin – ascended the statue, swift as a monkey, finding hand and footholds where there shouldn't be any, dodging missiles. She slipped through the eyehole of the belt-buckle face. Flashes of gunfire and curtailed screams told of severe damage done to guards who had kept out of Dravot's range. A ragged torso, shoulder gushing where an arm was wrenched off, stuck out of the mouth hole like an impudent tongue, splashing the statue's skirt as if the mighty warrior had gorily wet himself.

Would the child – who was probably older than me – be able to get close to Majin?

The small creature crawled out of an epaulette hatch on the statue's shoulder, arms gloved and sleeved with blood.

With a mechanical creak, the statue raised a hand and shooed the vampire off its shoulder as if brushing away a fly.

Majin's statue had moved – stirring to a semblance of life! Instinctively, the besieging crowd moved back, making space around the tree-trunk legs. If the statue could swat, it could also stamp.

The child smacked against the wall and clung there, head shaking.

'Give that one a medal,' said Kostaki.

'As far as I'm concerned, she can have a Fabergé Easter egg,' I said.

The Captain had blood on his face. His coat was slashed, but any wounds had healed quickly. He saluted me with his carrack. For him, this – a battle – is home.

Majin didn't deign to notice the child batted away by the statue. He was busy conjuring his earthquake. His gloves were white flames – sigils picked out in a filament so red it imprinted on my vision if I closed my eyes.

More and more cracks ripped through the streets, rocks grinding together and pulling apart. Buildings toppled but the wall stayed firm. Seismic activity was confined to Yōkai Town. Surely it couldn't be contained?

In the end, didn't Majin want to bring down all Tokyo?

'Seek safe ground,' said Kostaki.

'Easier said than done,' said Whelpdale. He wore a samurai helmet and breastplate over checked tweeds. His arms were longer than usual and double-elbowed. 'That johnny up there's doing all this, you know.'

We did.

'Something ought to be done about his ruddy cheek!'

'All suggestions welcome,' I said.

Whelpdale thought about it for a moment, and had a bright idea. He opened his mouth to tell us his blindingly simple, inarguably practical solution for all our woes and raised his finger like a pedagogue about to impress the class with a brilliant observation... then was shocked into silence.

A scythe claw pinned his borrowed helmet to his skull, piercing his head. A black barb stuck out through the fleshy part of his jaw.

Whelpdale's eyes worked and he tried to speak. His cheeks fell to his jowls and his nose melted like wax.

The claw was withdrawn with a liquid scraping sound. Whelpdale dropped like a scarecrow stuffed with potatoes.

The claw came towards me. I met it with the *katana*.

Silver bit into chitin, but didn't slice through.

I looked up and saw Clare Mallinger's face peeping over the side of the *jorōgumo* body. She had grown considerably. Her original head was a pimple on the neck of the huge spider-head that swung around to stare at me. Its eyes popped and reformed as Sergeant Dravot put silver bullets into them. Tears of yellow ichor dripped onto black fur.

'Clare, you've let yourself go...'

She opened her mouth to show teeth as black as Lady Oyotsu's and breathed a cloud of butterflies. Was this where they came from? Though I knew it was useless, I made sword-passes that cut through the cloud.

O-Same was still drifting overhead. Tossed away by Majin, she concentrated on pulling her flame-body back together. Even she could be injured.

The butterflies bit.

The claw-tipped leg – not one of the spider's usual eight, but an extra, many-jointed limb grown just for stabbing –

darted again. Though half-blinded by little wings and my own blood, I warded it off.

The creature swept *yōkai* and vampires away from the statue. Majin saluted the spider-woman and the statue raised its fist in the same gesture.

The *jorōgumo* fed its mouths with many hands, stuffing in whomever it could reach – *yōkai*, vampires, *oni*-soldiers, corpses. Mr Bats and I tried chopping at its legs. It was like attacking an ancient oak with butter-knives. Clare burped more butterflies. Curtains of ropy web spurted from her spinnerets, congealing into strings sharp as piano wires. They fell on the unwary and tightened, cutting through skin and into bone.

The *jorōgumo* was the statue's beast. The giant warrior stretched its arm in a 'good dog' gesture, then waved.

The statue mimicked Majin's quake-conjuring gestures. Gears wrenched in its shoulders and elbows. It was a vast automaton, not some stone golem. Steam hissed from its epaulettes. It wasn't all machinery, though. There was magic too. *Seiman* seals glowed on its palms, heated from within.

Artillery might have helped – shells with silver shrapnel – or a Gatling gun. Even so, Whelpdale wouldn't have bet on victory. The *jorōgumo* must have a heart – most spiders do, even if only a simple tube that pumps haemolymph through arteries. And Clare's original heart must be plumbed into the new works somewhere. It would take a skilled speculative anatomist with an advanced degree in unusual vampire-spider physiology to locate any organ worth staking. And a more skilled sea-hunter than Death Larsen – who'd shoot basking seals before daring anything as chancy as hurling harpoons at leviathans – to stick a length of silver through it.

I'd given up on appealing to Clare's better nature, as rare an animal as safe ground in an earthquake. Little of the human – or even of the conventional vampire – was left in her.

Take a moment to mourn a monster. Ghastly as Clare Mallinger was, this was not what she had expected of life. A doctor's daughter in a dreary market town. Cruel in small, pointless ways. With the Ascendancy, she was turned by some thoughtless shapeshifter barely out of the grave himself, then tinkered with by her amateur scientist father. Set loose to fend for herself, she killed without compunction. Humiliated in court, she was clapped in a box and packed off out of sight of decent people, got rid of in the hold of a tramp steamer, despatched like a parcel with a false address written on it to be infected and eaten from the inside by an insect-minded alien, and subsumed into the grotesque body of whatever she was now. Without Dracula in the world, Clare would be organising parish theatricals, setting her cap at the squire's son, gloating over dresses fetched from London months before her local rivals had a hope of anything as fine. Objectively, she'd have been a horrible woman but she wouldn't have a death toll to rival Messalina and her heart wouldn't be lost inside an arachnid behemoth.

But only a moment's mourning.

I still had to do my best not to get killed by poor dear Clare.

25

YŌKAI TOWN, DECEMBER 22, 1899

I nipped in and out of the alleys around Mermaid Ancestor Place, seeking cover to avoid being speared like Whelpdale. Kostaki and Mr Bats were close behind me. Clare the Spider was galumphing to squeeze into the warren of the market and get at us. She was staying close to Majin. The ground still heaved. I choked on brick dust, dead butterflies, smuts and ice pellets. The fog had burned away, but acidic smoke puffed up through the cracks in the pavement. Dragon's breath. Slow death in case anyone survived the quick variety raining down on Yōkai Town.

In the market, stray *oni*-soldiers popped up like ducks in a shooting gallery, too terrified to be much of a threat. Bloody foam bubbled through the wooden rictus grins of their demon masks. The boost was wearing off and the side effects were increasing. Had they known they were suicide troops?

I huddled in the sweet-smelling wreck of an incense stall. Kostaki and Mr Bats joined me.

Why now?

While I was in a cage in Castle Kawataro, things had changed. Drastically.

Lieutenant Majin didn't decide to abandon slow Go just because I was locked up. Until tonight, his strategy was death by a thousand cuts. Myriad little moves to wear down the denizens of Yōkai Town with the odd orchestrated earthquake and session of the Suicide Garden to shake things up. And implanting the *jorōgumo* egg in Clare Mallinger? The plan was working, too. Others supported Lord Kawataro's cry of 'death to all foreign devils' and we'd got bets down on which of our coffined elders would declare themselves the Count of Yōkai Town and try to massacre or enslave our hosts. On our passenger list are appalling rivals of Dracula: Baron von Rysselbert, Constantin Tirescu – packed off to the Orient following botched coups.

Framing me was a typical Majin tactic. He didn't even need to kill anyone himself, because he could get us to tear out each other's throats. Painting me black made the rest of our informal council seem culpable. Taking an interpreter out of the situation increased the likelihood of drastic misunderstandings.

Oh, *wonderful*, I thought bitterly – realising, days too late, that Goké was Majin's plant in Yōkai Town. A qualified replacement for me, even with a horror-gob in his forehead, was too convenient for belief, though Christina (and I) believed it all the same. Where was the smarmy, two-faced – at least, two-mouthed – worm? When last mentioned, he was in the Princess's deputation of 'respectable vampires'. Much potential for mischief there. In the event, wasted.

So, why the sudden hurry?

All at once: a giant spider-woman on the rampage, armies of masked killers let loose, a major earthquake, a warrior statue come to life, and an iceberg erupting in the middle of the district.

Death stones on the board!

More death stones than regular pieces.

'How did this start?' I asked Kostaki. 'The battle?'

'With the temple,' he said. 'We had just found Josef

Cervenka, dead like the others. I was arguing with Kawataro about you. Then, a burst of light… and the ice was there. A pyramid, built out of nothing.'

That didn't sound right.

'Majin did something at the temple?' I prompted. 'To get to Yuki-Onna?'

Kostaki shook his head. Mr Bats cocked an ear to listen to us.

'Majin wasn't there,' said Kostaki. 'He didn't make the ice mountain. He didn't start the attack until after it appeared. It was…'

I suddenly had a headache and sunbursts behind my eyes.

I knew what Kostaki was about to say…

Christina Light.

Majin didn't have the initiative. He was *reacting*. To a move the Princess made. She was the one who had tried to get to Yuki-Onna.

The result – a frozen explosion in the temple – took the Demon Man by surprise, and rattled him so badly he changed his game. The Princess put the fear of *something* into him. With his connection to Taira no Masakado, Lieutenant Majin ought to be immune to ordinary terrors. At Jisatsu No Niwa, he showed no fear of Christina. He stood by and watched me fix her arm when he could have finished her off. Something had changed since then. Majin set about destroying Yōkai Town and its inhabitants because his hand was forced. He must be suddenly, unexpectedly vulnerable. We could use that to our advantage. This wasn't his plan. This was improvisation.

Majin wouldn't put on such a display unless both he and his scheme were in jeopardy.

So, we knew what he was afraid of. Whom he was afraid of.

The Woman of the Snow.

Majin could be defeated like that long-ago *jorōgumo*

pretender with an unnatural winter. He wouldn't be the only one to lose. The country would be a frozen waste. Millions would die while Yuki-Onna slept on, serene under ice. If I was right, we vampires would sleep too. I doubted we'd be left in peace. If we weren't to be trusted not to kill a country, we'd burn. Was this why Dracula let us leave – to visit disaster on territory he couldn't conquer? Was he confident we'd become some other tyrant's problem?

Majin wants us to kill each other, but he's grown impatient, Christina had said in my mind. *If we won't do the job for him, he'll pour water on the ants' nest. He's started already.*

So, she *could* lie via her astral telegraph by omission. When she reached me in my cage, she knew it was her fault.

I supposed I should be grateful she'd sent Kostaki to fetch me – though that was at least as much his idea as hers. However, she had impressed on me that I was needed.

She needed me. To get her – to get us all – out of her mess. And where was she?

My headache was getting worse, so I thought I'd soon find out.

'A big quake's coming,' said Kostaki. 'I feel it in my knee.'

He was right. Pots of scented powder rattled and spilled. Tiles slid from roofs and broke on the rippling street, exploding into shrapnel.

Racing the tremor – which brought down shacks and walls as we passed – I ran out of the market, with Kostaki and Mr Bats close behind. We emerged from the cover of Mermaid Ancestor Place into thick, pelting snow.

A blizzard whirled through Yōkai Town.

Streets and parks I'd learned to recognise were under rubble. But the spouting ice mountain – a *snowcano*, if you will! – towered over Yōkai Town. We strove to reach it.

We made slow going over glassy sheet ice, using sheathed

swords as walking sticks. I felt the cold through the soles of my boots. Frail elders, in peril of losing our footing and taking nasty falls. The unnatural ice was hard as stone.

Ahead was the Temple of One Thousand Monsters. If anything was left of it.

Higo Yanagi was a fixed landmark. Snow piled up to her lower branches. Her human aspect was buried to the waist. She cradled Popejoy, who was broken and bleeding badly. A concave wound where his nose used to stick out suggested someone had heaved a chunk of granite at his face. Higo brushed his forehead with delicate fronds. Her human tears trickled onto him.

'You should've seed the other guy,' he said, coughing up blood.

'He murderalised the palooka,' explained Higo, proudly.

Popejoy managed a ruined smile at the willow woman's improved vocabulary.

For a warm man, the sailor had battled the odds. He had *biffed* goblins, *boffed* ogres and *outroughed* incarnate death gods! He had tossed immortal fiends about like shanty-town goons.

But he was finished now.

Kostaki and Mr Bats guarded my back as I looked over the battered sailor. Higo was a good nurse. She'd bound the worst of his injuries with her sticky bark. I'm not surprised that helped. The new wonder cure aspirin – sold as patent medicine around the world – is essentially willow sap. Higo could take away Popejoy's pain. But she couldn't put him back together.

He was dying... unless...

It's something I've always shied away from. Yes – vampire blood (like mine) is a cure-all, providing the patient doesn't mind the side effects: turning vampire, and what's more becoming my get. In centuries of treating the sick and dying, I have had precious few cases worth that roll of the dice. And they've always come up snake eyes. The turn is most likely to be a success if the aspirant vampire is in the pink of health. The dying are by definition less promising subjects, though the extremity of their need inspires foolish attempts. I have no get, but that doesn't mean I haven't wanted to pass on the Dark Kiss. When I realised Annie Marriner had let me bleed her to the edge of a precipice, I tried to force her to suckle from my wrist. She wouldn't let a drop pass her lips, and died – leaving me with an ache I'll never be rid of.

The closest I came to 'success' was Lacourbe, riddled with Russian grapeshot during the 'Battle of the Italians' in 1812. I dripped measures of my blood into him. He began to recover and turn. His fangs came through, then he choked to true death as hundreds of fresh teeth sprouted inside his throat and worked their way out of his body like sharp pebbles. A few drops of my blood saved you, Charles, once, but you weren't beyond healing without turning. Popejoy, broken inside and out, would definitely die, so the question was… would he come back? Dare I risk the procedure that made Lacourbe's death so much worse than it need have been? I believed I had no choice.

I put my fingernail to my wrist. Higo pulled the sailor away from me, into her arms. She was possessive of her protector.

'I shall do it,' she said, curling catkins around the patient's head.

She bent over him – her face a delicate green, skin become supple bark. Her right cheek split, under her eye, and vampire sap welled up. Her tears washed the sticky blood into Popejoy's mouth.

She cooed at him, urging him to drink. He licked the bitter blood from his lips.

We couldn't stay to see if Higo managed to turn her sailor.

The lights in my head were buzzing.

* * *

Christina calling…

Hello, ma baby, hello, ma honey…

Yes, very clever. Ahoy-hoy.

…hello, my ragtime gal…

Even in your own head, you can't carry a tune.

…send me a kiss by wire…

Clever! Think-singing in Drusilla's voice. Though that whispery warble is well below Paris Opéra standard.

Please yourself and 'listen' carefully, because this is important…

'What's the matter?' Kostaki asked.

'Her,' I said.

Mr Bats didn't ask what either of us meant.

We were at the *torii* gate. Only the top tier was visible above the sloping snow. Before us was a transparent wall. The misty shape of the temple roof was discernible, as through a barrier of frozen fog.

The ice wasn't just transparent. *Translucent.* Greenish-white light fluctuated inside the ice mountain.

I was reminded of early public demonstrations of the miracle of electric lighting. The bulbs flared for brief seconds, then popped with the tinkle of glass splinters and the stench of sulphur. Glow-worm wiggles burned into everyone's eyes. No wonder inventors wore goggles.

The Princess was *in the ice*.

'Oh, Christina.'

Kostaki saw at once what I meant.

The mountain was immune to earthquake. No cracks appeared in the ice-front. Taira no Masakado could not breach the fortress of Yuki-Onna. Christina was buried with the Woman of the Snow. I supposed she was safe. For the moment.

Pain!

That's not a nice way to communicate. I preferred ragtime.

A prick rather than a stab!

Better.

It's not me, she said, in my head. *It's your Ice Queen. You must free her. I tried… but—*

Made a bollocks omelette of it.

Ha ha. You're doing Dravot. A new talent. Mental impersonation. Please pay attention to the task in hand.

How?

You're resourceful. You'll find a way.

You're resourceful too. Why haven't you?

I have. I have summoned you here.

Why me?

Because the Japanese interpreter you left behind did not *prove satisfactory.*

I've some ideas about that. I believe he's a spy.

Of course he's a spy. Do try to keep up, Gené. I knew that from the moment the gash-faced ghastly stepped into the temple. The white European suit. The useful abilities. The letters of recommendation. Mr Gokey Kokey was trying much too hard to get in with the inner circle. I have been in enough revolutionary factions to recognise an agent provocateur *when one starts agitating provocatively.*

Cowards flinch and traitors sneer.

They do, you know.

So, I am here. What do you want translated?

It's not so much a matter of translation, as of persuasion. *You'll have to enlist the aid of a certain person.*

I was momentarily blinded by a fireball in my head.

I knew whom Christina meant.

I resented being dragged from my nice safe prison just to pass on a message like a bell-boy… but I understood.

'We need to find O-Same,' I told Kostaki.

'Which one is that? The tart with the snip-snips? One of those no-face women?'

'No. The burning lady with the dress on fire.'

Kostaki rolled his eyes. 'Makes sense, I suppose. Here

we are, troubled by ice. Send for a big candle. Like the fire brigade backwards.'

I hadn't seen O-Same since Majin blocked her attack. She might be injured, or dead – though it wasn't likely. As Kostaki had said, a woman of flame would be difficult to get the better of.

A long-tailed monkey *yōkai* bounded out of the dark, sliding down the ice slope, gripping outcrops with all four hands, chittering a mix of panic and glee. An acre of pink gum was exposed at us, along with sharp teeth.

'She's not smiling,' said Kostaki. He and Mr Bats drew their swords.

I stood between my comrades and the hissing monkey. 'It's all right,' I said. 'I know her.'

I turned to Topazia Suzuki and tried to calm her.

Her dress had been torn off and her hair was unbound. Her fur was brittle with frost and patches had been pulled away – like the skin on my hands, from contact with black ice. She was startled and afraid. That brought out her animal spirit.

'Topazia,' I said, 'they're not going to hurt you.'

'I've heard that before – tonight. From people who hurt me.'

I took off the greatcoat Kostaki had given me and offered it to her. Gratefully, she wrapped it about her shivering body. Her prehensile tail poked out of the back.

'Have you seen O-Same?' I asked. 'We need her here.'

Topazia sat on the gate. She turned round several times, as if testing out a tree branch for comfort. She was still distracted.

'I could summon her,' she said. 'All women can.'

Kostaki looked at me and shrugged.

Topazia still wasn't sure about us. We had been chatting pleasantly in the dorm and she liked the funny woman with the cricket and the tiny hat but we were still foreign devils. And I was accused of killing General Nurarihyon.

'I didn't do that. It was the *jorōgumo*.'

Now she was scared of me because I saw into her thoughts. Thank you, Christina. The Princess had connected us. She was a mental telephone operator, too. If she survived beyond the end of the month, the twentieth century was going to be all about Christina Light. The Edison and Marconi companies might as well burn their patents.

Let's not get ahead of ourselves.

Topazia was chewing her tail.

Give her peanuts.

No need to be insulting.

'My friend is down there, under the ice, with Yuki-Onna,' I told Topazia. 'We need O-Same to get to them.'

Now you've given it away.

Topazia had an animal's instincts for whom to trust. She liked being told the truth. If more people said in plain words what they meant—

You sound like my governesses, again... remember what happened to them?

Topazia now looked concerned for me. I must seem mad, distracted by voices no one else could hear. I tried to be reassuring.

The monkey *yōkai* looked up to the stars and opened her mouth in a smile wider than Kuchisake's. She gave vent to a high-pitched shriek I could feel in my fangs. After a pause, she did it again. A jungle cry.

Kostaki and Mr Bats winced.

But we saw a rocket jet across the sky.

O-Same descended, raiment of flame spread like angel wings, arms folded inside flickering sleeves. Inside her fiery head was the outline of a black skull.

I bowed low and humbly petitioned the Torch of Meireki for help.

26

YŌKAI TOWN, DECEMBER 22, 1899 (CONTINUED)

O-Same pulled her long hands – more fire than flesh – out of her sleeves. Magic lantern dragons woven from interlacing flames reared on her *furisode*. Arms outstretched like a sleepwalker, she floated towards the glacier, radiating intense heat. Ice retreated from her touch. Her burning sleeves trailed the ground, dissipating snow. Wet green grass turned brown. Scalding steam hissed like hot ground mist.

Where O-Same pointed, a cave mouth appeared.

Open sesame.

A trickle became a flow, then a gush. We stood either side of the sudden stream. Melted ice seeped into snow like lemon poured over sugar. Where the run-off fanned, opaque white became crystal transparence then froze solid.

The cave became a tunnel. I saw the ice mountain was hollow. The Temple of One Thousand Monsters nestled under a frozen vaulted ceiling. Unmarred white thick on tile roofs. Clear icicle lanterns hanging from trees.

I walked through the tunnel. Kostaki and Mr Bats followed.

Topazia was reluctant, for a moment – then scuttled quickly after us, cringing as if she dreaded the touch of a shadow hand.

I fancied I saw the flap of dark that perturbed her. A stray garland from a shrine, tossed on the wind, burned to ashes in O-Same's heat-wake. Or something else?

The air inside the dome was tart and chill but there was no wind. The din of battle was muted. The ice shielded the temple from the strife around it.

I looked back. The tunnel filled in as quickly as it had opened. O-Same's firelight was distorted by the thick ice window.

I trusted our Burning Lady would still be there when we needed to get out.

Cross that bridge when you come to it.

Thank you, Christina. Did you learn *Uncle Satt's Sage Advice and Helpful Saws for Boys and Girls* off by heart?

I have seldom found advice to be sage and few saws are helpful.

We're inside the snow globe now. Where are you?

A snow globe? How apt! Like the hideous cheap ornaments uncles bring back from Brighton or Bologna. Why do uncles go to such places, do you suppose? Don't answer. Yes, this is very like one of those gewgaws. We are in the basement. The temple is the tip of a veritable underground castle. Lady Oyotsu omitted to mention that, but Drusilla knew it at once. Upsidesy-downsy, remember? Bootscraper above the front door? You can't miss the way in. The trapdoor is open. It's in the room you went to that time to fetch the stuff you didn't need for the person who didn't want it. Remember?

Yes.

I led our party through the white gardens to the courtyard.

By the dragon fountain, we found Abura Sumashi and Rui Wakasagi, stiff as statues. The unseeing eyes of the potato-headed and musician *yōkai* sparkled with frost. Their skins were lightly dusted with rime. Even Rui's angry purple bruise had turned arctic blue. The effect must have been instantaneous; the frozen folk weren't contorted with pain like the petrified of Pompeii. Abura Sumashi was caught scratching behind his ear. Rui's fingers were pressed to the strings of a *samisen*.

I didn't know if the *yōkai* were still alive.

Topazia looked closely. With her tail, she touched the grotesquely bulbous half of Rui's face. Skin flaked from the poison bruise like very old paint. Topazia pulled her tail back.

'It stings,' she said.

I showed her my healed hands. 'Careful not to touch anything else,' I said.

Topazia chewed her lips and nodded.

I fancied Rui's eye – the one not swallowed by the mushroom growth of her disfigurement – glinted with anger. She might be still alive.

In agitated eagerness to avoid further touching Rui, Topazia elbowed Abura Sumashi. His arm came neatly off at the elbow and fell—

With lightning speed, Mr Bats caught the limb. He gently set it down.

'Well played,' I said. 'He might need that later.'

Mr Bats nodded at me. He nods expressively. This was a 'thanks for the compliment' nod. Usefully distinct from a 'touch that sword and die' nod.

We walked to the temple.

The screens were grouted shut by ice. Kostaki and Mr Bats kicked them in. We pushed through into the building.

Everything inside was coated in a thin layer of ice. The glacé surface was curiously tempting. Was it sweet to taste? Fruit glistened in bowls like sinister candies in the gingerbread house that tempted Hansel and Gretel.

Christina whistled the 'Dance of the Sugar Plum Fairy' in my mind.

Yes, very apt. Just what I was thinking. A sweet shop in a fairy tale.

The shaved, flavoured ice they sell outside the Colosseum is made from the dirtiest water and the foulest peaches. It's a miracle more tourists don't get the grippe and die of it.

We advanced cautiously. Statue people around. The monk Ryomen, both faces still for once. Aosagibi, the heron samurai, one leg drawn up. The miniature twin singers, sat in dollhouse chairs, glazed like Dresden figurines. Dimitri Denatos, one of our oilier refugees, in a pose of supplication. Zhang Fa, frosted hair knitted around her like a wickerwork egg, wisely not listening to him.

I didn't know Denatos was awake.

He's not the worst of them.

I saw what Christina meant.

In an alcove − on a futon piled with hard, cold, shiny cushions − we found Baron Carl von Rysselbert, putative father-and-furtherer of a line of Nietzschean overmen. His elite corps of fanatic get was to drag Dracula from his throne and boost him to the exalted status which was his destiny. The pretender went as far as engaging a Savile Row tailor to run up a gross of the utilitarian one-piece uniforms he had personally designed for his as-yet-unturned disciples. If he wanted his crusade of self-elevation to succeed, he should have paid his bills. But the blue-eyed, mighty-thewed overman cares nought for tradesmen and book-keepers. After repeated demands that the Baron's account be settled were ignored, Messrs H. Huntsman & Sons turned him in to Special Branch as a seditious wrong 'un. Somewhere, Nietzsche must write 'whoever fights monsters should see to it that in the process he does not lose his shirt… for if you gaze long enough into the abyss, your shilling will run out and your must needs shove another in the slot.' Von Rysselbert was earmarked as one of our likely future troublemakers. We could scratch him off that list.

The elder had swooped on the wrong woman.

Von Rysselbert's arms were tied with a familiar obi. He looked up at the Mantis, showing her a gargoyle face of terror. A film of ice sealed his screaming mouth, coating his dagger-fangs. The Mantis, grimly satisfied under her ice-mask, was savagely sticking a three-pronged hairpin between his ribs. Gouts of blood from the Baron's bursting heart were frozen between them like blooms of red coral. Vampire and murderess, welded by the cold in a tableau of death.

'I warned von Rysselbert off the local girls,' Kostaki said. 'He would not be told.'

'The Mantis is one of the few warm women in Yōkai Town,' I observed. 'We should have known she'd be bait to our more foolish, bloodthirsty shipmates and what would become of vampires who bit the hook.'

'She's not so warm now,' said Kostaki.

'You know what I mean.'

Mr Bats tapped the nape of the Mantis's neck with his *wakizashi*.

With a noise I'll never forget, the tableau – von Rysselbert, the cloak spread beneath him, the fascinating blood formation, the Mantis, her splayed kimono, even the *pillows* – cracked into a hundred thousand shards. Flesh, blood and cloth granulated, and collapsed into a strew of gravel, which poured out of the alcove.

I looked at Mr Bats, disapproving.

Governessy, again.

In my mind, I told Christina to go away – using mediaeval French idioms her tutors were unlikely to have used, at least not to her face.

I don't have to know what all that means to know it's rude, Gené.

Von Rysselbert and the Mantis were both murderers, many times over. The Baron was the worse villain. He chose of his own free will to be an utter brute and spat half-understood German aphorisms whenever his behaviour was called into question. The Mantis, whatever her name had been, couldn't help herself. Abused by some men, she took revenge on guilty and innocent alike. From their *liebestod* pose, the vampire was dead before the freeze. The mad woman was painlessly, mercifully killed by it.

Still, if they'd kept apart, one or the other or both might have lived through Christmas – three days from now, not that anyone has given the holidays much thought – and survived to see a new year, the Monday after next.

Kostaki has a Christmas present for you. Shall I tell you what it is?

That's a horrid thing to do. And childish. I thought you were the grown-up in this party?

In our secret selves, we're all children. Ladies and lords of the nursery. We want toys and candy and treats. I've learned that firsthand, visiting many, many minds. I have decided to take your advice and not struggle against my nature.

Don't blame me!

So you haven't got him anything? How embarrassing.

I looked at Kostaki, who was waiting patiently amid the glittering rubble of two dead people while I had a mental conversation with the Princess. At least he knew I wasn't mad.

'Christina says…'

This will be charming.

'… the trapdoor's in the dispensary.'

More romantic words ne'er were spoken.

Stepping around the mess, I led the way again.

The dispensary was more frigid even than the rest of the building. Draperies of ice hung from shelves. Breathing was painful, like inhaling little knives. The temple stocks a wide variety of dried herbs of a medicinal nature. The majority are non-lethal. Much of Yōkai Town's trade income derives from potions and salves brewed by Lady Oyotsu and her initiates. The Abbess also keeps a large selection of teas and blends of teas. The late General Nurarihyon was far from Yōkai Town's only *chai* addict. Tea ceremonies are important social and spiritual rituals here.

Kurozuka, a toad-tongued witch who serves as pharmacist, was cross-legged on her tatami mat. Her unkempt appearance earned her the nickname 'demon hag' (*onibaba*). The story goes that she used to swear by 'liver of unborn baby' as a cure-all. Try filling that prescription at Boots the Chemist. Understandably, she was unsuccessful in her original specialism. Few sent for a midwife who was as likely to harvest quack remedies from a foetus as deliver a healthy child. I'd trust her over Professor Cataflaque or Dr Gheria on a non-obstetrics case. She hadn't vivisected anyone in living memory.

Now, Kurozuka looked like a clumsily decorated cake. She was more thickly iced than others we had seen.

The nearer we were to Yuki-Onna, the colder it got.

'Ha,' said Kostaki, as something caught his eye. 'Dravot said as much and I didn't believe him.'

He pointed to a row of tins of Lipton's Yellow Label tea.

'"Ancient infusions gathered from haunted Aokigahara forests on the slopes of Mount Fuji", my eye!' he said. 'We've come a long way for a brew that can be had at any stall in London.'

Mr Bats and Topazia were puzzled by this.

Kostaki took a tin, rattled it, and slipped it in his pocket. 'For Dravot,' he explained.

Of course it was Christmas in three days. What with one thing and another, I'd not thought of the holiday season. What do you get for the man who has given everything up? *Sword oil. He'll look after the weapon even if he neglects himself.* Good grief, Christina – that makes actual sense. *You are welcome.*

Beyond Kurozuka's mat, a movable cabinet was shifted

out of its place so a trapdoor could be lifted. Stone steps, shiny with ice, led down into darkness. Somewhere, a greenish light burned.

Yes, this way.

Thank you, Christina.

I turned to advise caution in descending, but illustrated my point by slipping. I tumbled headlong into the room beneath the dispensary.

Kostaki followed, surefooted, and helped me up. Topazia skittered down, using all her hands and her tail. Mr Bats took up the rear.

Kostaki struck a flint on his tinderbox. He whistled at what came to light. The flame went out, but all four of us were vampires. We see in the dark. In my case, only reasonably well. But enough to get by.

We were in a large stone-clad room at a junction of several passages. Stairs led down in all directions. Using a bat trick, I shouted out 'white rabbits'. The echoes lasted a full minute. As Christina said and Drusilla had known, the temple was the tip of an underground castle. Crypts and catacombs feature prominently in vampire architecture. Warm kings look down from towers, palaces and skyscrapers – our tyrants prefer lairs, tombs and fortified cellars.

How had all this survived the earthquakes?

Mystic wards and enchantments.

Not Lipton's.

Don't be facetious. Follow my 'voice'.

We can see light. I suppose that's you.

Ego lux.

That you are, Princess.

'This way,' I told the others.

Without falling again, I led the party down a sloping path.

The freeze here had been more direct and fatal. We

walked through several drifts of multi-coloured ice chips and – thanks to what we'd seen upstairs – knew what they were. From one pile, Topazia took a flintlock pistol. Its powder was probably an icy paste. However, the relic – a European weapon, imported centuries ago – made her feel safer. She could probably do an injury by throwing her good luck charm at an enemy.

Approaching a personage like Yuki-Onna – Dracula comes inevitably to mind, and very few others – is like walking into a maelstrom or an inferno. Or the heart of a star. They shine such eternal light or exert such gravitational pull that everything else is dull, shrivelled or crushed out of shape. Your senses betray you and – even without Christina *talking very precisely* in your head – you feel you're displaced in yourself. For most of your life, you wonder if you're imagining them but, nearing their presence, you start to wonder whether they're imagining you.

As we descended, I felt shadows, listened for footsteps, fancied movements in the corner of my eye. If I paused, everything fell back into place but I couldn't suppress the thought that a threat had darted back into shadows and was watching with cold eyes.

We all kept looking around, imagining something following us or lying in wait. Topazia clung to her pistol, pointing it this way and that to ward off terror. She was with us because she was more afraid of being left behind than going on. Kostaki held up his hand, as if expecting a strangling loop to snag him by the neck. I was sure we had passed through the wall of ice alone, then remembered the shadow that spooked Topazia. Perhaps a bat had fluttered into the snow-globe after us, or perhaps... not a bat.

'Look at the ice on the walls,' Kostaki said. 'You can see the direction of the blast out from where we're headed.'

The tunnel narrowed as the ice thickened. We made slower progress, wading through shin-deep snow. No, not snow – this hadn't fallen, but manifested out of moisture in the air as dew becomes frost. There was an unnatural amount of ice powder.

Yuki-Onna made it – the way Christina made light.

The Woman of the Snow *inhabited* cold.

Even more bluntly than traditional *nosferatu*, she fed off the warm. Drawn to body heat, she could drain it all at once with a sharp intake of breath. If she took her time, she exhaled a freezing mist that slowly robbed her victims of all trace of warmth. She drank blood too, but liked it colder than body temperature, sucking salt slush from the veins of those unfortunate enough to attract attention.

The story was that she had a sentimental streak. Once – maybe many times with different men, for we all repeat our stories of love and loss – Yuki-Onna chanced on two woodcutters lost in the mountains, an old man and his young apprentice, both near death from hypothermia. She fell on the dotard like a blanket of snow, sucking his last drops of life. However, moved by the lad's comeliness, she spared him on the condition he never tell anyone of their meeting. She didn't want it getting about that she was capable of mercy. Storytellers are discreet, but the implication is that the bargain is sealed with more than a handshake. Later, the mortal meets and marries a (suspiciously) normal woman, who bears him many healthy children (the figure ten is mentioned) but gives the game away by not ageing a day in many years. Eventually, it strikes the handsome (but dim) husband that his unnaturally youthful wife looks exactly like the beautiful *yōkai* in the mountains, whom he now writes off as a feverish hallucination. Of course, the fool doesn't keep mum and recounts the long-ago 'dream' to his wife, who either kills him as promised or (more often) disappears, taking her children with her. There's a slim but important wedge of difference between 'never tell anyone' and 'never tell anyone *else*'. After all, Yuki-Onna knew all about the woodcutter's first meeting with her by virtue of being there at the time.

The Lilliput Twins have several songs about Yuki-Onna in their repertoire. One tune is distractingly close to 'Tit-Willow'. All one thousand of the Temple's monsters have their own airs. There'll be songs about us soon. 'Little Miss Mallinger Swallowed a Spider', 'How Do You Solve a Problem Like Drusilla?' There's already a ditty about the Carpathian Guard but Kostaki gets sulky if it's so much as hummed.

You're distracted, again. Concentrate.

There was something about the songs. Drusilla said the most important person in the song about the Ice Lady isn't named.

The husband is called Minokichi.

Not him, Christina. Dru meant one of the children.

The School Mouse.

Yes, that's what she said. She also says 'the mousey girl' sometimes. I've no idea what that means.

Join the club. Where is Drusilla, by the way?

We got separated in the battle.

She'll be fine.

Only Christina Light would react to the news that a close friend had disappeared in the smoke of battle by assuming 'she'll be fine'.

I 'heard' that.

I meant you to. I think.

You also believe me, you hypocrite.

Yes, I admitted. Dru will be fine. It's in her nature.

Here we were, puzzling over her footnote to a sad song. Knowing it was important, not knowing why. As ever.

We went down staircases. The chambers became less like rooms and more like caves. Clumps of frozen bats hung among stalactites like preserved fruit.

Mr Bats/Mr Icicles must feel welcome.

He was keeping up the rear. I thought he was looking around, as if expecting an attack… no, as if expecting *someone*. Good that he was on his toes. In this labyrinth, I trusted his instincts more than my own. Kostaki recruited wisely. Where had he been hiding the vampire samurai? Mr Bats was *nosferatu*, not *kyuketsuki* – a European bloodline. Had Dracula sent out missionaries to spread his taint to the Orient?

That's a surprisingly good guess.

The lights in the ice pulsated. A hundred candle points inside slabs clear as glass, like some species of Christmas ornament.

We came to a huge wooden door, quarter-way open. Beyond burned a light so bright it hurt my eyes. The light of seven suns – radiating all the colours of the rainbow.

I took an iron ring and tugged. The door wouldn't be pulled further open. It was stopped by solid ice – the floor was under a foot-thick skating rink surface.

I slipped round the door and into the chamber of light. It was the size and shape of a cathedral, with galleries of intricate ice-forms. The ceiling was so high that frost flaking off it fell like steady snow.

Topazia followed me, easily squeezing through the gap. Kostaki and Mr Bats had a harder time of it, and had to fiddle with swords and come at it sideways.

My eyes adjusted – *almost*. I wished I had my dark glasses with me. Unworn since we came to this fogbound district, they were still packed in my trunk.

Hanging in front of us was Christina Light.

She was behind a wall of ice… no, she was *inside* a wall of ice. She was mostly light, but held her shape. She retained just enough physical substance to be trapped. The freeze had blasted her off her feet and she floated dramatically, hair streaming behind her, skin glowing through her clothes. Only her bloodied eye was dull. The rest of her *shone*.

…O wad some Power the giftie gie us to see oursels as ithers see us.
You're welcome.
Now you see me, get me out…
She wasn't like O-Same. She was light, not fire.
Not yet.
You've tried to melt your way free, then.
I can set fires — but I need a magnifying glass to focus. I was hoping this ice would serve as a burning lens, but no, that would be too convenient.
We were so struck by the angel in the ice it took a moment before any of us noticed the other woman present.
Then Topazia made a monkey sound.
We all turned to look.
Yuki-Onna lay in an open tomb. It was like a sunken stone bath, filled with agitated ice. White, murderous razor-mist spilled over the rim.
This close to her, even vampire breath froze.
She wore a frosted gossamer shift. Her face was beautiful, if oval for a Japanese woman. She lay on her own unbound hair, which reached her ankles. It might have been a trick of the ice, but she seemed ten feet long. Her eyes were open. She was painful to look at.
Yes, yes, she's a wonder and a marvel, now—
Oh shut up, Christina.
I've been looking at the minx for hours. The awe wears off.
Really?
Since you mention it, no… but what use is awe?
Kostaki and Mr Bats stood either side of Yuki-Onna's bier. Topazia skipped up and crouched on the rim, gingerly probing an ice spout with her tail.
She smiled, genuinely — not in an aggression display.
'My Queen,' she said.
It hit me then that I'd been here before, in a situation like this, at least. A summons to a royal palace, a stalwart adventurer at my side, a captive queen, in need of freeing

from a curse, a secret mission, the fate of an empire in the balance, a flash of silver knife.

A flash of silver knife!

It was so cold in the chamber that I didn't feel the sword slide into my side. The sting came as the blade poked out of my ribs, tearing cloth.

Topazia screeched!

I half-turned – my side burned with a pain I'd seldom felt. The sword was slowly drawn out of me. I clamped my hands over my wounds. Blood welled and gushed over my fingers. I had been a flesh scabbard for a few seconds. One of my fangs jutted – another jolt of agony.

Through red, wavery ice – illuminated by an angry rainbow radiating from Christina Light – I saw Captain Kostaki.

His sword was slick with my blood.

Behind him stood a shadow. A Japanese vampire with red hair. A white scarf against a black vestment. An inverted cross. A hand on Kostaki's shoulder, with diamond-shaped nails.

My knees gave out and I fell.

27

A KNIGHT TEMPLAR V

*T*his is my command,' the Master had said, 'that you, Captain Kostaki, seek out the Yuki-Onna. Break through her defences, slay her protectors, penetrate her lair. In a cave of ice deep under her palace is a coffin. There you will find the Winter Witch. She has the face of Medusa, but you must look upon it without turning to stone. Strike her breast with iron so that her body shatters like ice in the spring. Then pull out her heart and bring me that so I may drink from it.'

As it had been decreed so had he done.

Kostaki looked at the blood trickling on the length of his black carrack. It was fascinating. Each droplet was alive, a tiny fish or insect. They broke apart and rolled back together, gathering into drips. He wanted to touch his tongue to the silvered steel... the taste would be worth the poison sting. For it was the only blood in the world, the blood he craved... the blood he *deserved*.

The witch's familiar fell, pierced in the side.

She was negligible – an obstacle, not an enemy. A stone to be removed from the path, not a foe worth the fight. Yet her blood, pouring through slits in her clothes, was an elixir, an ocean that called him to sail, a sky full of stars, a banquet laid out.

No – he would not falter! He was near the fulfilment of

his mission. Close to glory, to regaining the Master's favour. Promises had been made, on both sides. After the victory would come the reward. Restoration. Elevation. Ascendance.

A hand was on his shoulder, guiding him. A voice in his head whispered.

Strike her breast with iron… pull out her heart.

The familiar scrabbled at his boots, blood still leaking from her. She spoke, but he didn't hear. He was not to pay heed to her lies. A Templar was beyond corruption.

His comrades would approve. His Lodge Brothers. He heard them singing.

> *'He who would valiant be*
> *'Gainst all disaster*
> *Let him in constancy*
> *Follow the Master*
> *There's no discouragement*
> *Shall make him once relent*
> *His first avowed intent*
> *To be a Templar.'*

He took strength. His vows were heated armour, pressed to his bare flesh, mortifying him, rendering him pure. Everything but faith and honour and purpose was burned away. He was a knife, a sword, a fang.

He stood over the Winter Witch. She was buried in coals of ice. Frosty breath rose like smoke. He looked at her face – a white flame under the pool of jagged, broken ice – and was not turned to glass.

His faith gave him the strength to persist. To follow the Master who was behind him. Encouraging, urging, insisting.

Strike.

He heard the witch's heart. It was slow; one beat for every twenty of his, strong as a drum at an execution. He looked into her open eyes. Deep in the black chasms were tiny skulls carved of ice. The witch knew fear.

He could taste her blood, an arctic river in her veins, which would pass on her powers – her command of the elements – to the Master. When he squeezed blood from her heart, Dracula would become almighty, victorious, invincible, omnipotent.

More almighty, victorious, invincible, omnipotent.

He saw the rot beneath the beauty of the wretched familiar, the darkness behind the light of the Princess in the wall, the weakness in the heart of the Winter Witch.

In times to come, he would ride on a magnificent black horse under the banner of Nemuri, called Dorakuraya: Son of the Dragon, Son of the Black Mass, Son of Satan Himself. Kostaki would be honoured as one of the Seven Deadly Venoms, spreading the Master's cloak across this land, and all the lands beyond. Kostaki the Templar, Sanjuro Surnamed-What-Comes-to-Hand, Shurayukihime, the Avenging Daughter, Hanzo, the Swordsmith, Blind Ichi, the Masseur of Death, Ogami the Executioner… and his cold-eyed child Daigoro. A company without mercy, dedicated to the glory of Dorakuraya. A Guard worth joining. Feared, admired and exalted. The Seven would prevail, and the Master would rule by the square, by the level, by the plumb rule, by the compasses and by the all-seeing eye. The Seven were the scourge of Dracula, and they would strike heavy across the East.

As he would strike now.

'*Strike, good Kostaki,*' urged the Master. '*Strike, so that the blood may flow, so that I may ascend, and bear you up with me. A place awaits you, above others, on the left hand of Satan. Strike.*'

There were others in the tomb – a monkey and a soldier. They didn't matter. The Master would see them off.

In the wall of ice, he saw the Seven – himself included – standing ready, on the point of attack, and the Master, atop a fabulous armoured steam engine, behind them, arm raised, mailed fist to the sky.

The Seven.

The Number! There is no such thing as the Number!

The familiar, seeping into his mind. He shut out the womanly, cowardly voice.

He looked into the ice, and raised his sword to cut deep.

The familiar pawed his boots, feebly now. She had lost a lot of precious blood.

He could taste that too. The blood of a wretch. No, the blood of…

(He saw her face – fair as her spirit. He remembered her strength, her gentleness, her refusal to back down, her grace and wit…)

…of a lady elder.

Strike now. Strike.

'Don't,' said the familiar.

Why stay your hand, Captain? You have been given a direct order.

'It's not him, Kostaki,' said the injured woman. 'Not Dracula.'

Her words were a blow to his heart. A stiletto of ice to his brain.

There is no such thing as the Number!

Sword raised, he turned to the Master and saw red hair and deception. An inverted cross. The dream of glory was written across ice. The Seven were a phantasm – their image collapsed and ran, turned to water. The sun shone, melting the lies.

Not the sun: Lady Geneviève. And the one in the ice: Christina Light.

A gift, polished like silver. A light, bright as the sun.

Both pure, both poison to evil. And poison to *him*.

Something had tainted his mind. In this place, in the madness of fasting, in exile from his father-in-darkness and the fountainhead of his bloodline, he had let himself be fooled over and over. A tittering girl-thing with puppets, the cat-women, heartless and trivial, and this sham Dracula, this cast-off by-blow, this get of a fallen priest, this jumped-up faker.

Not Dracula, not Dorakuraya, not the Master, but Nemuri, Nemo, No One.

Fear sparked in the Japanese vampire's eyes, then cunning – and his shining sword came out from under his cloak.

The lady elder tried to pull herself upright, grabbing Kostaki's leg and the rim of the tomb. She coughed blood.

Kostaki knew what he had done, and burned with shame, terror, regret.

In his madness, he had lost something.

He would take it back.

28

YŌKAI TOWN, DECEMBER 22, 1899
(CONTINUED)

Don't just lie there, bleeding! Get up and stop the fool!
I knew it wasn't Kostaki but the vampire behind him.

Oh, the Captain had run his sword through me all right. It's just that he didn't mean it. He was on strings, like Tsunako Shiki's puppets. Kostaki's little pest shared Drusilla's penchant for unhelpful prophecy. She had told me to worry about who was playing the tune not who was doing the dance.

Don't get distracted. This is more important.

You are the distraction. *Nom d'une chienne qui fumée!* I need to concentrate on my *pain*… on the *blood* I'm losing…

You'll get it back in no time. You're a vampire, remember?

A vampire who's been impaled on a silvered sword.

Through the liver? No elder ever died from a stake through the liver.

You're not a doctor, Christina. I am. Severe trauma to any vital organ can be fatal to a vampire. Especially if enough silver remains in the wound to cause gangrene.

Excellent! You're boring me with medical lectures again. You must be recovering.

Kostaki's carrack was good quality. The silvering wouldn't come off. Shoddier electroplating made for deadlier (if dishonourable) weaponry. A true Carpathian Guardsman would kill enemies outright – not wait weeks

324

as they lingered on their deathbeds, ravaged by symptoms akin to tertiary syphilis.

Gené, talk to Kostaki. Get through to him.

As he's got through to me!

If you're going to be like that about it…

Now who sounds like a governess?

I do not *sound like a governess!*

Now *that's a* princess talking!

I do not believe in rank. That does not make me the same as a…

A servant?

A lackey of the corrupt bourgeoisie.

I tried to shut the buzzing voice out of my head.

In the delirium of pain, I saw black tendrils flowing from the red-headed vampire's fingers, wrapping around Kostaki's head like mummy bandages. A blindfold, a gag, tethers. Puppet strings.

I *saw* the trick.

Kostaki himself had warned me about the man, brother to Mr Bats. 'A red-headed devil in a black cloak. He has his own ambitions. A priest of Satan, he calls himself Dorakuraya. He sees himself as the Dracula of the East.'

Dorakuraya.

Kostaki stood over Yuki-Onna, and raised his sword.

'Don't…' I said. I sounded weak in my own head.

Dorakuraya's ribbons streamed like banners – they were not entirely visible, but as I bled out, I saw beyond the normal range. He raised his hands, fingers dramatically crooked, hands shaped into claws or grapples. So, another conjurer – like Majin, like Tsunako. Like Dracula.

Vampires with powers of fascination all have a repertoire of hypnotic gestures. The Marquis de Coulteray and I once spent an evening trying to learn the trick. Neither of us could twist our hands into the required shapes. At least, not without breaking bones. Giving up the effort, de

Coulteray concluded, 'It's no use… for this, you have to be double-jointed and Transylvanian!'

Dorakuraya, a long way from Transylvania. A conjurer – but also a poseur. Dressed in European style, hair redder than natural, assuming another vampire's mantle, even mangling his name.

And not doing his own dirty work.

There must be a reason for that.

'It's not him, Kostaki,' I said. 'Not Dracula.'

Good girl. That'll get through to the gallant Captain. Make him look at you, make him see what he's done. That'll rattle him back to his senses.

Kostaki didn't thrust his sword into Yuki-Onna's heart.

If Dorakuraya wanted her impaled, why *not* do it himself? He might have needed us – or at least O-Same – to penetrate the ice and reach the heart of the maze under the temple, but he had a sword, a strong arm and a clear shot.

Because it's dangerous to disturb the Woman of the Snow.

Ah, yes.

For instance… look at me.

Christina was stuck in a wall of ice. How had that happened?

How do you think?

Did you try to kill Yuki-Onna?

Certainly not, though I am opposed on principle to tyrants of all types, including vampire royalty. No better than warm monarchs. All of them murderers. No, I reasoned it out. Why didn't Majin just destroy us all?

As he is doing now?

Quite. Out of desperation. Proving my point.

Which is?

I thought you wanted me to stop buzzing.

You are *extraordinary*, Christina.

So noted, Sister Gené. My point is that Majin – the Demon Man – is afraid of Yuki-Onna, the Winter Witch. He doesn't think he can face her straight on. While she hibernates, he can pick away at us. If she wakes, he's got a problem.

So you tried to wake her. With what? A firm shoulder shake and a cup of tea?

Light.

Ah, that makes sense. You drew the curtains.

I illuminated the tomb, and this *happened… this explosion of ice.*

You were lucky. Anyone else would have been killed. Yuki-Onna would drain the life from them.

Which is why Count Carrot-Top is having a marionette do his killing for him.

Yes, of course.

You hadn't thought of that.

Now you mention it, it's obvious.

I saw it. You didn't.

Yes, fine, fair enough. Not really the best time to gloat, is it? You're embedded in ice and I'm bleeding to true death.

You'll be fine.

If Kostaki mortally wounded the Woman of the Snow, she would blast him to icicles before she died. Look what happened to Christina when she just tried to rouse Yuki-Onna. Dorakuraya would wade through the shattered, frozen corpse pieces of his catspaw and inhale the Ice Queen's final breath. He would assume her mastery of the cold. He would be the Man of the Snow, the Winter Warlock. Majin, the Emperor, Black Ocean and whoever else stood in his way would be slain. We refugees might rate a blast of chill air to clear us into the sea, but no more. Dorakuraya would eventually stand against Dracula. Those who venerate to the extent of copying always nurture secret desire to topple and replace idols.

A cunning, mean, cowardly path to glory, but so were they all.

While I shivered at a horrible, possible future, Kostaki overcame his most implacable opponent – himself.

He looked at me.

At last, I saw an expression on his dead face. Horror, at what he had done. Regret, close to hysteria. I'd feel bad if I stabbed a close ally too – but I'm flexible in ways Kostaki isn't.

I was no longer worried he'd try to kill me again. I don't believe he was even trying to kill me when he stabbed me. The Carpathian Guard are famously good at killing people, yet I wasn't dead. No – I'd just been in his way.

As Kostaki shook off Dorakuraya's puppet strings, I was afraid he'd realise what he'd done and be broken in himself. Honour was his straitjacket. He abided by a code Dracula's party had long since abandoned. Only someone as stubbornly idealistic could have been so sorely abused.

Idealistic? He's still Dracula's get.

Kostaki turned to face Dorakuraya, who produced a sword.

I tried to get up. Every move was agony. My wounds had healed, but my side was numb from silver. I couldn't feel my right leg or foot.

I got a grip on Kostaki's leg and hauled myself off the floor. I reached out to steady myself. My palm seared on the icy rim of the tomb.

The ice ground and cracked as Yuki-Onna turned to look up at us.

She was no longer asleep.

Mr Bats stood on the other side of the tomb, frowning. He chewed his attempt at a moustache. Would he side with us or his brother-in-darkness?

With shaking hands, Topazia pulled back the lock of her ancient pistol.

The ice wall shimmered. Christina, light with no heat, was coruscating… but still couldn't break out of her glacier prison. The cold grip wasn't just ice. It was the living aura of the Woman of the Snow. She controlled winter as Dracula controls wolves. And she kept the Princess away from her.

My blood was sprayed on the ice above Yuki-Onna's elongated face. It seeped down to her. Fine stuff, my blood. Of the line of Melissa d'Acques. Yet it has been spurned by so many. Annie of the Black Island refused it, that toothsome hussar in Russia didn't take to it, Lily Mylett of Whitechapel died despite it and, just now, Popejoy preferred bitter willow sap. Even you, Charles, had to have your nose pinched to make you open your mouth to swallow your medicine and a fruit pastille popped in afterwards to take the taste away. Finally, *someone* wanted my blood. A considerable someone, at that. The Woman of the Snow summoned my spillage. Rivulets wound between shards of ice. Rosy crystals formed and worked their way through cracks. Yuki-Onna's mouth opened slightly. Red on her lips... in her eyes...

So, the sacrifice that raised the Sleeping Beauty was me.

You knew you were the heroine of this song.

The *tragic* heroine.

Watch the men fight over you. You'll love that.

And you don't? What about those duels of frog lords and heron marquises? You were smug about that.

Politics. Not romance.

I sat up, hand pressed to my side. I still couldn't stand. Feeling was coming back – mostly itching. Aside from everything else, I had a bad case of red thirst. With so much blood lost, I needed to feed.

Mr Bats walked round the tomb with a distinctive slouching swagger. Taking a position midway between Kostaki and his brother-in-darkness, he looked at them both in turn. With a grunt, he aligned himself with the Captain and against Dorakuraya.

The two samurai regarded each other. Kostaki, honourable fool, stood aside.

'It was always going to end this way between us,' said Dorakuraya. 'My *tamiya-ryu* discipline against your *hyoho niten ichi-ryu* style. It has never been settled which is best. That falls to us.'

'You are my brother, Nemuri,' said Mr Bats. 'I thank you for cutting off the head of the apostate Rodrigues. You avenged our deaths. But I see our father-in-darkness in you now and nothing more. You must be ended.'

Mr Bats drew both his *katana* and *wakizashi* and assumed the 'Two Heavens, One School' stance, long and short swords raised over the head. Dorakuraya was master of the *engetsu sappo* – the full-moon cut. An anticlockwise circular motion, counting backwards to the moment of attack. This favours a long-handled sword. I anticipated impressing devotees of sword-fighting (*chanbara*) with accounts of how this ended.

Mr Bats advanced one step.

But Dorakuraya wasn't truly interested in the ancient question of which school of swordplay is best. He wanted to win.

Rather than counter Mr Bats' stance with his own, Dorakuraya threw himself to one side, thrusting his sword through the back of his cape, skewering Topazia through the heart – her eyes bulged with shock – and slamming her against the wall. Her pistol slipped from her grip and Dorakuraya snatched for it.

'*Ave Satani*,' he whispered, ecstatic in treachery.

Mr Bats scowled at such base behaviour but Topazia wasn't having it. Her eyes were dead but her tail had a final twitch.

Her pistol fell… and her tail batted it out of Dorakuraya's reach. The weapon flew across the chamber, turning over and over. It fell on the ice, and didn't go off.

His base gambit a failure, Dorakuraya tried to wrest his sword from Topazia's ribcage. All thought of an honourable match was abandoned – for who could duel with a killer of defenceless women? Kostaki and Mr Bats closed on the ginger poltroon. They executed precise moves. Blades passed through unresisting flesh and bone. A seeping diagonal cut Dorakuraya's face from forehead to cheek. The cap of his head slid away, eye still blinking. Petre Gheria would have marked the dissection A minus. The brain-pan was sliced like a breakfast egg. Grey matter, surprised by exposure to cold air, became solid. Pink frost formed on gnarled whorls.

Dorakuraya was transfixed by Kostaki's straight sword and Mr Bats' *wakizashi*.

Collapsing inside his black mantle, the half-headless vampire took three steps towards the tomb and pitched over the rim, splaying on the ice. Strawberry dust poured away from his bones. His skeleton crumbled and became a man-length heap of grit. His scarlet-lined cloak dissolved as if soaked in acid. In moments, Dorakuraya was just powder, settling into the ice, following my blood, inhaled by Yuki-Onna.

In aping Dracula, Dorakuraya had succeeded only in dramatising the end of Stoker's novel – where a *kukri* and a bowie knife sever the head and pierce the heart of the imaginary Count and he turns to ash.

All that was left of the Man Who Would Be King of the Cats was an upside-down crucifix. The damned thing was silver.

I wanted to go to Topazia, but my side still hurt too much. Nothing could be done for her anyway.

Alas, poor Monkey Minx.

She did better than either of us.

We're not done yet. Look at the Cold Girl.

The ice bed was crimson – stained by my blood and Dorakuraya's dust. Stately and with elegance, Yuki-Onna rose from her tomb, stiff as an unfolding knife blade. She stood, taller even than she'd seemed, cloak of hair draped over her shoulders, hanging to her ankles.

She was *hungry*. And the hunger of winter can never be satiated.

Ancient witch-queens tend not to distinguish between lesser folk. Those who would worship at their altars and those who would defile their graves look much the same in their eyes. Yuki-Onna might make an exception for the odd handsome woodcutter but this was not that sad song. This was the seventy-year winter. The battle that ended with one survivor. For cold is eternal.

As is…

Very clever, Christina.

As is?

Light. Light is forever.

So…

I scooped up Topazia's flintlock, trying not to think of Kawataro's ill-maintained Colt blowing up in Kostaki's hand. This pistol was centuries older than that. I didn't know who'd owned the weapon. Had it been lovingly kept in a case all these years? Or just tossed in a trunk and dug out in desperation? In this icehouse, the powder would be frozen and the flint wouldn't strike.

But we had one ball's chance. A silver ball, I trusted.

Brave heart, Gené, said Christina.

Mille milliards de monstres mauvaises! I responded.

I looked up at Yuki-Onna, the beautiful, the terrible. Hair black as night, face white as snow, lips red as roses.

She smiled, lacquered black fangs like a bear trap.

Kostaki looked at the gun and shook his head. He thought it a feeble weapon against such a monster.

And so it was.

I didn't fire at her.

I pointed at the wall – just above Christina's head…

Just above! You've aimed directly at my face, Gené dear!

'*Fiat lux*,' I said.

I pulled the trigger.

A miracle! The pistol discharged, with a sulphurous puff. The flash was mirrored, redoubled and repeated, all around the tomb. I closed my eyes, but was dazzled all the same. My ears rang from the percussive explosion.

I blinked uselessly. The flashes continued.

Ice cracked where the ball struck, as if a chisel hit a hidden fault. The pellet was held fast, inches from Christina's red eye. She was right about my aim.

Great slabs calved from the wall and crashed to the floor. The genie was out of the bottle. And the Princess was free.

The Woman of the Light flew into the Woman of the Snow.

So cold…

What did you expect?

You have no idea. So cold, *and so much* more.

Yuki-Onna still stood over us. One of her eyes was red. The other shone.

Are you in there, Christina? Are you *wearing* her?

It's not like that.

Then where are *you*? I only see *her*.

Look again.

Yuki-Onna was enveloped in a sparkling glow like a raiment of many jewels. The Princess wrapped around her – another puppeteer, but with a willing marionette. The lesson is work with the strings, not against them. From their entwined persons radiated an *aurora borealis*, though not very northern, so *aurora orientalis*, the Light of the East. They were heart-stopping in their beauty.

Have you done what Dorakuraya intended? Taken everything of hers? Declared yourself empress?

Yuki-Onna shook her head. A rainbow rippled across her glossy hair.

She smiled Christina's smile, but with black teeth.

We have come to an arrangement. That's all I ever intended. With her and with Japan.

So we're a country now? We have diplomatic relations?

If we must. And we must.

What are we *called*? Macedonia is taken. The Queendom of Eternal Light, pardon me, the Commune of Vampire Equals, Which Happens to Have a Princess in Charge?

Hush, Gené, you're hysterical.

What about Majin? He's still set on destroying Yōkai Town.

Yuki-Onna looked up at the ceiling. More frost fell around her.

We could feel the tremors now – no longer distant, no longer intermittent. A shaking, all the time. Even here, in the fastness of the ice tomb. I sensed the quakes in my teeth, like a form of red thirst.

Yes. Majin. The time has come to deal with him.

At that moment, I didn't think I could feel colder but Christina's tone – if words relayed without voice have a tone – chilled me.

In a flash that I will see for all days whenever I close my eyes, they were gone.

Yuki-Onna and the Princess.

The tomb was dark. Water trickled nearby.

'You'll have to help me up,' I told Kostaki and Mr Bats. 'Someone stabbed me and I can't walk as well as I used to.'

29

YŌKAI TOWN, DECEMBER 22, 1899 (CONTINUED)

Mr Bats held the trapdoor up and Kostaki helped me manage the stairs. In the dispensary, Kurozuka tried to kill us with a lancet. When she saw we weren't a threat, she looked at my wounds. Kostaki stood aside, not saying anything as I explained – without mentioning his name – what had happened. I was healing naturally, and getting feeling back in my side and leg. Kurozuka slapped fungus poultices on me front and back and cinched a bandage around my waist. Then she gave me a crutch and sent me on my way. She didn't have the most amenable bedside manner, but I didn't die of her ministrations. Should she wish to study medicine at the University of France, I would sponsor her application. She can apply experimental poultices to M. Modéran with my blessing.

Throughout the temple, *yōkai* were stirring. Christina had passed through as a ray of light, still wrapped around Yuki-Onna. Flashing from one reflective surface to the next, she thawed everyone in her way. The ice walls were gone, evaporated when Yuki-Onna woke. Dravot had organised Yōkai Town's scratch defences – everyone still alive who could pick something up and fight with it – to fall back to the temple. We found him in the courtyard, commanding a rag-tag troop of riflemen. Most of their weapons were scavenged from recently killed Black Ocean masked men. Lady Oyotsu's head was up in the air like an observation balloon. She relayed information to a busy group of intelligent folk – Abura Sumashi, the mirthlessly smiling Watson, double-faced Ryomen, a humbled Lord Kawataro – who were operating mortars jury-rigged from fireworks equipment. Dravot was in his element, ducking projectiles, striding back and forth, shouting orders and profane encouragement, and firing pistol shots at the creeping enemy.

'You've missed *everything*,' said Dru, who had exchanged her spiked parasol for Kasa-obake – and was presumably responsible for covering his blistered hide with sticking plasters. 'Christina's perfectly killed that bigsy-bugsy spider... oh, no, that hasn't happened yet. You've not missed it at all. I shouldn't have spoken. Just wait and see.'

A mammoth eight-legged juggernaut pushed through barricades of earthquake rubble towards the temple. The *jorōgumo* Clare Mallinger was too big to take in all at once. Black Ocean troops – hardy survivors after a few hours in this killing field, and likely the enemy's best men – advanced under cover of her bulbous abdomen. A battle had been fought and won inside the *yōkai*. Clare's head was five times the size of the spider's. She was in command. Moth-wings the size of battleship sails, wet and not fully formed, grew from her anterior cephalothorax. Eventually, she would fly!

'Peek-a-boo!' she shouted. 'I see you.'

A rocket burst against her forehead. Clouds of coloured smoke mushroomed. Strings of firecrackers popped. Some shrapnel had been stuffed in, but the pyrotechnics were more entertainment than ordinance. Clare shook off the burning fragments.

'Pook-a-bee!' she shouted. 'Can't hurt me!'

A bright light shone and a chill wind passed. The giant

spider-woman stiffened, hair frosted white, icicles bursting from spinnerets, face frozen.

Arcueid Moonstar loosed a stone from her slingshot.

Clare didn't just fragment into ice shards. The metamorphic processes inside her conglomerate body must have generated enormous heat... for she *exploded*. Molten innards burst through her flash-frozen skin, showering the troops beneath and around her. They screamed as they died of fire and ice. Some were crushed as her bulk collapsed on them. Clare's ice-sculpture face survived intact, the last remnant of a broken sphinx. A stray giant spider-leg – a *nunchaku* made from chitinous telegraph poles – thrashed, killing even after she was dead.

No one was in a mood to feel sorry for her.

It was hard to take in what Christina had become.

Yuki-Onna was there, twenty feet tall but insubstantial, skirts and cloaks of snow whirling about her. More like an apparition than a physical being. She still had Christina's eyes – one dead and red, the other alive and a small sun.

Yōkai rallied behind the Woman of the Snow.

The rest of us made do with Queen Christina.

'By the square, by the level,' said Dravot.

'By the plumb rule, by the compasses,' answered Kostaki.

'And by the all-seeing eye!' they said together.

Did I mention they were Masons?

Evidently, it was now revealed that the entire purpose of Freemasonry – as conceived by Solomon the Great in times of old – was to worship Christina Light and bring about her apotheosis.

Don't be ridiculous, Gené.

So you're still listening. I thought you might be too busy.

I am. You have no idea. Excuse me...

A bat-winged man-lifting kite swooped out of smoke

clouds. Hanging beneath, an archer swaddled in green furs unloosed silver-tipped arrows. Suzan Arashi fell, her shoulder pierced. The Green Bat must have an eagle eye to hit an invisible target. I hobbled to the next snowdrift and did my best to treat a patient I couldn't see. Even her wound was invisible, though I could tell the arrow had gone clear through. I snapped off the barb and extracted the shaft, then used the headband of a dead Black Ocean soldier as a bandage.

The kite swooped again... towards the column of cold light.

And its wings were frozen and shattered. The Green Bat plunged into a chasm.

There... that's his little hash settled.

So, Christina could talk to me and fight a war at the same time.

I had to be content with doing my best to save lives.

Suzan Arashi would be all right. She asked if she'd have a scar. I admired her for joking under the circumstances then realised she was serious. She is vain about her perfect skin, even if it can only be appreciated by the sighted when she stands in the rain or pours a bucket of flour over herself.

I felt a tug at my elbow and turned, ready to swing with my crutch. A *kappa* I didn't recognise – a junior officer, bedraggled and bloodied – held out my medical bag.

I took it and checked my stocks. Insufficient, but I would make do.

Next under my care was a Black Ocean soldier who'd had the fight knocked out of him and his head nearly knocked off. A warm man, terrified among vampires. I attempted a reassuring smile and set to work.

Dravot shot me a disapproving glare as I cleaned the dent in the unmasked man's head with snow.

'Sorry,' I shouted. 'Hippocratic oath.'

'Just fang the fellah and be done,' the Sergeant said. 'You need the blood!'

He was not wrong. Red thirst was making me light-headed and seepage from Kurozuka's fungus poultices altered my perceptions. Matters that should have been solemn and solid were hilarious and liquid. I hadn't thought to ask the mad midwife about side effects.

My patient tried to reward my conscientiousness with a knife in the stomach but was too feeble to do more than dimple my *haori*. My father told me a battlefield surgeon's duty was to treat a wounded enemy as if he were one of our own but secure *le salaud Anglais* with rope before cutting his arm off. I smiled at the ungrateful Black Ocean boy, glad of his blade-point spur to memory. I love my father and still resent his eclipse in my life by my father-in-darkness. The daggerman fell unconscious. With his own knife, I cut his arm and tippled. My red thirst abated a little. I tasted ergot in the soldier's blood and was more than tipsy.

I bandaged the ungrateful wretch and left him. Fortified by what I'd taken from him, I no longer needed the crutch.

Out of consideration for my feelings, Dravot didn't shoot the soldier in the head. When this was over, we would have precisely one live prisoner. The story of our terrible strength and cruel mercy would get about, Dravot said, disinclining other likely lads from putting on masks and giving us trouble. I didn't mention that the youth would most likely be obliged to commit *seppuku* or, at best, become a bonze and take a vow of silence.

Hah! Or get better and try to stab you with a longer knife!

Christina was still in my head.

Tremors continued. The temple grounds were riven by jagged cracks. Yuki-Onna's spells were weakened under the onslaught of the avatar of Taira no Masakado. Black rifts opened like wounds. Snow tumbled over the edges. Higo Yanagi shrieked, roots suddenly exposed. A party of *yōkai* worked to pull her out of the earth. She could be replanted. Popejoy was cradled in her branches, sleeping through the *rififi*, life in the balance.

Can you turn off the earthquakes, Christina?

All will be well.

And all is for the best in the best of all possible worlds.

Trust. Hope. Faith.

Leaving her to it, I took my medical bag and Hippocratic oath where they were needed. The temple antechamber was exposed to the elements with its wall shredded but still shaded by a roof. I made it my field hospital. Kage-Onna, a *yōkai* usually seen only as a shadow on screens, manifested as a dark shape and volunteered as a nurse. Kurozuka brought a selection of dubious remedies. It struck me that the opiates in her poultices were palliative not therapeutic. She was used to easing the pain of the dying.

I didn't give up as easily. I had a family reputation to consider and also, the honour of the ghouls, snubbed by better-connected medical students as meddlers with the dead rather than doctors to the living. Those boobs would be put in their place if they could see me now!

I tore the tiniest strip of bandage to make a sling for one of the miniature singers. Her arm snapped like a twig when she thawed. She and her sister trilled thanks in unison.

Ryomen was brought in, shot in his lower head. I prised the bullet out of his sternum-skullbone, but the angry face was dead. The placid upper head awoke, inconsolable. Yelling in a language I don't know, he took up a pike and rushed out into the fray.

Albert Watson – the Smiler – came to me with shaking hands, saying he couldn't hold a rifle any more. He had no obvious wounds. He kept looking over his shoulder at Kage-Onna, jumping each time he saw the shadow woman. I fished aspirin out of my bag and told him it was a miracle remedy. For a moment after he swallowed the pills he believed me but his hands still shook. I diagnosed a bad case of the terrors.

The Smiler turned vampire in the hope of stilling a worm that crawled into his gut after a hard campaign on the North-West Frontier. Armies call his condition cowardice because generals and politicians can't afford to admit that seeing and doing things seen and done in war can break a man as surely as torture. Watson wore a Victoria Cross ribbon – a charm to prove his fled valour. And being a vampire was no more use to him. I knew from Dravot that the Smiler more than earned Britain's highest honour, given only to those who display extraordinary courage in time of war. But his rope had run out. In all fighting forces, his sickness is known. In the Royal Navy, the favoured treatment is the rum ration. If symptoms persist, the medicine preferred by senior officers is summary execution.

Dravot poked his head into the clinic and shouted, 'Smiler, we need you at the line!' Watson looked at me, imploring. His mouth couldn't close over his huge fangs.

I didn't know what to say. My heart was stabbed. I saw glowing shapes. Christina's light was in my head. Dru sang 'Twiggy-Voo'. Dravot yelled 'The British Grenadiers' with dirtier words.

The Smiler turned and bumped into a veiled woman. He recoiled in terror, as if she'd stuck a tent peg in his heart. She unwound her veil to show her ruin of a mouth.

'Do you think I'm pretty?' asked Kuchisake, brazen.

Watson's eyes goggled.

Kuchisake raised gardening secateurs.

'Do you think I'm pretty?' she repeated, shy.

A long pause.

'Yes, miss,' said the Smiler. 'I does… I thinks yer *beautiful.*'

She pressed the tips of her shears to the tears on his cheek.

I wasn't fast enough to intervene. And we were short of iodine. Watson's smile would be wider – but Kuchisake's eye was moist.

'*Do* you?' she asked. (In English – she had hidden talents.)

'Not 'alf,' said Watson.

She dropped the shears and kissed him, swarming the flaps of her mouth around his whole jaw. He returned her embrace.

Was I dreaming?

I had been wrong about Kuchisake's question. I thought she cut your face whether you said she was pretty or not. But there *was* a correct response, one only a madman could give. To tell her she was pretty *and mean it.*

That kiss lasted for minutes. I'll be seeing it long after Christina's light-flashes have faded from my eyes. Some of the wounded – those not close enough to see properly – cheered.

In the end, the Smiler kissed Kuchisake on the forehead, said, 'Good-bye, Dolly,' and asked for his gun. For once, his smile looked real. His fear worm yanked out, he snapped to and followed Dravot's orders. Kuchisake primped and wound her veil back round her mouth.

'Happy now?' I asked.

She didn't answer, but did help with the wounded.

Several weren't reassured, but she didn't ask her question and used her shears only to cut bandages.

One Thousand Monsters.

However many of us there were – and I didn't ask Dru for a running total, for fear she'd give it – we outnumbered the Black Ocean masked men. They were easier to kill than us. They were cut off from supply lines. The ergot was wearing off. Many in our ranks were so horrible I'd be afraid to face them myself.

O-Same.

Mr Yam.

Kostaki.

Dravot.

Mr Bats.

Albert Watson, VC.

Tsunako Shiki.

Arcueid Moonstar.

Yuki-Onna.

And Christina Light, who could win battles on her own.

Why ever should I want to?

To get the job done?

I have always believed in collective action.

But you went behind our backs when you gave sealed orders to Marit Verlaine?

You remember her? Good. All this is distraction.

A distraction with a high cost in corpses.

Yes – the fallen will be mourned. When we have time.

Very gracious, I'm sure.

Verlaine has been successful. Provided we do the Emperor a trifling service, we have won concessions. Our mission here will light a beacon. It'll illuminate the world. Yes, even London.

Trifling service? When emperors ask for those, you start digging graves.

That's not an inaccurate assessment. But, for once, the graves are not our own.

I stepped out, leaving my infirmary to the Three Ks: Kage-Onna, Kurozuka and Kuchisake.

Majin's statue stood outside the temple grounds.

The thing had walked from the gate. A stone war

machine. Steam belched from its lower face, knees and elbows. Maxim guns stuck out of its eyeholes. Blasts of flame poured from vents in its sides. Lieutenant Majin was still perched on its helmet, arms raised, a violet crackling arc between his glowing hands.

The guns opened fire. The entrenchments Dravot had ordered dug in snow were pocked with silver.

The *noppera-bō* Go master Kokingo was stitched across the blank curve where he didn't have a face. The gouges looked like bloody eyes. He melted to nothing.

Death stones on the board!

Arcueid Moonstar was cut to pieces, but not killed.

Dravot gave orders to pile the dead – theirs, ours, anyone's – and use them as sandbags.

Mr Yam leaped up at the walking statue. I'd wanted to see him matched against Majin.

A plume of flame shot out and the *jiang shi* was blasted into the air, robes and pigtail on fire. O-Same streamed across the sky, took hold of Mr Yam, and pulled him to safety on a rooftop. She flew at the statue, drawing another fire jet into herself. The statue's midriff exploded. *Oni*-soldiers died. There were men in there, working the machinery. It wasn't all magic.

With horrible deliberation and a creaking slowness, the giant stepped onto the temple grounds and stamped across the courtyard, crushing everything under its feet. The *torii* gate, the dragon fountain, the dead, a Black Ocean soldier who was playing dead. Where the colossus trod, the ground split. Sulphur smoke belched from below. Lava bubbled and snow melted.

In the middle of Yuki-Onna's winter, I felt heat.

A dragon hatching!

Then a blizzard enfolded the statue.

Yuki-Onna's cold poured into the stone giant, freezing it where it stood. An arm broke off and crashed down.

The iron sword came loose from the stone belt. The big blade shattered a stone leg, then scythed through a pile of wicker baskets. A scabby, ragged warm man scurried out of hiding. He looked up in terror at the unsteady giant. An engine exploded. Hot metal parts rained on the unfortunate bystander. Bleeding from a dozen glinting wounds, he howled until frost reached him. Greenish-grey stone whitened, and became brittle enough to smash.

Dravot ordered volleys. Kostaki had the Sergeant's tiger rifle. He fired at the joints, at the weak spots.

Lieutenant Majin still grinned. Bullets and other projectiles turned to water when they struck his bubble. The statue was smashed out from under him, in pieces... but he floated, kept aloft by waves of magical energy. He drew strength from powers under the earth. He called to his masters.

Taira no Masakado, the dragon sorcerer. Enma Daio, the shogun of Hell.

They were undefeatable. We were lost!

Then an angel of light descended on Majin.

Don't look!

I shoved my face into a snowdrift. I still saw the *flash*.

I was deafened too. I heard only ringing.

I pulled my face from the snow and opened my eyes. The statue was rubble. *Yōkai* swarmed over it, dragging out dazed or dead Black Ocean men. But Majin hovered in mid-air, hands brimming with black flame. Christina, a shining ghost, was separate from Yuki-Onna now, one arm hanging limp. She wound wings of light around Majin's bubble. Violet sludge − liquid, gaseous or ectoplasmic − poured out of the Lieutenant's open hands and pumped into her aura. It flowed faster than she could suck out the colour. The powers of the earth were feeding her poison.

So much... so much...

I would never be deaf to Christina. My hearing

was coming back anyway. Winds roared, shouts and alarms, screams…

A black-fire dragon shape formed around Majin, *seiman* sigils for eyes. The Demon Man was becoming more demon than man.

Our angel's wings looked ragged and thin, bleeding rainbows.

Christina, come away.

No. As I said, I believe in collective action.

What does that *mean*?

I'm sorry, Gené, it means this*!*

A spear of light pierced my heart and I screamed.

I am a vampire. We bleed people. So we may live, usually. I am a doctor. We bleed people too. For their own good, mostly.

Before I turned, I was bled empty.

Chandagnac gave me his vampire blood first. It was what we now call a reagent. In 1432, it was black magic – tainted by Satan. As my father-in-darkness-to-be guzzled from my throat, I felt myself diminishing inside my body. Darkness closing in and the far-off light.

The *something bright* reported by those who nearly – or actually – die is not Heaven. It's an effect of the optic nerves shutting down. The eye specialist Dr Doyle wrote a paper on it.

For me, the far-off light faded. And I opened my eyes to a changed world.

No, to a changed *me*.

Now here was the light again. Not far off but all around and inside.

Unbearable light.

Even Chandagnac did not use me as comprehensively as Christina did. He took only blood, while she bled me of much more. I wasn't her sole donor. From her phantom wings came a thousand tendrils of light, tipped with barbs of Yuki-Onna's ice, and she latched on to us all. Vampires, *yōkai*, the warm, dragons, witches, Gods, shrines, rocks, trees, ghosts, spirits, elementals. She *fed* on us. She treated us as prey and called us her army.

We haven't talked about it.

We don't need to. Because we *know*.

Collective action meant giving the Princess all we had; every drop of blood, every spark of life.

Wearing Yuki-Onna — an elder as powerful as Dracula — was not enough.

She needed us *all*.

She had known this all along. That she needed our lives. Remember her fuss about shipboard casualties? She was worried then that we wouldn't be enough. We were important to her, collectively. Less so as individual pieces.

She took from us all. She didn't ask permission. If she had, we would have given it. She was like Kuchisake. There was only one answer to her.

Yes. Take me to the light.

I was on my hands and knees, convulsing as she emptied me.

Before my eyes, my hand withered. At the end of my arm was the claw of a four-hundred-and-eighty-year-old woman. I tried to flex my fingers. It was as if a crucifixion nail were driven through my palm. I felt the weight of years on my heart.

All around, colour drained. I thought it was me. I thought I was becoming colour blind. But there was a rainbow around the Princess in the sky.

Seventeen of us died. I counted. Five of my casualties were bleached white, then turned to dust. They might have died anyway. Twelve others, including Rikard Moritz, a vampire priest; Aosagibi, the heron duellist; *kyuketsuki*; Hartlieb von der Wies, minutes after being pulled from his coffin and slapped awake. Others I didn't know and can't name.

But the rest of us lived. Were saved.

Seventeen is a bigger number than three.

Dafydd, Sergei, Annie…

Not fair, Christina. Recite your own names.

I forget them. I must. I will not *take a rod to myself.*

No, you won't.

We were mostly unconscious when Christina Light broke the spell.

But we all woke when Lieutenant Majin fell out of the sky.

The sun rose above Yōkai Town, casting less light than our Star Princess. Fog seeped back. The ground cooled and quieted.

My hand was unwrinkled again. I could make a fist without pain.

'Upsy-daisy, call me Maisie,' said Drusilla.

She helped me stand. The white streak through her hair is annoyingly fetching – as if done on purpose.

All around, *yōkai* and vampires were dazed but recovering. Rui Wakasagi and Francesca Brysse walked by, arguing – each speaking with the other's voice and in the other's language. We had been drawn out of ourselves into the light. Not all of us were put back properly.

Details, details.

I saw Kostaki, wearing a Japanese straw hat against the sun.

'My lady elder,' he said, nodding.

'Captain,' I responded.

I've no idea what's in his head.

Liar.

Shush.

348

Dravot turned his defence force into a fire brigade. Blazes raged. Roofs and walls had collapsed. Boats with hulls cracked by ice were sinking. People were trapped and people were hurt. Kurozuka brought me my bag and I got back to work. I went out with a rescue party.

In the ruin of a Christian church, we found the wretch who caught the brunt of the exploding statue: Kichijiro, formerly Dorakuraya's minion. An interesting case. The ghouls would love him. Cogs and gears mortified his flesh and half a wheel stuck into his spine, but being frozen by Yuki-Onna had deadened pain. Things had been done to him by his master to keep him alive beyond his natural span. Now his versatile body was incorporating – perhaps making use of – junk forced into it.

I clacked my forceps and offered to extract what I could. Kichijiro was offended by the suggestion, intent on protecting the metal in his meat. He scuttled off, flapping and clanking. Some new-hatched *yōkai*, perhaps? A tin Renfield.

A few Black Ocean men were still alive – desperate, coming out of ergot fugues, dangerous. Smiler Watson and Kuchisake took charge of these stragglers – to talk them into surrender or subdue them with pistol and scissors. My ungrateful patient was sitting up and drinking tea served by the shadow *yōkai* Kage-Onna. He didn't look in the least ashamed. I've a good mind to send him a bill.

Mr Bats stood guard by the temple, arms crossed, retained by the Abbess. No longer a scurvy *ronin*, but a proud household samurai. Lady Oyotsu sat on her palanquin, watching and nodding. By her, playing with dolls, was Tsunako Shiki. All three were calm, as if this were an ordinary morning – not the day after they were supposed to die in the ruin of Yōkai Town. They looked like a vampire family.

A cry went up. The deep, throaty, nerve-scratching was a voice new to me. Gokemidoro – hair now white as his unblemished suit − shouted out of the cleft in his face, expelling air over rough strings, which passed for vocal chords.

Goké had found Majin in the ruins, and raised the cry.

As if he hadn't been the Lieutenant's spy, Goké was kicking the broken, crawling sorcerer.

Duty like a knife in my chest − as Kostaki would understand − I went to see what I could do for the Demon Man who'd intended to kill us all.

A cat-girl got in my way. Over her furry shoulders was draped a white tunic with pearly brass buttons. A stolen Black Ocean uniform, bleached by the Light.

'Meiko-o-o-o,' she miaowed.

A group of *bakeneko* stood around the Lieutenant, idly scratching him with toe-claws, directing his crawl, bending over to lick his wounds, hissing laughter.

Meiko, leader of the pussycats, wore Majin's cap at a jaunty angle, peak over one big slit-pupiled eye. A cigarette dangled from her mouth. Smoke curled around her whiskers. She looked me up and down, shrugged, and let me close.

There's nothing left.

I turned Majin over. He was blind. And his mind was empty.

Be grateful. Feeding off him − and the dragon he served − let me give back to you what I borrowed.

Took.

Borrowed.

I'm too tired to argue.

Majin's hands were burned to stubs. His *seiman* sigils were ash on overdone meat.

I organised the *bakeneko* into a stretcher party. Meiko let me give orders, tough enough not to be insecure. I wasn't a threat to her position as top kitten. With effort, we tipped

Majin onto a whitened Black Ocean banner. We carried him to the gate.

He writhed, then swooned.

We left him for collection.

They'll just behead him, Gené. They'll say he was a traitor, acting on his own.

Which he was.

Of course.

The gate opened. Soldiers came in and scooped up Majin. They dragged him off – not gently. I was too tired to complain, criticise or make suggestions. Too tired for justice, revenge or mercy.

After the rubbish was removed, a deputation proceeded into Yōkai Town. Baron Higurashi, in his diplomatic togs. A European man in Japanese traditional dress. He introduced himself as Yakumo Koizumi. And Marit Verlaine, getting along very nicely thank you very much, not in chains.

They all bowed to me.

No. Not me.

I turned and saw the Princess Casamassima, glittering only slightly, dressed in white, arm in a pale pink sling, hair arranged to cover her red eye. She walked towards us, as if floating.

She was the Number Incarnate. And the Number was One.

30

AT SEA, JANUARY 1, 1900

Anew year – a new *century* – and I am again cast out of Eden.

Christina said I wouldn't stay. Drusilla too.

Dru's here, on the ship. She misses her umbrella, but is fonder of the new captain.

Popejoy has changed.

He turned vampire, but his bloodline is unusual. He choked on the first blood he tried to drink. With willow sap in his veins, he can only subsist on near-liquid vegetable matter. It has to have as high an iron content as human blood. Luckily, he has a penchant for greens. Eddie Joe stocked the ship's larder with tinned spinach.

Popejoy's face resembles a gnarled, knotty tree. Nothing I can do about that. Even stripping the bark doesn't help.

As for Higo Yanagi – she's rooted on a hillside overlooking the sea, abandoned by her faithless American. Now she's a wailing willow. She can't be uprooted again, and the sailor has returned to the sea. An old, old story. I don't even think Dru's responsible. It's the sea. Just the sea.

There are already songs about her hopeless sacrifice.

* * *

Death Larsen is not aboard.

When Popejoy returned to the *Macedonia* a changed man, the crew mutinied and threw the former captain over the side. He was last seen splashing towards the shore. Like many seamen, he's a poor swimmer. I doubt he'll be welcome in Tokyo.

The men expected Popejoy would kill the man who put out his eye. But he saw too much death in Yōkai Town – or whatever it's to be called now it's the Principesality of Light – to take revenge.

I worry Death will find a new boat and come after us, like Ahab hunting the whale. He harpooned his own brother for less than we have done to him.

The crew are emboldened. They think, with their tree trunk of a captain, they can beat Death. And maybe they can.

Popejoy did change the name of the ship. We now steam on the good ship *Tomcod*.

Drusilla freed her cricket.

At the ceremony where Lady Oyotsu placed Topazia Suzuki's urn in the shrine of the fallen behind the temple, Dru uncaged the insect, which is now named the Blue Fur Lady, in honour of her dead friend.

If there's a tragic heroine in this song it's Topazia. Not me.

Without the last twitch of her tail, Dorakuraya would have slain us in the ice tomb. He'd have eaten Yuki-Onna's heart and then risen from the winter temple to face Majin.

Whoever won, the city – the world – would have lost.

Kostaki is with the ship. With Sergeant Dravot. And very few others.

Christina *let* us go.

I know this is the truth. She could have kept us.

Maybe we would be too much trouble? Opinionated busybodies she would have grown tired of overruling all the time. Distractions like Dru. Idealists and cynics like Kostaki and Dravot. Nags like me.

Voices she doesn't need in her head. Maybe it's her idea of mercy. Or sacrifice – getting rid of vampires whose company she might enjoy, so she can focus on her purpose.

Her higher purpose.

There were cool goodbyes. All said out loud. She didn't come to the dock to see us off. She sent Francesca Brysse to represent her.

Can she feel guilt? Or would that be another distraction?

She has done what she has done. By her lights, she acted for collective good. She was empowered by our need for immediate salvation. She believed she was entitled – *obliged*, even – to act as she did. As an electric vampire, bleeding us all at once.

Her arm is still lifeless – when she's in her resting form – and her eye is red. But she's *better*. I might say *healed*, though I think her faint spells and lapses into lassitude weren't symptoms of sickness but effects of her process of change, like Clare in her cocoon or any of us in the first throes of the turn. All along, she has been changing – *becoming*. She won't fly apart into sparkles or dissipate like moonbeams in fog. She is increasingly confident.

In every sense, she is not who she was.

I still cannot love her. As she said.

Yet she's so alone, so cold…

But it may be that we need her.

The world still has Dracula in it.

Kostaki has avoided speaking directly to me since he pulled his black carrack out of my side. I can understand that. He gave Dru a Christmas present to pass on to me – a Japanese fan – which I have put up in my cabin.

I asked Dravot – who guards his tin of Lipton's as if it were the Agra treasure – what I should get his comrade in return. He nudged me towards a stall in Mermaid Ancestor Place, which specialises in exotic imported delicacies.

The closest to a smile I've seen on Kostaki's lips came after he unwrapped his present – a halfpenny box of Bassett's Aniseed Imperials.

I have hopes for Kostaki.

He remains a *ronin*. He follows *bushido*. Not the low path of bloody revenge but the higher road of atonement.

He will wipe my blood off his crab sword.

He will wander the face of the earth, a pilgrim.

The rest of our party remain in Japan – if Yōkai Town still counts as Japan. According to the hundred-year lease that went into effect at midnight, it's an international settlement now. Christina needs them as she believes they need her. She is the new avatar of Yuki-Onna. Whisper it, for she is Princess of the Cats. The *yōkai* have accepted her. She saved them all and they are properly grateful.

She says she will never again use them as she did.

I believe she thinks she means that. I do not believe she will keep her promise.

Silence.

This far out to sea, I don't hear from her.

I don't miss her voice… but the absence is strange.

So, I am writing for you, Charles – and Mycroft Holmes, of course.

What will the Diogenes Club make of Christina Light's utopia?

It is a strange thing, her vampire *bund*. The Temple of One Thousand Monsters stands, but the rest of the enclave is in ruins. Christina is not unhappy about that. It's as if Majin wiped her slate for her. She can design and build to her own specifications. She has called on architects and builders. Everyone she needs to throw her light up into the sky. It's her intent that a beacon be lit.

Already, I understand, other ships are *en route*. We were not the only refugees on the seas. Now there is a port that will – no questions asked – take vampires off your hands. Some will flee there, some will be sent unwillingly.

It's not the vampire city the Marquis de Coulteray envisioned. But that may be for the best. Two days ago, Dorga arrived, with a retinue of *rakasha* from India, and *jiang shi* priests from China's Temple of Golden Vampires. De Coulteray's *pishacha* mother-in-darkness may finally get her pagoda. The lesson of Paris, where the Marquis was vivisected, and London, where Dracula rules, is that no city – no place – is safe for vampires. I think of de Coulteray's hopes, and wonder whether they could have been fulfilled under Christina Light. Looking back at where we came from gives me scant insight into where we are going – where the Princess will take us.

I think of that 'family portrait': Lady Oyotsu seated, Mr Bats standing, Tsunako Shiki playing with dolls. For the moment, they are content to let Christina keep busy. But she should watch them. She may be close to all-powerful, but she will need them; if not their support, then their neutrality.

Kostaki says we were the Shiki girl's puppets all along. Well before Dorakuraya or Christina got their hooks in us. He was certainly her favourite playmate – or, perhaps, toy. I see why he thinks of her as an infernal nuisance, though he still keeps quiet about the exact nature of the tricks she played on him. While the rest of us fought monsters, she was fighting boredom.

That little girl's black eyes still haunt me.

* * *

Since this account will function as an intelligence briefing, I will do my best to set down the facts.

Realising Lieutenant Majin was intent on destroying all of Tokyo, Christina took it upon herself to stop him. In this, she served the cause of self-preservation, but had the genius to see an opportunity to earn the grudging gratitude of the Emperor, even of the Black Ocean Society. Her woman, Marit Verlaine, petitioned Baron Higurashi, and entered into protracted negotiations. The Japanised Yakumo Koizumi – a Greek-Irish journalist and former West Indies correspondent of the New Orleans *Times-Democrat*, born Lafcadio Hearn – acted as go-between. Both sides could say things to Koizumi as estranged couples talk to each other by addressing everything to the butler, knowing full well that every complaint and insult is heard by all parties in the room. It's a matter of conditional clauses *without prejudice or favour*.

The 'trifling service' Christina offered was stopping Majin before he could wake the city-destroying Taira no Masakado. She was also responsible for returning Yuki-Onna to her rest after making use of her. Deep under Tokyo, fire and ice are in balance. There may be a future cataclysm, but at present there is a pleasing harmony of *in* and *yo*.

What has Christina achieved? A reservation for vampires where the warm can keep us penned? Her own country, where she may put her revolutionary socialist principles in effect? Will she grow tired of squabbling comrades and cut out inefficiency by reluctantly taking on supreme command?

A safe haven for the world's unwanted undead?

A wide-open town, like Shanghai or Deadwood?

A capital for an empire to come?

The lease runs a full hundred years. Once that would

have seemed a long time. We must strive to live through the twentieth century to see how the experiment turns out.

In 1999, will Christina's camp still stand? Will it still be necessary?

What will succeed it?

Dracula could plunge the world into war before even a tenth of the century is done, so it may not matter.

As our resident oracle, I've asked Drusilla.

'It depends on the School Mouse,' she says.

So, that's comforting.

Our holds are empty. And, frankly, our money has run out. Popejoy has set a course for Hawaii. The seas are against us.

As usual.

MR RICHARD JEPERSON... PLUS ONE
THE DIOGENES CLUB,
LONDON SW1Y 5AH
UNITED KINGDOM

MISS CHRISTINA LIGHT REQUESTS THE
PLEASURE OF YOUR COMPANY TO SEE IN
THE NEW MILLENNIUM.

AT DAIKAIJU PLAZA, CASAMASSIMA BAY,
TOKYO, JAPAN.

DECEMBER 31ST, 1999 – DUSK TILL DAWN.

SIGNIFICANT ANNOUNCEMENTS WILL BE MADE.
DRESS CODE: CYBERFORMAL.
INVITATION NOT TRANSFERABLE.

RSVP.

Miss Mouse, this means you...

ABOUT THE AUTHOR

Kim Newman is a novelist, critic and broadcaster. His fiction includes *The Night Mayor*, *Bad Dreams*, *Jago*, the Anno Dracula novels and stories, *The Quorum* and *Life's Lottery*, and *The Man From the Diogenes Club*, all reissued by Titan Books, *Professor Moriarty: The Hound of the D'Urbervilles*, *Angels of Music*, *The Secrets of Drearcliff Grange School* and *The Haunting of Drearcliff Grange School* published by Titan Books and *The Vampire Genevieve* and *Orgy of the Blood Parasites* as Jack Yeovil. The critically acclaimed *An English Ghost Story* was nominated for the inaugural James Herbert Award. His non-fiction books include the influential *Nightmare Movies* (recently reissued by Bloomsbury in an updated edition), *Ghastly Beyond Belief* (with Neil Gaiman), *Horror: 100 Best Books* (with Stephen Jones), *Wild West Movies*, *The BFI Companion to Horror*, *Millennium Movies*, *BFI Classics* studies of *Cat People* and *Doctor Who*, and *Video Dungeon*, a collection of his popular *Empire* magazine columns of the same name.

He is a contributing editor to *Sight & Sound* and *Empire* magazines, has written and broadcast widely on a range of topics, and scripted radio and television documentaries. His stories 'Week Woman' and 'Übermensch' have been adapted into an episode of the TV series *The Hunger* and an Australian short film; he has directed and written a tiny film, *Missing Girl*. Following his Radio 4 play 'Cry Babies', he wrote an episode ('Phish Phood') for Radio 7's series *The Man in Black*.

Follow him on Twitter @annodracula. His official website can be found at www.johnnyalucard.com.

ALSO AVAILABLE FROM TITAN BOOKS

ANNO DRACULA

It is 1888 and Queen Victoria has remarried, taking as her new consort the Wallachian Prince infamously known as Count Dracula. His polluted bloodline spreads through London as its citizens increasingly choose to become vampires.

ANNO DRACULA: THE BLOODY RED BARON

It is 1918 and Dracula is commander-in-chief of the armies of Germany and Austria-Hungary. The war of the great powers in Europe is also a war between the living and the dead. As ever the Diogenes Club is at the heart of British Intelligence and Charles Beauregard and his protégé Edwin Winthrop go head-to-head with the lethal vampire flying machine that is the Bloody Red Baron...

ANNO DRACULA: DRACULA CHA CHA CHA

Rome 1959 and Count Dracula is about to marry the Moldavian Princess Asa Vajda. Journalist Kate Reed flies into the city to visit the ailing Charles Beauregard and his vampire companion Geneviève. She finds herself caught up in the mystery of the Crimson Executioner who is bloodily dispatching vampire elders in the city. She is on his trail, as is the un-dead British secret agent Bond.

TITANBOOKS.COM

ALSO AVAILABLE FROM TITAN BOOKS

ANNO DRACULA: JOHNNY ALUCARD

It is 1976 and Kate Reed is on the set of Francis
Ford Coppola's movie *Dracula*. She helps a young
vampire boy, Ion Popescu, who leaves Transylvania
for America. In the States, Popescu becomes
Johnny Pop and attaches himself to Andy Warhol,
inventing a new drug which confers vampire powers
on its users…

PRAISE FOR THE SERIES

'Compulsory reading… glorious' Neil Gaiman

'A *tour de force* which succeeds brilliantly' *The Times*

'*Anno Dracula* is the definitive account of that post-
modern species, the self-obsessed undead'
New York Times

'Politics, horror and romance are woven together in
this brilliantly imagined and realised novel' *Time Out*

TITANBOOKS.COM

ALSO AVAILABLE FROM TITAN BOOKS

THE SECRETS OF DREARCLIFF GRANGE SCHOOL

BY KIM NEWMAN

A week after her mother found her sleeping on the ceiling, Amy Thomsett is delivered to her new school, Drearcliff Grange in Somerset.

Although it looks like a regular boarding school, Amy learns that Drearcliff girls are special, the daughters of criminal masterminds, outlaw scientists and master magicians. Several of the pupils also have special gifts like Amy's, and when one of the girls in her dormitory is abducted by a mysterious group in black hoods, Amy forms a secret, superpowered society called the Moth Club to rescue their friend. They soon discover that the Hooded Conspiracy runs through the school, and it's up to the Moth Club to get to the heart of it.

'Kim Newman stands among speculative fiction's finest, and his new book is no less impressive than the best of the rest of his writing… I had a hunch it would be wonderful and it was' Tor.com

'I can see myself re-reading this book time and again' Fantasy Book Review

TITANBOOKS.COM

ALSO AVAILABLE FROM TITAN BOOKS

AN ENGLISH GHOST STORY

BY KIM NEWMAN

The Naremores, a dysfunctional British nuclear family, seek a new life away from the big city in the sleepy Somerset countryside. At first their new home, The Hollow, seems to embrace them, creating a rare peace and harmony within the family. But when the house turns on them, it seems to know just how to hurt them the most – threatening to destroy them from the inside out.

'Immersive, claustrophobic and utterly wonderful' M.R. Carey, *New York Times* bestselling author of *The Girl With All the Gifts*

'Thoroughly enjoyable, master storytelling' Lauren Beukes, bestselling author of *Broken Monsters*

'Deserves to stand beside the great novels of the ghostly' Ramsey Campbell

'An intoxicating read' Paul Cornell, bestselling author of *London Falling*

TITANBOOKS.COM

ALSO AVAILABLE FROM TITAN BOOKS

VIDEO DUNGEON

BY KIM NEWMAN

Ripped from the pages of *Empire* magazine, the
first collection of film critic, film historian and
novelist Kim Newman's reviews of the best and
worst B-movies. Some of the cheapest, trashiest,
goriest and, occasionally, unexpectedly good films
from the past twenty-five years are here, torn apart
and stitched back together again in Newman's
unique style.

Everything you want to know about DTV
hell is here.

Enter if you dare.

TITANBOOKS.COM

For more fantastic fiction, author events, exclusive
excerpts, competitions, limited editions and more

VISIT OUR WEBSITE
titanbooks.com

LIKE US ON FACEBOOK
facebook.com/titanbooks

FOLLOW US ON TWITTER
@TitanBooks

EMAIL US
readerfeedback@titanemail.com